# PRAISE FOR
# JODI PICOULT

## *MERCY*

This title is also available as an eBook.

"A quietly powerful book that examines the boundaries of love and loyalty, courage and forgiveness."

—*The Boston Globe*

"A graceful stylist, Picoult entertains her readers not only with feel-good storytelling and irresistible characters but with consideration of such serious moral dilemmas as euthanasia and forgiveness."

—*Booklist*

"I would be surprised if anyone who reads the first 20 pages of *Mercy* could put it aside again. This is the Real Thing, a novel about plausible people and important ideas told with riveting cinematic clarity. The story's edge, and the economy with which Jodi Picoult hones it, positively gleam."

—*Portland Oregonian*

## *CHANGE OF HEART*

"Picoult engineers . . . provocative and relevant moral dilemmas rich in nuance, mystery, and wit. . . . Picoult's bold story of loss, justice, redemption, and faith reminds us how tragically truth can be concealed and denied."

—*Booklist*

"Picoult bangs out another ripped-from-the-zeitgeist winner. . . . An impressive book."

—*Publishers Weekly*

"Jodi Picoult writes novels mothers and daughters can agree on even if they disagree about most everything else. While her stories deal with 'issues,' they are bathed in intimacy, often domestic in nature. . . . Her books manage to be disturbing and comforting in the same breath."

—*Daily News* (New York)

"Picoult is a skilled writer, with tautly written chapters that earn her the title of master of the page-turner."

—USA Today

# NINETEEN MINUTES

"Adept character development and intelligent plot twists. . . . *Nineteen Minutes* is both a page-turner and a thoughtful exploration of popularity, power, and the social ruts that can define us in ways we may not wish to be defined."

—Rocky Mountain News (Denver)

"No reader can possibly foresee the book's stunning denouement. This is vintage Picoult, expertly crafted, thought-provoking and compelling."

—Entertainment Weekly, Grade: A

"Picoult approaches the troubled (and troubling) psyche of the high school students with empathy and respect."

—The Washington Post

## ALSO BY JODI PICOULT

# MERCY

## Jodi Picoult

WASHINGTON SQUARE PRESS

New York    London    Toronto    Sydney

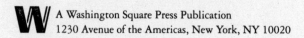 A Washington Square Press Publication
1230 Avenue of the Americas, New York, NY 10020

ISBN-13: 978-0-7434-2244-4
ISBN-10:    0-7434-2244-9

First Pocket Books trade paperback printing April 2001

50  49  48  47  46  45  44  43  42

WASHINGTON SQUARE PRESS and colophon are
registered trademarks of Simon & Schuster, Inc.

For information regarding special discounts for bulk purchases,
please contact Simon & Schuster Special Sales at 1-800-456-6798
or business@simonandschuster.com

Designed by Liane Fuji

Printed in the U.S.A.

I'm indebted—again—to Ina Gravitz and Dr. James Umlas. Thanks also to Fran Kaszuba, Christopher Gentile, Aaron Belz, Laura Gross, Laura Yorke, Jane Picoult, Jon Picoult, and Paul Constantino, chief of police in Sterling, Massachusetts. Hats off to Andrea Greene Goldman, legal guru, who didn't mind consultations at midnight and who graciously waived her hourly fee. And special thanks to my husband, Tim van Leer, who gave me fly-fishing lessons on our perfectly dry back lawn, and all the time I needed to write.

*For Hal and Bess Friend, my grandparents, with love.*
*I could write volumes about how much you both mean to me.*

What power has love but forgiveness?
In other words
by its intervention
what has been done
can be undone.
What good is it otherwise?

—William Carlos Williams,
    "Asphodel, That Greeny Flower"

# PROLOGUE

When she had packed all the artifacts that made up their personal history into liquor store boxes, the house became strictly a feminine place. She stood with her hands on her hips, stoically accepting the absence of old Boston Celtics coasters and the tangle of fishing poles, the old dartboard from a Scots pub, the toolbox and downhill skis, the silky patterned ties which sat in the base of one box like a writhing mass of snakes. Without these things, one tended to notice the bright eyelet curtains, the vase filled with yawning crocuses, a needlepoint pillow. True, it looked more like a scene from a Martha Stewart magazine than a home, but that was to be expected.

She packed away the matching mugs hand-lettered with their names, and the video camera they'd bought for their last anniversary, and a framed sampler some relative had stitched to commemorate their wedding. She painstakingly dismantled the frame of the big brass bed, lugging the pieces into the living room until all that remained was a thick and silent mattress.

She thanked God, and in advance, the groundhog, for the unseasonably warm day. When it hit 50 degrees in the shallows of January, people came out of their houses, and the more people to venture outside, the more people there would be for the sale. She dragged the boxes outside and turned them over and arranged the items on top of them. She ran a line between the two elm trees in the front yard and neatly hung his clothes up, even his spare and dress uniforms. She emptied his bedroom drawers and organized the things she found in smaller cartons: socks, ten pairs, for fifty cents; sweatshirts, two for a dollar. She set the bed up behind her folding chair, where she wouldn't have to see it.

She went back into the house for a final quick check, since curious neighbors were already milling on the front lawn. The walls were bare of his ancestral paraphernalia. The living room seemed empty, now that his old leather wing chair was sitting in front of the azaleas. Overall, the house looked much like her apartment had eight years ago, before she had met him.

There was only one thing left in the house that reminded her of him. It was the panel of stained-glass, the daffodils on a blue border, that he'd given her just a few months before. She stopped in the bedroom doorway, staring as the sun filtered through it and burned the colors and pattern onto the mattress. When he gave it to her that day, she'd held it up to the light, turning it back and forth, until his hands had come over hers, stilling. "Be careful," he had said. "It's fragile. See the soft lead? It bends. It can break."

She wondered why she had not perceived that conversation then the same way she did now: as a shrill and distant warning. Instead she had only smiled at him, smiled and said that she knew this; that of course, she understood.

Glancing around her, she took a quick calculation of what had sold, what still remained. The strongbox in her lap held over seven hundred dollars at last count; she could easily believe that half of the people in the town had stopped by at some point to browse, if not to buy. The fishing tackle and his grandfather's bamboo fly rod had been among the first things to go. All of his suits were gone. The head teacher at the nursery school had bought every last uniform, saying the four-year-olds loved to play policeman, and wouldn't this be a wonderful addition to the dress-up corner?

The only things left were his boxer shorts—she supposed they would have to be sent to Goodwill—and a stack of travel magazines that she'd found quite by accident behind his band saw. Inspired, she stood up and took the stack, then walked to the edge of the driveway. She handed the one on top—blue ocean, white beach, "200 Top Caribbean Hotels"—to a man with a little girl in tow. "Thank you for stopping by," she said, offering the magazine like a theater *Playbill,* or a parting gift.

At ten past five, she sat down on her folding chair. She remembered reading once about tribal Indian societies centuries earlier, in which women had the power to divorce a husband simply by stacking his shoes outside a tipi. She pressed her knees together and tried not to think about the sun that was blinding her eyes and giving her a headache.

Her husband drove up at 5:26. "Hi," he said. "I made good time."

She did not say anything.

He glanced at the overturned boxes, the pile of underwear to the left of her feet, the bare strung clothesline, the box on her lap. "Getting rid of some stuff? It was a good day for a garage sale."

She did not turn to face him as he gave her a strange look and walked into the house. She counted how many breaths it took before he thundered down the stairs and out the door, to stand in front of her. His face was red with anger and he blocked out the low sun so that the edges of his hair and his shoulders seemed to be on fire.

"I'm sorry," she said coolly, coming to her feet. She gestured gracefully around the lawn. "There's nothing left." Clutching the strongbox beneath her arm, she walked down the driveway and into the street. She put one foot mechanically in front of the other in the direction she knew would lead to the center of town, and she did not allow herself to look back.

# PART I

Who will not mercy unto others show,
How can he mercy ever hope to have?

—Edmund Spenser, *The Faerie Queene*

A man gazing on the stars is proverbially
at the mercy of the puddles on the road.

—Alexander Smith, *Men of Letters*

After a while, I couldn't remember whole pieces of you, as if part of the punishment was a recollection through a filter that grew hazier with time. On certain Sunday mornings when I dreamed you, I could not picture what your teeth had looked like, or the exact curve of your jaw where it fit in my hand.

I used to imagine us sitting down for a drink at a bright little restaurant, maybe one of those specialty coffee shops that have become so popular. I swear I could smell the blended beans and the starch of the white napkins, even the milled soap that you would have used that morning. I was able to see your easy smile, which always seemed to startle its way across your face—your smile, but not your teeth—and the way your fingers tapped a light tattoo against the mug. I did not give us conversation: no _You look great,_ no _What have you been up to?_ no _It has been hell._ Like your teeth and the line of your jaw, this part was unclear to me. I was not sure if there was a protocol to follow when I welcomed back from hiding my other half.

# ONE

*I*n the moments before, she laid a hand on his arm. "No matter what," she said, giving him a look, "you cannot stop."

He turned away. "I'm not sure I can even start."

She brought his hand to her lips, kissed each finger. "If you don't do it," she said simply, "who will?"

For a long while they sat side by side, staring out a streaked window at a town neither of them knew very well. He watched her breathing pattern in the reflection of the glass, and tried to slow his own heart until they were equally matched. The quiet dulled his senses, so that he became fixated on the clock beside the bed. He would not blink, he told himself, until the next minute bled into the last.

With a fury that surprised him, he turned his face into the bow of her neck, trying to commit to memory this softness and this smell. "I love you."

She smiled, that crooked little curving of her mouth. "Now," she said, "don't you think I know that?"

In the end, she had struggled. He wore the scratches like a brand. But he had held the pillow to her face; calmed her by whispering in her ear. *My love,* he had said, *I'll be with you as soon as I can.* At the words her arms had fallen away; then it was over. He had buried his face in her shirt, and started himself the very slow process of dying.

*F*or the hundredth time that day, Cameron MacDonald, Chief of Police in Wheelock, Massachusetts, closed his eyes and dreamed of the Bay of Biscay. If he got it just right—the thrum of silence in the station, the afternoon light dancing over the corner of his scarred desk—he could make himself believe. There *was* no Smith and Wesson jabbing into his side; there *was* no mountain pass outside the window; hell, maybe he wasn't even Cameron MacDonald anymore. He opened his mind as wide as he could, and let himself tumble into the beautiful blue of it.

He blinked his eyes, expecting the bobbing shoreline of Prest, or the sweet scent of the Loire Valley that you could carry in your pocket when you were within a reasonable distance, but he found himself staring at the pale, pasty face of Hannah, the secretary at the police station. "Here's the file," she said. "He was indicted." She turned to leave, but stopped for a moment with her hand on the door. "You sure you're not coming down with something, Chief?"

Cam shook his head, as much to clear it as to convince Hannah. He smiled at her, because if he didn't, he knew she'd be on the phone with Allie and within a half hour, his wife would have him drinking a tea made of nettle roots and feverfew.

He put the file down, glancing longingly at *Gall's Buying Guide* catalog for public safety equipment, inside which he'd stuffed a *Travel* magazine. Hannah was right—there *was* something wrong with him. It was the same thing that happened every year since he'd returned to Wheelock, as was expected, to become police chief after his father's death. He was suffering from wanderlust, complicated by the tension of knowing that he was rooted to this town by something as simple as his name.

*W*heelock looked like other small western Massachusetts towns: the center consisted of a simple white church and a lending library, a joint building for fire and police, the local coffee shop, and a dotting of old men who sat on stone benches and watched their lives slouch by. But what made Wheelock different from Hancock and Dalton and Williamstown was the fact that had it not been for a twist of fate, nearly every family in Wheelock would still be living in Scotland.

At first you wouldn't notice. But then you'd see that the town restaurant served its specials on "ashets," not plates; that its serviceable stocky white china was decorated with the fat square rose of Bonnie Prince Charlie. You'd attend a marriage at St. Margaret's, and realize that the ceremony still ended with a blood vow. You'd drive through the winding side streets and see the name *MAC-DONALD* painted on an alarming number of mailboxes.

And if you happened to travel to the Scottish Highlands, you'd notice that a small town called Carrymuir on the banks of Loch Leven was an uncanny twin to Wheelock, Massachusetts.

In the 1700s, the Clan MacDonald was the largest and most powerful clan in Scotland, spread from the western isles through the main Highlands. One particular sect of the clan lived in Carrymuir, a small town north of Glencoe which was nestled between two jagged crags of mountains. In spite of the rampant clan warfare in Scotland, Carrymuir had never been defeated, built as it was in a natural, easily defended fortress.

*Clann* was the Scottish Gaelic word for children, and a clan was made up of relatives, some more distant than others, who happened to live on a given piece of land. The clan chief, or laird, had the power of life and death over his tenants and tacksmen, but the authority wasn't quite as one-sided as a king's. After all, the chief's subjects were his brothers and nephews and cousins, and the trust and respect they offered up to him came at the price of his protection and his promise to care for them.

Cameron MacDonald of Wheelock, Massachusetts, had been named for his great-great-great-great-great-grandfather, a legendary soldier who had fought in the battle of Culloden, where the English routed the Highlanders. Cameron had heard the story over and over as a boy: When his namesake realized that Bonnie Prince Charlie's Highland army didn't stand a chance against the English soldiers, he tried to save his clansmen from being killed in battle. He secured their honorable discharges by promising, in exchange, his own remarkable skill in a fight to the death against the British. But he hadn't died, as he had expected. And after Culloden, when the victorious English came through Scotland burning towns and slaughtering livestock and raping village women, the first Cameron MacDonald realized he had to again save his clan.

So while he went to jail as a Jacobite prisoner, he arranged for the families of Carrymuir to leave, one by one, on packets bound for the American colonies. Which explained why, when most Scots were being hanged or sold as indentured servants to the West Indies, this small sect of Clan MacDonald remained intact and resettled in the wilderness of Massachusetts.

They found a spot that looked like home, with a brace of rolling mountains and a narrow body of water that was more of a pond than a lake, and sent word back to Scotland about this place. *Wee loch,* they wrote. *It's set by a wee loch.*

And eventually, the laird and his family came over too, leaving a trusted uncle to watch over the land in Scotland. They traded the comfortable kilt for trousers; they proudly flew the Stars and Stripes; they accepted the Americanized name of the town. And as a natural extension of inbred responsibility, the man who was the figurehead of the Clan MacDonald also became Wheelock's police chief.

In 1995, that position belonged to Cameron MacDonald II, having been handed down from his great-grandfather to his grandfather to his father, passing along the same line of succession as the honorary title of clan chief. He'd be the first to tell you that things had changed. Obviously, although he was considered the chief of a clan and duly noted in the Scottish records, he was no longer directly responsible for the welfare of the townspeople. At least three-quarters of the town had never even seen the lands in Scotland that technically belonged to them. Hardly anyone spoke with a burr; fewer still knew more than a smattering of Gaelic.

On the other hand, old habits died hard. There was no tarnished silver bowl or royal edict that proved that Wheelock was MacDonald land, but it was theirs just the same, in the way that their ancestors had laid claim to that narrow pass in the Scottish Highlands. It was land, quite simply, they'd lived on forever.

At age thirty-five, Cameron MacDonald knew he would stay in Wheelock for the rest of his life; that he would be the police chief until he died and passed the office to his firstborn son. He knew these were things he did not have a choice about, no more than he had a choice about tossing off the choking obligation of being the current laird. Sometimes, in the very still parts of the night, he would tell himself that an honorary title did not mean today what it meant two hundred and fifty years ago. He'd reason that if he picked up his wife and moved to Phoenix for the climate, everyone would take it in stride.

Then he would remember how Darcy MacDonald, his third cousin's daughter, had tripped right on Main Street when Cam was no more than three feet away, talking to the town barber. She'd had seventeen stitches in her knee because he hadn't moved quite fast enough, or been in the right place at the right time. In fact, some days he felt that every arrest, every conviction, was a reflection of something he'd done wrong as a leader.

He'd press up against the soft, snoring curl of his wife, Allie, because she was as solid as any truth he could spin. And he'd try to push himself back into sleep, but his dreams were always of chains, link after link after link, which stretched across the vast Atlantic.

When Allie Gordon was in high school, she was not the most popular girl in her class. She was nowhere even close. That honor belonged to Verona MacBean, with her cotton-candy puff of hair and her Cover Girl mascara and her pink mohair sweater molded like skin to what the boys referred to as the Hoosac Ridge.

And today, fifteen years out of nowhere, Verona MacBean herself stepped into Glory in the Flower and ordered three large centerpieces for a library luncheon to be given in her name.

"Verona!" Allie had immediately recalled the name. There was something disconcerting about seeing her classmate dressed in a severe beige suit, her hair scraped into a knot at the back of her head, her cheeks flat beneath a sheer layer of foundation. "What brings you to town?"

Verona had made a little clicking noise with the back of her teeth. "Allie," she said, her voice just as thin and breathy as it had been in high school, "don't tell me you're still here!"

It was not meant as an insult, it never was, so Allie simply shrugged. "Well," she said, drawing out her words and savoring them like a fine French delicacy, "since Cam's here to stay . . ." She let her voice trail off at the end, peeking up at Verona from the order form she was filling out. Then she stared her in the face. "You *did* hear about Cam and me, didn't you?"

Verona had walked over to the refrigerated case, as if inspecting the quality of the flowers she had already commissioned. "Yes," she said. "I seem to recall something about that."

A few minutes later Verona had left, specifying the *exact* time for the centerpieces to arrive (it was an author's luncheon; it wouldn't do to have wilted roses for an author who, as she put it, was just coming into bloom). Allie had walked to the back room of the flower shop, where she kept her foam and moss and desiccants, her raffia and wire. She stood in front of the tiny mirror over the bathroom sink, assessing her complexion. Then, rummaging through a bookshelf, she found her high school yearbook—kept solely for putting together names and faces that walked into the shop. She let the book fall open to Verona's page. It was much easier to believe that she, Allie, had grown older and wiser, while Verona MacBean, in glossy black and white, was trapped in time. It did not matter that Verona had gone on to Harvard and then to Yale, that her first book—philosophy— was the talk of the town. It only mattered that in the long run, Allie Gordon had married Cameron MacDonald, which no one in Wheelock would have guessed on a long shot.

On the other hand, it was no great surprise when Verona MacBean became Cameron MacDonald's steady girlfriend in the fall of 1977, although Cameron was a high school senior and Verona was a freshman. They were both undeniably beautiful, Verona in a collectible doll sort of way, and Cam towering over nearly everyone else in the school, his wide, strong shoulders and bright shock of hair always easy to spot.

Allie fell in love with his hair first. She used to sit in the school library bent over a slim volume of Plath's poetry, waiting for him to come through the double glass doors that blocked off the bustle of the hall. He came in every day during the period she worked at the counter checking out books for the grateful, understaffed librarian. She'd straighten the shelves behind the spot where he sat down, imagining her fingers weaving through that hair, separating it so the strands that looked like fire prismed off into reds and rangy yellows. At the end of the class period, she would pick up the books he'd left behind and tuck them back in their Dewey decimal places, trying to hold on to the heat Cam's hands had placed on the protective plastic covers.

The truth was that Cameron MacDonald did not know Allie Gordon existed for most of the time they had lived in the same town. She was far too quiet, too plain to attract his attention. There was only one incident in high school where Cam had ever truly come in contact with her: during a blood drive, they had been lying beside each other on the donor tables, and when she sat up and hopped from the stretcher to get her promised juice and cookies, the world spun and went black. She awakened in Cam's arms; he'd jumped off his own table to catch her as she fell, unintentionally ripping the intravenous from the crook of his elbow so that when Allie went home that afternoon, she realized that Cam's blood spotted the back of her blouse.

Allie had trouble convincing herself that the reason they had gotten married years later did *not* have to do with the fact that after college, they were two of the few who had come back to Wheelock. Cam had returned because it was expected of him, Allie because there was nowhere else she really wanted to be.

If she stood on the bottom ledge of the refrigeration unit for the fresh flowers and craned her neck in a certain way out the window, she could see Cam's office at the police station, even make out his shadowy form hunched over his desk. It was the reason she'd chosen this particular real estate space when she opened the flower shop eight years ago.

She saw that he was in, not out on patrol, and decided now was as good a time as any to bring him his arrangement and tell him about Verona. She crawled down from the ledge, rubbing her hands against her knees to warm them up, and closed the sliding glass door of the cooler. Absently, she ran her fingers over the sweet chestnut and barberry foliage that made up the greens in the piece she would bring over to Cam.

Allie knew the language of flowers—the idea that every bloom stands for some quality of human nature. Bouquets sent from the shop for the arrival of a baby were stuffed with daisies, for innocence, and moss, for maternal love. Valentine's arrangements had roses, of course, but also lilies for purity, heliotrope for devotion, and forget-me-nots for true love. To Cam, she often sent designs that were full of messages she knew he could not understand. She eyed her latest work critically, nodding over the tulips which made up the bulk of the piece. In Persia, a man would give a tulip to his betrothed to show that as red as the flower was, he was on fire with love; as black as its center, his heart was smoldering like a coal.

She filled out the vase with Michaelmas daisies, China asters, and fire thorn. And then, as she always did for Cam's arrangements, she added as many sprigs of purple clover as she could without making the lines of the flowers seem overblown. Clover, which simply meant, *Think of me.*

When she walked out the door to take the flowers to Cam, she did not bother to lock it. Very few people would try to rob the wife of the Wheelock police chief.

Hannah was on the telephone when she walked through the door of the police station, but waved her toward Cam's closed office door to tell her he wasn't in a meeting. "No," she was saying firmly. "We don't use psychics, but thank you."

Allie set the tall vase in the center of the main desk, where bookings were done, and then walked to Cameron's office. She gave a quick knock and pushed the door open with her shoulder before Cam could tell her to come in. He was asleep, his head pillowed on his arms on top of his desk.

Smiling, Allie crept around behind his chair, running her fingers through the hair at the back of his neck. She bent close to his ear to whisper. "While justice sleeps," she teased.

Cameron came awake with a start, snapping his head up so abruptly he clipped Allie's chin. Allie staggered back, seeing black for a moment, until Cam grabbed her and pulled her down onto his lap. "Jesus, Allie," he said. "You scared the hell out of me." Allie rubbed her jaw, testing it gingerly by setting her teeth. Cam's fingers came up to brush her throat. "You okay?"

Allie smiled. "I brought you your flowers."

Cam rubbed his hand down his face. "I told you you don't have to do that."

"I like to."

Cam snorted. "This is a police station, not a hotel lobby," he pointed out. "People who are arrested aren't much interested in interior design. They don't even notice."

"But *you* do," Allie pressed.

Cam looked up at her wide brown eyes; her hands, gripping each other. "Sure," he said softly. "Sure I do."

He glanced out the open doorway to the front desk where Allie's latest arrangement stood. She was an artist; he told her that often. The mixtures of reds and blues, of stark lines and soft curves, and the overall whimsy of her floral designs gave her creations a comfort and an ease that did not exist in Allie herself. Once he had peeked at her personal journal when she was at work, hoping to find a layer to his wife that she didn't have the courage to reveal. But there had been no racy thoughts or dreamy recollections, just a review of how she had acted and what she had said to Cam, and then notes on what she might have done differently.

Sometimes he woke up in the middle of the night, sweating, worried that after years of marriage to Allie he, too, would wind up editing his life, instead of simply living it.

"Guess who came into the store today." Allie moved off his lap to sit on the corner of the desk, swinging one leg.

"Am I supposed to go through everyone in the town?" Cam asked.

"Verona MacBean." Allie frowned. "Well, I don't know if it's MacBean anymore, but she's here, all the same. She's a famous writer now. They're doing some hotshot lunch for her at the library."

"Verona MacBean," Cam said, grinning. He tipped his chair onto its two rear legs. "Good old Verona MacBean."

"Oh, cut it out," Allie said, lightly kicking him in the leg. "She's pinched and pruny and her boobs don't look nearly as big now as they did when she was sixteen."

"Probably grew into them."

Allie picked up a catalog and whipped it at Cam's head. A glossy travel magazine fell onto the desk between them. Her eyes widened at the white spray of beach and the weaving red sloop splayed across the front cover. She picked it up and curiously thumbed through it. "Well, at least it's not *Playboy*," she said. She skimmed a list of all-inclusive resorts, and peered closer at an advertisement depicting a tastefully nude sunbather.

Cam reached across the desk and plucked the magazine out of Allie's hand. His face felt hot, his collar too tight; he didn't want Allie to know what he spent his time daydreaming about.

Allie raised her eyebrows as a blush crept across Cameron's face. "I'll be damned," she said. "You're trying to keep a secret." She leaned close to Cam. "Not that it's up to me or anything, but I'd rather go sailing than skiing." She hesitantly moved forward an inch, keeping her eyes open, and touched her lips to Cam's.

For a moment, Cam let her breath brush his mouth and then he kissed her quickly and pushed her back. "Not here," he murmured.

"Then where?" Allie whispered, before she could stop herself.

They both looked away, remembering the previous night. Allie's hands had stolen across the bed, slipping under the blue T-shirt he was wearing, moving in quiet circles. That was her invitation. And Cam had simply turned toward her, his eyes setting a distance, his fingers staying her own.

"Oh," she had said, her hand dropping away.

"It's not you," he'd explained. "I'm just exhausted."

Allie wondered where the myth that men wanted to make love more than women came from, since in her experience it was always the other way around. She did not like being less beautiful than her husband, or being the one who always made an advance. Sometimes Cam did not even bother to tell her he was tired. Sometimes he simply pretended to be asleep.

She questioned if it might have been different if she were a classic beauty, or if she were sexy. She told herself that she'd lose ten pounds and cut her hair and mold herself into someone irresistible, and then when Cam came grabbing for her she'd simply turn away.

Maybe she'd find someone else.

And then she'd laugh at the very thought of letting anyone touch her the way Cameron MacDonald had.

As if she had conjured it, Cam reached for her wrist and began to stroke it with his thumb. He did not know what else to do. There were some things he just could not tell Allie, not even after five years. There were some times he needed to be alone with thoughts of what he might have otherwise done with his life, and unfortunately that was often in the hollow of the night when Allie needed more from him. But in spite of what she thought when he rolled away from her, there was never any question in his mind about his feelings for Allie. Loving her was a little like taking the same seat day after day on a commuter train—you couldn't imagine how it might feel to be in the row behind, you could swear that the dimensions and hollows of the seat were made just for you, you came back to it repeatedly with a whoosh of comfort and relief that it was still available.

Allie was staring at him. If only she'd stop looking at him like that, her eyes catching his excuses and throwing them to the wind. He wished he could make her happy, or even spend as much time trying to as she did for him. Cam dug his thumbs under the loops of his heavy ammunition belt; out of the corner of his eye he saw a two-page spread of Acadia National Park. "I'm sorry," he said.

*No,* Allie thought, *I am.*

The woman stood behind the counter of the flower shop with her hands flying over a mix of fan palm, angel wings, bells of Ireland, gaultheria, oats, and milkweed. Cuttings carpeted the Formica and the black and white tiles of the floor. For a moment, Allie stood shocked in the doorway of her own store, watching a stranger do her job. Then she focused on the arrangement to the right of the cash register.

It was bell-shaped and quiet, a delicate arch of every shade of greenery that Allie had stored in the refrigerated case. At two spots, a splash of bright red caladium peeked from behind feathers of grass, shocking as blood.

Allie took a step forward, and the woman jumped, her hand at her throat. "You're in my place," Allie said.

The woman smiled hesitantly. "Well, then . . . I'll move." She hastily gathered up the tools she'd filched from the back room, and in her hurry dropped a pair of shears on the floor. "Sorry," she murmured, dipping below the line of the counter to pick them up. She stepped around the counter and handed them to Allie like a peace offering.

It was the most presumptuous thing Allie had ever seen— some stranger walking into the store and making her own flower arrangement—and yet this woman seemed to blend into the shadows, like this had all been a mistake and out of her range of control. Allie glanced at the plum beret on the woman's hair, the nails bitten to the quick, the heavy knapsack slung against her right foot. She was about the same age as Allie, but certainly not from

Wheelock or anywhere nearby; Allie would have remembered someone with eyes the wet violet color of prairie gentians.

Allie walked up to the counter, letting the softer greenery graze her palms. "I thought you might be looking for an assistant," the woman said. She held out her hand, which was callused at the fingers from florist's wire, and shaking slightly. "My name is Mia Townsend."

Allie could not tear her eyes away from Mia's arrangement, which brought to mind rolling fields and nickering horses and the hot, heavy press of a summer afternoon. She knew it had nothing to do with the actual flowers and ferns Mia had chosen, but rather the skill of the placement and the thoughts that had gone into it.

Allie had not been looking for anybody; in fact in a town the size of Wheelock most of her business came from the shop's association with FTD. But then again, Christmas was coming, and Valentine's Day, and she'd kick herself if she let someone with Mia's talent walk out the door before she could learn a thing or two from her.

As if she knew that Allie was equivocating, Mia suddenly reached down for her knapsack and pulled out a carefully wrapped package, which she began to unwind. Allie found herself looking at an exquisitely twisted bonsai tree; miniature, gnarled, ancient.

"Lovely," Allie breathed.

Mia shrugged, but her eyes were shining. "This is my specialty. They remind me of those babies you see sometimes, the ones with tiny little faces that look like they know all the wisdom of the world."

*The wisdom of the world.* Allie looked up. "I think," she said, "we can work something out."

H annah, who had a talent for eavesdropping, told Cameron that Verona MacBean had written a book on the image of hell.

"It's not like it used to be," she said, tracing the top edge of her coffee cup. "You know, fire and brimstone and all."

Cam laughed. "Don't tell Father Gillivray; he's looking forward to that stuff."

Hannah smiled at Cameron. "Verona says that instead of physical pain, it's more mental. Like, you know, if you marry this gorgeous guy only to find out in hell that he really married you for your money."

"I wouldn't worry," Cam said. "I don't pay you nearly enough."

She smirked. "And suppose that in order to marry this hunk, you gave up someone who was *really* in love with you. The pain you'd feel knowing you picked the wrong guy is supposedly what hell is like." Hannah wrinkled her nose. "Not that I can see where Verona MacBean, Wheelock Queen, would know what hell is like at all."

Camerona's full-time sergeant, Zandy Monroe, stuck his head out from the locker room. "You forget, Hannah, that Verona used to date the chief."

Cam threw a stack of mail at him. "Don't you have anything better to do?"

"That depends," Zandy said, grinning. "You taking me out to lunch?"

"No," Cam said. "I'm taking Allie out." He surprised himself; this wasn't something they'd planned when she stopped by earlier, but he knew she'd jump at the offer to spend an hour with him. He pulled on his heavy blue coat and locked his office door behind him. "If the town comes under siege," he said to Hannah, "you know where I'll be."

Walking down the half block to Allie's flower shop, he started to smile. He'd step into the store and tell her he was looking for a bouquet, dahlias and lilies in colors that called back August. He'd say it was for someone special and he'd make her play along and give him a gift card and then he'd write, *What are you doing for the rest of your life?*

Humming, Cam threw open the door of the flower shop and came face-to-face with a woman he had never seen before. Allie's name died on his lips as he stared at the tangle of hair that bobbed just to her shoulders, the soft swollen curve of her lip, the pulse at the base of her throat. She was not beautiful; she was not familiar; and still all the breath left Cam's body. As he grasped the hand she extended in greeting, he realized that her eyes were blue-violet, the shade that he'd dreamed as the Bay of Biscay.

*O*h," Allie said, coming out from the back room. "This is Mia." And that was all she had time to tell Cam before Zandy Monroe burst through the door of the shop, throwing it back against its hinges hard enough to crack one pane of glass.

"Chief," he said, "you'd better come."

Years of instinct had Cameron flying out the door behind his sergeant, left hand trained and ready on his gun. He saw a growing crowd of people in front of the police station; from the corner of his eye he noticed Allie and Mia shivering their way closer to the commotion.

With adrenaline pulsing through his limbs, Cam stepped into the center of the group, where a red Ford pickup truck was parked. Zandy walked up to the driver's-side window. "Okay," he said, "this is the chief of police." With a shrug at Cam, he murmured, "Wouldn't talk to anyone but you."

"Cameron MacDonald?"

The man's voice was strong but strained; an officer with less experience than Cam might not have noticed the pain that ran ragged over the syllables. "Yes," he said. "What can I do for you?"

The man stepped out of the car. He did not live in Wheelock, but Cam thought he'd seen him around town this past week. At the post office, maybe the tavern at the Inn. He was every bit as tall as Cam, but thinner, as if being alive had simply taken its toll. "I'm James MacDonald," the man said, loud enough for everyone to hear his last name. "I'm your cousin." He took a step back toward his truck, gesturing toward the passenger seat, in which a woman was slumped over, sleeping. "My wife here, Maggie, is dead." He looked up at Cameron MacDonald. "And I'm the one who killed her."

# TWO

Notwithstanding Verona MacBean's standards, all hell broke loose. Two women fainted, one striking her forehead on the sidewalk so that a thick red pool of blood puddled under her cheek. In a pointless act of chivalry Art MacInnes, the local barber, walked up to James MacDonald and punched him in the nose. Two children on bright neon bikes wove around the pickup truck and through the festering crowd.

"All right!" Cam yelled. He gestured to Zandy, who started to walk around to the other side of the pickup. For all Cam knew, this guy could be some nut; the lady in the front seat could be napping or in a diabetic coma or playing along. Cam turned around to face the crowd. "You all go home," he said. "I can't take care of this if you don't leave."

No one moved.

Cam sighed and took a tentative step toward James MacDonald, his arms stretched out in front of him. James was slightly hunched over, holding his hands up to a face streaming with blood. Cam reached into his pocket for a handkerchief. "Here," he said, waving the small white square in front of James's face, in a gesture that looked much like a surrender.

James MacDonald hadn't done anything threatening; there was no reason to bring him into the station in handcuffs. Cam would sit him down, offer him coffee, try to get him talking. He wouldn't arrest him just yet.

"Chief," Zandy Monroe said, "the door's stuck."

At the sergeant's voice, James MacDonald whirled around to see Zandy tugging at the passenger door of the pickup truck. When it wouldn't budge, Zandy slipped two fingers into the partially unrolled window and tried to reach the woman's neck to get a pulse.

With a feral cry, James MacDonald ripped out of Cam's grasp and ran to the other side of the truck. He pulled the sergeant away from the door, throwing him backward with the bodily force that a tall, strong man learns to keep in check. "Don't you touch her," he screamed at Zandy, his fists clenched, his teeth obscenely white against mottled skin. He turned back to the door and wrenched it open, and that was when Cam saw the door hadn't been stuck, but locked; that James MacDonald had ripped it from its bearings. He caught the body of his wife as it slumped up against him; pressed his cheek against hers. He spoke against the white curve of her neck. "Don't you touch her," he whispered.

Cam's eyes met Zandy's over the hood of the truck. He started to walk around to the passenger side as Zandy moved closer to James MacDonald. But James did not resist as Cam pulled him out of the cab of the truck. "Mr. MacDonald, I'm going to have to put you under arrest." He snapped handcuffs over the man's wrists. "Uh, Sergeant," he said, nodding at the body in the truck, "you want to take care of this?"

James began to strain against the handcuffs. "No," he whispered to Cam. "You can't."

Cam had to lean close to hear him. "We've got to go inside, Mr. MacDonald."

"Please don't leave her alone with him."

Out of the corner of his eye, Cam saw Allie step out of the crowd. She was shivering as she walked up to them, and she did not look Cam in the eye. "I'm Allie MacDonald," she said. "I'm Cam's wife." She laid her hand on James's arm. "I can stay with Maggie, if you'd like."

James looked her over, and then nodded his head. Cam let his breath out in a long sigh, and motioned for Zandy to hold James's arm. Then Cam steered Allie away from the truck. "You don't really want to do this," he said. "You could be implicated as a witness when he goes to trial."

"Oh, Cam," Allie whispered. "You're not really going to arrest him, are you?"

Cam grabbed her upper arms. "He killed a woman, Allie."

"But he came to you for protection."

Cam snorted. "That's a little like locking the barn after the horse has run out."

Allie squared her shoulders. "I'd just listen to his story, if I were you. It's obvious that he loved her."

Cam bowed his head. "Still," he said, "that isn't going to bring her back to life."

James MacDonald glanced one last time at the still and lovely body of his wife in the front seat of his truck and remembered his wedding day eleven years earlier, during which everything had gone wrong.

Maggie had picked Memorial Day weekend, hoping to stand outside for the ceremony, but the balmy weather that was forecast had dissolved into torrential rain. Wanting privacy, they'd opted for a justice of the peace, and had made an appointment. But they showed up at the man's door only to be told by his wife that he'd come down with the stomach flu, and so Jamie had driven from Cummington to the next town to the next, trying to find someone who hadn't gone away for the holiday and who would be willing to marry them.

By the time Jamie and Maggie were standing in the front parlor of a justice of the peace in Great Barrington, the cuffs of Jamie's trousers were soaked from puddles and Maggie's bouquet of violets was limp over her fist. In the background, they could hear the splintered laughter of the justice's guests, who were having a free-for-all Memorial Day cookout in the warm, dry confines of his garage. "We are gathered here," the justice of the peace said, "to . . . Oh, shit."

Maggie's head had snapped up. Her hand, tucked inside Jamie's, shook a little.

Jamie realized then that she was waiting for him to ask, on her behalf, if there was a problem. Chauvinistic and old-world as it might have been, nothing more clearly drove home to Jamie what it was going to mean to be a husband. He would be Maggie's mouthpiece. And at other times, she might speak for him.

"Is something wrong?" he had asked.

The justice of the peace squinted over James's shoulder. "Witness," he said. "Can't do it without one." He cupped his hands and yelled in the general direction of the garage, until a sweaty, wild-eyed man appeared in the doorway holding a Coors. "Jesus," the man said. "You don't have to shout." He thrust the can into the justice's hand.

"Not *now,* Tom," the justice said.

Tom frowned. "I thought you yelled for a beer."

"I yelled *Come here.*"

"Excuse me," Jamie interrupted. "Could we get going again?"

Tom was wearing a Chicago Bulls tank top and Lycra biking shorts that outlined his belly. A loose, wet smile splayed across his face. "Hey," he said, looking from Jamie to Maggie. "You getting hitched?"

The justice asked him to just sit down in the corner and be quiet, and he'd put his name on the marriage license in a few minutes.

"No way," Tom said. He grabbed Maggie's free hand, scattering her violets, and yanked her away from Jamie. "You got to do a wedding right, or you don't do it at all." With a quick jerk he anchored Maggie to his side. "I'll give you away, honey," he said. "We'll do a whole grand entrance."

At that point Jamie did not want the man's name on his marriage license, much less his hands on his fiancée. But before he could object, Maggie smiled easily. "That would be lovely," she said to Tom, although she was looking at Jamie. *Let's just get it over with,* her eyes seemed to be saying, *so that we can laugh about it later.*

Jamie thought of the women he had dated, their images shifting like smoke. Some had told him their plans for an elaborate marriage on the second or third date; one had even drawn him a sketch on a cocktail napkin of a wedding gown she'd had made up and stored in the back of her closet, just in case. Not one of the women he'd known in his past would have made it through this fiasco of a wedding without being reduced to tears. Not one of the women he'd known in his past could hold a candle to Maggie.

He had never really asked her to marry him, he realized. They had simply both assumed that it was going to happen.

"Under the Boardwalk" was blaring from the garage as Maggie, on Tom's arm, began to walk across the small parlor. Her heels crushed the violets she'd dropped on the way out. Her perfume was overshadowed by the alcoholic cloud surrounding the man beside her. Next to Jamie, the justice of the peace began to flip through his book, having lost his place.

Maggie reached Jamie's side and slipped her arm through his. He could feel her shaking, so he patted her hand gently. He would apologize to her for this. He would spend the rest of his life making it up to her.

"We are gathered here . . ." the justice of the peace said.

"For the free beer," Tom finished.

Maggie covered her mouth with her hand, and then burst into laughter. Her head tipped back so that Jamie could see the long, smooth line of her throat, and the spill of russet hair over her shoulders. There were tears in her eyes; Jamie thought it made them seem like jewels.

"Marriage," the justice recited sternly, "is not something to be entered into lightly and unadvisedly."

"I'm sorry," Maggie said, trying to compose herself. She tightened her hand on Jamie's and looked down at her shoes and snorted, then bit down on her lip.

The justice began to speak, but Jamie didn't listen. He had turned to face Maggie. Beyond her was not a glittering ballroom or the hallowed glass panel of a church, but a weaving line of people doing the bunny hop and a barbecue that belched out large drafts of smoke.

He realized that there was nowhere else on earth he would have rather been.

Suddenly Jamie went cold. Maggie must have sensed it, because she dropped his hand and placed her palm against his cheek, whispering, "What is it?"

He shook his head. He, who could have told Maggie anything, did not know how to put into words this feeling: Did you ever look down at yourself and realize that finally you had it all? Did you ever feel that everything was so right in your life you'd have nowhere to go but downhill?

Misunderstanding, Maggie touched her fingers to his mouth. "I'm fine," she assured him. "This is fine."

He nodded once, a jerk of his head. He pushed away his thoughts and concentrated on the hope he'd been fed from his own wife's hand.

As soon as Cam began to lead James MacDonald into the Wheelock Police Department, the crowd outside began to disperse. At the front desk, he unlocked the handcuffs and asked James to empty his pockets. He watched a handful of pennies, a packet of gum, and some lint fall onto the Formica, but nothing that would incriminate the man as a murderer.

Hannah was out to lunch, so the station was empty, silent except for the intermittent static and calls of the dispatcher on the radio. "Mr. MacDonald," Cam said, "why don't you come on in here?"

He led the prisoner into the booking room and gestured to a chair. Then Cam sat down and pulled a custody report out of a file in the drawer, laying it facedown on the desk in front of him. He'd listen to what the guy had to say, but he'd bet his gun this was going to end in an arrest.

He looked up to find the man staring at him with a grin turning up the corner of his mouth. "They say you look like him, you know," James said.

"Look like who?"

"Cameron MacDonald. The first one. The famous one."

Cam made a big production of arranging the spill of pens and pencils on the desk. "I wouldn't know," he said. He took a deep breath. "Look, right now I'm just the chief of police, and you've confessed to murder. So let's forget the other crap."

"I can't. I came to Wheelock on purpose, because you were here."

Cam narrowed his eyes. "How exactly are you related to me?"

"Your grandfather is my great-uncle. Ask Angus, if you don't believe me. What is he now, eighty? Eighty-two?"

"What he is is senile, at least most of the time," Cam admitted. His great-uncle Angus had been the keeper at Carrymuir during the years that Cam and his father had prospered in Wheelock. When Ian MacDonald died, Cam had flown to Scotland, brought his uncle Angus home with him, and signed Carrymuir over to the Scottish National Trust.

"Mr. MacDonald—"

"Jamie." He leaned forward, as if he was about to confide a secret. "I was named for our own uncle Jamie," he said. "The one who
was killed in the war."

Cam's mouth fell open. No one talked about his uncle Jamie,
the hero, because it used to make his grandmother weep. Jamie had
been the firstborn son, the one who would have been clan chief if
he hadn't been shot down over the Pacific in 1944. Cam's father,
the second son, had taken the title by default.

Cam swallowed, recovering. "Well, Jamie," he said. "Tell me
what brought you to Wheelock."

He hesitated only a second. "I came here to kill my wife."

Cam stared right into Jamie's eyes, almost the same color as his
own—sea green, a MacDonald trait. He looked for a swift check of
rage, a curl of remorse, or God willing, the blaze of insanity. He
saw none of those things. "Jamie," he said, rolling the custody report into the typewriter, "you have the right to remain silent."

Jamie MacDonald had made a career of creating alternative
worlds. He let young couples designing their first home walk
through houses that had not yet been built; he gave paraplegic men
a chance to walk again; he let medical students do surgery on patients that did not suffer or bleed. As the president and founder of
Techcellence, a conceptual-design computer company specializing
in virtual reality, he had joined the cutting edge of a radical technological movement and had become a symbol for the entire field.
Maggie, whose computer skills extended to booting up WordPer-
fect, used to say it was much simpler than that. "You're the Wizard
of Oz," she would tell him. "You make people's wishes come true."

He'd sort of liked that image. It was true—people tended to
seek out Techcellence to do things no other conceptual-design firm
would do. Because Jamie wasn't afraid to take a challenge and
shape it with his mind and his hands until it fit on a seven-by-nine
screen, his company often produced the systems and models for virtual worlds that became prototypes for other firms to copy.

Jamie had a high-end computer system at his house in Cummington, complete with a bodysuit and glove and head-mounted
device, but most of the design work was done in his lab. Located
downtown, it had computers with more technological expertise, as

well as the big equipment—the SGI Onyxs, graphics machines which could generate the real time in the virtual world. There were about ten people who worked full-time for Jamie, and when Techcellence secured a contract with Nintendo or the Defense Department or a teaching hospital, there were two hundred more people he could hire on as subcontractors—digital sound mixers, artists, story writers, texture mappers, producers, directors, programmers. In many ways, Jamie was like a chef—finding cooks who had already made dishes that he could combine into something even more flavorful, in spite of the fact that he'd grown none of the ingredients himself.

He often came into work on weekends, when it was quietest; and he'd bring Maggie with him. One Saturday, a few years after they were married, Jamie had come in to fiddle with a program for a private client, a formerly seeded millionaire tennis player who had become quadriplegic after a heli-skiing accident. Maggie, who openly admitted to being terrified of so many computers, sat curled with a book on a Salvation Army wing chair where some of the best brainstorming was done.

Jamie was stuck. It wasn't creating the virtual world—any savvy hacker could jump on the Internet and download to do that. This client had a specific request: he wanted to play tennis again.

Had Jamie wanted to milk him for his money, he could have simply set the program up like some of the other virtual reality systems developed for handicapped people. A sweatband around a quadriplegic's head could measure the magnetic field given off by the optic nerve, so that the guy would be able to move a cursor—or a virtual tennis racket—simply by shifting his eyes. But Jamie, who had always been something of a perfectionist, wanted to give his client more. It would not be enough to see a racket swing on a computer screen and know you had connected with a ball, like those archaic Pong games on the old Atari video game systems. He wanted his client to *believe* he was on his own feet again.

Ordinarily, this wasn't a problem when creating a virtual world. A good HMD tracked your head movements and isolated your views to computer-generated images, in a 190-degree field. With the addition of a glove, a bodysuit, and a motion platform, there were three kinds of feedback a designer could generate. Tactile feedback produced vibrations at specific parts of your body, which your brain would interpret along with visual and auditory clues—if you see and hear oozing slime, you'll feel it. Auditory and visual feedback employed subtleties, such as subfrequencies outside the hearing range, to give the sensation of motion, or flight, or vertigo. And force feedback—actual shoves applied to the body—could make you feel like you were in microgravity, or blasting off in a rocket.

The problem was, on someone who couldn't sense anything beneath his neck, these types of feedback would be lost.

Jamie pulled the HMD off his head and rubbed his hands over his face. He wasn't even aware he'd sighed in frustration until Maggie put down her book and came to stand beside him. "Tough day at the office?" she said, rubbing his shoulders.

"Impossible," Jamie admitted. "How do I go about making someone feel something they're not physically capable of feeling?"

Maggie frowned. "I'm not following you."

"VR for the handicapped," Jamie explained, passing her the HMD. "Quadriplegic wants to play tennis."

He knew, by the smile that curved Maggie's lips beneath the high-tech helmet, that she was delighted with the visual images of the tennis center in Flushing Meadow—the lined courts, the perspiring crowds, the smoggy blue of the sky. He watched on the flat screen as Maggie flickered her eyes, making a tennis racket appear at the edge of her virtual vision and swing in a forehand. "He wants other friends to be able to connect into the virtual space. And he wants a neural network thrown in, a 'smart enemy,' in case no one else is around to play against him."

"Why are you stuck?"

Jamie shrugged. "Because I can't make him feel the sweat on the grip of his racket. Because I won't be able to make his legs tired from running."

"That's hardly your fault," Maggie said. "Couldn't you overcompensate somewhere else? You know, like a scent—suntan lotion waving in from the stands, or that rubbery smell you get when you open a can of tennis balls?"

"He can already smell," Jamie said. "He wants to walk."

Maggie sank down on his lap. She pulled off the HMD and

touched her hand to the screen, shaking her head. "It always amazes me how much better it looks with the helmet on."

"That's the idea." Jamie smiled.

"Imagine," Maggie said. "To be so active, and to have that taken away from you. If I ever get into an accident and become a quadriplegic, you have my permission to shoot me."

Reflexively, Jamie's arms tightened around her. "You shouldn't even joke about that," he said. "And you don't really mean it."

Maggie raised her eyebrows. "You'd want to live as a vegetable?"

"You're not a vegetable. You still have your mind."

"And you're stuck in it," Maggie added. "No thank you."

"You have all five of your senses," Jamie argued. "You can still see, you can feel with the skin on your face, you can smell, you can taste, and you can hear."

"Taste is a stupid sense," Maggie muttered absently. "No one would miss it."

"You would if you didn't have it," Jamie said.

"I'd rather be blind, deaf, and dumb than quadriplegic."

Even with the whir of the computers in the back of the lab, the room was too silent for Jamie's liking. He kept thinking that if they continued to talk like this, they'd be tempting fate. "I hope you never have to make that choice," Jamie murmured.

Maggie took her hand and pressed it to his cheek. "You could stand not feeling me touch you here," she said, moving her fingers to his forehead and over his lips. "And here, or here." Then she slid her hand down his chest, between his thighs, to cup him. "But to forget what *this* feels like?"

He felt himself growing into her palm. He could not believe that the sensations Maggie could create by touching him were something he would ever have trouble remembering. Maybe that was the clue for his program, too—evoke a memory of what used to be, so that the mind made up the parameters the body physically couldn't. He would use the sounds and smells of a game of tennis, and mount a small fan in the HMD to give the sensation of wind caused by movement. If there were enough bombarding stimuli to elicit a recollection of running, of serving a tennis ball, why couldn't your head make you think it was really happening again?

Maggie squeezed him gently.

Jamie swallowed. The problem was, the same mind that could suspend its disbelief had the capacity to be rational. A man who had walked for forty-two years before surviving an accident wouldn't be fooled by bells and whistles. A man who had touched his wife and moved within her body and felt her sweat drying on his own skin would not remain satisfied with a resurrected memory. When you came down to it, no matter how good Jamie was at what he did, a virtual world could never be the real thing.

Jamie cupped his hands over Maggie's breasts and grazed his teeth along her neck. "You have a point," he said.

If you aren't spooked about that kind of thing," Zandy Monroe said, "I can go find Hugo."

Allie shrugged. Sitting in the driver's seat of the pickup truck beside the body of Maggie MacDonald, she wasn't frightened, and surely Cam would have wanted his sergeant to dispose of the body with the local undertaker, even if he hadn't explicitly said so. "We're not going anywhere," she said, smiling at Zandy.

She had sent Mia back to the flower shop and told her to make as many funeral decorations as she could until Allie herself returned. *Roses,* she had said. *Use as many as we've got.* She also told her to find bluebells, which stood for constancy, and gillyflowers, for the bonds of affection. Now, she glanced at Maggie's smooth, pale skin. *Rue,* she thought, *for sorrow. I should have told her about rue.*

With Zandy gone, Allie leaned closer to the dead woman. She glanced out the window up and down the street, then laid her palm against Maggie's cheek. It was cold and firm to the touch. Allie drew back her fingers and tucked her hand inside her pocket.

Hugo Huntley came back with Zandy a few minutes later. He was the local mortician, and like everyone else on Main Street, had been in the crowd when James MacDonald had driven up to the police station. "Allie," he said, by way of greeting. He peered at the body through thick-lensed glasses that made his eyes look very tiny and sunken in his face.

"She's dead," Zandy said flatly.

"Well yes." Hugo nodded. "I can see that."

Zandy carried Maggie MacDonald across the street to Huntley's Funeral Parlor, downstairs to the embalming rooms. To Allie's shock, Maggie's body had already begun to freeze into the rigid position of sitting upright, so that even slung over Zandy's shoulder, her knees bent stiff and jutted into his abdomen instead of hanging slack.

Zandy laid the body on its side and turned to Allie. "You can probably go now, Mrs. Mac," he said.

Allie shook her head. "I made that man a promise. If you stay, so do I."

They both turned to look at Hugo, who had donned a white lab coat and rolled Maggie MacDonald's body onto her back, so that her knees peaked in the air. For a horrible moment, Allie remembered how funerals were done centuries ago, and she had a brief vision of the laying out on a scarred kitchen table, where strong arms broke bones knotted by rigor mortis until the body lay flat enough for a coffin. She turned away, the sweet mix of disinfectant and embalming fluid making her feel sicker.

"I don't think you should really do anything yet," Zandy said to Hugo. "Least, not till Cam says so." Hugo doubled as the town's forensic expert, although his police experience was limited to an autopsy some ten years back that had turned out to be much less of a mystery than originally thought: the deceased, believed to be poisoned, had died of cirrhosis of the liver.

Hugo peered closer at the body. "I won't do anything, but I'm going to get her out of these things and take some Polaroids. No matter what, that's the first step."

Allie swiftly glanced at the door before crossing her arms over her chest and steeling herself to bear witness. Zandy leaned against a tray of medical instruments, scratching at a brass button on his heavy coat and pretending not to watch as Hugo wrestled with the stiff body to remove the clothing. In the end, both Allie and Zandy simply turned away.

"Not a scratch," Hugo called cheerfully. "No bruises at the neck. Not even a hangnail." Allie could hear the whip of a sheet being snapped open and laid over the body. "My educated guess is death by asphyxiation. Smothering."

Allie shook her head, trying to erase the image of James MacDonald lunging for his wife before Zandy could touch her. "Why would you do that to someone you love?" she murmured.

Hugo touched her arm. "Maybe because they wanted you to." He gently led Allie to the embalming table, pointing to several tiny tattoos that looked like the marks of a pen on Maggie's face. "They're for radiation therapy," he said. "The eye's a secondary site for cancer." And then he pulled down a corner of the sheet, to reveal an angry red zag of weals and scars where Maggie MacDonald's breast had been.

You ready?"

Jamie turned around at the sound of Cam's voice. He had already signed the top half of the voluntary statement that acknowledged his right to wait until a lawyer had been provided, but that was not his intent. He knew he was going to be punished; he just wanted to get it over with. Cam had taken the handcuffs off an hour ago when the secretary offered him a cup of coffee. He had been waiting for Cam to set up the booking room with a tape recorder. Now he stood in front of the most beautiful array of fall flowers he had ever seen.

They were red and purple and musty yellow, and the different fronds all seemed to swoop low, like the trajectory of a leaf from a tree. He kept staring at the arrangement, thinking how rich and warm the colors seemed to be; and then, in the next blink, it seemed their own beauty was dragging them down.

Jamie turned to Cam. "I've never seen a police station with flowers in it."

Cam looked at the arrangement. "It's my wife. She owns a shop here. She does one every week." He watched Jamie finger the fragile petals of a lily, rubbing it gently so that Cam could smell the light rain scent all the way across the room.

"You love her?"

Cam took a step backward. "My wife? Of course."

"How much?"

Cam smiled a little. "Is there a limit?"

Jamie shrugged. "You tell me. What would you do for her? Would you lie for her? Steal? Would you kill for her?"

"No," Cam said shortly. He turned Jamie away from the flowers abruptly, so that the lily fell to the floor and was crushed beneath the heel of his own boot. "Let's go."

*I*t started almost two years ago, when we were ice-skating. Maggie was good at it; she'd do little axels and toe loops and impress the hell out of the kids who came to play pickup hockey on the pond. I was goalie, and feeling every bit of my thirty-four years as I blocked the shots of these high school guys. When the action was down at the opposite goal, I'd turn to my right to catch what Maggie was doing.

It was only chance that I happened to see her fall down. Something stupid, she said when I raced across the ice to her side. A twig sticking out of the surface that caught on the pick of her skate. But she couldn't stand up; thought maybe she'd heard something pop when she fell. I pulled her up the hill on a Flexible Flyer we borrowed from a little girl, and even though she was crying with the pain, she managed to make a joke about us trying out for the Iditarod next year.

They showed me her X rays, not just the clean break of her ankle, but the little holes in the white spaces, like bone that had been eaten out. Lesions, they said. Bone cancer was a secondary site.

When they found the original tumor, they removed her breast and the lymph nodes. They did CT scans, bone scans, sent for estrogen receptors.

It stayed dormant for a while, and then it came back in her brain. She would hold my hand and try to describe the flashing red lights, the soft edges of her fading vision as this tumor ate away at her optic nerve.

The doctor said that it was a guessing game. It was only a matter of time but there was no way to determine where the cancer would show up next. Another lobe of the brain, possibly, which would mean seizures. Maybe it would depress respirations. Maybe she would go to sleep one night and never wake up.

A few months before our eleventh wedding anniversary, we went to Canada. The Winter Carnival, in Quebec. We danced and sang in the streets and in the thinnest hours before morning we sat on benches in front of the ice sculptures with only each other to keep ourselves warm. Maggie unzipped my coat and unbuttoned my shirt and placed her cold hands on the flat of my chest. "Jamie," she said, "this thing is taking me from the inside out. My bones, my breast, my brain. I think I'm going to look down one day and realize that nothing is left."

I hadn't wanted to talk about it; I tried to look away. But directly in front of us was the ice sculpture of a woman, all curves and lines and grace, her arms stretching over her head toward the limbs of a tree she would never be able to reach. I stared at the sculpture's dead eyes, at the lifelike form that was a lie—it was only a shell; you could see right through to the other side.

*Maggie tightened her fingers, pulling at the hair on my chest until I stared at her, called back by the pain. "Jamie," she said, "I know you love me. The question is, how much?"*

*B*y the time Jamie MacDonald finished telling Cameron how he had killed Maggie, he was kneeling on the floor, his hands clasped together, tears running down his face.

"Hey," Cam said, his own voice thick and unfamiliar. "Hey, Jamie, it's all right." He reached down awkwardly to touch Jamie's shoulder, and instead Jamie reached up and grasped his hand. Instinctively, Cam put his other hand down, too, cupping Jamie's clasped hands in a silent show of support.

It was also a gesture of obeisance, Cam realized with a start, the one a Scots clansman had used two hundred years back to accept the protection of his chief.

According to the sworn voluntary statement of James MacDonald, his wife had been suffering from the advanced stages of cancer, and had asked him to kill her. Which did not account for the raw scratches on his face, or the fact that he'd traveled to a town he'd never set foot in to commit the murder. Maggie had not videotaped her wishes, or even written them down and had them notarized to prove she was of sound mind—Jamie said she hadn't wanted it to be a production, but a simple gift.

What it boiled down to, really, was Jamie's word. Cam's only witness was dead. He was supposed to believe the confession of James MacDonald solely because he was a MacDonald, a member of his clan.

Except for the time he had come back to Wheelock against his own wishes to succeed his father as police chief, Cam hadn't given much thought to being chief of the Clan MacDonald of Carrymuir. It was an honor, a mark of respect. It meant that when he married Allie, he did so in full Highland dress regalia, kilt instead of tuxedo, snowy lace jabot instead of bow tie. It was an anachronism, a cute link to history, and it might have made him a little more protective of his town's inhabitants than other police chiefs, but it did not override his other responsibilities.

He certainly wasn't about to let a murderer off the hook because the man was his cousin. And bending the laws would be unethical. If there was any principle Cameron MacDonald lived by, it was doing things the way they were supposed to be done. After all, as both po-lice chief and clan chief, it had been the pattern of his entire life.

But Jamie MacDonald had specifically come to Wheelock, Massachusetts, to kill his wife because he wanted to commit a mur-der in a place that was under the jurisdiction of the chief of Clan MacDonald. He was not expecting special treatment, but he knew he could count on being listened to, understood, judged fairly.

Cameron suddenly remembered a story about Old MacDonald of Keppoch, who centuries ago had punished a woman for stealing gold from his castle. He'd chained her to the rocks on the islands, so that when the tide came in she drowned. None of the clan had helped her; none had protested their chief's judgment. After all, the woman who had stolen from the chief had indirectly stolen from them as well.

It was premeditated murder; Murder One.

It was done out of mercy and love.

He knew the town would take sides on a case like this. He also knew that, like three hundred years ago, whether he chose to let Jamie MacDonald go free or whether he recommended life in prison, no one in Wheelock would contradict his decision.

But that didn't make it any easier.

It was after four-thirty when Allie returned to the flower shop. She pushed past Mia, slipping on cuttings that were strewn across the floor, and locked herself in the bathroom in the back. She vomited until there was nothing left in her stomach.

When she stepped out of the bathroom, Mia was standing nearby with a bowl of water and a Handi-Wipe. "You should sit down," she said. "The smell of all those roses is going to make it worse."

"It's a little overwhelming," Allie agreed. She sank into her desk chair and leaned her head back, letting Mia's cool hands posi-tion the towelette across her brow. "Oh, God," she sighed.

When Allie closed her eyes, Mia started for the door. She paused with her hand on the frame. "Is it true? Did he kill her be-cause she was dying?"

Allie's head snapped up. "Where did you hear that?"

"A woman named Hannah called. I told her you weren't here." Mia paused. "I made the cemetery baskets and the wreaths," she said. "You can take a look."

With her head throbbing, Allie pulled herself to her feet. She'd glance over Mia's work, although she was sure they were fine, put them into the cooler, and close up a half hour early.

Mia's arrangements were lined up at the bottom of the cooler, three simple conical shapes that did not look much like cemetery baskets at all. They were very traditional arrangements of carnations, fennel, barberry, larkspur, yellow roses, and Michaelmas daisies, colorful but standard. Allie's eyes swept their lines, a little disappointed. After what she had seen of Mia's green, grassy setting this morning, she had hoped for something original.

"Oh," Mia said, wiping her hands on an apron Allie had forgotten she owned. "Those aren't for the funeral. I saw the purchase order for that MacBean woman, and I didn't know whether you'd be back in time to fill it for tomorrow's luncheon." She lifted a thin shoulder. "I figured a library wouldn't want something that goes against the grain, so I tried to remember what the centerpieces looked like at my cousin Louise's wedding." Allie lifted her eyebrows, and Mia blushed, filling in her nervousness by tumbling her words one after another. "You know, the kind that's done at a VFW hall, with some tacky band in blue tuxedos that sings 'Daddy's Little Girl.' "

Allie laughed. "Let me guess. The flower girl carried a little ball made of miniature pink carnations."

Mia smirked. "You were invited?" She helped Allie lift the centerpieces into the cooler, and then gestured to the far corner of the store where a string of cemetery baskets and wreaths were taking shape beneath the dried flower rings Allie hung on the walls for browsing customers.

Allie sucked in her breath. Mia had found the rue, all right, but had steered clear of the bluebells and the other suggestions Allie had offered. And she had been absolutely correct to do so. Instead of the traditionally shaped baskets, she had placed side by side six trailing bouquets more fashioned to a wedding than a funeral. Snowy lilies of the valley, orchids, and stephanotis nestled between heather sprigs, rue, rosemary, ivy, and ferns. And at the heart of each pale, creamy arrangement was one spiraled rose as red as blood.

"Oh, Mia," Allie said. "These are perfect."

"You really like them?" She twisted her hands in the hem of her shirt. "It isn't what you asked for."

"It's *more* than I asked for." She looked up at Mia, taking in the florist's moss trapped beneath her nails, the leaves clinging to the soles of her shoes. "Mr. MacDonald will love them."

"If Mr. MacDonald ever sees them," Mia said, and then abruptly looked away. "I would assume he'd be in jail when they have the funeral."

"Oh, Cam wouldn't do that," Allie said easily.

"Cam?"

"The chief of police. He's my husband."

Mia thought back to the early afternoon, to the tall red-haired man who had burst into the flower shop with such a presence that the air around her had started to hum. Of course he was the police chief; he'd been in charge at the scene with Mr. MacDonald. Mia had seen him put his arm around Allie when she volunteered to sit with the body. He had bent low to talk to her, but to Mia it seemed he was curling over Allie, a method of protection.

"Mia," Allie said, "where in town are you staying?"

Mia had thought about it during the day; in fact had even called the Wheelock Inn to see how many nights she could afford to stay in a room before her dwindling stock of money was replenished with a paycheck from Allie. But the Inn had suddenly found itself blockaded by the police, the site of a murder investigation.

"To tell you the truth," Mia said, "I'm not entirely sure."

Allie glanced at the row of funeral baskets. It was very likely her own fault that Mia hadn't had any time to find accommodations. She thought of Maggie MacDonald and knew that the last thing she wanted was even a moment alone by herself. "Why don't you stay with me, for the night? Cam isn't going to be home until late, and it'll be nice to have some company."

Mia smiled. "I'd like that." Then she bit her lip. "I have a cat out in my car."

Allie waved her hand. "It can't possibly do anything to the house that Cam hasn't already done." She picked up a broom and began to sweep the cuttings into a pile, concentrating, with a stroke that bordered on violence so that her mind would not wander. She raked the heavy bristles across the wooden floor, over and over and over, until the scrape of the raffia against the polyurethane rang like a scream in her ears.

She stopped sweeping, balancing her forearm on the knob of the broom, taking deep breaths so that she would not break down in front of this woman she hardly knew.

"Do you want to talk about it?" Mia's voice came softly from behind.

Allie shook her head, letting her throat close with tears. "I don't know what's the matter," she said, trying to smile. "I guess I just keep thinking how much you'd have to love a person, to be able to do something like that for her." She wiped her eyes on the shoulder of her shirt. "It's a horrible thing to imagine."

"Maybe," Mia said quietly. "Maybe not."

Mia Townsend believed in love, she really, truly did. She knew it could strike certain people like a stray line of lightning, leaving them prostrate and burning and gasping for breath. After all, this had been the case with her parents. She had grown up surrounded by their consuming love, constantly in its presence, but always on the outskirts. In fact when she thought of her childhood, she imagined herself standing in the snow, her nose pressed to a small, cleared ring of glass on an icy windowpane, watching her parents waltz in circles. She pictured the circles getting tighter and smaller and warmer, until her mother and father converged into one.

So when asked if she believed in love, Mia said yes—without hesitation—but she did not count herself as a participant. She thought of it as the chemical reaction it was, and saw herself not as part of the equation but as the by-product you sometimes find after the combustion.

Allie MacDonald had driven her to the small Colonial she'd lived in for five years with Cam. She'd made tea and soup and told Mia the stories behind certain objects in the house: the old oak trunk with the bullet stuck in the center, the basket-hilted sword hung over the fireplace, the red tartan blanket that Mia was beginning to recognize as the Carrymuir MacDonald plaid. Then she'd tucked embroidered sheets around the cushions of the living room couch and had given Mia two pillows and one of the blankets and told her to sleep well.

Mia fell asleep with Kafka, the cat, tucked under her arm, and almost immediately started dreaming of her strongest childhood memory: the time her parents had left her behind.

Mia had been four years old when they went for that walk in the woods. She had trailed behind them, passing in front when her parents stopped for several minutes to kiss in a copse of bushes. Knowing it would be a while, Mia had wandered off to listen to the trees. She was sensitive to sounds—she could hear blood running through veins or buds opening on flowers. So while her parents moaned in each other's arms, she flopped down on her belly in the moss and waited for the telltale hum and stretch of bark as the branches sought out the afternoon sun. When she remembered to look up, her parents were gone.

She had tried to listen very carefully for the traces of their laughter on the breeze, or of her father's fingers brushing her mother's neck, but the only sound she could distinguish was her own unsteady breathing.

Mia had sat down and hugged her knees to her chest. It wasn't on purpose, she told herself. It wasn't their fault. It wasn't that they didn't love her either; it was simply that they loved each other more.

After about three hours, she had wandered to a road, and a driver she did not know took her to the closest police station. Mia could remember, even now, certain things about the officer: how nice he was when he helped her climb into the chair behind his desk; how his hair smelled of peppermint and did not wave in the wind. He had driven her home in a police cruiser and they walked in through the unlocked door. She poured him a glass of milk while they waited in the kitchen for her parents to appear. Mia had sat very quietly at the table, wondering if it was only she who could hear through the ceiling the rush of her mother's breath, the square pressure of the big four-poster on the bedroom floor, the pound and ache of her parents' love. . . .

Mia woke up when she heard the first tumblers in the lock giving way. Quiet footsteps traced their way into the living room. Blinking, she let her eyes adjust to the darkness. She sat up to see Cameron MacDonald raise his arms over his head, stretch with an animal grace, and turn in her direction.

His first thought was that Allie had been waiting up for him, and had fallen asleep on the couch. But he had talked to her at dinnertime; told her she'd best go to sleep. Years of instinct had him reaching for a gun belt he'd removed in the kitchen, so his hand was riding on his hip when he realized he knew the woman on the couch.

She was wearing one of Allie's nightgowns and her hair was in even greater disarray than it had been when he'd first seen her in the flower shop. Her hands clutched at a MacDonald plaid and her eyes were wide and bright.

He tried to move, and couldn't.

Then she smiled at him, and with an instinct he could only consider self-protection, Cam whirled and ran up the stairs.

Allie was asleep on her back, wearing a fine lawn nightgown blued by the light that was ribboning through the bedroom window. She was snoring. Cam held his breath and eased down beside her on the bed. He untied the laces at the throat of the nightgown and gently peeled the fabric away, so that Allie's breasts lay exposed like an offering.

He bent his head to her nipple, running his tongue along the edge until her hand came up to his hair. She made a small sound in the back of her throat and tried to sit up. "No," Cam whispered. "Just stay there."

He pulled off his shoes and socks and uniform, tossing them across the room. His badge hit the corner of the dresser with a metallic ping. He stood naked in front of her, watching her eyes darken and her nipples peak harder, knowing that he did not even have to touch her to get her started.

When he brushed his lips down Allie's ribs, she tried to sit up again. Cam shook his head. "But I want to," Allie whispered. "I want to touch you."

"Not now," Cam said. "Not tonight." He turned toward her again, making love with a methodical rhythm, as if he was cataloging each inch of her somewhere in his mind. By the time he moved up to look in her eyes, he was heavy. He tried to push away the churning thoughts of Jamie MacDonald in the holding cell, of Maggie's body lying in the yellow light of the embalming room, but he found himself thinking instead of the woman downstairs on the couch.

With his head pounding, Cam buried himself in Allie, moving more roughly than he'd ever intended to. When it was over, he rolled her onto her side, noting the red abrasions of his beard stubble on her neck and her breasts; the bite he'd left on her shoulder.

Jamie MacDonald had murdered his wife more gently than Cam had made love to his own.

I see us like we're in a movie, sometimes, except I'm not a participant, but someone watching the action. I'm tracing my forefinger down the soft stubble on the back of your neck, and there's moonlight the color of cream on the terry-cloth towel you let fall from your body.

# THREE

*H*e didn't so much mind the dying.

That surprised him a little; at twenty-five, he still pictured his life like the long ribbon of a river, spread out farther than the eye could see in twists and gullies that caught one unaware. He'd been fighting to protect what was his for nine years now, and he'd certainly accepted the fact that one careless moment, one running sword, could kill him. But the odds had never seemed quite so bad.

The sleet and rain sluiced beneath the folds of his plaid, and the wet ground of the moor rooted his feet. Suddenly the mist parted, revealing a flash of a gold button here, a fluttering standard there, the steaming breath of a mounted soldier's horse.

He looked to his left, and to his right, but for the first time in his life he did not know the men who were fighting beside him. His own men, his tenants and tacksmen and cousins, would be on the road to Carrymuir by now.

Like him, they had seen the sea of ten thousand sassenachs, heard the rolling cannons, listened to the conflicting commands given to the Highland army. They had seen the zealousness on Prince Tearlach's smooth face and had known that they simply could not win.

When, in the wee hours of the dawn, he had gone to strike his bargain with the Duke of Perth, he knew that his argument was purely a matter of logistics. He had agreed to lead his men, he told Perth. That did not mean he himself would be fighting.

*It was a technicality; any oath he'd made would naturally imply he'd be fighting alongside, since no laird would expect his clan to do what he himself would not. But in this case, he was willing to bend the truth to protect the others. And he knew when he offered the commander the choice of a ragtag band from Carrymuir or his own skill in combat, it wouldn't be much of a choice at all.*

*He wondered, as he slogged across the moor for the third time, his leg bleeding from a lucky round of* sassenach *grapeshot, whether any of these fools realized he did not want to be here at all. He didn't want to face one more bloody English soldier, or step on the still-heaving backs of Scots fallen four deep.*

*He wondered what God was like. He hoped that heaven resembled Scotland.*

*He murmured the paternoster over and over to hear the sound of his own voice. Seeing a* sassenach *just turning his way, he lifted his left arm high in the air. He brought the sword down at the man's neck, cleaving it wide, feeling the hot blood melt the sleet on his chest.*

*Cameron MacDonald sank to his knees and vomited; tried to remind himself that he had given his word to fight to the death. He did not much relish dying, but aye, it was a fair trade. He loved the people of his town too much to see them suffer.*

*And had he the chance, he'd do the same all over again.*

A ngus MacDonald sat up in his narrow bed. Having heard the gossip during one of his lucid moments during the day, it did not surprise him when the ghost of his great-great-great-great-uncle Cameron came to haunt him in the hollow of the night. And it surprised him even less that Cameron MacDonald I was, in death, no less unconventional than he'd been when he was alive. No rattling chains and slipping through doors, not for him. No, he came to Angus in the guise of a dream, a spectacular frenzy in which Angus seemed to be seeing through Cameron's own eyes as he thundered across a moor, waving a broadsword.

"I shouldna have expected anything different," he muttered, talking to himself as he pulled on a pair of twill trousers and a pilled Shetland sweater. Once, when he'd been caretaker of Carrymuir, he'd seen the ghost of Mary Queen of Scots herself, sailing away from Loch Leven Castle dressed as a laddie, as she'd been when she escaped its prison hundreds of years before. It had left him with a queer feeling in his stomach and a beating in his head not unlike a hangover—sensations he felt right now.

Angus knew that although most people would dismiss him as someone in the throes of Alzheimer's, he was really a victim of collective memory. It was a sort of reincarnation, a resurrection of some other clan member's thoughts. He happened to be privy to whatever was plaguing Cameron MacDonald I. And tonight, Cameron MacDonald I was not pleased with the actions of Cameron MacDonald II.

"I dinna know what he can be thinking," Angus said, pulling slippers onto his feet, because they were the first footwear he could find in his bedroom. "Young Cam always has to be reminded about the way of things."

Angus, in fact, had been the one to convince Cam to return to Wheelock and become police chief after his father's death. Almost exactly eight years ago, Cameron had come to Scotland to tell Angus about Ian's accident. At the time, Angus had been seventy-four, caretaker at Carrymuir all his life, although his wife had died twelve years earlier and all his relatives were living in Massachusetts. Young Cameron, who was a bit of a wanderer, had volunteered to sit at Carrymuir for several years to spell Angus, but Ian's early death had altered the plans. Cam had taken Angus to the tavern for a wee dram, knowing that he, like everyone else, would take the loss of a clan chief hard. He spread his palms over the scarred wooden bar and told him of the ice, the tractor-trailer, the bend in the narrow road. He said this all in a monotone, because it wasn't quite real to him yet, and he mentioned, as the doctors had, that his father had felt no pain. When he was finished speaking, Angus looked up at him, his eyes bright and dry. "Aye, well," he said, "so I'll be stayin' here a wee bit longer."

To Angus's horror, Young Cam had wanted to trade. He'd stay at Carrymuir, he said, and Angus could go home and take over the clan. The thought had shaken Angus more than his nephew's death; you simply couldn't cross the lines of leadership like that.

Even now, Angus remembered the shine of Cam's brow and the set of his jaw as he fought his own birthright. *It's no' a real title,* he had said. *There's nothing I can do as chief that ye canna do better.*

Angus had shrugged, finished off his whiskey, and stared at the boy. He wondered if Cam realized that he had slipped into Angus's own Scots burr, not because of a familiarity with the pattern of speech in Carrymuir, but simply because it had been bred into him. "Duty is duty," Angus had said, "and a laird is a laird. And be there a clan or no', lad, ye canna doubt your own blood."

Of course, stubbornness had also been passed down over the generations of MacDonalds, so Angus had accepted a compromise. Cam returned to Wheelock, but so did Angus, and the lands and grand house at Carrymuir were left to the Scottish National Trust.

Every morning over his rainbow banquet of vitamins and heart medication Angus forced his mind back to Carrymuir, so that he would not wake up one morning and find that he could not remember it any longer. He pictured the strong stone house, the fireplace in the great hall, the sheep that spilled about the old crofters' huts like a current. He did not let himself dwell on the fact that Carrymuir, which had never been taken by Campbells or English or anyone else, was now overrun with tourists.

But he did not have time for that now. Angus pulled his bathrobe on over his clothes, and at just after three in the morning, began to walk in his slippers the mile from his small home to the Wheelock police station, where once again he would be his great-nephew's conscience.

INVESTIGATION REPORT
Wheelock Township Police Dept.
Case # 95-9050


STATE vs. MacDONALD, James Reid
                White male, age 36,
                D.O.B. 3/14/59.
                Place of birth: Boston MA
                Ht. 6'4", wt. 200 lbs.
                green eyes, auburn hair


CHARGES:   Murder One


PLACE:     Wheelock Inn, Main St., Wheelock MA

DATE:       September 19, 1995

EVIDENCE:   1. Pillowcase
            2. Rug samples
            3. Shoes worn by suspect
            4. Samples of hair (victim)
            5. Samples of hair (suspect)
            6. Autopsy report
            7. Photographs of crime scene and
               victim
            8. Voluntary statement from
               suspect

*A*llie brewed her own tea. It was a very English thing to do, and Cam sometimes laughed at her, saying she'd better keep quiet about it or all the good Scots would run her out of town. At first she did it because she was a stickler for detail. In the same way she could sense a stray frond of grass ruining an arrangement, she could taste the commonplace seeping from a bag of Lipton's as strong and as bitter as arsenic. But she'd learned to tolerate it and now she brewed her own tea only because Cam usually made a comment about it.

Allie did at least a hundred things each day simply because of their effect on Cam. They bound him to her: she'd drop his shirts off at the cleaners without being asked, or lay out a bowl of cereal for him before she went to bed so it was there in the morning, or, as in the case of the tea, open herself to teasing just to guarantee an exchange of conversation. She made his life run so smoothly that he never had to wonder about those little details that plague everyone else—like turning the clocks back in the fall, or always having enough milk in the refrigerator, or keeping handy the right size batteries for whatever piece of electronic equipment he was fixing. She told herself this was something she wanted to do, a silent promise she'd made on her wedding day to the handsome, magnificent man standing beside her. If every day flowed seamlessly into the next for Cam, he'd never have reason to wonder, *What if?*

It never occurred to Allie that this was very similar to behaviorally drugging Cam. Or that every selfless errand she ran for her husband was another silken strand that wrapped him tight, like a spider trapping her prey with guilt. Or that Cam was strong enough, and sure enough, to break out of any hold or system Allie could ever create.

Then again, maybe this *had* occurred to her, and that was the reason she continued.

Sometimes, when Cam was working the midnight-to-eight shift, and Allie was lying in bed, she let her hands move restlessly over her own body. She pretended that Cam would notice something ridiculously simple—like the fact that all his socks were neatly paired and folded in his underwear drawer—and would turn to her with the same look on his face that Allie often gave to him. *Allie,* he'd say, his eyes burning with wonder and worship, *have you done all this for me?*

Cam had gone back to the station in the middle of the night to relieve Zandy, who was watching over Jamie MacDonald. When Allie heard the car pull into the driveway, she slid the egg from the bowl where it had been waiting to the sizzling pan. By the time Cam had kicked the dirt off his boots and hung his coat up in the mudroom, Allie was already slipping the egg onto a slice of toast.

She placed her hand on the back of his neck as he settled heavily at the kitchen table, rubbing his face with his hands. "Tired?" she asked.

Cam made an indistinguishable noise in the back of his throat. He picked up his fork just as Allie laid the steaming plate in front of him. His mouth watered at the sight of the hot food, but he carefully set the fork on the edge of the plate and turned back to Allie.

She was at the sink, scraping the frying pan. She had a thing about letting food sit in a frying pan, and was obsessive about scrubbing it clean the second it came off the stove. Her shoulders were tense with effort, but she was humming.

"Allie," he said, but she didn't hear him over the running water. *"Allie!"*

She turned around quickly, pressing up against the basin of the sink as if he'd scared the hell out of her instead of just raising his voice. "What's the matter with your egg?"

"Nothing." Cam took a deep breath. "Allie," he said, "do you think he was right?"

Allie slid into the chair across from her husband. There was no question in her mind what he was asking. "Do *you?*"

Cam stared at her so forcefully Allie could feel his gaze. She covered her chest with her palms, picturing in a quick flash Cam's mouth drawing deep at her breast the night before. "I don't know," he admitted. "But my hands are tied. He killed a woman; we've got the body. He's got scratches on his face and Hugo found skin cells that match up under Maggie MacDonald's fingernails." He paused a moment, cocking his head. "If I was dying of cancer and in god-awful pain and I asked you to kill me, would you do it?"

Allie didn't hesitate. "Yes. But then I'd kill myself, too."

Cam's mouth fell open. "Because you'd murdered me?"

"No," Allie said. "Because you'd be dead."

*M*ia put her toothbrush down at the edge of the sink and stared at the medicine cabinet one more time. She'd done it before at other people's houses—peeked inside—but this was a little different. This wasn't simple curiosity, but a burning desire to put together the pieces. And it seemed patently wrong to invade the privacy of a woman who had gone out of her way to give her employment and shelter all in one day.

Mia opened the mirrored door, watching her own image lengthen and swerve and then fall away to a neat array of glass shelves.

Tylenol, and iodine, and syrup of ipecac. Gauze pads and Band-Aids and Laura Ashley perfume. Ban deodorant, Brut after-shave. Kaopectate.

The only prescription medicine she recognized was a form of penicillin. Well, that, and the birth control pills. She had used the same kind at one point.

Mia took out the shell-shaped box and ran her finger over the lid. She flipped open the pills and counted the number missing.

It occurred to her that if she pushed a couple of pills out with her thumb and washed them down the drain, she could quite possibly change the life of Cameron and Allie MacDonald. She quickly snapped the lid shut and put it back in the medicine cabinet, shaking with this sense of power.

A s Cam put down his empty glass, Allie refilled it. "It's Murder One," he said, as if he could not believe it himself. "He knew he was going to do it; he drove to a specific goddamned town to do it; and he voluntarily admitted to killing her." He shook his head. "I don't know what Jamie thought I could do for him," he said. "I've got to assume it was a premeditated killing."

"A lot of people aren't going to see it that way."

Cam stood up and wrapped his arms around her. She fit just under his chin. "Too bad you're only the wife of a clan chief. You'd make the perfect political mate."

"Cam," Allie said slowly, as if a thought had just occurred to her, "I made funeral decorations. Cemetery baskets and things like that. Well, actually, Mia did."

Cam nodded. "You're the town florist. No one's going to think you're making a statement."

Allie pulled away from him and opened the refrigerator, pretending to search for something. "But what if I *did?*"

"What if you did what?"

"What if I wanted to make a statement?"

Cam sank back into a chair. "Allie, even if *you* killed someone, I'd have to turn you in." He ran a hand through his thick hair, spilling it over his face. "I'd still be the police chief."

Allie nodded, briefly imagining Cam's own hand locking her into the small, dark cement cell in the center of town. "Yes," she said, "but you'd also still be my husband."

That was Cam's breaking point. He bolted upright, knocking the chair behind him onto the floor. "This is *not* what I came home for. This is *not* what I need from you."

A switch snapped in Allie. She dropped the dish towel and closed the refrigerator door and moved right in front of Cam, pushing past his frustration and anger to wrap her arms around him. "No, of course not."

Cam let Allie guide him to the chair and gently press him into it again. He clenched his fists and closed his eyes, wishing he could be anywhere else but in Wheelock, Massachusetts. Instinctively, his mind began to picture his favorite places. He envisioned a white elephant in Thailand, splashed with a bucket of water to turn a dusky gray; the shutters of nine hundred shops flapping open in Cairo's souk; the pink stone cathedrals of Mexico City.

Something brushed across his leg and he jumped a foot.

"Excuse me," said a voice, and Cam opened his eyes to see the woman who had been sleeping on the couch the night before.

"Oh, Mia," Allie said, turning around with a smile. "Was there enough hot water?"

Mia nodded. She was staring at Cam, seeing him as he had looked when he'd stepped into the living room and stretched toward the rafters like a sleek and stunning mountain cat. She stuck out her hand. "Hi," she said. "I don't think we've really met."

Allie stepped behind Cam and placed her arm around his waist. "You're right. We got sidetracked yesterday. Cam, this is Mia Townsend, my new assistant. Mia, this is—"

"The police chief of Wheelock," Mia interrupted, a smile lighting her eyes. She gripped Cam's hand firmly.

"Assistant?" Cam was speaking to Allie, but he kept his gaze trained on Mia, even as she pulled her hand away and bent over the bowl of cereal that Allie, like a mother, had placed in front of her.

"Well," Allie said, "there's just something about her. Wait till you see what she can do."

*There's just something about her.* Cam swallowed, reaching up to find Allie's hand on his shoulder. It was warm and small and smooth and he knew all its knobs and textures. It felt completely different than Mia's hand had, moments before. "I can't imagine it being any better than your stuff," Cam said.

"Oh, just wait."

Cam shifted his weight. This stranger had come to Wheelock and in a single day had charmed Allie, had infiltrated her way into his own house. He instinctively tensed, realizing that every time he'd been in the vicinity of the woman, he'd felt a nervous energy, a hunch that she wasn't quite comfortable in her own skin. And a niggling sense that he had spoken to her, or seen her, or been somewhere near her before.

Suddenly Mia jumped to her feet. "My cat," she explained. "I think I left him in the bathroom." She darted her eyes overhead. "He's probably clawed your shower curtain to shreds."

Allie laughed. "Eat your breakfast. I'll get the cat."

Mia remained standing several seconds after Allie had left the room. Then she smiled hesitantly at Cam and sat down.

Cam watched her pour milk into the cereal. She scooped the corn flakes up toward the back of the bowl, the way he'd seen the English eat soup. "What's the cat's name?" he said, willing to call a truce.

"Kafka."

Mia did not look up.

"Kafka?" Cam pressed, amused.

She nodded. "He'd rather be anything but a cat."

"And how do you know that?" In spite of himself, Cam found that he was leaning forward.

Mia's dark blue eyes locked tight on his. "When we lived in India, he thought he was a cow. He crossed streets in front of cars and learned how to moo. In Paris he tracked a finch onto a windowsill and leaped off, thinking he could fly." She lifted a shoulder. "With him, you never really know what's going to happen."

"No," Cam said. He could smell her now, clean like rain, not at all like the Zest in the shower upstairs. His thoughts of Jamie MacDonald were gone; all he could see was Mia running through the streets of places he'd imagined his entire life. "You lived in India? In Paris?" When she did not answer, he leaned a little closer. If he moved his thumb, he would brush her wrist. He wanted to ask the question that had been dancing at the back of his mind since yesterday. "Do I know you?" he whispered.

Mia could hear Allie's footsteps coming down the stairs, and the healthy mew of Kafka in her arms. She turned away from Cam, stayed silent. *Yes,* she said to herself, *I think maybe you do.*

# FOUR

When Cam walked into the police station later that morning, his uncle Angus was sitting with Jamie MacDonald in the lockup, dressed in his bathrobe and playing a game of chess.

"For God's sake," he muttered, unlocking the cell. "Angus, what are you doing in there?" He looked around for Casey MacRae, the patrolman he'd left guarding the prisoner.

"I told Casey I'd spell him," Angus said. "I havena seen wee Jamie since he was seven."

Cam threw his cap onto the booking counter. He glanced at Jamie MacDonald. "Sleep well?"

"No," Jamie admitted. "Did you?"

Cam turned his back and began to leaf through the court book, praying he'd get Jamie MacDonald in front of a magistrate before lunchtime.

"What are you doing here, Angus?" Cam sighed. "And get out of the damn lockup. I can't let you in with a prisoner."

Angus tightened the sash of his bathrobe, grumbling, but stood from the cement slab that doubled as a bed in the cell. "Young Cam, I dinna think that's any way to be speaking to your elders."

Cam hated it when his uncle called him that, as if he were still six years old, as if the old Cameron MacDonald hadn't been dead for two hundred years. He gestured at Angus's wet bedroom slippers. "You come here in your pajamas and get yourself locked up with a murderer, and you can't understand why I want to hire someone to take care of you during the day?"

Angus stepped out of the lockup. "I dinna want some wee lassie telling me how to eat my parritch in the morning and washing my privates for me in the bath." He tapped Cam on the shoulder. "I didna come to speak about that, anyway."

Cam sighed and began to swing the heavy cell door closed again. "We're going to court within the hour," he said to Jamie, matter-of-fact, and then he slammed it shut.

He turned around to find his uncle in his office, sitting behind the desk with his feet propped up. Cam shrugged out of his coat, hanging it on a hook on the back of the door. "Sometimes I think I should have left you at Carrymuir," he said.

"Sometimes I wish that ye had."

Cam sat down in the chair opposite his uncle and rested his elbows on the desk. "Angus, I know what you're about to say to me, and don't think I haven't thought of it myself. But the fact is I've got a body lying across the street, and a signed confession that the man in that lockup killed her."

"Aye, well," Angus said, as if he hadn't heard a word Cam had said, "I was on Culloden Field last night."

Perhaps because they were the very last words Cam had anticipated as a response, he sat forward, speechless. Recovering, he shook his head. "You were *where?*"

"Culloden. Ye canna tell me that in spite of everything else ye've forgotten, ye dinna remember that."

For a long time Cam had resisted sending Angus to a retirement home because the closest one was over the mountains, a good forty-five minutes away. Moreover, someone who had grown up fenced in by nature would not take well to antiseptic-washed floors and Bingo in the cafeteria. But he was beginning to see that he had little choice. "Angus," Cam said gently, "this is 1995."

"It may be at that, but all the same, I fought the English last night with Prince Charlie." He settled forward, as if he could not believe that Cam was not quick enough to pick up what he had been trying to say. "Your great-great-great-great-great-grandfather isna happy. That's why Cameron's come to haunt me."

Cam laid his head down on his desk. He'd humor the old man; he'd talk for five more minutes; then he'd usher him onto Main Street and drive his prisoner to the district courthouse on the other side of town. "Cameron MacDonald has come to haunt you," he repeated.

"In a matter of words," Angus said. "It's a bit like I've crawled right into his wee brain." He paused, remembering. "He didna want to be on Culloden Moor at all."

Cam did not lift his head, so his words were muffled by his sleeve. "He was an incredible soldier. He supported the Stuarts. Where else would he have been?"

"He would have rather been home with his kinsmen, I imagine."

Cam's patience was wearing thin. "Angus, we all grew up with the story. The damn public school probably uses it as a primer instead of *Dick and Jane.*" He snapped his head up, reciting in a singsong, "Cameron MacDonald offered his own life so everyone else could go back to Carrymuir."

"Aye," Angus said, pointing with one finger. "But do ye ken why he did it? Why he was willing to die?"

In a flash of insight, Cam suddenly realized where this was heading. "Because he was their chief?" he said smugly, ready to launch into an explanation as to why Jamie MacDonald would still have to be arraigned.

"No," Angus said, "because he couldna stand to see the people he loved hurting." He stood up and came around the desk, laying his thin, white hand on Cam's back. "Dinna fash yourself, lad. You'll come up with something." And with a goodbye knock on the Flexon-covered bars of the lockup, he walked out of the police station.

*T*he art of bonsai, Mia told Allie, had to be fashioned in harmony with nature, in a desire to dominate it and to re-create it, although on a different scale. She told her its history in China, then Japan; how the French were fascinated by the power the bonsai artists had—being able to make such a towering, magnificent tree grow in such a tiny space. Allie watched carefully as Mia sketched for her the different forms of the trees, single trunks curved to the left, cascading trees, upright ones, knotted ones, trees that rooted to rocks. She repeated their Japanese names like mantras: Chokkan, Moyogi, Sabamiki.

They had bought some small Japanese maples at a nursery a half hour away, and Allie was going to turn them into bonsai trees, like the one Mia had shown her yesterday. Mia had a complete set of tools for pruning trees: saws, scissors, clippers, branch cutters. "I'm a surgeon," she had said, and Allie had laughed until she realized that Mia was serious.

There weren't many rules. Mia cut back one of two opposite branches on the first trunk with a saw, which would produce alternate branches. She told Allie to make the cuts clean, so the tree would heal quickly. She had her pluck off the leaves.

"It looks bald," Allie said.

Mia stood back, assessing her work. "It'll grow. You don't want it to be bushy."

Wiring was the most difficult part. It was to spiral at an angle of 45 degrees, wound around the branches of the tree to train it in the direction you wanted it to grow. The wire would remain on for several months, but was unwound daily and repositioned to keep it from cutting into the tree.

For a few minutes, Mia watched Allie work. It was easy to talk to her, to teach her, and to learn from her. She did not know if she really liked Allie—really, truly liked her—or if Allie had become a fast friend simply because she was the first person Mia had met in Wheelock. Mia could remember making friends in sixth grade when she'd had to change schools and did not know anyone—after a moment of solitary panic, she had laughed with the two girls whose seats had flanked hers in homeroom. By the time they left ten minutes later, Mia had traded her small secrets, receiving in return the information that Jenna was in love with Billy Geffawney and that Phyllis could swallow a hard-boiled egg whole. It was months later, with a knot of her real friends woven tight around her like a winter cloak, that Mia realized how little she had in common with these first girls she'd latched onto, how shallow and strange they seemed, how foolish she had been to doubt her future. For years she avoided them, thinking how much they knew about her, afraid that a single desperate act of friendship might one day be used against her.

While Allie worked on her new bonsai, Mia unloaded her works-in-progress from the back of the rental car she'd driven to Wheelock. It had been parked overnight in front of the library. After several trips, Mia returned, breathless, holding a pile of terracotta plates and an army-green duffel bag. "Well," she said, glancing at the floor, which was littered now with gnarled trees and hunched trunks in a smattering of containers and pots. "I feel like we're in Kyoto."

"You've traveled a lot, haven't you?" Allie asked, twisting a length of copper wire. "You're not from around here?"

Mia shook her head and began to carry the pots into the back room. "I'm from everywhere. I haven't stayed long enough in one place to really say I'm from 'around there.' "

"Were you an army brat?"

Mia stopped at the threshold of the door. "No. My parents still live in the house where I grew up." She set two of the containers down on Allie's desk and then dragged the chair into the workspace of the flower shop. Absently she took the wire from Allie and corrected a loop around a branch. "Did you grow up in Wheelock?"

Allie nodded. "So did Cam." She smiled. "I think I've know him my entire life."

Mia did not find this unlikely; for a moment she could picture a toddling Allie grasping at Cam's shirt to hold herself upright. "You were high school sweethearts?"

Allie shook her head. "No, in fact, those awful baskets you made for the library luncheon are for a program being given in honor of Cam's old girlfriend."

"I can honestly say you have better taste."

"That," Allie replied, "isn't saying much." She began to pinch the leaves off one side of the tree, as Mia had shown her earlier. Thin light filtered through the high windows to skitter on the wood floor. "I knew Cam in high school, but he didn't really know me or pay any attention to me. I mean, *everyone* knew Cam. He went to college in Scotland, and then he traveled around a little, and he came back to Wheelock when his father died."

Allie had explained to Mia the night before the strange chain of command that stretched backward in Cam's family all the way to the Scottish Highlands. "I met him in a hardware store," she said, clipping a maple branch that grew too close to the roots. "I knocked him unconscious."

She had been buying lumber for this very store. With careful instructions, Allie was going to fashion her own workbench out of several two-by-sixes. Cam, once again new to town, had been behind her in line. While Allie was rummaging in her purse for the correct change, the wood balanced precariously at her shoulder, she heard Cam's voice behind her. "I have some change," he offered. She had turned around to take it from him, inadvertently swinging the two-by-sixes, and clubbed him on the back of the skull.

He had awakened with his head in her lap and a vicious pounding behind his eyes, but other than a mild concussion, he was fine. When Cam told the story, he liked to say that from the first, Allie had made him see stars.

Allie shrugged when she finished, a little self-conscious talking about herself at length. Mia was sitting at the workbench, her chin propped on her hands. Beneath her elbows was a puddle of Japanese maple leaves, some as big as a fist. "You remind me of my mother," Mia said.

Allie laughed. "Because I made you breakfast?"

"No, I always did that myself. Because of the way you look when you talk about your husband." She thought of her parents, and the way they would tell a story: they'd sit close, continuously interrupting each other, and their hands would flutter together and apart, like mating butterflies, coming to rest on each other's knees.

"And does Cam remind you of your father?"

Mia envisioned Cam's large hand pressed to the checkered kitchen tablecloth, and the shining line of auburn hair that brushed his collar. She tried to picture Allie in his arms, Allie under his solid body, but she could not. "No," Mia said, "he doesn't."

Graham MacPhee never got to do the divorces. He'd joined his father's law practice four years earlier when he passed the Massachusetts bar, earning the dubious distinction of being the second lawyer in a town that barely needed one. His father, who had been Wheelock's attorney for forty years, did a smattering of everything: wills, real estate, contracts, bankruptcy, neighbor disputes, personal injury.

Although Graham had plea-bargained and had done some civil

suits, his father always saved the messy marital disputes and shady cases for himself. Said it was a question of experience, to which Graham had answered that if he was never given a chance, he'd never get the damn experience. He wanted to go to court.

He was reviewing a torts case when the bell over the door tinkled. Cleo, the paralegal/secretary, wasn't at her desk, so Graham went to the front of the office himself. In the process of standing he knocked the torts file off his desk, scattering papers at his feet.

"Shit," he muttered, kicking them into further disarray. He walked down the hall of the office and came face-to-face with the chief of police.

"Where's your father?" Cam said abruptly, glancing out the window. "I need to speak with him."

Graham watched the man turn his regulation hat around and around in his hands, as if he were feeding a seam. "He's in court." Graham drew himself up to his full height. "What can I do for you?"

Cam stared at Graham, who he knew was scared shitless at having to be with him in the same small room. When Graham was eighteen, Cam had caught him with a group of friends at the construction site of a house, drinking Coors and pissing on the newly erected staircase. He'd fingerprinted him, read him his rights, and detained him to put some sense in his head, but he'd never filed the arrest report.

Graham cleared his throat. "Was there something you needed, Chief?"

Cam nodded shortly and then tilted his head, as if he were assessing Graham's physical strength. "Let's go to your office," he said, striding down the hall to a place that would afford privacy.

Graham thought of the papers all over the floor, of the fishing magazine and the Walkman right smack on the desk. "The conference room," he suggested, steering Cam to his left.

Cam didn't even bother to sit down. "You know about the MacDonald murder," he said, gesturing for Graham to take a chair. Graham watched him pace in front of the oak table, listened to the way his voice crowded the corners of the room, and realized that Cameron MacDonald would be quite a presence in a court of law.

"I've heard some things," Graham hedged.

Cam slapped his hat against the smooth surface of the table. "I want a defense lawyer for this guy."

Graham frowned. "He's hiring this firm?"

Cam shook his head. "*I'm* hiring *you* on his behalf. I'll pay the bill. In return, you don't breathe a word about who's funding your client—not to your father, not to a judge, not to my wife. Your job is to make him look like Mother Teresa in front of a jury." He took a deep breath, and when he looked down at Graham again, Graham almost believed he could see fear in the police chief's eyes. "Just get him off the hook," he said softly.

Graham stared at Cam. "What are *you* going to do?"

Cam picked up his hat. "I'm going to book him for murder, and fight you every step of the way."

When Cam went home after meeting with Graham MacPhee, he found the door unlocked.

He knew Allie was at work; he'd just talked to her. It was clearly a B & E. He pulled his gun out of its holster and swung himself into the doorway, checking right and left and right again as he'd been trained to do. Wild connections began to take root in his mind: Jamie MacDonald was part of a drug ring; the murder had been a setup to cover a larger crime; someone was right now in his bedroom stealing cufflinks and stray buttons and rug fibers, trying to implicate Cam himself.

A thorough search of the downstairs revealed nothing. He crept up the stairs and threw open his bedroom door, fully expecting to find some vermin going through his drawers, and pointed his gun at the moving figure on the bed. "Police," he yelled, his throat dry and pounding.

"Oh," Mia Townsend said, her face blanched and drawn at the sight of the gun. "Jesus."

Cam flicked the safety and jammed his gun into his holster. "Fuck." Trembling, he crossed the room in two steps. "I could have killed you. I could have *killed* you." He grabbed her by the shoulders and shook her, speaking through a clenched jaw. "What the hell are you doing here?"

Mia's teeth chattered. "I came for the cat," she said, and then she started to cry.

She had never been held at gunpoint; she hadn't expected Cam to come home in the middle of the day; she was in the bedroom snooping when she shouldn't have been. The pressure of Cam's fingers tightened on her upper arms, and then she felt him pull her against him. He stroked her back, which felt fine-boned and light.

"I'm okay," she said, working her hands up between them.

Cam stepped away, and Mia sat down on the edge of the bed. "Where's Allie?"

"At the shop. Working on bonsai. I taught her." She listened to the patterns of her own voice, frail and stilted, and shook her head to clear it. She wondered why she could not think or manage to form a complex sentence.

"Bonsai? That's what you do? Force trees to grow the way you want them to?"

Mia tried to smile. "I guess you could look at it like that."

Cam sat down beside her. "You and I, we do not have a good track record."

Mia shook her head. Cam watched her bend down to pick up a fallen spray of photos, resettle them in a heart-shaped striped box that Allie had found at a tag sale. "What's this?" he said.

She could feel the blush creeping from between her breasts, all the way to the high points of her cheekbones. Stupid, stupid. She had never in her life done something like this—violated another person's privacy.

In fact, she had learned how to fade into the woodwork at a very early age, since the best way to please her parents had been to simply stay out of the way. She had made unobtrusiveness an art that, as she grew older, naturally spilled into bonsai, where restraint and blending into the background were the measures of success. She was not accustomed to being anything but an outsider; never *had* been, until yesterday's hectic events had dragged her from a vantage point on the outskirts of Wheelock smack into Allie MacDonald's world.

And with the MacDonalds, her interest was fast becoming an obsession. She had parked her car at the curb so that she'd have more time to explore, figuring the neighbors wouldn't worry if they didn't see a strange vehicle in the driveway. Then she'd gone inside to piece together all the blank spaces in the life that Allie had spent the morning drawing. By ten o'clock Mia knew how Cam and Allie had met; the names of Cam's childhood pets; the tradition they had of celebrating Valentine's Day—a florist's nightmare—early, when Allie wasn't overwhelmed with work.

Presented with her first chance to get close to people in over ten years, Mia wanted to become totally immersed. It was why she had become obsessed with Allie and Cam, or at least this was what she told herself. She did not notice that she spent far more time looking at Cam's things than she did Allie's, that for a full five minutes she had traced his monogrammed initials on a pressed white dress shirt. She did not notice that as she moved from room to room, she tried to seek out certain places—the snug hollow of an armchair, the spot in front of a dresser—where she knew Cam must have been.

Mia had come to the house to get Kafka, but she was far more interested in spying. She'd checked the books on the nightstand— Allie favored romance novels, Cam—to her shock—poetry; she'd sat, like Goldilocks, on all six different cushions of the living room couches. She'd even sprayed a line of Cam's shaving foam across her forearm and sniffed at it, trying to determine if that was the scent that had stayed with her all morning. And Mia, who was so sensitive to sounds that she could hear a fly brush a window screen and the moon shifting in the middle of the night, had become so absorbed in the contents of the bedroom that she had actually been discovered in the act.

Cam took a few of the photographs from her and held them up to the light. Mia did not look at him. "You caught me," she said quietly. "I was snooping."

To her surprise, Cam laughed. "And?"

She raised her chin, figuring if she could not be brave about this she would never survive it at all. "You wear boxers, not briefs; you had more blond in your hair than red when you were little; you get your uniforms dry-cleaned in Hancock."

"And Allie?"

Mia plucked at the quilt on the bed. "I haven't gotten around to her, yet." The corners of her mouth lifted. "I found your stash, too. The travel magazines inside your tool chest."

Cam took a second group of photographs from Mia's hands. It

didn't bother him that she knew about the magazines, not nearly as much as it had bothered him yesterday to think of Allie knowing this. Maybe it was because he knew that Allie would not even begin to understand. You simply could not define freedom to someone who did not realize they were caged.

"I read the article on Tibet," Mia admitted.

Cam nodded. "Ever been there?"

She shook her head. Stooping low, she took the last collection of spilled photographs from the floor. She leafed through a few shots of Allie as a young girl; a wedding picture of Cam, breathtaking in full Highland dress regalia. She seemed to be looking for something in particular, so Cam uselessly shuffled through the pile of photographs he held, as well, as if he could divine what she was missing.

"Here," she said, holding out a photo of a lush green valley ringed by mountains, with an imposing white stone keep to the left. "I've been here."

"You've got to be kidding," Cam said.

"It's in Scotland, isn't it? Near Glencoe?" She ran her hand over the folded tartan blanket at the foot of the bed. "Is this the place where you're all from?"

He stared into Mia's dark eyes, thinking this all hit a little too close to home to ring true, and folded his arms over his chest. "Prove it."

Later, Cam wondered whether things might have worked out differently if Mia had been able to tell him the number of cobblestones in the front walk of the Great House, which he'd counted as a child when he was bored by the adult conversation inside; or if she had remembered that under the rosebush to the left of the gate was a small gravestone for an old terrier who used to stand guard beneath it. As it was, Mia simply shook her head. "It was a long time ago," she said, "and anything I would be able to remember is something I could have seen on a postcard." She shrugged lightly and stared at the skin at the base of his throat, which was so fine and white she could see the blue veins mapped beneath it. "I guess you'll have to trust me."

That was the moment Cam thought it was possible he had seen someone who looked like Mia Townsend at Carrymuir, maybe the time he went when he was eight, maybe when he was eighteen. Perhaps she had walked with a lighter step; perhaps her hair was a little shorter, but surely he remembered that delicate carriage, those spiraling curls. And because he felt it was the only way to be perfectly sure, he leaned across the inches between them and kissed her.

She fit. Through slitted lids he saw that her eyes were still open and this became his goal: he wanted to see them drift shut. So he ran his tongue across the line of her mouth and kissed the edges. He was not thinking clearly. He told himself that if she tensed just the tiniest bit beneath his hands, he would break away. He told himself he would count to ten and see if this happened.

At about the same time his heart began to beat again, one curl of her hair wound its way around his finger, as if it could will him to stay.

Mia's eyes began to close and she wondered what in the name of God she was doing. Her blood was running fast, not simply because of this man with his big hands framing her face, but because she had known this was coming and now it had finally happened.

Cam buried his face against her throat. For a man who longed to travel, who had known the comfort of a wife and a job and a mortgage, he had the strangest sense of coming home. He felt the vibrations of her voice against his lips, motions that hummed through him for several seconds before he realized they were words.

"I have to go," Mia was saying. "I have to go now."

Afraid she would stand up and run out the door and possibly straight out of this town, Cam reached for her hand. "I'll take you back to the flower shop," he said, the sounds thick and unfamiliar to his own ears.

"I have my car."

"Leave it," Cam said. "Allie will drive you back later."

They stared at each other, unwilling to even suggest that this might happen again; that either one might want or not want the other to be in the same house another night. Finally Mia nodded, having based her decision on the fact that she could not stand knowing what Cam would say to Allie if she was not present in the room when he got there.

He did not touch her while they were walking downstairs. He stayed a single step behind Mia, walking quickly to catch the scent she left behind. With every movement it got harder to believe that he had kissed a woman he hardly knew in his own bedroom, and he let the guilt grow. He had a wife that he loved. A murderer who still had to be arraigned. He did not know what he had been thinking. He did not want to acknowledge that he simply had not been thinking at all.

At the bottom of the stairs, Mia scooped Kafka into her arms and headed for the front door. She paused at the threshold. "I need to know what you're going to tell her," she said, trying to sound glib and failing miserably.

Cam let her walk out the door and then started to lock it behind them. "That I thought you were a burglar and pulled a gun on you. That I scared you to death."

"Well," Mia said, moving to the police cruiser, "it wouldn't be a lie."

After Allie had finished her bonsai wiring for the day, and had dropped Verona MacBean's centerpieces off at the library, she decided to visit Jamie MacDonald. She told herself that it wasn't really going against Cam's wishes. If anyone, like Hannah, asked what she was doing visiting a man Cam was going to book for murder—well, she'd just say he was family.

She made him a nosegay of flowers that she thought might help: roses for love, marigolds for grief, violets for faithfulness, chrysanthemums for cheerfulness during adversity. She filled these in with statice and quaking grass. She knew it wouldn't be allowed in the cell, but even Cam couldn't object to having it hung on the swing lock outside. She waited until Cam's police cruiser had been gone from its spot for fifteen minutes. Then she checked her hair and brushed dried bits of petals off her clothes and began to walk down the street.

Casey MacRae was the only person, other than the prisoner, inside the police station. Hannah had called in sick, and Cam was, as Casey put it, God knows where. "Hey," he said, looking up from a game of solitaire he was playing on the booking counter. "It must be MacDonald day at the station."

Allie unbuttoned her coat and hooked it on the knob of Cam's locked office door. "Who else has been here?"

Casey smiled. "Old Angus. Middle of the night, in his bath-robe."

Allie laughed. "Cam must have loved that. Do we know for a fact he's still in town? Or did Angus ride him out on a rail?" She sat down in Hannah's swivel chair and pushed it back on its ball bearings, whizzing on the scratched linoleum floor.

"Allie," Casey said, "I really don't know when Cam's coming back."

Allie set her feet and smiled. "Oh, I didn't come to see Cam. I want to talk to Jamie."

"He'll *kill* me."

"He doesn't have to know." Allie jumped out of the chair and walked past Casey into the booking room. "We can sit right in here. You can cuff him and even stand by to referee." She knew she was going to win. In the end, she promised him a free coupon for a dozen roses sent at Valentine's Day to the woman of his choice—a seventy-dollar value—in exchange for fifteen minutes with Jamie MacDonald.

He came into the booking room looking a little the worse for wear. His shirt was wrinkled from having been slept in; a fine red stubble traced the line of his jaw. Casey's beefy hand was locked around his upper arm, and his wrists were ringed with old hand-cuffs. "Mr. MacDonald," Allie said, her throat suddenly dry. What did you say to someone who had killed his wife?

"Please," he said, sitting down across the desk from her, "call me Jamie."

"Then I'm Allie," she replied, taking a deep breath. She smiled at him, started to speak, and then stopped. Finally she shook her head. "I can't very well ask you how you're doing, can I?"

"You can ask whatever you like," Jamie said. "I just may not answer." He leaned forward to rest his arms on his knees, and the sudden movement made Allie shift back in her chair. Jamie stared at her. "I won't hurt you."

"I know," Allie whispered. She folded her hands in her lap and realized she still carried the dried flowers. Nervous, she thrust them at Jamie. He reached for them with his manacled hands, his fingers brushing hers briefly. She was surprised at their warmth and their softness, as if their very substance seemed incapable of violence.

"A housewarming gift," he said dryly, turning the small bouquet over in his hands.

Allie bit her lip. This wasn't going the way she had planned. She had figured, oh, she'd walk in like some kind of Florence Nightingale and let Jamie pour out his heart before being arraigned. Sort of like being shrived before justice. Instead, she had nothing to say, and Jamie wasn't in the mood for confidences. She was just about to wish him the best at his arraignment and bolt from the booking room, when he shifted in his chair, catching her attention. "Did you come in spite of him?" he said.

Allie froze. "I don't know what you mean."

"It can't look very good for the chief of police when his wife pays a mercy visit to the guy he thinks is a murderer."

"This isn't a mercy visit," Allie said automatically. Her eyes scanned behind Jamie's head to a row of clipboards Cam had hung strategically for the part-time officers to peruse at their leisure: staff notices, weekly schedules, the FBI's Most Wanted.

"No? Then it's a social call." He stared at her. "What would happen if your husband found out you came to see me?"

Allie shrugged, but it seemed more like a shiver. Cam wouldn't yell, he certainly wouldn't threaten her, but he'd withdraw. He would think that she didn't support him or believe in him, and because that hadn't happened in the five years they'd been married, it would cut him to the quick. "It has nothing to do with you, Jamie, or what you did," Allie said slowly, carefully picking her way through her own words. "I just don't want to hurt him."

A smile stole across Jamie's face, so completely transforming him that Allie would not have recognized him if she'd seen him on the street. "Then you're the one."

Allie blinked at him. "The one what?"

"The one who loves more." He moved closer to the desk, and the handcuffs tapped against the metal edge as he inadvertently made gestures. "You know it's never fifty-fifty in a marriage. It's always seventy-thirty, or sixty-forty. Someone falls in love first. Someone puts someone else up on a pedestal. Someone works very hard to keep things rolling smoothly; someone else sails along for the ride."

Allie opened her mouth to protest, but saw that Jamie wasn't even looking at her anymore. "When I first saw Maggie, she was standing knee-deep in water at this little duck pond, scrubbing the bottom with a long-handled brush. I thought she worked for the town, but she told me later that she did it once a month because nobody else bothered to. She was wearing a yellow slicker and baggy striped shorts and diamond earrings. That's what made me come closer. They kept catching the light of the sun and winking at me. I mean, here she was covered in mud and droppings, but she was still wearing diamonds." He shook his head. "I took the scrub brush from her and helped her onto the grass. I lived right on the other side of that park; I passed it ten times each day, and suddenly I knew that the next time I passed it, if she wasn't there, it was going to look all wrong."

Allie covered her mouth with her hand and turned away. She pictured Maggie MacDonald on the embalming table. She tried to remember if Maggie had been wearing earrings.

"I'm the one like you," Jamie said. "The one who fell first. The one who would do anything to keep it the way it was at the beginning."

Allie felt the room closing in on her. She forced herself to her feet. "I have no idea what you're talking about."

"Seventy-thirty," Jamie replied.

"But you *killed* her."

Jamie shook his head. "I loved her," he said quietly. "I loved her so much I let her go."

From the corner of her eye, Allie could see the door of the police station swing open and for a horrible moment she thought it would be Cam and she would be well and truly caught. Her stomach flipped as she waited for the newcomer to step into the main area of the station. A young man, someone she'd seen before but couldn't quite connect with a name.

"Not Cam?"

"No," Allie breathed, before realizing that Jamie had just proven his point.

Casey MacRae stuck his head in the door of the booking room. "Allie, I'm going to have to ask you to leave. MacDonald's counsel just arrived."

Allie nodded, and Casey ducked back out. She turned to Jamie. "I wish you luck," she said stiffly.

Jamie reached out and took her cold hand between his own. She tried to imagine him pressing those hands over Maggie's nose and mouth, pressing hard and not relenting, but she could not really do it. "Allie," he asked softly, "do you think I'm guilty?"

He had let his guard down; in his eyes she could see the effort it cost him to simply sit upright; the pain caused just by breathing; the shimmering memories of a slow, moonlit fox-trot around a duck pond. "That depends," she said, allowing herself to smile, "on what you think you're guilty *of.*"

Within five minutes of meeting Jamie MacDonald, Graham MacPhee realized the man would have gladly welcomed the death penalty, had it been an option in Massachusetts. He did not want counsel, especially not someone who was a notch above your average public defender. He simply wanted to be convicted and to spend the rest of his life wasting away in a bigger cell.

"Tell me again," Jamie said, pacing in the small booking room. "Who hired you on my behalf?"

"A friend. Someone who wants you free."

"I don't have any friends in this town." Jamie thought of Allie, and Angus—neither of whom would have access to the funds necessary to retain a criminal defense attorney.

Graham was beginning to lose his patience. This was his first real case—a whopper of a court case, at that—and his goddamned client didn't even want to defend himself. "Look, it doesn't matter if your fucking fairy godmother hired me. I think we can get you off the hook for this and I intend to do so."

Jamie remained very still for a moment, and then, as if all the energy had simply left his body, he slowly folded into a chair.

Graham sighed. "Tell me what happened."

For forty-five minutes, Graham took notes on a yellow legal pad. Finally, when Jamie fell silent, he drummed two pencils on the table and reviewed what he had written. And as he did, Jamie MacDonald watched Graham through lowered eyes, his head bent down, tracking Graham's moves. Graham wondered what he was getting himself into. In criminal defense, it was common for an attorney not to trust his client; this was the rare case where the relationship seemed to have been turned around.

Then Jamie locked his gaze on Graham's, and Graham froze. He found himself thinking about what kind of man could have done what Jamie had done. Was it really out of love? What else might have provoked it? For all he knew, Maggie and Jamie Mac-Donald could have been in the middle of a knock-down-drag-out divorce, and the killing was the result of one snide remark that took Jamie over the edge. For all he knew, Maggie might have held a million-dollar life insurance policy with Jamie as beneficiary. For all he knew, Jamie MacDonald could have been the consummate actor.

But he didn't think so.

"You've lived in Cummington for the past sixteen years, you've been married for eleven of those, and your wife was suffering a long and painful death. You were overcome with emotion and distraught and in a moment of weakness you killed your wife, hoping to put her out of her agony." Graham smiled tentatively. "Not guilty by reason of temporary insanity."

Jamie knew better than to tell Graham it hadn't been quite like that. Still, he did not know if he could put his faith in a lawyer so new at his job that his cordovans squeaked a bit when he walked the length of the room.

Sensing Jamie's hesitation, Graham sat down on the edge of the desk in front of him. "Did you sleep last night?"

Jamie glanced up. "No," he said.

"Why not?"

Jamie stared at this man, this gift from an unknown benefactor, as if he were crazy. "Because I'd killed someone I loved hours before? Because I kept seeing those few minutes every time I closed my eyes? Take your pick." He turned away, disgusted; angry at Graham for being such a novice, angry at himself for revealing even that much. For a few moments neither man said a word. When Jamie spoke again, he had to strain to hear his own voice. "Because it was the first time in eleven years I had to sleep without her next to me."

Graham grinned. It took all his self-control not to jump off the corner of the desk. "That is why we're going to win this case."

Jamie shook his head slowly. "They have a body, a signed confession, fingerprints, scratches."

"Maybe so," said Graham MacPhee, "but we have *you*."

Martha Sully, one of the magistrates at the Wheelock District Court, was a *sassenach,* but she usually agreed with Cam when it came to setting amounts for bail. She sat behind her podium desk reading Cam's arrest and custody report, noted that the complaint was based on "information or belief." She had already asked Jamie to enter his plea.

"So," she said, glancing up at Cam. "Been busy out on your end of town?"

Cam grinned. "You could say that."

He liked Martha Sully; he liked her clipped English voice, with its trilling dips and draws. She sounded remarkably upper-class, like she was hiding cakes and crumpets just behind her gavel stand. Cam knew her to be a fair magistrate. He had only been the subject of her wrath once, when Angus, in a fit, had started screaming at her in the town coffee shop about the need to get those god-damned Windsors off a Stuart throne.

Martha ran her courtroom very casually, at least at the beginning stages. She lifted her eyes, signaling to Cam that she was ready to begin. "Your Honor," he said, having done this a thousand times, "in light of the evidence uncovered by the voluntary statement given by James MacDonald and taken from the scene of the crime, we've booked him on charges of Murder One. Because he was the perpetrator of such a violent crime, we recommend that bail be set at fifty thousand dollars."

When he said the sum, Jamie's eyes sought his out. Cam was not certain if he read disillusionment there, or respect.

"Your Honor," Graham began, clearing his throat, "my client is an upstanding citizen of his community. He's never received a traffic ticket, he's a member of the Small Business Association, he's served on the Cummington selectmen's board for three consecutive terms. Since he does not in any way pose a threat to the Wheelock community, we feel that he should be released without bail, provided he stays in the area pending trial."

Martha rubbed her temples and scanned the papers before her once more. She had, of course, heard of this case yesterday when it happened; had in fact been waiting for it to appear in her courtroom today. She knew what Cam was up to; she also knew what he was up against. She doubted he really wanted James MacDonald locked away at the county jail, in spite of his outrageous request.

"Conditions for bail are as follows: Mr. MacDonald will remain within Wheelock proper pending trial; and he is obligated to check in with Chief MacDonald at the police station every day, excluding Sundays, before noon." She peered over her half-glasses at the small group in front of her. "Bail," she said, "is set at five dollars."

Cam stayed in the courtroom after Jamie and his lawyer had left. He sat down at the prosecutor's table and stretched his legs in front of him, peering at the seal of an eagle over the judge's podium and squinting to read its motto.

The last thing he wanted was to be Jamie MacDonald's keeper. *Damn Martha Sully.*

With a sigh, Cam got to his feet and headed out of the court. He had a hundred things to do at the station, administrative duties that hadn't been finished in the bustle of the past two days. He had to talk to Allie too. He hadn't seen her yet this afternoon. He had driven Mia to the flower shop, but Allie had only left a note saying she'd be back soon.

At the foot of the stairs he saw Jamie, standing before the bail bondsman's office, talking to someone. He considered just walking out the door, but realized it went against his better judgment. Taking a deep breath, he walked forward.

"Fifty thousand dollars?" Jamie said.

Cam opened his mouth, ready to reply, when he realized who Jamie had been speaking to. Allie was just shoving her wallet back into her purse, having obviously sprung Jamie free on his ridiculously low bail. "Really, Cam," she admonished, smiling up at him.

Her heart-shaped face was pink from the cold and her tongue came out to wet her lips. Her hair spilled over her shoulders, catching here and there in the collar of her coat.

Within an hour, everyone in Wheelock would know that Cam had asked for fifty thousand dollars bail, that it had been set at five dollars, and that Allie had been the one to pay it. He found himself wondering how high she would have gone. A hundred? Five hundred? Five thousand?

She slipped her hand through the crook of his arm, and at her touch, he felt his fury begin to recede. "Jamie's going to stay with Angus," she said, as if she were announcing the seating at a dinner party. She smiled a goodbye and steered Cam out the door.

They had taken separate cars, so they stopped at the center of the parking lot, hands bunched into their pockets against the unseasonable cold, like two fighters squaring off. "Allie," he said, "I have to know what you were doing here today."

Allie stared at him as if he could create a whole different world for her, as if he already had. He thought of Mia, and suddenly he could not breathe. "Why, Cam," Allie answered, her voice clear and true and comfortable, "I came because of you."

I have questions for you that I never got the chance to ask:

Do you look like you did back then? Would it make a difference, anyway?

Do you think of me, when you least expect it—when you're unwrapping a garden hose or tilting your face to the shower or making love to someone else? And can you leave it at that, or do you find yourself compulsively sifting through the memories?

If I had been the one to leave, would you have written out your heart to me?

# FIVE

When Mia was in seventh-grade Latin class, she learned that her name derived from the classical word for "mine." The teacher made a joke about it, saying it was surely the most selfish name in the class. But Mia had only smiled weakly, wondering what her parents had had in mind. Whose was she, exactly? Her father's? Her mother's? In spite of their devotion to each other, they hadn't named their daughter "Ours," leaving her to believe she had to choose a side.

She had played hooky for the rest of the day, coming home to sit in the rose garden her mother had abandoned several years earlier when she found that pruning took her away from Ed Townsend too many hours of the weekend. Mia had remade it into her own image, twisting the thorny bushes around wire frames and clipping them so that they resembled dragons and centaurs and big-bellied ships, trained to stay exactly as they'd been told. Her parents thought she was very clever, quite a little horticulturalist. They had set a hammock in the garden, big enough for two, so that they could watch her work.

But they weren't in the garden when Mia arrived, and she didn't go to her gardening shed immediately. Instead she sat on the cool, damp grass, picking apart a leaf with her nails. She thought about her name. She reached the conclusion that even at birth, her parents had wanted her to be separate and apart from the magical unit they fashioned when they were together. Self-sufficient, she was. Independent.

*Mia.* Mine. And she knew then, perhaps had always known, that she could only belong to herself.

*C*am sat in the middle of a dark pew, staring at the body of Christ. It was a waxy sculpture that hung over the altar at the town's church. When Cam was a young boy at Sunday mass, he'd held himself awake by keeping his eyes wide and unblinking until the sheen of tears made the painted blood at Jesus' hands and feet look real.

MacDonalds had always been Catholics. It was why some of the clan chiefs had decided to support the restoration of Prince Charles—and the Stuarts—to the British throne. By now, most of Scotland was Presbyterian, but the MacDonalds of Carrymuir, when they came to Massachusetts in the late 1740s, had brought with them their original religion.

Cam was not a terribly religious man, but he knew that when he was overwhelmed, he had somewhere to turn. He had several reasons to be in church at this time: He wanted to light a candle for Maggie MacDonald; he had to pray for Jamie MacDonald's soul. He wanted to talk to someone about his own indiscretion, too— and although the confessor he had in mind was Mia Townsend herself, he knew this was not possible.

Unfortunately, as he sat there waiting for Father Gillivray to begin hearing confessions, he could only picture his wedding day five years before.

Allie had been a beautiful bride, small and elegant in white satin that curved at her breasts and her hips. Cam had watched her walking down the aisle, and all he had been able to think was, *She's so light.* It seemed that with every step she hovered inches above the ground, and when her father placed her hand on top of Cam's, he had clutched at it with his fingers, determined to keep her from floating away.

Allie had been beautiful, but Cam had stolen the show. After all, it was not every day that a clan chief took a wife. He had worn his father's full-dress regalia: the black velvet coat with silver buttons, the heavy kilt in the strong MacDonald tartan, the white linen shirt with a festival of lace at the throat and the wrists.

When they went back to their honeymoon suite at the Wheelock Inn, Allie had laughed, saying he had more clasps and buttons to undo than she did. . . .

Cam sank to his knees, as if in prayer, hoping the hard bench below him would center his thoughts.

Even in this church, where he could feel God sitting next to him, Cam could not get the image of Mia Townsend out of his mind; the slight tilt of her eyes, the spiral of her ear. She had been rooting for Jamie MacDonald, just like Allie, but somehow he did not hold it against her.

Cam bent his neck so that his forehead touched the pew in front of him. He did not even know what exactly he was going to confess to. Was it adultery if you kissed a woman who was not your wife? Was it adultery if you thought about her so often you could hear her voice when you closed your eyes?

It didn't seem right that he'd only sinned in a matter of the flesh. For some reason, kissing Mia seemed less of a betrayal to Allie than having Mia running through his thoughts like stunning mountain scenery seen from a train: you did not keep looking after a while, yet you couldn't help but notice it was there just outside the window.

The whole time Cam had been holding Mia on a bed he shared with Allie, on a quilt Allie had sewn one summer in a craft class, in a room that Allie had wall-papered and furnished, he had not had a single thought of his wife.

He saw Father Gillivray's round, black-clad body shuffle from the vestibule to the small confessionals at the back of the church. Giving him a minute to settle in, Cam stood and drew open the curtain of the little booth, then sat down on the folding chair. "Bless me, Father," he began, "for I have sinned. It has been four months since my last confession."

He could see Father Gillivray's profile through the latticed opening of the confessional. Impulsively, Cam pressed his big hand up to the partition, as if by blocking it off he would guarantee a greater anonymity. "I've been thinking a lot about this one woman," he said. "I can't get her out of my head. I see myself . . .

well, with her. She's not my wife. And I kissed her. I kissed a woman who wasn't my wife."

*And I'd do it all over again,* he thought.

"Think about what you're doing," Father Gillivray said. "Think long and hard."

He was given his penance and knelt in a different pew to say the round of the rosary. It was not the first time he'd been a hypocrite to the teachings of the Catholic church. He and Allie had been using birth control, after all, and he didn't make it to Mass every week.

He looked up at the plaster face of the Holy Mother and pictured Mia, and knew that he was damned.

When he broke from the heavy double doors into the fading daylight, he was sweating. He hadn't finished his rosary. He certainly hadn't been capable of thinking of his actions. Cam walked down the street toward the station to pick up his car, feeling the wind wrap about his neck. He did not realize until he was on his way home that he had never lit a candle for Maggie MacDonald, never prayed for Jamie at all.

*T*he ten men who had worked for Jamie at Techcellence were part computer geeks, part philosophers, and part geniuses. Two—Flanders and Rod—had been with Jamie from the company's conception over a decade earlier. Like Jamie, they were obsessed with pushing the envelope in their virtual designs. And like Jamie, they spent a good deal of their free time in the lab, shooting the breeze with each other and brainstorming tomorrow's toys.

It was the fall of 1992, and they had just won their first big Sega contract. While Jamie tinkered with one of the huge graphics machines, Rod had run out to get a case of Rolling Rock. The three of them were halfway through the package, toasting their own success and their unquestionable brilliance. "Hey," Rod said, his eyes lighting up. "Give me an HMD." He reached for the high-tech helmet, switched on a couple of computers, and downloaded a program they'd recently finished for an architectural firm in Nova Scotia—a virtual walk-through of a hospital that had not yet been built. "You ever get into VR when you're shitfaced?"

Jamie looked up over his shoulder. "You fuck with that program, and I'll kill you. That took me months to get right."

Flanders had picked up the program at a different monitor, sliding his hand into the glove and fitting the HMD over his skull. On the two-dimensional screen, Jamie watched images of the men appear as they stepped into the glass-domed hospital foyer.

Rod whistled, staring up at the impressive ceiling. "Nice," he said. "But how are they going to scrub the bird shit off the cupola?"

"It's virtual bird shit," Flanders said. "Jamie thinks of everything."

"You ready?" Rod asked, turning to the right so that the tracking device in his HMD picked up Flanders. Flanders nodded. "Let's rock," Rod said, and he took off down the main hospital hall at a breakneck run.

Flanders was close at his heels, his feet flying on the motion-platform treadmill that was attached to the computer system. Jamie took a sip of his beer, smiling at the antics of his colleagues in someone else's virtual world as they sent wheelchairs careening and leaped up to touch the fluorescent ceiling lights. Flanders crouched down on the platform, pushing against something invisible that let him vault over a nurse's desk in the simulated hospital. "Hey," he said, "let's be derelicts."

He tossed a virtual felt-tipped marker at Rod, who stretched out his gloved hand to catch it. "Too heavy," Rod commented. "Jamie, you're going to have to finesse the tactile feedback."

Flanders began to scribble on the pristine white walls. "God, I was always too good. I should have been doing destructive things all along."

"Graffiti?" Rod said. "Graffiti's for kids." He walked into an adjoining surgery suite and dumped a tray of instruments all over the floor.

"For Christ's sake," Jamie said. "Get out of there. Now."

Reluctantly, Rod and Flanders tugged off their HMDs and gloves. "What's the big deal?" Rod sulked. "You can boot up the system again and it'll look just as sterile as it was before we went in."

Flanders pushed away from the terminal. "Who's to say it

will?" he asked. "I mean, if VR is so realistic that you feel, see, and sense an experience, who's to say it didn't happen?"

"Oh, Jesus," Rod said under his breath. "Three beers and he's Aristotle."

"No, I'm serious. If I think I walked through that hospital and left a graffiti mural, who can prove I didn't?"

"When they build the hospital," Rod yawned, "your artwork won't be there."

"That's the ticket," Jamie said. "For something to be real, it has to have an impact on the outside world. If you create a program that lets you think you've robbed a bank, it won't matter what you remember about it, because you didn't come away with hard cash, and you didn't hurt anyone else in the process."

Rod leaned back in his chair. "All right. But what if you commit a virtual act that—even in the real world—wouldn't leave a visible mark? All you've got to go on is the memory of carrying it out." He grinned. "And what if someone's hooked up with you to a system? Then you *both* have the same experience of participation. Proof positive."

Jamie arched a brow. "What act wouldn't leave any kind of mark?"

Rod smirked. "Adultery. Good old computer sex. You're at one terminal, she's at another. You'd swear on your grandmother's grave that you can feel her skin and smell her. Shit, with a good bodysuit you could even come. And she feels it all on *her* end, too. Can you prove that it didn't really happen?"

"No exchange of bodily fluids," Flanders said primly.

"Yeah, but in this case, there wouldn't be a perceptible impact in the external world, so all the evidence would lie in the memory of the two people—whether they had sex in a real bed, or at a terminal." Rod hooted with pleasure. "Go ahead, Jamie. Shoot holes in that one."

Jamie shook his head and started picking up the empties. "If a tree falls in the woods and no one's around . . ." he said, letting his words trail off.

"C'mon. You're telling me that even in a highly sensitive system, you'd be able to tell real sex from virtual sex?"

"You boys wouldn't understand," Jamie said, grinning.

"Oh, the old married man," Rod sang.

"That's right. There's nothing that could fool me into believing virtual time spent with Maggie would be anything like the real thing."

"Tell us, Confucius," Flanders said.

But Jamie went around slowly and deliberately switching off the hardware and then the lights. You could not explain to someone who had not been there that to join with a woman in cyberspace, all you needed was a savvy program and a certain degree of skill—no roll of your soul, no heart. You could not explain to someone who had not loved as well and as strongly as he had that being with Maggie let him walk in a world he could never create on his own.

Mia checked into the Wheelock Inn at a reduced long-term room rate. It was the tiniest room in the little two-story hotel, tucked next to a broom closet in the west corner. It had its own bathroom, and a claw-footed tub with a curtain drawn round for a shower. There was a tiny kitchenette. The bed was covered with a tartan blanket just like the one she'd used at Cam's house, and a small dresser was topped with a chipped blue ewer and washstand.

She tossed her duffel bag on the bed and carefully set her knapsack down on a tipsy table. When she unzipped it, Kafka bounded free, happy to be unconfined. If she was careful about a litter box, the pinched clerk downstairs would never know she had a cat.

She took the bonsai tree she'd been carrying in her other hand and began to unwrap it from its protective gauze layers. It was the one she'd shown Allie yesterday in order to get a job; a fig tree with exposed roots, twenty-eight years old, just like Mia. Of course she'd started to work with it some time ago, but it was still quite an achievement. Twenty-eight years, and thriving in this tiny terracotta plate. Mia ran her finger over its twisted, exposed roots, its whispering dime-size leaves. "Hello," she said softly, setting it in a place where it could begin to turn an unfamiliar room into a home.

She had taken a room at the Inn because she did not want to see Cameron MacDonald again. She knew this was unlikely in a town of less than two thousand people, especially since she was working with his wife, but that did not keep her from setting her distance.

She stood in front of the dresser, peering into the antique mirror. Her face seemed bronzed and foggy; and her mouth was wide and straight, the way it always was. Her lips no longer looked swollen, as they had after Cam had dropped her off at the flower shop. When she discovered that Allie had gone out, Mia locked the front door and stood in front of the bathroom mirror in the back of the shop, holding her fingertips to her mouth as if she could keep the sensitivity at a peak.

She began to rummage through the drawers of the nightstand and the dresser, not so much because she expected to find anything but simply because it was what one always did when settling into a stock hotel room. There was a votive candle in the bottom drawer of the dresser that smelled heavily of peaches, and a King James Bible—King James of *Scotland,* she now knew—in the nightstand to the left of the double bed.

Under the Bible was a stack of paper imprinted with the town seal, and a small, chewed-off pencil. Mia lit the votive candle, then took the paper and pencil and sat down on the bed, using the Bible as a lap desk.

*Cameron,* she wrote, because she liked the length of his name, *I have been thinking of you.* She thought of the fairness of his skin, and the way the sun brought to life the rich autumn colors in his hair. She remembered how, when he thought he had frightened her with the gun, he had gathered her close so that her head was pressed against his chest. She had listened to the rhythm of his heart, so remarkably strong that Mia believed her head was being pushed fractionally away with every beat.

Mia picked up the pencil again and crossed out what she had written. *Cameron,* she began again, *I have been thinking of nothing but you.* Then she stood up and fed the paper to the flame of the votive candle, watching the traces of her folly fall to ash.

Allie closed the flower shop early and drove to Angus's house, which stood beside a cornfield that belonged to Darby Mac. He was the only farmer in Wheelock, nearly as old as Angus himself, and had been called Darby Mac all his adult life, in an effort to keep at bay the jokes about Old MacDonald's farm. In late September, the corn was quite high, almost hiding Angus's house from view. Allie glanced out the window at the field, and then slowed as she noticed the high color spotting the stalks. A bright red Mylar balloon emblazoned with *Congratulations!* bobbed in the light breeze. There were ordinary balloons too, pink and white and yellow, and a silver string of letters that spelled *Happy Anniversary* stretched the length of the front row of corn.

Angus opened his front door before she knocked. "How festive," she said, still looking over her shoulder at the corn.

"Aye, well, Darby Mac says it'll keep off the crows."

Somehow, Allie felt disappointed. For maybe the slightest moment she had imagined there was a celebration under way, a party just inside Angus's door.

"Lassie," Angus said, "are ye going to be stayin' out or in?"

Allie turned and stepped inside. "Is Jamie ready?"

Angus's house could politely be described as Spartan. With the exception of a hearth rug Allie herself had braided for him and a wing chair he'd had sent from the Great House at Carrymuir, there was little decorative furniture. He had a kitchen table, but no chairs, insisting he did not want to linger over dinner when the only person to hold a conversation with was himself. The mantel over the fireplace was empty, and the conspicuous absence of pictures on the walls only called more attention to the tiny brass frame on the side table that held a postcard of the mountains and rolling glen he'd always called home.

"Jamie's as ready as he'll ever be," Angus said. He picked up an umbrella from a stand by the door and rapped it against the ceiling. "Jamie, lad," he yelled. "It's Allie come to see ye."

Jamie came down the narrow stairs quietly, twisting a coat that must have been Angus's in his hands. "Are you sure you want to do this?" he said brusquely.

Allie smiled at him. "You're going to have to get out sooner or later," she reminded him. "Where's that MacDonald pride I've heard about all these years?"

Jamie shrugged himself into the coat, a shapeless tweedy brown jacket that was inches too short at the sleeves. Allie turned to Angus. "You're sure you don't want to come?"

Angus snorted. "To a lecture about hell?" He shook his head. "I'm old enough. Why tempt fate?"

Allie kissed him on the cheek and walked out the door. She was settled in the car, adjusting her seat belt, when she realized that Jamie was still standing outside, his fingers clutching the handle of the passenger-side door. She unrolled the window. "You don't want to be late," she said, and then she saw the direction he was gazing.

She watched a breath of wind stir the rainbow of balloons. "I've never seen anything like this," Jamie said.

Allie turned the ignition. "Darby Mac says it works."

Jamie sat down and pulled the door shut. He stared straight out the window. "You know, when I got to Angus's house yesterday, the farmer only had that one balloon. The *Congratulations!* one." He smirked. "I thought it was for me."

Allie pressed her foot on the brake to slow the car, and turned to stare at Jamie. "Well," she said, "you never know."

The arraignment of James MacDonald had created such a stir in the sleepy little town that anyone who might have attended Verona MacBean's reading from her book on the nature of hell completely forgot it had been scheduled. Consequently, the Friends of the Library had judiciously postponed the reading until today, asking Allie to keep the three centerpieces in her cooler overnight. And because she'd agreed to do so without any additional charge, Verona herself had given Allie two tickets to the event.

They were small black rectangles, printed with gold lettering. "Wheelock's Daughter, Verona MacBean," they said. "Reading from her critically acclaimed book, *Damnation in the '90s: To Hell and Back*." Allie had, of course, offered Cam a ticket, but he had politely declined. Even if he had the time to go, he wouldn't need more than a smile to gain admission; it was one of the perks of being Chief of Police. "Maybe I'll meet you there," he had said, pulling on his socks that morning. "I wouldn't mind seeing how Verona turned out."

"Then I'll just find another date. There are plenty of men in this town who'd like to escort me to a lecture on hell."

Cam laughed. "You've already asked Angus?"

Allie tossed her head. "Who says it has to be Angus? Maybe I'll take Jamie."

At her words, Cam had gone still. He'd glanced up at her, his eyes dark. She thought he would become angry, or flat out forbid her to go, but instead he simply nodded. "Maybe you should," he'd agreed.

Allie pulled up to the library and parked in a spot at the curb. She walked in and handed her ticket to the lady at the front of the conference room, turning to ask Jamie where he wanted to sit. He was standing awkwardly in front of the woman, who had started to walk away.

"Excuse me," Allie said, grabbing the ticket from Jamie and ripping it in half and then dragging him into the room. She tapped the woman's back. "Is there a problem?"

The woman glanced at Jamie and then looked away. "I don't think it's entirely proper for him to be here," she said, loud enough to make others turn their heads.

"My cousin has not been convicted by a court of law. He's a guest of this town."

"That doesn't mean we have to like it." Allie whirled around to find Jock Farquhason, a thin, reedy bank teller, staring her down.

"Let's go." Jamie started to tug at the sleeve of Allie's sweater.

"Absolutely not," she hissed. She led Jamie to a table at the front of the room. It became crowded in a matter of minutes, and although some people nodded to Jamie as they passed, no one else came to sit beside them—those unwilling to cast the first stones didn't want their lot thrown in with a mercy killer, either.

Allie did not realize that Cam had seen the whole thing. He was standing in the back of the room, more comfortable with his shoulders against the cement-block wall than he would be sitting beside Jamie MacDonald with all of Wheelock watching. He could have said something to that asshole Farquhason, but he didn't have the heart or the inclination. If Jamie MacDonald was planning to win, he'd have to play by the same rules as anyone else.

When the lights dimmed and Verona MacBean stepped onto the stage in all her glory, Cam could not suppress a smile. The woman in the severe black suit with her hair braided tight against her head was a far cry from the hot little number who used to go

down on him after-hours in the boys' locker room. He tried to un-
dress her with his eyes, picturing the creamy skin and swelling
curves that had kept him in a permanent state of semierection in
high school, but Verona's face and form kept giving way to the
image of Mia's frightened eyes, the fragile bones of her spine.

He turned and left before Verona even started speaking.

A 1994 Gallup poll, Verona began, found that sixty percent of
Americans believe in hell. That was up from fifty-four percent in
1965. Hell, she said, had developed in religion out of the sense that
some people were getting away with sin in this life, and deserved
punishment in the next one.

She stood in front of a small podium someone had transported
from the elementary school auditorium. "Jews had Gehenna," she
said, "named for a dump near Jerusalem where animal carcasses
were thrown into bonfires. The New Testament mentioned a lake
of fire, an outer darkness." She paused and smiled at the crowd.
"And in 1990, a tabloid ran a story about a Soviet drilling fleet
who found hell when looking for oil. They had it closed off after
smelling the ashes and smoke, hearing the shrieks of the inhabitants."

Any schoolchild could describe a laughing, teeth-gnashing
Devil, a pit of fire and brimstone. But, Verona said, the latest the-
ology on the matter postulates that although hell exists, it isn't in a
literal space.

"We now believe that people don't get sent to hell," she said,
stopping to take a sip of water from a tumbler. "That would make
God into a horrible sort of magistrate. Instead, we see hell as a
choice people make for the afterlife. People who decide during the
time they're alive that they don't need God will have to spend eternity without Him too."

Jamie, who hadn't wanted to hear Verona MacBean, hadn't
even wanted to leave the safe haven of Angus MacDonald's home,
found himself wholly entranced with her words. And as she began
to speak of the popular image of hell, with its rings of Dantesque
fire and burning walls, he had a sudden image of Maggie. She was
getting into bed in the middle of the night, like she always did.
She awakened at least once or twice to pee; she used to say she had
a bladder like a thimble. By the time she came back to the bed-

room, she'd be freezing. She'd slide under the covers and put her icy feet on Jamie's calves, and he'd pull her close, her back to his front. "You're burning," she would whisper. "You're on fire." He'd concentrate on the soft curve of her bottom, pressed to his groin, and he'd selflessly give her all his heat until he fell asleep, now clutching at Maggie for warmth.

He did not necessarily agree with Verona MacBean's vision of hell. It could be much simpler than the theologians seemed to believe. You knew you were damned when you woke up in the morning and realized, with a jolt, that you were still alive. You knew you were damned when you went to sleep at night, and you kept seeing the love of your life just at the reach of an arm's length, but every time you went to touch her face she vanished like a reflection in a pond.

He turned to watch Allie, still and intent on the lecture. She had come to the courthouse yesterday for his moral support; he knew this just as surely as he knew that she had not told Cam that was her reason for going. Jamie would have bet her husband didn't know he was with her now. Not that Jamie blamed her—he understood that sort of relationship, perhaps better than anyone. A lie of omission was much simpler than admitting to yourself you were going against the wishes of the person you idolized.

And suddenly, in the middle of the Wheelock Public Library, the pieces fell into place. Jamie understood why he had been able to kill Maggie. He had been telling himself over and over during sleepless nights that he would have done anything Maggie had asked of him; that was the nature of love. But he was starting to see that he had wanted to do it, and for a purely selfish reason: he did not wish to see her sick and pained and beaten, because that wasn't the way he wanted to remember her. He had held her head when she vomited after chemotherapy; he'd kissed the scar where her breast had been; he'd been a paragon instead of a husband. But when he first woke up in the morning and turned to see her sleeping—bones taut under stretched skin, hollow asymmetry of her chest rising and falling with battered breaths—he had always shuddered. Slight, small tremors; they were easy enough to suppress before he put his arms around Maggie and woke her up with a genuine smile.

He had wanted back the old Maggie. The woman he had fallen in love with.

He hated himself for this.

But it had been a strong current in him, strong enough to make him take her life when she asked, although he had to have known she was not—could not have been—thinking clearly.

It disgusted Jamie that the last six months he spent with Maggie had been a well-constructed lie. It infuriated him that he had not been brave enough to see past what the cancer had taken away and to find instead the wonderful, indefatigable qualities that remained.

And it was agonizing to know that in spite of what he had done, it had all been for nothing. Killing Maggie had not brought her back whole and shining as she used to be. Jamie looked at Verona MacBean, black-clad and confident and artsy, and knew that she didn't really understand hell at all.

Graham MacPhee was sitting in his office with a bottle of Rolling Rock—it being far after hours—and scribbling down defense possibilities on the back of a take-out Chinese menu.

*Absence of Malice.* Murder One was defined as having malice aforethought. This defense was the most likely possibility, and yet the one no one could really prove. Who knew what went on behind locked doors? Who said that an intentional killing motivated by grief or love even fit into the same category as an accidental killing? He considered Jamie's confession, which stated that Maggie had asked to be killed. If a victim consented to her own death, was the killing still a criminal action?

He knocked his head against the edge of his desk. There were big enough holes in that argument to drive a herd of elephants through. The prosecution would laugh him out of the courtroom.

Graham twirled his pencil around his fingers like a miniature baton. *Suicide,* he wrote, *Accomplice to the Act.* He was reaching a little, since Maggie MacDonald had certainly been capable of slitting her own wrists or swallowing a bucket of pills. What would she need Jamie for?

In some states, a botched suicide attempt was considered a crime. This wasn't the case in Massachusetts, thanks to generations of Democrats. If committing suicide wasn't a criminal act, aiding a suicide should not be one either.

"Sure," he said aloud. "Tell that to Jack Kevorkian."

*Temporary Insanity.* This was what Graham had suggested to Jamie at their first meeting; the catchall for defense strategies when there were extenuating circumstances. It meant that Jamie was not in control of his faculties at the moment he had killed his wife. He would not have been able to understand the nature and the quality of the act he was committing. Which basically said that when he picked up a pillow, Jamie didn't really know it could be used to smother; when he held it to his wife's face, he didn't know it could be fatal. Temporary insanity meant that Jamie did not know at the time that what he was doing was wrong.

Graham snorted. Jamie had known damn well what he was doing; he simply thought it was *right*.

In other cases, where killing had been a means of mercy and the defense had been psychiatric, the record of acquittals seemed to follow a pattern. The more violent the method of killing—bullets, knives—the more likely the defendant was to go to jail. The more incapacitated the victim had been at the time of the killing, the more likely the defendant was to go free. Jamie had used a pillow; you couldn't get gentler than that. But Maggie had been walking, talking, laughing, in the minutes before.

Graham swallowed the last of his beer and set the bottle upside down on the polished surface of his desk. He was pussyfooting around the truth, which suddenly seemed to have a startling presence, as if it had taken the form of a carrion bird that was perched on the edge of his windowsill. The reason Jamie MacDonald had killed his wife was because she was going to die, she was in pain, and she simply didn't want to suffer anymore.

Mercy killing was too gray an area to be a suitable defense. Jurors weren't reliable enough to guarantee acquittal. Prosecutors talked out of both sides of their mouths, saying euthanasia was merciful, of course, but that didn't justify breaking the law.

Graham had known when he got into trial law that his business was not judging morality but securing acquittals. His father had defended clients who were as seedy as the bottom of a sewer, and had won his cases anyway, because it was what he was paid to do. But to defend Jamie on the basis of the truth?—well, that meant challenging the way the laws had been written.

Graham didn't know how he felt about euthanasia. He had never loved a woman enough to even contemplate what kind of thoughts had run through Jamie's mind leading up to the killing. He tried to see it from Maggie's point of view—if he was going to be sentenced to such a life, would he want someone to help him out of it? Was it the same as wanting someone to pull the plug if you ever became a vegetable?

It was easy to mull over after three Rolling Rocks, when he was in full control of his faculties and every cell in his body was screaming with health. He was too young to make that kind of choice.

Maggie hadn't been all that old either.

Taking a deep breath, Graham began to draw circles around the words he'd already written on the menu. Were there certain variables, certain instances where the law should not have control over death? What kind of law could you possibly put on the books, when there were so many different issues to consider? To Graham, defining mercy killing would be like peeling an onion. Every case involved another layer, and another, and you'd keep stripping these and making exceptions and before you knew it there'd be nothing left at all.

He tossed the empty bottle into the trash can and shut off the banker's lamp on his desk. *Don't sweat it,* he told himself. *You've got time.*

But as he was locking the office door behind him, a thought tugged at his mind. *You've got time,* it said. *Jamie doesn't.*

*C*am thought of the total-immersion technique in which people learned languages by speaking them exclusively, living in the origin country, sleeping with Berlitz tapes murmuring beside their heads. He knew of people who had done this successfully and had come to love the language. And with this in mind, he took the next day off from work and asked his wife to go fishing.

He hadn't asked her in three years, but he thought that if he spent every waking minute of the day with Allie, listening to her and watching her and only her, he could surely drive Mia Townsend from his mind.

Cam was just propping up against the banister the bamboo fly rod that had been his grandfather's, when Allie appeared at the top of the stairs. She was wearing a faded denim shirt and a baggy pair of khaki pants rolled up to the knees. She sat down on the top step and slipped on a pair of Tretorns riddled with holes. "We're going to be getting wet, right?" she said, knotting the laces. "I figured after what Arbuth did to these, there's very little left to damage." Arbuth was the neighbor's mastiff. Cam smiled, remembering how Allie had chased him with a Wiffle bat when she found the dog chewing on her new sneakers.

Cam tucked a short-handled net into his belt and jammed a red felt hat on his head. It was dotted with bucktail streamers and woolly boogers and nymphs, several dry flies as well. He held his arms out to the sides and pirouetted slowly. Allie whistled. "You're a vision."

She scrambled down the stairs and wrapped her arms around Cam's waist. "You see how lucky we are that Mia came to town?" she said, and Cam stiffened in her embrace. "If it wasn't for her, I couldn't just take a whole day off."

"Lucky," Cam repeated, pulling away. He reached for the fishing rod. He did not want to look at Allie. Having heard Mia's name again, he knew what would happen—he'd turn to his wife and he'd start comparing her flushed cheeks and pointed chin to Mia's smooth brow and tumbling curls. "Let's go," he said curtly, and moved toward the door. He left Allie standing alone, rubbing her upper arms and wondering what she'd already done wrong.

Recovering, Allie followed Cam out the front door and, to her surprise, watched him walk toward the backyard gate. "Come on," he said, waving her closer. "We don't have all day."

"I thought we did," Allie murmured. "I thought that was the point." She watched Cam move to the center of the slightly sloping lawn, holding the fishing pole in front of him. He pulled free some of the bright yellow line, and then with his left hand, he began to swing the rod back and forth, back and forth, like a human metronome, until the line had whizzed through the guides and was arcing over him like a monochromatic rainbow.

"You know, I may be a novice, but wouldn't we have a better chance of catching fish if we did this near water?"

Cam smirked at her. "You think I'm going to let you hold my grandfather's fly rod without practicing on dry ground?" He let the leader rest on the crabgrass and looked at Allie. Her hands were on her hips, her ponytail was curling over her shoulder; her feet pointed out to the sides, as if she was getting ready to do a plié.

The last time he'd taken Allie fishing, it had been deep-water. Not his favorite kind, but he hadn't the time or the inclination then to teach Allie how to fly-fish, which in his opinion was more of an art than a sport. They had gone out for blues, and Allie—who'd had to be shown how to work the reel—had caught the biggest fish. He could remember her dancing in little circles in her borrowed slicker when the captain presented her with a free day's pass to return, a prize for the catch of the day.

Pulling his thoughts back, he tugged at the line. The leader had snagged on a piece of grass. "Shows you what you know." He grinned. "I have a bite." He tugged gently, until the neon-bright line snapped into the air. "Now," he said, closing his mind to anything but the beauty of what he was about to do, "it's all in the presentation." He started swinging the line in rhythm again as he backcast and false-cast, over and over. "You've got no weight on the end of your line. You're using the weight of the line itself to cast. Well, hell, you're not even really casting. You're just kind of suspending your line above the water."

"Grass," Allie murmured.

"Whatever." He closed his eyes, letting the sway and the motion lead him. "You want to roll the line out in front of the fish, like a red carpet . . . rolling . . . rolling . . . until finally the fly just drops"—here he made a light popping noise—"into the water."

Then he stopped speaking. He let his arm sway from front to back, occasionally pulling out more line and feeding with his casts until the leader reached even farther. He felt the sun on the back of his neck and watched the juncos fly toward the narrow purple pass in the mountains several miles away. He breathed in with each backcast, out with each false cast, and lost himself.

He was in New Zealand, fishing for giant rainbow trout. In the wilds of Alaska, tall grass burning his legs while he cast for salmon. With a deep breath, he pictured himself in Montana, tying two leaders in a blood knot as he prepared to fish for cutthroat. He was on Loch Leven, which had always felt like home, a small boat rocking beneath him with the currents that hid both the char and the kelpies.

"Where are you?" Allie said.

He blinked his eyes. She was smiling at him, and he was surprised that she could read him so well.

Cam shook his head. "Your turn," he said, holding out the rod.

She moved into the circle of his arms. Cam came close behind her, tucking the rod under the band of her watch. "There," he said, fitting her hand over the cork grip. "Now you won't bend your wrist." He began to move her arm back, watching the line overhead, then pushed her arm forward. "You don't want to hear the line snap. When you backcast, watch the line come out. It'll unroll and you'll see this loop unfolding itself . . . when it hangs like that, see? That's when you bring it forward."

Allie felt her shoulder pressing against his chest, his fingers closing over hers. He arced her arm in a slow and gliding pendulum, lending her the grace she had witnessed in him moments before. She closed her eyes, beginning to feel that this was simply Cam's way of asking her to dance.

*Back,* two, three, *front,* two, three. *Back,* two, three, *front,* two, three. Allie saw herself whirling about a glittering columned ballroom, Cam's cutaway evening attire smooth and fine beneath her hands. There was a moment when she could smell the winter coming and sense the heaviness of the air and feel her blood running and knew, at the same time, that she and Cam were in perfect rhythm. *Oh, yes,* she thought, *this is lovely.*

"Now you do it," Cam said, stepping away, and Allie awkwardly found herself standing alone. She lifted the fly rod, trying to listen to Cam's senseless comments about lifting at ten o'clock, lifting at one o'clock, keeping her wrist straight and presenting the line. She tried to keep up the rhythm by humming music, but she could only focus on the fact that Cam was watching the twist and furl of her body as she had watched his. Her cheeks flushed, and she wished that he'd hold her close again.

It was afternoon before Cam pronounced Allie proficient enough to hold his sacred fly rod on Wee Loch, the lake for which the town had been settled. Cam tied the Old Town canoe onto the roof of Allie's car and drove to the boat launch. Then he settled Allie in the front of it and paddled to the far shore of the lake, where they were likely to find bass.

"Okay," Cam said finally. "This is the magic place." Allie glanced around at the lily pads and stumps that dotted the little cove Cam had rowed into. Then Cam reached across the boat. The canoe tipped gently from side to side to balance itself, and Allie clutched at the gunwale, her face whitening. "Cam," she choked out, "please don't."

Cam was casually tying a fly onto the leader of the fishing rod when she felt composed enough to turn around. "Don't what? Use the dry fly?" He frowned down at his hands. "Maybe you're right. Maybe a nymph . . ."

"Cam," Allie began again, "I hate boats."

That was an understatement. She truly disliked the sensation of having the world move beneath her feet, but she wasn't fond of anything outdoors. While Cam had spent the pleasant journey across the lake pointing out the different kinds of birds and trees in passing, Allie had been counting the mosquito bites on her arms. She did not much like the wilds of nature, but she knew that it was the only setting that did not dwarf Cam or seem to leash his energy, and she never missed the opportunity to watch him in his element.

"Allie." Cam tugged on the leader to test it. "You're in six feet of water. There's nothing to worry about." He smiled at her, and handed her the fly rod. "Go ahead," he said.

He knew that Allie did not like to spend time outside. Hell, her chosen profession involved cutting down the most beautiful ornaments nature had made and arranging them to look good on a dining room table.

It was gorgeous out; the sun was high and bright and dancing on the loch, the greenheads were gone, the mountains in the distance looked too lovely to be real. Cam glanced at Allie, who was carefully tangling the line around her forefinger like he'd shown her. If she spent more time doing things like this, she'd fall in love with it too. It was simply a matter of exposure.

He absently watched Allie begin to cast again, coming uncomfortably close to a tangle of branches, and fantasized about taking her with him when he went duck hunting, ice-fishing, hiking over the Wheelock Pass. He pictured her legs getting strong and sun-tanned, her features lit by the jumping glare of a campfire. He wondered how long it would take from that point to get her to want to see Madagascar, or Crete, or the Rockies. He considered why he didn't just plan a trip—Allie would go if he asked her, he knew that—but he realized he did not want to see her staring out a tiny fogged airplane window and wishing she were somewhere else.

He wondered if it bothered her to see *him* look like that, every day of his life.

"I've got something," Allie said, her voice leaping with the gentle sway of the canoe. "I think I saw it."

Cam watched the splash of the surface as the bass moved away with her line. He coached Allie in a low, firm voice, telling her when to let the fish run and when to pull gently in on the reel. As the bass became visible through the dull brown layers of the water, Cam sat forward and pulled the net from his belt.

"Now lean back," he told Allie, pushing her away and holding her wrist up high to bring the fish closer. He leaned in the opposite direction, over the gunwale of the boat. He scooped the net halfway in the water, watching the fish's tail beat frenetically against the nylon ropes. "What a beautiful fish," he said, hoping to excite Allie. "This is one of the biggest bass I've seen come out of this lake."

"Really?" Allie crowed. She relaxed her hold on the fishing rod and scooted to the same side of the canoe as Cam, peeking into the net to see her prize. "Look at its eyes," she said, reaching to brush its scaly head, and that was when the canoe flipped.

Allie popped up instantly, gasping and treading water and thinking of all the slimy things that lived on the bottom of a choked lake like this one. To her surprise, everything was black, and she wondered for a moment if she'd hit her head and lost her vision, when suddenly she realized that she'd come up beneath the overturned canoe.

She was about to duck beneath and resurface to find Cam, when she heard him laughing. Not just a chuckle, a *how could this have happened to us?* kind of laugh, but a gut-busting guffaw that

Allie knew could only be at her own expense. He was laughing at her eagerness and stupidity, which had tipped the canoe. Raising one eyebrow, she gripped the gunwale of the canoe and floated. She took calm, deep breaths. *Let him stew,* she thought.

Cam did think it was hilarious. Oh, she'd be pissed; hissing and shaking like a wet cat, he imagined. But if she'd only seen her own face seconds before she realized she was going to hit the water . . . He wiped his eyes and tried to swallow his laughter and realized that Allie had not surfaced.

"Allie," he called, spinning around 360 degrees to see if he'd missed her. "Allie!" His eyes took in the several stumps lying to the side of the boat, the side that Allie had fallen on, as well as the tangle of lily pads whose roots, he knew, could catch your leg and drag you down.

Cam's pulse began to pound in time with the throb of his head. She was a good swimmer, but that didn't count when you were knocked unconscious. "Allie!" he screamed, his voice carrying on the smooth surface of the water and sounding like nothing he'd ever heard before. "Allie!"

He ducked beneath the water and opened his eyes to the grimy underworld but he could not see more than five inches in front of him. He began to feel around the bottom of the lake with his feet, hoping to brush something he could dive for. His teeth began to chatter and his heart had frozen in his chest.

Allie popped up not two feet away.

"Jesus Christ," he exploded. "Jesus fucking Christ!" He took one long swimming stroke toward her and crushed her against him, half dragging and half swimming her toward the shore where they could both stand.

When he set her on her feet, he was still shaking. He grabbed her so tightly he could feel the ridges of her ribs against his skin. "You scared the hell out of me," he said roughly, shocked at the vehemence of his own reaction and the strength of his need. "You scared me to death."

He held her away from him, touching her forehead, which was ringed with silt; and her hair, still tangled with wet leaves and one of his flies. He tilted her chin up to his face. "Don't ever do that," he murmured.

She had wanted to tell him it was all a joke, that she hadn't liked him laughing at her, but Cam was holding her close and staring at her as if he had to memorize her features, as if he had just seen the yawn and chasm of a life that did not include her.

Jamie MacDonald's words flew into her mind: *Seventy-thirty.*

Cam was looking at her, she realized, the way she always looked at him. Fascinated, she touched her hand to his cheek, and felt him shiver. "I won't," she promised, and she clenched her fists tight into Cam's soaking shirt in an effort to hold on to the moment.

# SIX

Jamie MacDonald was on the lookout for angels. He had spent yesterday wandering through a card shop, picking up the Victoriana to stare at fat-faced cupids and ethereal silver-haired girls in pleated Corinthian dresses. He examined these closely, looking for a sign, but he did not see in them any trace of Maggie.

He knew she was going to come to him. He knew this as surely as he knew that he would wait, if necessary, forever. Sometimes he would close his eyes and smell on the air the lily-of-the-valley smell that had threaded Maggie's clothes; the clean, honey scent of her hair. He'd picture her wearing a white turtleneck and a swingy white skirt, downy feathers brushing her shoulders and sweeping her back.

He was waiting for Graham MacPhee to come out of his goddamned office. It wasn't like the man had any other clients, so he did not understand why he was being made to wait. He cast a glance at Allie, his unofficial chaperon in town, who was calmly reading a *Good Housekeeping* magazine with most of the recipes cut out.

She seemed to feel him looking at her, and lifted her head. Giving him a nod of support, she smiled.

Allie had taken him to the post office, the minimart, the dry cleaners. She had paved the way for him to enter the video rental establishment and the barbershop, both of which were run by men who made no effort to hide the fact that they considered Jamie a blight on decent society. She had gone out of her way to steer him toward the one teller at the bank who had gazed at Jamie with moon eyes and told him he was a saint; to the waitress at the coffee shop who kissed his cheek and said he had brought back her faith in true love.

Twice now at noon, when Jamie went to the police station to check in with Cameron MacDonald as per the conditions of his bail, Allie had gone too, her arm firmly locked through his. Cam had yet to do more than grunt at him and wave him away, but he did not do anything worse, either. And this, Jamie knew, he owed directly to Cam's wife.

He stared at her now from his perch by the faux fireplace. She was not a conventional beauty, but she was pretty enough, with her whiskey-colored eyes and shiny, straight hair. She looked about as substantial as a twig, but Jamie had learned differently. Whether Allie MacDonald chose to admit it or not, she had an overwhelming depth of strength. Twig, maybe, but made of willow—able to bend and twist and give way, rather than break.

Maggie would have loved her.

With that thought, Jamie swung his head to the fireplace again. For the first time, he noticed that the bas-relief carved into the mantel was a pastoral scene: Shepherds and cows and milkmaids scampered across the line of the fireplace, and overhead were clouds and angels. He stared into the white faces of each one, burning to see the curve of Maggie's eyebrow or the ordinary jut of her chin.

Allie put her hand on his shoulder as he stood clutching the mantel. "Jamie," she murmured, "why don't you come sit down?"

He spun toward her with tears in his eyes. "I can't find her," he said.

"You will," she assured him, leading him to the facing chair. She sat across from him and patted his knee. As he ran his hands through his hair, Allie stood and walked over to the secretary. "Really, we've been waiting a very long time."

As if she had summoned him, Graham MacPhee appeared from the hall. He was springy and lively and his hair was damp and combed back, although it was after one o'clock. "Jamie, Allie," he said, running their names together as if they were one. "The time got away from me."

He waved them down the hall to the conference room, where a file stood open, its contents knocked haphazardly across the table. Allie took a seat, but Jamie remained standing just inside the door. "The paperwork's all drawn up for Techcellence," Graham said. Jamie had opted to transfer temporary control of his company to Rod and Flanders. "I still don't like the idea of not specifying how long that interim time should be," Graham added, frowning. "You can change your mind, and set a limit."

Jamie shook his head. "Let's just say I'm not quite the optimist you are."

Graham cleared his throat, then fixed a smile on his face. "The preliminary hearing is next Wednesday," he said brightly, as if this were good news.

Allie glanced at Jamie, but he was staring out the window at the dull traffic of Main Street, his face closed and inscrutable. She licked her lips and leaned forward, crossing her legs. "Which means?"

Graham shrugged, making a trickle of water from his hair run over the collar of his olive herringbone suit. "It's a formality. We go back to court and the DA tells a judge they've got a body, and then they'll make Cam get up on the stand and connect Jamie's confession to the evidence, and the judge decides there's probable cause and we all go home."

Allie shook her head. "What about Jamie? Why can't he give his side of the story?"

Graham turned to look at his client, who was still staring out the window. "It's traditional that at a preliminary hearing, the defense doesn't present evidence. We save that for the big shebang. Don't want Jamie to have to go through a prosecution's cross-examination twice."

Jamie surprised everyone by walking across the room to the window and banging the flat of his hand against the glass. "How long?"

"How long till what?" Graham said.

"How long till this is over?" Jamie asked, turning to face him. "How long till I'm just locked away?"

Graham stood, but still had to crane his neck to look up into Jamie's face. "Hopefully never. That's the point."

"But assuming we don't win," Jamie said slowly, "then I just spent a precious half hour waiting for you to get your ass off the Stairmaster at the gym."

Graham flushed all the way to his hairline. "It won't happen again." Flustered, he sat heavily in one of the swivel chairs at the table and began leafing through the manila file. "Speaking of which, we ought to discuss your defense. I'm going to need a list from you of people who can testify to Maggie's illness, and neighbors or friends or relatives who knew the two of you—"

"Relatives," Jamie snorted.

Graham darted a glance at Allie and began to draw tiny circles at the corner of the page he had before him. "Well, we're going to have to find someone to swear to your character."

"I will," Allie said.

Graham grinned at her. "I need someone who knew him before he showed up at the station. But you might be helpful in collecting witnesses, since they're likely to cooperate with a police chief's wife." He thrummed the pen against the edge of the table and turned to Jamie. "We need other people. We need a parade of witnesses who look appropriately shocked that you'd be brought up on charges of murder."

Jamie lowered himself to the swivel chair beside Allie's. He swung from side to side, pushing off the balls of his feet and almost letting a smile ghost its way across his face. "And who is going to break the news to these paragons that I'm pending trial?"

Graham blinked. "I will, of course." He nervously fingered his tie as he felt Jamie's gaze slide from his Adam's apple to the notch of his belt buckle and back up to his face.

"No," Jamie said, and leaned back in the chair, crossing his ankles on the mahogany conference table.

"No?"

"No." Jamie smiled pleasantly, a neat baring of his teeth. "I want Allie to go." Allie started at the sound of her name, which seemed like a lullaby on Jamie's tongue. He sat up and rested his elbows on the table. "Who's going to sway a prospective witness more? A wet-behind-the-ears lawyer or the proverbial police chief's wife?"

Allie turned to him, knowing he understood that she did not

like being credited for her role rather than for herself. She put her hand over Jamie's, slipping her fingers between the cracks of his own. "I'd be happy to go," she said, surprising herself. "I'll talk to people in Cummington, and I can walk through the house and pick out photos and the marriage license and things like that."

"You can't," Graham said, although he couldn't think exactly why not.

"Can't you deputize her or something? Give her a warrant to break into my house. I don't care."

"That's not the issue here—" Graham began.

"The issue," Jamie interrupted, "is that I trust Allie. I do not trust you."

Jamie had raised his voice, and he rose from the table, his palms pressed flat, to stare Graham down. At that moment, Duncan MacPhee, the elder lawyer in the practice, stuck his head through the cracked door to see his son cowering before a client who was charged with murder.

"Is there a problem?" he asked.

"No," Allie said, at the same time that Graham did. Jamie sat down in a single movement, the wind gone from his sails.

Graham nodded. "We're just arranging the best way for Mrs. MacDonald to feel out the citizens of Cummington." He stood up, excusing himself for a minute, and walked to the door, wondering if Jamie MacDonald could see that his knees were shaking.

As soon as Graham disappeared down the hall, Allie rounded on Jamie. "You were very hard on him," she scolded. "He's only trying to help you."

Jamie grinned and pulled a sheet of yellow paper off the pad in the manila folder. "Don't you know, Allie, that you can't help someone who doesn't want to be helped?"

Allie swallowed and stared out the window. Her eyes naturally fell to the police station, where someone was walking out the front door. He moved too quickly and Allie was too far away to see who it was, but she pretended that she had gotten a glimpse of Cam, and this made her feel better.

Jamie had picked up a pen beside her and was neatly printing a list of names. "I don't have all the addresses," he said. "You can get them from a phone book."

Allie nodded. She wondered how she was going to tell Cam

what she'd spontaneously agreed to do. She wondered if Mia would be able to handle the flower shop all by herself, having been an employee for less than a week.

"You can stay at the house. I've got the keys at Angus's." He hesitated only a second. "Feel free to look through whatever you want. Take whatever you think I'll need." He finished scribbling a name and tossed the pen down. "There." He smoothed the paper with his palms, and let his hand linger when he passed the paper over to her. "Thank you," he said quietly. "I know you don't want to leave him to do this."

There was no question in her mind as to whom Jamie was referring. "It's only a few days," she reasoned aloud. "Cam'll be here when I get back."

Jamie kissed her forehead and stood up. He paced a few times in front of the chalkboard behind the table, then crossed to stand at the window again. He glanced up at the sky, looking.

He imagined himself locked up in one of the maximum-security prisons in Massachusetts—maybe Concord, where he would hear the traffic screaming around the rotary all night—cut off from Wheelock and Cummington forever. He thought of Maggie, dancing through the streets of these towns on translucent feet, peering through windows and cracking thick doors in an effort to find him. He considered heaven, empty and aching without her, as she soundlessly searched for someone who'd left without a trace.

"You need to do me another favor," Jamie said, resting his forehead against the cool glass. "When she comes, when Maggie comes . . ."

"I'll tell her," Allie replied, standing so close behind him he could feel her breath against his shoulder. "I'll tell her where to find you."

Unlike other New Age believers, Ellen MacDonald didn't much care who she had been in her past life, unless it had something to do with her late husband.

Eight years ago, when Ian was still alive, if someone had mentioned the word "crystal" to her, she would have asked if it was Waterford or Baccarat. Now, she wore a small dagger-shaped pendant about her neck made of quartz that had been dug out of a holy cave in Arizona. She wore clothes made of recycled cotton, she believed in thought projection and chakras, and she was getting a degree in naturopathic medicine through a correspondence course with the Mothers of Light New Age Community School, run out of a farm in northern Vermont.

Most of the people in Wheelock thought she'd lost it a little when Ian had died, her son Cameron included. If she was not a subject of ridicule, it was only because she'd been the clan chief's wife for so many years—it was a measure of respect that allowed for eccentricities, sort of like being a dowager duchess or the Queen Mother.

They would have all been surprised to learn that she didn't give a damn about bamboo panpipes and personal flower essences and barbecued tofu and all the other things she discussed with people, instead of holding genuine conversations. They would have all been shocked to learn that the only reason Ellen MacDonald believed in New Age phenomena was because the day after Ian was buried, she had received a brochure by mistake from a commune whose bold black headline read: *A Soul Mate Stays with You Forever.*

It had been a mishap in the post office, which was not extraordinary in a town with a plethora of MacDonalds, a simple flier of junk mail from a New Age network that supposedly hooked up singles by means of their birth charts and karma. But for someone who had just lost the love of her life, it seemed too true to simply throw in the trash.

For a week, Ellen had left the flier tacked to her refrigerator. This same week, Cameron's wife had moved in with her, making sure she ate and took the sleeping pills prescribed for her at night. Ellen grieved for ten days, and then asked Allie to take her to the library; she had some things she wanted to look up. Three months later, she had become a different person.

It was not that she believed in channeling or reincarnation. There was just something about involving yourself in a network of people who truly thought that love lasted through generations and centuries. It seemed healthier to steady your body for an inner peace and to accept that she'd see Ian again in a matter of lifetimes than to pine away with one foot in the grave. *You never know,* she told herself, over and over.

Allie was the only person Ellen knew who seemed truly happy for her new path in life. At least once a week, she brought over fresh and dried flowers and they'd practice making poultices and decoctions and infusions to cure minor maladies. The best success they'd had yet was with feverfew, which did wonders for Allie's menstrual cramps. Once, they'd made up an infusion of elder and Allie had slipped it into Cam's orange juice in the morning; she said that by noon his cough had disappeared.

She was in Ellen's kitchen now, plucking the heads off calendula. Ellen walked through the hall and set down the mail on the kitchen table. "Get anything good?" Allie asked over her shoulder.

"Bills," Ellen said. "Coupons for things I don't use."

Allie laughed. "Give them to Angus. He still hasn't gotten over American supermarkets. If he gets a coupon, he buys it, no matter what it is." She looked at her mother-in-law. "I actually saw him buy Tampax once."

Ellen smiled and moved to Allie's side. "You think this is going to work?"

Allie bit her bottom lip. "I don't know. Creams are tricky. I've never made one." She glanced at the beeswax and lanolin, sitting in unmarked containers on the counter. "We've got to make the infusion first, in any case." She filled Ellen's teapot with a pint of water and set it to boil. "You think we've got an ounce yet?" she asked, running her fingertips lightly over the crushed flower heads.

Ellen nodded. "At least." She crossed the kitchen and sat down in a chair, resting her elbows on the table. "You know, I think you and I would have made rather good witches."

Allie grinned. "Imagine. I'd get to *ride* a broom instead of using it to clean up the shop floor twenty times a day."

The teakettle began to whistle. Allie scooped up the calendula and dropped it into the boiling water, firmly setting the lid back in place. "Twenty minutes," she said, marking the time on her watch.

Ellen liked her daughter-in-law. She was sweet and dedicated; she was crazy about Cam. A bit of a pushover, sometimes, but Ellen knew better than anyone how hard it could be to live day to day with someone who had as much force and fever as a hurricane. "Is Cam speaking to me yet?" she asked.

Allie blew a strand of hair off her forehead. "I don't think so," she said good-naturedly. "He's still pretty angry about the plot."

Ellen had offered Jamie MacDonald a piece of the family cemetery in which to bury Maggie. Jamie MacDonald was no different than she was. No matter how Maggie's life had ended, Jamie would have been twice as happy to go with her rather than be left picking up the pieces on this earth, which was something Ellen had been dealing with for eight years. So she had immediately written off for a gift subscription for him to a New Age magazine, while offering him the spot in the rear of the MacDonald family plot. And Cam had nearly taken her head off over it.

"I like to think that Maggie and Ian will watch over each other," Ellen said.

Allie had taken a double boiler out of the cabinet and was heating almond oil, beeswax, and lanolin to a melting point. "But who'll watch after Jamie?"

"Why, you."

Allie was not about to say anything to Cam's mother about her son's obstinacy when it came to Jamie MacDonald, so she strained the tincture and poured it into the double boiler. In silence the two women waited for the water to bubble off, and then removed the mixture from the heat to cool.

"Well," Allie said, wiping her hands on her jeans. "Too bad we can't test it."

Ellen dipped a finger into the lukewarm cream. "What's it supposed to do, again?"

Allie frowned at her. "You're the one who's taking the holistic medicine course," she scolded. "It's supposed to take care of minor burns, sunburn, eczema." She glanced down at her hands. "None of which we have."

Ellen smiled and turned away. "Give me a minute," she said. She walked to the sliding glass door which led into the backyard. She unbuttoned her caftan and pulled free the ties, uncovering her bra. She slipped the strap free, revealing smooth white skin, and held her palms crossed over her chest. Then she pictured Ian's face. With Allie watching, she lowered her hands to expose her left breast, which was now marked with a new and painful burn just over her heart.

Allie covered her hand with her mouth. Ellen reached for the calendula cream, which was supposed to ease such scars and inflammations, and gently rubbed it in a circle over the red welt. "Ah," she said, smiling for Allie's sake. "Much better." The redness faded a bit, and Ellen admitted that the cream helped a little with the smarting of the skin. But it did nothing at all for the deeper sting and ache, since any fool could tell you that neither calendula nor any other potion known to man could possibly soothe right through to the soul.

Cam was late to the funeral because Miss Emily Kerr, who was eighty if she was a day, wanted to purchase a gun permit. "Why?" he had asked, the standard routine question before the permit was issued.

Emily had drawn herself up to her full five-foot height. "Well," she'd said, "to protect myself from the likes of *you*."

She left the police station abruptly. It was the second time that day someone had come in for a pistol permit. Donald Burns wanted a gun, he said, because he had season tickets to the Bruins, and Boston was a dangerous place.

Cam knew better. Pistol permits were rare in Wheelock. The sudden interest had more to do with Jamie MacDonald's arrival in town than anything else.

*Jamie MacDonald.* At the thought, his eyes flew to the clock on the wall. Swearing under his breath, Cam pulled his coat from the hook on the back of the office door and ran out of the station to his unmarked cruiser. The funeral had started a half hour ago.

As it was, Cam missed the service entirely. Father Gillivray had already reconvened the tiny group in front of the gaping raw mouth of the newly dug hole at the Wheelock cemetery. To his surprise, a good number of townspeople were gathered around the coffin. Allie stood on one side of Jamie, holding his arm. On his other side was Cam's mother, Ellen.

She was wearing one of her long purple caftans and was fingering the ankh she wore about her neck. She must have sensed Cam the moment he stepped on the hallowed ground, his hat in his hands. Glancing up, she caught his eye and stared him down, the same way she'd done when she caught him hiding *Playboy* magazines between his mattress and box spring.

Mia was there too. She was standing somewhat to the back of his immediate family, wearing a baggy black jumper that looked like a cross between a nun's habit and a flight suit. A wide-brimmed black hat hid her eyes and her nose, but Cam recognized her.

He looked up and found Allie tugging at his sleeve. She gave him a hesitant smile, and led him over toward Jamie. She laced one arm through Cam's, and then she laced the other through Jamie's again, and at that second Cam could feel an uncontrollable flow of grief, as if skin-to-skin contact had opened the lines of current.

Maggie MacDonald was being buried, at Ellen's request, in the MacDonald family plot. The grave was a little distance from Ian's, farther still from Cam's grandparents and great-grandparents and heroic Uncle Jamie. Cam had yelled at his mother for over an hour when he heard she'd offered the plot for Maggie's burial. It meant that one day, he'd be buried in the same piece of ground as Jamie MacDonald, and he did not think he could stand that for eternity.

As Father Gillivray droned on, Cam could feel himself swaying on his feet—a by-product of having the midnight-to-eight shift the night before. He stared at the baskets of flowers surrounding the casket. They were flawless and pure and ivory, marred only by the teardrop shape of a blood-red rose. He let his eyes drift shut, imagining the skirl of bagpipes that had sounded the departure of his father's soul from Wheelock. He heard the creak of the coffin being lowered into the ground.

Allie's fingers tightened on Cam's arm as he realized that the sound he had imagined as the mourn of bagpipes was coming from Jamie MacDonald. He had heard of the Chinese practice where wealthy families hired professional women to keen for the dead during the burial procession. It was supposed to be a sign of honor to have so many grieving for you. Maggie MacDonald might have had only one, but this made it no less powerful.

Jamie crumpled before Cam's eyes. Tearing free of Allie's and Ellen's arms, he slipped to his knees in the soft earth, covering his face as the casket sank by inches. Behind Cam, the townspeople began to shift, uncomfortable and itchy. Father Gillivray looked up from his Bible. "My son," he said softly.

"*Mo chridhe,*" Jamie murmured, his eyes wide and dry. He stood suddenly, woodenly, and grabbed for Allie's arm. "Please," he begged, "get me out of here."

With a quick glance at Cam, Allie started to walk Jamie from the open grave. Father Gillivray recited the prayers quickly, and with Jamie already gone, everyone began to disperse. The cemetery workers began to shovel earth back over the casket, making a neat rounded hump in the spot where there had been a gaping hole.

Cam watched it all with his hands in his pockets, figuring that this could be his penance for missing the church service. He'd make sure everything was finished all right. He watched the two men prop their shovels against a nearby oak and wipe the sweat from the backs of their necks. Then he turned around to see Mia standing behind him.

He stared at her as if he were not going to be allowed to look at her again. He waited, his fists clenched, until the broad black hat tilted enough so that he could see her eyes. When she looked up, his stomach dived in a roller-coaster drop, as it hadn't since he was in high school.

It was totally inappropriate to feel this way, here and now, but Cam could sense the heat of his body rising in fits and starts. *Ah,* he thought, as he remembered again to breathe, *she's lit from the inside.*

Mia did not say a word, but stepped up to the grave and lifted one of her floral arrangements. Carefully unwrapping the wire around the single red rose, she pulled its stem from the Oasis that anchored the flowers and handed it to Cam.

He twirled it between his fingers and brushed it against the side of his hand. Allie didn't like roses much—called them plebeian—but he'd always found them pretty. He liked their texture, smooth and downy as a woman's skin.

With great care he pulled the green stem base from the rose so that a flutter of petals settled into the palm of his hand. He lifted these to the wind and let them swirl and dance in the air, coming to rest on the packed dirt.

"What does it mean?" Mia asked.

"What does *what* mean?" Cam said, startled, a million possible answers rushing through his mind.

"Those words. *Mo chridhe.*"

Cam shook his head, pretending he didn't know. But in Wheelock, everyone knew a little bit of Scottish Gaelic, especially the endearments a mother or lover might use. He walked Mia back to the center of town in silence, his mind branded by the image of

Jamie MacDonald on his knees in front of the grave, as if he were praying; Jamie MacDonald leaning toward the body of his wife and whispering, *My heart.*

*H*e had managed to crawl to a ditch when the English cannons stopped firing, and now he was facedown in a puddle, using all his strength to roll onto his back so that he would be able to breathe. Not easy, with both his kneecaps broken and his eyes running red with blood that streamed from a gash at his scalp.

*He was still holding his sword, though. He grimaced, thinking that at least he wouldn't be forsworn. He'd given his word to fight the English until he could not stand, and that was completely beyond his power right now.*

*Cameron prayed for a quick and timely death.*

*He had wished for his own death only once before, on the day he'd acquired his illustrious reputation. He'd been fighting beside his father, and the left arm that had surprised so many right-handed Highland enemies had also been the reason his father had been wounded: when Cameron had raised his left arm to strike, a gap had been created where there was usually a shield.*

*His father had been run through the gut, and had asked Cameron for his help. There had been no question that his father was going to die, but he was too weak to take his own life quickly. And so Cameron had loaded the ball into his father's pistol; had held it to his temple while his father pulled the trigger.*

*He had not killed his own father, but that was only a technicality.*

*On the day that his father died, he had run back to fight the Campbells clothed only in his long white shirt and the impenetrable weave of his fury. He'd wanted to die, right there next to his father. He had not wanted to be the one who would have to go home and break the news to his mother and his brother and sisters. He did not want to be the laird of Carrymuir.*

*He was only sixteen, and he killed forty Campbells himself that afternoon. He did not even receive a flesh wound.*

*He'd carried his father's body home in his arms.*

*The bards that went from castle to castle began to weave tales about the magic of Cameron MacDonald's left arm. When the storytellers came to Carrymuir, Cameron would leave the room. No matter how many Campbells or English soldiers he killed, it could not bring his father back. He kept trying and trying, but not even this day, this slaughter at Culloden, could do it.*

*Cameron glanced up to see hooves circling toward him at an astounding speed, and he closed his eyes, praying and preparing himself, hoping he'd be knocked unconscious first.*

*A man rolled from the horse not three feet away from him, and the horse magically stopped dead in its tracks. Cam turned and found himself staring at the dusty red coat of another English soldier, holding a gun.*

*He smiled. "Go ahead,* mo charaid," *he said, throwing his arms wide. "Put me out of my misery."*

*The soldier's eyes widened. He looked at the pistol and then down at his own midriff, which was saturated with blood. "I hope you linger for days," the Englishman said flatly, and he pulled the trigger on himself.*

*It was several seconds before Cameron's ears cleared from the blast at such close range. He could reach the pistol, and he could also reach the reins of the soldier's horse, which stood patiently, stomping at the muddy ground from time to time.*

*Cameron looked from one to the other, and then back again. He closed his eyes, and he saw his father's face, and he started to cry.*

*Who would have known that given the choice, he would not take the easiest path after all?*

Angus woke up to the fading hoofbeats, his heart pounding, his head spinning. He ran his hands lightly over his limbs, checking his knees, which were spiny and knobbed with arthritis but otherwise hale. With a muffled swear at the soaked, sweaty condition of his bedsheets, he pulled himself from the bed and set off down the hall to the linen closet.

He heard the sounds through Jamie's closed door, and his first thought was that Cameron MacDonald had galloped straight from his own mind into Jamie's, but then he shook his head at the impossibility. Ghosts, real ones, didn't behave such as that. No doubt the laddie was remembering the funeral earlier today, or even having a visit from Maggie. Angus laughed at this; they'd have to have breakfast sometime, the four of them—Angus and Jamie and the two ghosts that frequented the house.

Gathering clean sheets into his arms, Angus tiptoed down the hall toward Jamie's door. He pushed it open gently, swearing as it creaked on its hinges. Jamie lay on top of the sheets, his hands fisted, his body twisting from side to side.

For a moment Angus stood in the doorway. Then Jamie let out

a little cry, the kind that sounds like a whimper to someone awake, but, in one's dreams, is a scream.

The linens hit the floor with a soft sigh as Angus crossed the room and crawled into the bed with Jamie. He wrapped his arms tight around the boy and tried to keep him from tossing and shaking any more. Jamie was not seeing his Maggie, that much was clear. More likely he was seeing himself.

And no sooner had Angus let this thought enter his mind than Jamie buried his face in Angus's neck, clinging to his uncle as if his life depended on it, and gave himself up to his grief.

A llie had read somewhere that husbands and wives spend less than four waking hours together, and this statistic terrified her, since with Cam's crazy scheduling, she sometimes went a whole day without talking to him. She had read another statistic that said women use twice as many words in the course of a day as men do, and she wondered if this was because women were garrulous by nature, or because it took twice as long to make men understand what was being said.

She didn't remember how, but both of these surveys tied in, somehow, to divorce.

She considered it her personal duty to keep herself actively engaged with Cam whenever he was around. Their relationship was far too important to fall by the wayside over something as mundane as language.

Allie climbed into bed and turned toward Cam, who promptly reached to his nightstand to shut off the light. She sighed and flopped onto her back, crossing her arms over her belly. "You're mad at me."

"Don't put words into my mouth," Cam said.

But he hadn't spoken to her since she'd casually mentioned over dinner that she'd be going to Cummington the next week to assist Graham MacPhee in Jamie's defense. "Then how come you aren't talking to me?"

"I'm talking to you. I'm talking to you right now." He sighed and glanced at Allie. "You going to shut off your light?"

"You don't want me to help Jamie."

"You're a big girl, Allie. That's up to you."

Allie furrowed her brow and reached for the light switch. "But you'll be on the stand for the prosecution. And I'll be with the defense."

"I'm a witness," Cam said. "Not the DA. I don't really care one way or the other."

She stared up at the ceiling, where the moonlight had gathered in faint white kaleidoscope patterns. "He's a very nice man," she murmured.

"Like I said, I'm not the DA. He's the one who wants to hear that." He fumbled over the heaps of the quilt and tartan to find Allie's hand, which he raised and kissed on the knuckles. "Good night," he said, glancing at the digital clock beside Allie's head.

"I'll be gone for at least three days," Allie announced. "Maybe four."

Cam nodded and mumbled sleepily, "Have a good time."

"Don't you want to tell me you're going to miss me?"

"I'll miss you." He rolled to his side, taking most of Allie's covers with him.

For a few moments, Allie watched the patterns on the ceiling shift and congeal into the shapes of a whale, a llama, an angel. Then she reached over the nightstand and flicked on the light again. "We can't go to sleep."

Cam flopped onto his back, shielding his eyes with his hand. "*You* can't," he corrected.

Allie bit her bottom lip. "Do you now that husbands and wives spend less than four waking hours together?"

"Couldn't this be one of the other twenty?"

"No," Allie said. She chewed on her thumbnail. "I think we should talk more. We've hardly spoken at all this week, between Jamie and Mia and God knows what else."

Resigned, Cam sat up and propped the pillows behind his back. "And what," he said, "do you want to talk about?"

"Things," Allie hedged. When she'd pictured them having a lively conversation, she hadn't gotten to the specifics.

"I'm not going to list my arrests for you," Cam said.

Allie hesitated. "We could talk about what you're going to say at the preliminary hearing."

"No," Cam said, "we can't."

They sat beside each other until Cam leaned over to kiss her shoulder. "I like not talking to you. I like knowing that I don't *have* to talk."

Allie was silent. "What did we used to talk about?" she said finally, more to herself than to Cam.

She already knew the answer: Five years ago, they had not known each other. Then, they had discussed the future, the names of their unborn children, the design of the grand mansion they would build on prime Wheelock acreage. Now, they could say entire sentences over breakfast with a simple connection of their eyes. Now, they knew each other's surprises.

She and Cam had always been different, and Allie had clung tenaciously to the idea that opposites would attract. She had told herself that two like jigsaw pieces, after all, would not fit.

They had started dating in the coldest days of January, and after several brandy-laced dinners at her apartment, Cam had invited her out for a walk one Sunday. It had been below zero, and he'd bundled her up in his own jacket and snow pants and gaiters and had taken her through the woods at the base of the Wheelock Pass. She remembered staring at the thick of the forest and thinking she was walking right into the heart of winter on its wafer-thin crust. She had listened to Cam speak of the Chimborazo foothills, the Costa de la Luz, the city of Belfast, watching his breath fog in little circles over the words as he spoke.

"Wouldn't you like to travel?" he had asked, and she had simply shaken her head. She told Cam that the very thought terrified her and brought back a recurring nightmare she had had as a child. She was in a strange city made of stone, and everyone around her spoke in odd clicks and whirs she could not understand. She kept thinking if she listened more closely or held her back a little straighter, it would all fall into place, but instead she only felt more isolated and she always woke up not comprehending what she had done wrong.

"That's the point," Cam told her. "You aren't doing anything wrong. You're doing something different."

"All the same," Allie said, "I like to know what's coming next."

At the end of the day he had kissed her goodbye, looking at her intently and saying that traveling was all very well and good as long as you knew there was a place or a person you could call home.

"Do you think we're opposites?" Allie said now, her own voice sounding loud and dramatic in the quiet of the night. "Do you?"

She turned to Cam and found his eyes closed, lashes feathering his cheek. She rested her head against his chest and put her arms around him, breathing in his scent and his silence, taking—as always—his lead.

C am sat on the stool at the local coffee shop and broke apart his muffin. He poked at the crumbs with his finger, not really wanting blueberry but accepting it in lieu of the alternative, a doughnut, which he would not let his officers eat on duty simply because it made them a likely butt of community jokes.

"You want something else?" Jenny was a third cousin, one of the waitresses in the shop.

"I'm all set," he said, letting her scurry to one of the four booths lined against the wall. He glanced up at the clock, which hung beside a stuffed boar's head, and settled back. He had ten more minutes before his shift began.

Allie was going to be leaving the day after tomorrow, and it felt strange. He'd been apart from her before during their marriage, but not because *she* had instigated the separation. There had been training in New Braintree for him, and the time he had gone to the hospital for knee surgery. But Allie was the homebody. Allie held down the fort.

She'd already given him a list of food he'd have to buy when grocery shopping and tasks she normally did. Was it really possible that in five years he had not learned how to work the dishwasher?

He wondered what the hell Jamie MacDonald had said that had made her willingly agree to leave Wheelock.

He stared down at his list, and thought of the one Allie had been writing for Mia before he left the house this morning. Twice as long. He'd almost volunteered to deliver it to the shop, when he realized that of course Allie would be going there herself.

A jingle of year-round sleigh bells heralded the opening of the door of the coffee shop. As if Cam had summoned her with his thoughts, Mia walked up to the counter.

"Hi," he said.

She froze at the sound of his voice, and then turned to face him, smiling shyly. "Hi."

He gestured at the neighboring stool and she climbed onto it, accepting the cup of coffee Jenny placed in front of her. She took a long sip, closing her eyes, and then looked down at the square of paper in Cam's hands. "So we're both going to be orphaned," she said.

Cam waved the paper in front of her. "I've got less to do than you do."

"Then I'll have to give you some of my chores. You want to buy the fertilizer, or call the customers with back payments?"

"Oh," Cam said, laughing. "Back payments. I'm much better at threats."

She laughed with him, and he let his own voice drop out solely so he could hear the silver of her own. He stared at her, knowing he should not be doing this, especially in the coffee shop, the nesting bed of community gossip, and also knowing he could not help himself.

He wanted to touch her hair. God, he wanted to touch it.

She tore her glance away to look at her wristwatch. "I've got to go."

Cam jumped off the stool. "Me too." He hesitated, unsure of how to best phrase what he wanted to say. "If you need anything over the next couple of days," he began, but then stopped, watching Mia empty her thin purse of two dollars to leave on the counter. "Mia," he said, as she turned to the door, "you left a hundred-percent tip."

She shrugged. "I know. I always feel bad when I only get coffee. I used to be a waitress."

"Where?"

Mia stared at him for a long moment and then walked out the door. He followed her, falling into step on the street. "Italy, 1986," she said finally. "A café near the Rialto Bridge. It was called La Mano del Diavolo. The Devil's Hand."

Cam's feet stopped moving. Mia kept walking, but he could not go forward. He had stood on the bridge in Venice and had seen the little café in the distance. He remembered the striped purple umbrellas and the wrought-iron chairs and marble parfait tables.

But he hadn't stopped. He had been on his way out of Italy, en route to visit Angus, in Scotland. He looked at Mia, who had turned around, imagining her as she had been almost ten years earlier, her falling hair a river of curls, her black serving apron wrapped around her willowy form, her voice asking, *Cosa desidera?* He pictured her glancing left and right to see if anyone was looking, and then sitting on the terra-cotta wall to slip her shoes off, one at a time, then massaging her feet.

He thought now that not stopping at The Devil's Hand was the biggest mistake of his life.

"If I didn't know better," Cam murmured, "I would think you've been following me." He rubbed a hand over his jaw. "I was there."

Mia crossed her arms over her chest. "You were where?"

"Venice, in 1986. On the Rialto. I saw your café."

Mia felt a trickle of sweat run between her shoulder blades. "Prove it," she said.

She had not liked being a waitress; it was one of the jobs she'd had on her self-supported Grand Tour, where she worked for a few weeks or a month in a country she chose to explore. Still, The Devil's Hand had not been as bad as some: the midnight-shift truck dispatcher in Sydney, the bathroom attendant at Schönbrunn Palace—these were the difficult jobs. She could remember watching the café patrons, trying to determine who would give her the biggest tip. Would it be the old man with long white hair like Benjamin Franklin? The lovers who had shaved matching hearts into their scalps? The Pakistani with a shifting blue jewel in his turban? She could remember the tiny gold circles of lire, spread across the mauve tablecloths and rococo menus like a connect-the-dots puzzle. She'd pick them up and stuff them into her apron pocket, letting them sing all day with her movements.

At least once during her shift she'd look to the Rialto, making a wish as had become her habit. She had asked for money, she had asked for adventure, she had asked for love. She pinned her wishes onto the foot traffic on the bridge, believing that, like a falling star, she had a better chance if someone walking by could carry her desires farther away.

She never looked at the faces of the people on the bridge to whom she had entrusted her dreams; she figured that they were only messengers, after all.

She thought that maybe this had been the biggest mistake of her life.

Mia remembered, with a jolt, the moment days ago that Cam's hand had taken the picture of Carrymuir out of her own. She recalled the shadow that passed over his face when he refused to believe that they might have had a history which began before they'd met. She thought of him standing on the Rialto, his hair as bright as the lire in her apron, and she lifted her chin a fraction. "Prove it," she said again.

It seemed incomprehensible to Cam that he could have been within a mile of Mia Townsend without knowing it. Proof? He could have told her about the violet tablecloths and the heart-shaped backings of the ironwork chairs, but as Mia had said before, these were things he could have learned from a postcard. "I wanted to go there," he said simply. "I didn't have the time." He shifted his weight to his other side. "What were you doing at a Venetian café?"

*Waiting for you.* The words were at Mia's lips; she held her hand over her mouth to keep them back. Then, with a brittle smile, she jammed her hands into her coat pockets. "Well," she said brightly. "What a coincidence. We'll have to tell Allie."

Bringing up Allie's name made her feel a little better; she was able to breathe, and her skin didn't feel flushed. Cam nodded, smiling too, and took a step backward. He told her to have a nice day.

Mia watched him walk in the direction of the station. Then she turned and ran down the street. But instead of going to the flower shop where Allie was expecting her, she flew back to her room at the Wheelock Inn. She rummaged through her knapsack, tossing papers and pencils and small bags of seedlings out of the way until she found what she was looking for.

*Dear Cameron,* she wrote on a scrap of paper from the desk, *Better late than never. Mia.* She addressed a matching envelope to the police station and marked it personal and confidential. Then she picked up the cocktail napkin she'd taken out of her knapsack. It was from The Devil's Hand; it was one of the things she had taken with her—she made it a point to take at least one item from everywhere she'd been, to give her at least the semblance of a history.

She stuffed the note in the envelope and took one last look at the napkin. It was frayed at the edges and emblazoned with the café's logo: two faceless lovers in a circle of fire, which—even in silhouette—seemed to leap and burn and ruin.

Mia took a deep breath and jammed the napkin into the envelope. She licked it and closed it, sealing her future.

Don't laugh: what I miss most is talking to you. I imagine running into you in a busy market, even though I don't go to the market. And we decide to have lunch and we talk over margaritas; and then we walk back to where you are staying and we talk some more, and we talk in the hotel lobby and we keep talking until the moon is high in the sky and the bellhops change shifts and the night manager kicks us out.

I want to talk to you, but I don't have the slightest idea what we would have to say.

# SEVEN

*I*n between the bill from the lighting company and a pamphlet from the local mechanic who serviced all the cruisers was an envelope from the Wheelock Inn. Cam sighed and ran his hand through his hair. Probably a complaint about the way Zandy had handled the investigation of the room that Jamie MacDonald had been using; maybe even a mention of some scrap of evidence—his officers were always instructed to ask the parties at the scene of the crime to contact the station if they came up with anything else. He picked up the sterling letter opener on his desk and slit the corner of the envelope.

He pulled out the napkin first and what he noticed was not the stygian logo of The Devil's Hand, but the scent of Mia Townsend—cloves and rainwater and sweet grass—that now seemed to fill the room. He picked up the tiny ragged square and held it to his cheek.

He noticed the note as he went to throw the envelope in the wastebasket. The lettering was done in pencil, neat and precise, and he smiled, knowing that as a third-grader she had never strayed outside the lines. He read the short letter, and then read it again. He held it up to the light to see if there was anything that had been erased.

He took the note, hid it in the folds of the cocktail napkin, and placed it in his coat breast pocket.

Then he pulled a piece of stationery out of his desk drawer. *Mia,* he wrote, staring at her name on the page. He crumpled it up into a ball because the three letters drooped down.

*Mia,* he wrote a second time, on a different sheet of paper. Then he wadded the page up and threw it hard into the wastebasket. What the hell was he doing?

He sat back down at his desk, slicing open the light bill and the other pieces of mail and putting them in piles for Hannah to pay or to type suitable replies. He braced his hands, palms flat, on the desk.

He closed his eyes and made a bargain with God. *If You send someone into this office by the time I count to twenty,* he thought, *I will not write this note.* Then he held his breath and began to count.

He heard Hannah shuffling through the overstuffed filing cabinets outside, and Zandy picking up his things before going home for the day. He heard the front door open and close again, and an unknown voice muffling through a request at the front desk. He heard footsteps in front of his office.

Fourteen, fifteen.

He opened his eyes, picked up the pen and began to write.

*Mia,* he said, *Now the only thing I need is a cappuccino. I hate drinking alone. Will you meet me?*

He did not sign his name. He sealed it in a Wheelock Police Department envelope and, walking from his office, set it on Hannah's desk with the outgoing mail.

Allie wiped her hands on the white baker's apron, scattering bright yellow nasturtium petals over the kitchen floor. She had packed a suitcase to take to Jamie's house in Cummington; she had cleaned the bottom half of the house; and now she was preparing dinner for Cam and Mia, a thank-you in advance for taking care of things while she was away.

She was roasting a chicken, stir-frying asparagus, and making her nasturtium-lettuce salad. It was lovely to look at, all that red and orange and yellow against the greens of spinach and endive. She served it with walnut oil, and when people got over the shock of eating flowers for dinner, they always complimented her on her originality.

Cam hated it, said it made him feel like Robinson Crusoe, making do with twigs and weeds. But she knew that Mia would appreciate it. She liked the idea of showing Mia something she did not already know how to do.

"Cam," she yelled, "was that the door?"

In the living room, Cam was trying to read the evening paper. He had heard the doorbell, had known it was Mia, and tried to stuff the information into the back recesses of his mind. When Allie told him that she had invited Mia for dinner, he'd felt the blood rush from his head. He could not imagine anything more uncomfortable than sitting across a table from both his wife and the woman he could not stop thinking about.

"I'll get it," he said, pushing to his feet. He walked to the front door and leaned his forehead against it for a moment, considering whether by sheer will he could prevent this evening from taking place.

She was wearing a huge beige sweater and an ivory turtleneck and skinny little leggings the color of oatmeal, as if her clothing was her way of blending into the background. Cam wished he'd thought of it.

"Hi," he said.

She did not meet his eye. "Hello." She reached into her big carpetbag knapsack and pulled out a bottle of blackberry wine. "I brought this. I think it goes with any kind of entrée."

"Allie's in the kitchen." Cam stared at Mia. He wondered if she had gotten his letter. Occasionally, letters that were being sent somewhere within Wheelock boundaries were delivered the same day they had been mailed.

Mia pushed past Cam and walked toward the kitchen. He could hear the two women talking and laughing, high runners of music that reminded him of the conversation of birds.

He did not know how long he had been standing there staring at nothing when Allie touched her hand to his shoulder. Mia was a few steps behind her. "Cam," Allie said, "can you open the wine? I'm almost done. If you don't mind taking care of Mia."

"No," Cam said, surprised by the steadiness of his voice. "Of course not."

He poured the blackberry wine into fancy glasses they had received as a wedding present, belled like tulips with thin golden stems. When he handed Mia her glass, her fingers shook a little and spilled wine over the back of his hand.

"Oh," she said, turning around to find a napkin. "I can't believe I did that."

Cam brushed his hand against the leg of his pants, not giving a damn if it was going to stain. "It's nothing."

They sat for a few long, quiet minutes at the far ends of the couch, sipping the wine, until Allie fluttered in with a tray of spanakopita. "This isn't seventh grade," she said, laughing. "Boys and girls don't have to stand on opposite sides of the gym."

Cam watched her move back to the kitchen, wondering as always how she managed to turn simple motion into a dance. He wished she would stand beside him. Then he'd be able to chatter about the weather and the news and he wouldn't have to worry about trusting himself.

Mia was running her finger along the rim of the glass, making an unholy sound like the keen of a ghost. "My first boyfriend taught me how to do that."

"Oh?" Cam said, his throat closing. "And who was that?"

"Freddy Hornburger. No joke; that was really his name. He was my best friend's brother. He took me aside at her fourteenth-birthday party and asked if I wanted to see an owl turn its head all the way around. But when we got to the backyard there wasn't an owl, and he pushed me onto a chaise and kissed me so badly I thought I was being swallowed."

"And you still became his girlfriend?"

Mia shrugged. "I figured we had nowhere to go from there but up. I spent one week ignoring him, though, and swearing that I was never going to kiss anyone ever again." She lifted her glass in a toast. "I changed my mind eventually."

Cam raised his glass too. "Here's to Freddy," he said, but found when he took a sip he could not seem to swallow.

Mia shifted on her side of the couch, which Cam could feel all the way down to his end. "I have a lot of trouble talking to you," she admitted. "I don't feel very comfortable."

"I know what you mean. I feel like that too." And he truly did not understand it. In a way he felt as if he knew Mia better than he knew himself, and vice versa, but he could not seem to get past the polite simplicities. He wondered if, like him, she sensed that there was a dam to their conversation, and that the tiniest trickle would rush into an unstoppable flood. He wondered why she did not mention his letter, or the fact that she had sent him a note in the first place.

"Dinner," Allie called.

Allie was a very good cook. She said it was only a matter of being a voracious reader, since finding the right cookbooks made all the difference. "God," Mia said, slicing into her chicken, "I could never make anything like this."

"It's not too hard. You stick it in the oven and wait for the little button to pop out its side."

"Still," Mia demurred. "I haven't gotten much past Spaghettios."

At this, Allie frowned. "I was going to ask you to have Cam to dinner over the next few days, but I guess he can heat his own can of Spaghettios."

Cam dropped his fork. He listened to its ring, and all the subsequent echoes. "I can take care of myself."

Allie placed her hand on his forearm. "I know that. I just didn't think you'd *like* to."

"Besides," Mia said, "the kitchenette in my room isn't equipped for much past boiling water."

Allie took a helping of asparagus and passed the serving bowl to Cam. "That settles it, then. Cam will have you over here."

*Cam will have you over here.* For a moment, Allie's words hung in the air in front of Cam, palpable and festooned and so conspicuous that he marveled no one else was commenting on them. *Cam will have you over here.* He pictured Mia, flushed and waiting, the quilt upstairs pulled haphazardly over her bare, fine limbs.

"So," Mia said, "how long do you think this will take?"

"Cummington, you mean? Or the trial?" Allie did not wait for an answer, but began to speak again. "I don't know, really. I'm figuring on three or four days to speak to the neighbors and people Jamie left on his list; a day to go through his house." She paused. "I feel so strange about it. Like I'm stepping into someone else's place."

"It's not snooping." Cam was careful not to look at Mia. "You have Jamie's permission."

"Well," Allie said, chewing thoughtfully. "There is that."

When there was only a scatter of platters and bones, and circular bruises on the tablecloth from spilled blackberry wine, Mia pushed back her chair. "I'm doing the dishes," she said, "I'm not taking no for an answer."

After Mia had cleared the table and the water began to rush in the kitchen sink, Allie pulled Cam out of his chair and propelled him toward the living room. He sank deeply into his leather wing chair, surprised when she chose to sit on its arm beside him. They each had their spots in the room: his was the wing chair, hers was the couch. Allie wrapped her arms around his neck and yawned with her cheek against Cam's hair. "I hope she'll go soon."

Cam looked up at her. "Why'd you invite her?"

Allie grimaced. "I feel responsible. She doesn't know anyone else around here, and I'm leaving her with a whole store to run." She bit her lower lip. "I mean, it was a nice dinner, but I'd like to say goodbye to you without an audience."

"I'm sure she'll leave," Cam said, tightening his fingers on Allie's shoulder. "I know she'll leave." He thought of Allie as she would be an hour from now, her white cotton nightgown buttoned to the throat so that he could take his time removing it, the nightstand lamp on his side of the bed casting her body into a familiar pattern of shadows. He knew she would brush her teeth and then go to wait for him in bed; he knew that she'd be the first to reach out under the covers. He knew the exact pattern their lovemaking would take, and in spite of Allie's intention of saying goodbye, he knew it would be a familiar welcome.

He suddenly did not want Mia Townsend in his house. If you removed the temptation, you had nothing to worry about.

Cam stood abruptly. "Where are you going?" Allie said, recovering her balance without him in the chair.

He smiled at her. "I'm going to hurry things along."

He walked into the kitchen and found Mia standing at the sink, her sweater rolled up to reveal sharp pink elbows. He stood silently, watching the natural grace she exhibited even when using an S.O.S. pad, seeing the curls at the bottom edge of her hair jump when she scrubbed particularly hard. In retrospect, he did not understand how he had managed to survive dinner, to say the right things, preoccupied as he was with the rhythm of Mia's breath, the pitch of her questions, the curve of her brow.

He picked up a dish towel and began to dry.

"You left Allie alone?" she said, the very name putting a thick, viscous barrier up between them.

Cam nodded. He ran the striped blue and white cloth along the edge of the oval roasting pan, feeling the material dampen and give with subsequent strokes. He picked up a serving fork and worked the cloth between its tines. When he realized there was nothing left to dry, he looked up to find Mia watching his hands.

"What did you do with the napkin?" she whispered.

"I kept it in the pocket of my shirt all day." Cam watched Mia reach for his hand, slowly, as if it were an action beyond her control. She laced her fingers through his and he could feel the soap and warm water sealing them.

He thought of the old Scots custom of handfasting, by which two people could marry simply by clasping palms and announcing their intent in front of witnesses.

"That drink," she murmured. "I'll meet you tomorrow at seven."

*T*he moon sat cross-legged on the windowsill, its white skirt reaching to the plush bedroom carpet. It turned Allie into a creature of light, someone she would not recognize in a mirror; someone who was as sure of her worth as she was of her beauty. She lay with her head propped on the pillows, watching Cam.

He kissed the curve of her throat and then traced a snaking path between her breasts to her stomach. Allie watched Cam's hair spill over her ribs and she touched it, surprised for a moment by the soft, cool strands she'd been picturing as fire.

She liked foreplay. She knew she had the better end of the deal; Cam would, by ritual, move gently over her body, and then when she started to feel guilty she'd push him onto his back and run her fingertips over his chest and between his legs. But Cam always built to a fever pitch quickly, and it would be only a matter of minutes before he pressed her against the mattress and drove into her for release.

He began to skim his way up her, pushing her knees apart. "Not yet," she whispered, and Cam looked at her from under a fringe of hair. He took her hand from his shoulder and kissed it, then brought it down between them to rest on the folds of herself. She could feel his fingers between hers, and the sweet, damp heat.

"Now," he said.

She clawed at his back as he came deep inside her so forcefully they scooted inch by inch across the sheets. She waited until his head was thrown back and a moan tore from his throat before she let herself go.

As always, Cam immediately jumped to his feet and walked into the bathroom. Allie heard the water running and knew that he was soaping himself and washing off whatever remained of her.

She knew this was nothing but force of habit, but she always wondered exactly where Cam thought she'd been. She liked to imagine that just once, he would lose himself so completely during sex he'd be unable to move afterward, incapable of doing anything more than reaching for her hand in a silent, joyous connection.

Once, shortly after they were married, Allie had been sick at home and had watched "The Newlywed Game" on TV. One of the questions the wives had been given was, "When you're making whoopee, it's most like which Olympic sport: marathon running, gymnastics, or ice hockey?" When Cam came home from the station, she'd asked him what he thought. "Hockey," he had said, without hesitation. And he was right—there was a fury to their lovemaking, as if they were punishing each other for being something different from what they each had hoped. Many nights after that game show she had lain awake, listening to the tide of Cam's breathing, wondering why one of the multiple choices hadn't been something slow and lovely, like pairs' skating or water ballet, something partnered in grace and beauty and trust.

Cam slipped back under the covers, smelling of mouthwash. He gathered her against his chest. "That was nice," he murmured into her hair.

Tomorrow she would sleep in Jamie and Maggie MacDonald's bed. Allie wondered how firm it would be, what secrets would seep into her dreams. "Goodbye," she said.

Just so you know," Maggie MacDonald had said, "I'm against this on principle."

Jamie laughed and pushed her down into the chair that had been set up in the deserted lab. "You won't feel a thing."

"It's not that. It's the very *idea* of it. I feel like a Barbie doll, and everyone knows that no living woman has *her* measurements."

Jamie walked over to the device that could produce a design of a female body with lasers that would map a three-dimensional scan of Maggie's form. "You're not a Barbie doll," he said.

Maggie lifted her eyebrows. "Is that supposed to be a compliment?"

He walked to the chair and crouched in front of her, grasping her hands. "To me, you're the perfect image of a woman. So what's the matter with cloning you?"

It was 1993, and Jamie was doing a body scan of his wife to use as the model for an architectural firm's VR program. Their contract to build an elementary school in a rich New York suburb led them to ask for this particular application: a walk-through in which a user could be made child-size, and thus see if there were sharp edges at eye level, or cubbies too high to reach. But they'd also asked for a grown-up prototype, so that teachers might be able to assess the best spots for storage and educational aids, as well as the potential for hazards. Since they hadn't specified the sex of the prototype, Jamie was giving them a male and a female model. The user would be able to texture-map his or her own face over the model's digitized one.

"Who'd you use as the perfect man?" Maggie asked.

"Rod."

She laughed. "Rod? How come you didn't scan yourself?"

Jamie grinned. "Flattering as that might seem, I'm too tall. Rod's just under six feet, which fits in more as average."

"Ah," Maggie said. "So I'm not the perfect woman. I'm just average."

"Your words. Not mine." He pushed several buttons on a keyboard, and the pale green lasers that would translate the physical points of Maggie's body to the computer shimmered and waved into a direct, striking line that ran down the center of her face. "Sit still," he said. "Here we go."

He watched the beam of light pass over his wife's body, sliding over the curve of her breast and the valley of her stomach to her arm and the angle of her elbow. The laser rotated on its axis, glowing between her shoulder blades.

Jamie turned his attention to the computer screen. As if it were a Polaroid, an image of Maggie was coming into focus by bits and pieces. Her eyes blinked blindly out from the inside of the screen, her hands materialized to rest at her sides. Her legs, eerily foreshortened at the knees for a few moments, sprang into view in a dotting of color. "Okay," he said, "now stand up."

He wanted to make sure that the coordinates matched, while the lasers were still working. "Raise your right arm," Jamie ordered, and when Maggie did so, her computer image repeated the motion. "Touch your waist. Turn around." Every move she made, her prototype did as well. There was nothing missing.

He watched on the screen as Maggie lifted her hands to her hair and skimmed them down her body. Jamie cupped his hand against the computer screen; she was small enough to stand in his palm, to carry around in his pocket, to set on a shelf like an object of rare and priceless beauty. "How is it?" she asked, her mute lips on the screen puckering with silent words, looking for all the world like a kiss.

Jamie stared at Maggie's body on the screen, young and firm and healthy no matter how many times the program was switched on, no matter how old they all got in real life. "Perfect," he said.

Glory in the Flower had been decorated to look like someone's living room on a rainy autumn afternoon. Instead of having tables spread with dried flower arrangements and herbal wreaths, Allie had set two enormous overstuffed sofas in the center of the shop. There was a coffee table sporting a fresh arrangement every day, as well as magazines and a small tea service. The only indication that one was in a flower shop came from the unexpected details: the ivy trailing over the fat arm and leg of the couch, the bowl of rose petals that stood beside the cream and sugar, the lampshade overhead, which was fashioned entirely out of dried primroses and statice in luxuriant jewel tones.

In the back of the store, behind the sofas, was the cooler and the workbench where Allie did most of her arrangements, set under the spill of sun from a skylight. Behind a Chinese screen was the storeroom, as well as shelves stuffed with metallic foil and fabric, a palette of ribbons, birdcages, baskets, and brocade hatboxes that were all used as containers.

Mia walked to the cooler first and placed her lunch—yogurt—next to a large black bucket of persimmon roses. Then she shrugged out of her coat and set it on the desk chair in the storeroom. Absently, her eyes scanned the tools of the trade: rubber bands, green wire, scissors, Pokon leafshine, Floratape, and huge boxes of Spanish moss and Oasis.

It had taken her until yesterday to figure out Allie's system of organizing flowers. The cooler was not arranged by availability or popularity of flowers, or even by color, but by what the flowers were supposed to represent. She knew that once, bouquets had been sent as a message, not just as ornaments of beauty. When Mia had first become interested in floral arrangement, she'd been fascinated by this philosophy. Evidently, Allie was fascinated as well. She'd bunched the flowers with positive qualities on the left side of the cooler, those with negative connotations on the right. So jasmine and lilac and camellias and passionflowers—representing grace, first love, perfection, and faith—were gathered together in serviceable black florist's buckets. Acanthus, crocuses, thorn apples, and peonies were bunched in dishonor on the other side, signifying artifice, abuse, deceit, and shame.

It almost made Mia afraid to open the right door of the cooler, for fear that all the evil would seep into the world, like it had from Pandora's box.

She jumped as the phone rang. "Hi," she said, "Glory in the Flower." She expected it to be Allie, checking up to make sure that Mia had arrived on time and had opened the store without any catastrophes, but even as she thought this she realized it was not Allie's way. Allie would give her the benefit of the doubt, whether Mia deserved it or not.

"Oh, Antonio," she said, relaxing at the voice of one of her distributors. She scanned the nails stuck into the shelf above her eyes at even intervals, each marked with a day of the week and spearing various orders to be filled. "I need jacarandas and some tree fern." Allie had told her to order whatever she could from Antonio instead of from the other wholesalers; his prices were a little higher but his flowers were always fresh.

She haggled with him over the price of alstroemeria, finally agreeing on $4.75 a bunch, and said that she would indeed like to see the Washington State purple tulips. Then she got off the phone and closed her eyes and listened.

The quiet had a noise; it pulsed through the air vents in the flower shop. And if she cracked the cooler a little, she knew she would be able to hear the whistling silk of the roses as their pursed heads began to open.

Mia turned toward the storefront. Allie had set her bonsai tree on a low table across the room, along with the seven other trees they had wired together in hopes of future sales. With a smile, she crossed the room and unwrapped the wire from Allie's tree, keeping it from cutting too deeply into the bark and listening to the sigh of the roots and the cambium at this freedom. "Sorry," she said, carefully rewrapping the bronze wire. "I can't let you go just yet." She did the same to several other trees, snipping leaves and branches where she thought Allie might have underestimated the future tree. Then she sat down on the couch that faced the front of the shop.

There were a hundred things to do; Allie had left her that god-awful list, after all, but Mia only wanted to close her eyes and think about Cam. She knew she had to send him word of where she was going to meet him for this drink, but she did not think it would be prudent to waltz into the police station with the whole town watching. Not that what they were doing was at all out of sorts. A drink was just a drink. And Allie had asked Mia to watch over Cam.

She walked to the cooler and gathered in her hands a bunch of sad-eyed pansies and delicate apple blossoms. She braided the stems around the branch and tied them with a French-wired ribbon. Then, after hanging the Closed sign, she ran down the street to the police station and tucked the tiny bouquet under the driver's-side windshield wiper of the unmarked cruiser she recognized as Cam's.

Mia was out of breath by the time she arrived back at the flower shop, her pulse racing from more than the exertion. She sat back down on the couch, staring at the mess of petals that she'd made when she wrapped and wired the bouquet.

Somehow, she knew that Cam would figure it out.

Pansies meant, *I'm thinking of you*. And apples, since the days of Eve, had always meant temptation.

A llie did not go directly to Jamie MacDonald's house. Instead, she drove to the office of Dr. Dascomb Wharton, the family practitioner who had taken care of Maggie after she fell sick in 1993.

She found herself without an appointment, sitting on a cracked black Naugahyde chair and reading a magazine that dated back to the Gulf War. From time to time, when she knew that the receptionist was watching, she would glance at her watch.

Two hours after she'd arrived at Dr. Wharton's, she was ushered through the winding corridors behind the reception desk and into his private office.

The doctor was a tremendous, shaggy-haired man who seemed to have learned about the dangers of cholesterol too late. He was eating a calzone, dipping it at regular intervals into a small vat of spaghetti sauce, when Allie pushed open the door. "Sit down, sit down," he bellowed. "You don't mind me eating lunch while we chat?"

Allie shook her head. She had never seen anyone quite so large, except of course for the terribly sad cases on the Oprah show, and she wondered why the spindly-legged chair beneath the man's bottom did not simply give way. The doctor wiped his mouth with a napkin and smiled at her.

*What big teeth you have,* Allie thought. She smiled back.

"What can I do for you, Mrs. MacDonald?"

Allie pulled a Polaroid photo of Jamie from the front pocket of her purse. It was certainly not a good picture; in fact, Cam had loaned it to her from the police file that had the copy of the arrest report. "I'm here on behalf of this man," she said, offering the photograph to the doctor. "Do you know him?"

Dr. Wharton pursed his lips. "Why, of course I know Jamie. But I know Maggie better, being her doctor."

"Knew," Allie said, before she could think. The doctor stared at her. "She . . . died a few days ago."

"Oh." Dr. Wharton looked nonplussed. "Oh, well, yes, that was to be expected."

Allie stuffed the photograph back into her purse. "She was very ill, then?"

Dr. Wharton leaned forward. "My dear, this is a matter of patient confidentiality."

Allie nodded, having anticipated this. She withdrew a letter from Graham MacPhee, on a piece of paper emblazoned with the legal firm's letterhead, and handed it wordlessly to the doctor. "I see," he said, scanning the few lines. "So Jamie did it."

"We've yet to go to court." She leaned forward. "That's why I'm in Cummington. I'm trying to find people who knew Maggie, who knew Jamie, who would think that this kind of charge is ridiculous."

Dr. Wharton stuffed the last of his calzone in his mouth and held up a finger. When he swallowed, he rested back in his chair, tipping it precariously. "What I will tell you, and any court that subpoenas me, is this: Maggie MacDonald would not have lived out the year, in my opinion. Her breast cancer, diagnosed two years ago, had spread to her bones, and finally to her brain. It had not responded to chemotherapy or radiation, and the last time I treated her it was because the tumor had infiltrated the optic nerve." He paused, as if trying to see how sharp Allie was. "The eye."

"What kind of tumor was it, originally?"

"Ductal carcinoma," Wharton replied. He rapped his fingers against the smooth surface of his desk.

Allie looked away before asking the next question. She pictured Maggie laid out on the embalming table of the funeral home, her knees grotesquely bent into the air. "Was she in a lot of pain?"

The doctor made a strange sound through his nose. "Well, now, pain is a relative thing. Some women breeze through childbirth, for example, and others beg to be unconscious."

"We aren't talking about having a baby."

"No," Dr. Wharton agreed. "We are not." He steepled his fingers and rested his chin on top of them. "I think Maggie MacDonald was in physical pain, yes," he conceded.

"But . . ." Allie prompted, hearing the qualification in his tone.

"But I don't think it was what hurt the most." Allie raised her eyebrows, and Dr. Wharton smiled so gently all the pockets of his face dimpled and folded into each other until he looked like an entirely different man. "I think what was killing Maggie was knowing that she would be leaving Jamie behind."

Anyone who wondered why the town's flower shop was open late at night would suspect that Allie was working on a wedding. Sometimes it took two or three days to wire all the flowers in a bridal bouquet, and Allie often stayed into the witching hours to get the painstaking work finished. So when Cam walked down the street from the station, passing several families en route to dinner at the coffee shop, he did not turn away or try to hide. He simply tucked the limp knot of flowers into his coat pocket and smiled at Geordie MacDonald and Sarah Murray and said yes, the weather was getting colder much quicker than usual.

Mia had locked the door, so Cam had to knock. This took him by surprise; he was always yelling at Allie to lock the door, to which she simply replied she wasn't a target: if by any chance a thief ever *did* happen to set foot in Wheelock, he wouldn't pick a store that barely turned a profit. Cam had almost succeeded in pushing that last thought of Allie out of his mind when Mia's small face appeared in one glass pane of the door.

She was wearing jeans that looked very soft, and a man's white shirt rolled up at the elbows. For one irrational moment Cam wanted to grab her shoulders and demand that she tell him whose shirt that was. But instead he smiled at her, and pulled the tiny bouquet out of his pocket. "I got your flowers."

Her face was as pale as the collar of the shirt, but that only made her eyes stand out in relief. They were shining and sapphire; they reminded him of the trappings of royalty. He unbuckled his gun belt and laid it gently across the counter by the cash register When he turned, she was standing two feet in front of him. "What makes you think," she asked quietly, "that I'm safe?"

He sat down on one of Allie's couches, which he personally had lugged out of a cousin's pickup truck when Allie found them at a tag sale in a town over the mountains. Mia had set the fine bone china tea set on the low table, along with a bigger vase full of the same flowers she'd tacked to his windshield.

"They're pretty," he said, brushing one pansy. "And they smell like spring."

Mia sat down on the couch opposite Cam and plucked one branch from the arrangement. "Apple blossoms. They're very hard to get in October." She stared at the patterns of the flowers, dotting the bark in a neat spiral. "Do you know that, supposedly, if you cut an apple in half on Christmas Eve, and put the left half close to your heart and the right half by the front door, the person you want will be found near the right half at midnight?"

Cam watched her hands absently strip the bark from the branch. "Is this something you've done?"

"No," Mia said. "I've just heard of it."

"How do you know which is which?"

"What do you mean?"

Cam touched the branch closest to him. "Which is the left half and which is the right half of the apple?"

Mia raised her eyebrows. "I don't know. I suppose it all depends on your point of view." She ran a finger over the rim of one of the two teacups, but did not make an effort to pour out, or even ask Cam if he wanted some tea. He saw her knees bounce as she tapped the floor with her feet, and realized she was even more nervous than he was.

Suddenly she bolted up and walked past him to the flower cooler. From his seat, Cam could see the reflection of her face in the glass. Her features seemed so drawn that the slightest motion of her mouth might make her shatter. "When I was traveling," she said, "I learned everything I could about flowers. On Corfu, the natives wear sunflowers as hats. And in France, the country wives use clematis as a clothesline." She passed a hand down the chilled front of the glass case, grasping for the handle as if she were drowning. "Did you know Allie keeps fresh herbs, too? Here's basil. It's supposed to be a symbol of hatred." She turned quickly, and offered a fragrant sprig she'd broken off to Cam, who had come to stand behind her. He took it from her, set it on the edge of the couch, and then closed his fingers over hers.

Mia tugged free and crossed her arms over her chest. "But in Romania," she said, her voice high and thin, "if a woman gets a man to take basil from her own hand, he'll be faithful for the rest of his life." Suddenly she sank against the cooler, as if her knees had simply given out. She buried her face in her hands. "Oh, God," she murmured. "Oh, my God."

Cam drew her into his arms and held her until all the brittleness melted from her carriage and left her soft and sobbing against him. "Sssh," he whispered into her hair. His eyes fell on the basil, balanced on the edge of the couch. "Sssh."

Jamie MacDonald lived in a modest Colonial on the north side of the Cummington duck pond. It had been painted white, and its black shutters were beginning to peel. When Allie pulled up in her car and parked in the driveway, a neighbor waved to her, as if she had been expected.

There was a pretty wreath on the front door. Curly willow had been twisted into the shape of a heart, and dried red and white roses were snaked through its turns. Allie dug Jamie's house keys out of her pocket and opened the door.

The house was neat and very quiet. Allie knew from Jamie that he and Maggie had left Cummington in a hurry, but there didn't seem to be any dust, and the polished wood floor that ran down the length of the hall was unmarked by muddy boots or black heel prints. The house smelled of lemon wax, evergreen, and something that Allie could not put her finger on but would have bet was a fragrance that simply signified Maggie herself.

"Well," she said aloud, more to hear the way her voice sounded in someone else's home than anything else, "we've got work to do." She hung her coat over the knob of the banister and dug Jamie's list out of the back pocket of her jeans. "The file boxes are in the study," she read, and she poked her head into the first room off to the right.

It was a dining room, decorated with a large oval cherry table and an Irish lace runner. An oversized pewter goblet sat in the center of the table, filled with chubby wax grapes. From the dining room she stepped into the den, where the vacuous black eye of the TV screen stared back at her, and the simple dips of the couch showed that Maggie and Jamie liked to sit side by side.

*I should be in forensics,* she thought, tabulating the hundreds of things she had already learned about Jamie and his wife simply by stepping through a few rooms of his house. She went into the kitchen and opened the refrigerator, wrinkling her nose as she poured the sour milk down the sink drain and threw some moldy bread into the trash. Then she found the study.

It was painted an old-world blue, and one wall was filled with ancient yellowed books that Allie could not imagine anyone having the patience to read. There were two desks in the room: one the wide, tilted run of an architect's workspace, the other a simple oak structure with hideaway cabinets. Allie moved to the architect's desk first. Jamie had mentioned that Maggie was an illustrator, or she had been before it became too difficult to work. There were no pictures-in-progress tacked to the surface, but a small bowl painted with Mickey Mouse's face held markers in all the colors of Allie's own roses: sage and lemon and honey and shell pink; sky blue and aubergine, topaz and ivory. Allie picked the markers up and rolled them between her palms, resisting the urge to draw a rainbow.

Clipped to the corner of the white desk was a photograph of Jamie and Maggie. Allie peered closer, fascinated by the mobile smile of Maggie's mouth and the shine of Maggie's eyes. Jamie's arm was looped around her shoulders, his face was turned in profile as he pressed a kiss onto her cheek.

Allie touched her finger to the spot on Maggie's cheek that Jamie was kissing, then touched her own mouth. Feeling slightly guilty, she pulled the photo from its clip and tucked it into the pocket of her chamois shirt.

Jamie's desk held all the bills and all the tax records. She found the fire-resistant strongbox under the right drawer, just as he'd said she would. The key was already in the lock; she had only to turn it to reveal their marriage certificate, their passports, the deed to the house, and their insurance. She took a manila envelope from the desk, emptied its contents, and placed these things inside. Then she removed the picture from her pocket and slipped it gently on top of the other documents.

If *she* was the jury, she knew what she'd believe more.

Allie walked upstairs to the bedroom and opened the three doors inside to find two closets and the bathroom. One entire shelf in the linen closet was filled with ovulation-predictor tests, carefully stacked. She took one out and stared at the fuzzy picture of a mother and child on the package. Maggie and Jamie had no children, neither did Allie and Cam. The difference was, Maggie and Jamie had *wanted* a baby. Allie did too—she had from the moment she'd started dating Cam—but even now, years later, he insisted he wasn't ready. And in this, like all other things, she would wait for him.

Allie closed the linen closet and walked to the other side of the bedroom. She sat down in front of Maggie's vanity table and sprayed a bit of perfume from an atomizer onto her neck. Joy. She knew the smell; she had never been able to afford it. To the left of the perfume was deodorant. To the right was an army of amber plastic vials containing Demerol, Valium, and a host of other medicines that Allie did not recognize.

*Oh, Maggie,* she thought, staring into the mirror, *I would have moved them. I would not have kept them in a place where I could see them every time I looked for my own reflection.*

With the precision of a research scientist, Allie wrote down the names of the prescription drugs and their dosage strength on the front of the manila envelope.

In retrospect, she could not say what had made her do it, but Allie methodically began to get undressed. She tucked her sneakers under the vanity table and hung her shirt and jeans over the chair and walked into Maggie MacDonald's closet.

She dressed in a filmy camisole the color of apricots, and an ankle-length skirt made of silk faille in all the shades of a sunset. It was big at the waist, so she hiked it tighter with a leather belt embroidered with a Native American bead design. Then she found a big blue turtleneck sweater that reached to her knees and seemed to swallow her alive.

Maggie had been much taller.

In a hatbox on the top shelf of the closet she found a wig that was the same color as Maggie's hair. She didn't think Maggie had been wearing a wig; surely that would have come out during the autopsy. More likely this was from a year or so ago, when she had undergone chemotherapy that did not work.

Allie crouched in front of the vanity table and tugged and pushed her own dull brown hair under the neat mesh cap until a swing of artificial hair came to touch in two points at the base of her chin.

She went through the drawers of the lingerie chest, pulling on thigh-high stockings and then argyle socks and tennis Peds over those. She wrapped a scarf printed with exotic fruit around her neck, and a longer, more diaphanous one about her hips. In the top drawer she found Maggie's old bras, as wispy and thin as a memory, buried beneath the sturdy white cotton prosthetic ones for a mastectomy patient.

Feeling sick, Allie clamped her hand to her mouth with the intention of running to the bathroom, but when turning around she faced the bed. For the first time she noticed that it was unmade. In a house where everything had its place, where dust didn't deign to settle, the tangled blue sheets and knotted, rolled comforter seemed to be a violation. She inched closer, dropping down to the edge of the bed and reaching for a pillow. She brought it to her face, smelling Jamie's aftershave and Joy.

It was possible that Maggie had felt too sick to make the bed on the day they left, or that Jamie had been the last one to leave it. For all she knew, Maggie might not have even been sleeping upstairs at that point, too tired to go up and down. But Allie could see them as clearly as the bright patterns woven into the skirt she wore: Jamie and Maggie, about to walk out the door of their house, until Maggie turned suddenly and grasped Jamie's hand and dragged him back up the stairs to make love one last time in their own home.

She lay down on the bed in Maggie MacDonald's clothing, pulled the sheets over her head, and wept.

Cam's face turned the same way as Mia's when they kissed. They scraped teeth and mashed noses before getting it right, but the simple act of finding their way together instead of having an expected pattern made his head swim. They sat on the couch, kissing like teenagers, their hands trapped between their bodies like gypsy moths, darting beneath clothing and batting against skin.

She smelled, felt, and tasted different than Allie, and Cam allowed himself to think this just once. Then he concentrated on learning the texture of the backs of her hands; the feel of the pulse at her temple; the clear, heady scent of her hair.

He undressed Mia slowly, waiting for her to clutch at the sides of her shirt or make a tiny cry of protest, but when she did nothing he simply continued. She sat on the couch on the white blur of her big shirt, which unfolded beneath her legs like the opened petals of a lily. Then he stood up and began to unbutton his uniform.

The badge struck the edge of the table when he tossed it away, reminding him of exactly who he was and why he should not be doing this, but he pushed the thought aside to step from his shoes and shuck his way out of his pants. When he was naked in front of her, Mia reached out to touch his thigh. She got to her feet and walked around him in a little circle, trailing her fingers so that they were always brushing his skin. "Oh, my," she said softly, coming to face him. "Where are the mistakes?"

He caught her up close then, lifting her to the tips of her toes so that they pressed together at the shoulders and stomach and legs. He kissed a curl that had worked its way to the corner of her mouth. He followed her down to the couch and came into her slowly.

She saw Cam's beauty not in its entirety, but in bits and pieces, like a camera's eye swinging slowly. She panned from the russet of his thick hair to the veins beneath the white stretch of skin, to the simple sculpted V where the muscle of his shoulder joined his bicep. She ran her hands down his chest and stomach to the spot where they were joined, and felt him shake.

Their hearts were pounding between them, slightly out of rhythm. Cam knew he could not hold on, so he buried his face against her neck and, in the strongest effort of will he had yet to face in his life, pulled out of Mia and crushed her against him.

He felt the spot, milky and sticky between them, as binding as guilt. "I didn't have anything," he said, by way of explanation.

Mia nodded. "You'll have to do something about that next time."

Cam felt his heart jump. She wanted to see him again. She wanted to do this again. He rolled to his side, nearly knocking her off the narrow couch, and draped her body over his, realizing for the first time that Mia was crying. With his finger, he wiped away a tear that was balanced over her nostril. "Why?" he said, not sure he wanted to know the answer.

Mia shivered. "I was thinking of my parents," she whispered. "I was thinking I've waited far too long for you."

Cam shifted his weight, still afraid that she might break, or in the blink of an eye puff into a little cloud and disappear. He reached blindly behind him to the edge of the couch, and retrieved the sprig of basil. He tucked it behind Mia's ear. "About that tea," he said, and he watched her turn like a sunflower into the light and strength of his smile.

# EIGHT

*I*n 1692, forty MacDonalds of Glencoe, a town not five miles from Carrymuir, were murdered by Campbell soldiers who had enjoyed their hospitality for two weeks.

The MacDonald laird had been delinquent in pledging his support to William of Orange, waiting until the last day of the prescribed time to swear his allegiance. But he *had* given his word, so when a troop of Campbell soldiers came to Glencoe and asked to stay in the name of the English crown, the laird had no misgivings.

However, the English had decided to teach the Highlanders a lesson. The Campbells, longtime enemies of the MacDonalds, were all too happy to do the honors for William of Orange. After staying at Glencoe, they arranged a massacre in the early hours of the morning, shooting the MacDonald laird, biting the rings off his wife's fingers, and leaving her to die naked in the snow.

In Glencoe, and in Carrymuir for that matter, it was still said that you should never trust a Campbell.

Which was why, when Jamie MacDonald heard the name of the district attorney prosecuting his case, his knees gave out beneath him.

Audra Campbell, Assistant DA, stood in front of Martha Sully, the magistrate assigned to the preliminary hearing of the State of Massachusetts versus James Reid MacDonald, and held up a picture of a moon-white, lifeless body that was the very last thing Jamie wanted to see.

"Your Honor," she said, "we have the autopsy report on Margaret MacDonald; a signed confession from the defendant attesting to his role in her death; Polaroid photos taken upon the arrest of the defendant by Police Chief Cameron MacDonald that show signs of resistance by Margaret MacDonald to her attacker; and various pieces of evidence that link the defendant to the scene of the crime." She raised her brows, as if to convey, *Don't we all have somewhere else we'd rather be?*

Graham shifted uncomfortably beside Jamie. He'd explained the procedure to him before arriving in court; Jamie had understood that they wouldn't be offering any evidence of their own, because it would be subject to cross-examination. *This isn't about your guilt or innocence,* Graham had said. *This is just a decision about whether or not to go to trial.* And although Jamie had seemed to understand while sitting in the confines of Graham's Honda, it didn't explain why his client had taken one look at the prosecuting attorney and had wilted as if he had seen a ghost.

Audra Campbell was a tiger lady, an attorney with an immense chip on her shoulder that did nothing to soften her severely cut suits and her no-nonsense clipped boy's haircut. She did not particularly care for most of the cases she tried in the Berkshire area, but she liked to win. She did not consider defendants to be rapists and thieves and murderers as much as opponents to break down and send slinking away.

She moved in front of the wooden table set up for the prosecution and glanced at the people sitting in the back of the courtroom. "I have a witness here, Your Honor, who would be prepared to verify that the defendant drove to the Wheelock police station on the afternoon of September 19, 1995, and admitted in front of a crowd that he killed his wife. This same witness was the arresting officer who took the defendant's signed confession. In addition, I have another witness who will testify that the defendant attacked him in front of the police station, and had to be brought under control."

She glanced coolly at Graham MacPhee, who was too busy looking at the gathered crowd to catch her eye. Zandy Monroe, the sergeant who would apparently be willing to testify to being assaulted by Jamie, was sitting beside Cam, his head bent as Cam whispered something.

Graham wondered if Cameron MacDonald could do it. He wondered how he'd sleep at night knowing he'd put his cousin in jail for what would most likely be the rest of his life.

Graham stared down at the yellow pad he'd brought to the preliminary hearing. He'd drawn triangles and his own initials, but nothing else of import. With great deliberation, he wrote Cam's name and underlined it. Allie was off in Cummington getting key witnesses, but Graham knew that part of the defense strategy at Jamie's trial would be Cam. Graham pictured a cross-examination where he leaned against the witness box, casual as could be, and asked Cam to explain the intricate family ties of the Wheelock MacDonalds. He imagined asking Cam to recite the Carrymuir chief's motto, the same words that graced the Wheelock town seal: *Ex uno disce omnes*—From one, judge of the rest.

If Cam testified that his cousin was a killer, what would that say about Cam himself?

Graham smiled. All he had to do was make the prosecution's star witness look the tiniest bit unsure of himself on the stand, couple that with Jamie's testimony, and he'd be golden.

Now if only he could prepare a valid legal defense.

"Counselor," Martha Sully said, "do you have a response?"

Graham felt Jamie stiffen at his side. He stood up and cleared his throat, smoothed his Brooks Brothers jacket over his pleated suit pants. "Your Honor," he began, "while some of the contentions made by the prosecution are accurate, my client would argue that he is not guilty for the following reason: Overcome by grief, he was simply not himself. At the time of Margaret MacDonald's death, James MacDonald was a victim of temporary insanity. We would be prepared to testify and present evidence to that effect at a trial."

He sat down abruptly and Jamie looked up at him, an amused smile quirking across his face. Jamie leaned close to Graham, his breath hot upon his ear. "Well," he whispered, "the ugly duckling becomes a swan after all."

Graham raised one eyebrow. "You ain't seen nothing yet."

Martha Sully looked down her nose at the people assembled in front of her. She slipped on her half-glasses and began to make markings in the file that lay open on the podium. "The court finds that there is sufficient evidence to submit this case to a grand jury for further consideration," she said, and she snapped the folder shut.

Audra Campbell began to stuff her papers and notebook back into her leather briefcase. She stood, ran her hands down the back of her skirt, and walked over to the defense table. "I'll be seeing you soon," she said to Graham, and then she glanced at Jamie, a feral smile slicing her face in two. "Mr. MacDonald, I give no quarter."

Jamie looked her straight in the eye. "Well," he said evenly, "I'd expect no less from a Campbell."

*E*llen MacDonald would not have scared the hell out of her if Mia had been doing something ordinary, like pruning the bonsais or making dish gardens, instead of writing Cam's name over and over on an order form.

"Hello," Ellen called, just inches away from Mia's shoulder, and she jumped a foot. Mia stood up and faced Cam's mother, whom she'd met briefly at the funeral, and slipped the paper she'd been dreaming on into the back pocket of her jeans.

"Mrs. MacDonald," Mia said, trying to smile. "Didn't Allie tell you she was going out of town?"

"Of course." Ellen walked over to the Mr. Coffee and poured herself a cup in a mug Allie usually used. "But she told me you'd be running the business, and that I should just stop by as usual and take what I want."

Mia stared at her blankly. *Take what you want?*

Ellen crossed to the cooler and began to finger the herbs that Allie kept on the right-hand side. "Fresh lemon balm and dried linden," she said, more to herself than to Mia. She stood up, frowning. "I know she's got them somewhere. She orders what I need every week."

Mia thought of the latest shipment Antonio had brought by, the strange twigs and leaves she hadn't recognized and had left for Allie on her desk. "Oh. You must mean these."

Ellen took the flowers into her hands, rubbing the petals with her fingers as if to assess their frailty. "Wonderful," she said. "These are both supposed to do wonders when it comes to calming you down."

Mia looked at the ugly little branches in Ellen's hands and raised an eyebrow. "I like a little more color."

"Oh, no. I use them for medicine. I boil them up. Natural healing." She waved the lemon balm in the air, so that several of the flower heads drifted toward the floor. "Allie's a godsend when it comes to organic ingredients."

Mia wouldn't have expected any less. She smiled uncomfortably, not knowing if she was supposed to do anything else, like offer Ellen MacDonald a teakettle to make her infusion, or pluck the petals off for her. Ellen did not say anything, but she didn't seem inclined to leave, either.

"So, you're Cam's mother," Mia said, realizing only after the words were out of her mouth how intimate they sounded.

"The very one." Ellen reached deep into a pocket and drew out several small polished stones. "You seem a little piqued, dear," she said, rattling the stones in her palm like they were dice. When they fell, she began to sift through them. "This is rhodonite, that's for calming—here, you take it—and this is rose quartz, for love; and no, not this one, that's carnelian for sexuality . . . Ah!" With a flourish, she presented a tiny smooth green stone to Mia. "Aventurine. For tranquillity."

Mia touched all of the stones, scattered like bright marbles across Allie's desk. "Do these really work?"

Ellen shrugged. "I suppose it depends on how much you want them to. When old Angus had a stroke the year after he moved to America and the consensus was that he was going to die in a matter of days, I sewed malachite into the lining of his hospital gown. It's supposed to strengthen the heart, the circulation. Wouldn't you know it, he walked out of the hospital on his own two feet the next morning."

Mia's mouth dropped open. "That's amazing!"

Ellen smiled. "It probably was not so much the malachite as the fact that he was a MacDonald," she admitted. "They're too stubborn to die until they're good and ready."

The swing of the door on its hinges sent Mia running to the front to greet a potential customer. Bent over the worktable, carefully arranging two paper plates and utensils, was Cam. "Hi." He grinned when she came into the room. "Since it's in my best interests to keep up your strength—"

"Cam," Mia said. "Guess who's here?"

Ellen walked out, her coat buttoned again, her hands clutching fistfuls of stubby flowers. "Well. Two birds with one stone."

Cam leaned down to kiss his mother on the cheek. "What are you doing here?"

"Allie got me some linden," she said, holding it up for Cam to sniff. "I'm making a soporific today."

"Well, hell." Cam smiled, in too good a mood to take issue with his mother's crazy ideas. "Somebody has to."

Ellen glanced at the table, set cozily for two; at the calzones that Cam had purchased, leaking greasily through the bottom of the paper bag. She looked up at her son. "Don't tell me *you* forgot Allie's gone."

"It's for Mia," Cam said smoothly. "Allie asked me to make sure she gets regular meals."

For a moment Ellen could not put her finger on what was the matter. But then she understood: Cam was feverish; he was burning up. He didn't seem to be acting sick, but she would have recognized anywhere the flame behind his eyes and the flush that worked up from his neck.

Ellen stared at her son, who was unwrapping something that looked like Parmesan cheese and whistling an old Scots lullaby. Then she looked at Mia, whose hands were moving restlessly at her sides. There was an amethyst in Ellen's pocket, which represented the strength of will, and she considered giving it to Cam, but realized this was something he'd have to discover himself.

Then she thought of Allie, who was not there to bear witness; Allie with her back curved over Ellen's stove as she mixed beeswax and lanolin and what have you. She thought of the time she, Ellen, had oversteeped a tincture, so that when Allie tried to rub it over her face as a restorative, it had dyed her skin green. She thought of the way Allie had looked at her own wedding, how she'd stood in the receiving line clutching Cam's hand so tightly that she left behind faint bruises that lasted a week.

Ellen set down her flowers and unbuttoned her coat. She perched on one of the work stools and propped her elbows up in front of a paper plate. "My," she said, smiling. "I hope there's enough there for three."

The spare bedroom in Jamie and Maggie's house had been converted into a home office for Jamie, complete with a state-of-the-art computer system and virtual reality aids. Allie stepped into the room cautiously; computers made her nervous. She had taken an adult education course the year before which taught her how to inventory her stock and do billing on a computer system, but she'd never even *seen* some of the paraphernalia that littered Jamie's study.

Strange geometric patterns were swirling on the screen, as if the user had stepped out to the bathroom and was planning on coming back in a moment. This, Allie had seen before—they were screen savers, or something like that; they were supposed to save energy when the computer was turned on but unoccupied. It surprised Allie that Jamie hadn't thought to shut off the system before leaving with Maggie; then she realized other things had probably been on his mind. Still, with Jamie away in Wheelock, the drain of electricity would be costing him a fortune. Almost shyly, Allie sat down at the swivel chair and reached for the power switch on the computer.

As soon as she stretched out her hand, the geometric patterns vanished and a bright yellow ball blinked at her, like the flash of a camera. The ball skidded from left to right, leaving a string of letters behind. WELCOME, Allie read. PLEASE PUT ON GLOVE AND HMD.

Entranced by a computer that seemed to know just when she'd arrived, Allie reached for the glove. She slid her hand inside and wiggled her fingers, then stared at the headpiece lying beside the computer. She had no idea what an HMD was, but this was the only other piece of equipment attached to the system. Gingerly she lifted the helmet and fit it over her head and eyes.

She jumped. Instead of staring at a computer screen, she was *in* it. Allie's peripheral vision, even when she swung her head back and forth, revealed a simple cell with gray walls and aqua carpeting, like a doctor's waiting room. Words began to form inches from her face, trembling in the air like hummingbirds. *You have entered Northrup Architectural's Virtual Design System,* Allie read. She stretched out her hand, allowing the letters to balance on her palm, delighted to discover they had weight and texture. Then, in smaller print: *Conceived and implemented by Techcellence, Inc., copyright 1993.* Frowning, Allie wondered about that. She would have expected Jamie to be working on something more current.

But before she could let herself question any further, the room fell away around her and she found herself staring at three hovering holograms: a skyscraper, a hotel, and a flagpole. A disembodied TV-announcer voice began to speak. "Please indicate which project you'd like to tour by pointing with your gloved hand," he said. As Allie reached out, he enunciated each choice. "Rystrom Towers," he boomed. "The Four Seasons, Toronto . . . Carter S. Wilder Elementary School."

Allie curled her fingers around the flagpole. "You have chosen Carter S. Wilder Elementary School," the voice said. "If you would like to proceed with your tour, please say so now."

Allie cleared her throat, feeling a little foolish. "I'd like to proceed with my tour."

All of a sudden she was standing on a grassy slope, staring down at the new brick building with its shiny bike racks and wooden jungle gyms. She could feel the wind stirring her hair; she could hear the cries of children playing. Astounded, Allie squatted down and rubbed her hand over the grass. Inside the glove, she could swear she'd felt the crisp spikes and stubby needles of a just-mowed lawn. "Jamie," she whispered, "you are a genius."

She stood up, walking and wondering why she wasn't bumping into the computer unit that she knew was right in front of her—there must have been a moving platform she'd missed seeing. At the front door of the school, she reached out and pulled at the heavy aluminum door. It swung open at her touch, but not before Allie noticed that her hand, which was surely wrapped around ordinary air, had felt a handle, and resistance.

There was a trophy case in the main hall, and bright children's paintings on paper that curled at the edges like eyelashes. Allie examined the stick figures of one artist, and was brought whirling around by the sound of the disembodied voice again. "Please choose the image you'd like to assume for your walk-through." Again, hovering before her eyes, were several forms: a woman, a child, a man, a wheelchair-bound boy. Unsure of why she was being asked her sexual orientation and physical capabilities, Allie pointed to the figure closest to her. "Female," the voice boomed. "Adult."

The tiny image grew and grew until Allie realized she was standing face-to-face with someone. Narrowing her eyes, she took in the thick hair, the guileless smile, the unmistakable image of Maggie MacDonald.

"Step forward," Maggie invited, and Allie wondered if it was her real voice. She took one step and then, as Maggie urged her, another, until she realized that the Maggie-image wanted Allie to literally walk right into her. Of course, Allie realized. This was the way Jamie had chosen for the computer user to "see" him or herself in the school. Allie remembered the quick flash when she'd sat down at the computer—it must have been an internal camera, capturing her own features to map onto this programmed female form. That way, during the walk-through she would be able to reach for things and see a female hand; she would be able to look in a bathroom mirror and see her own face.

With her eyes wide open Allie walked into Maggie's body, shuddering at the feel of being under someone else's skin and staring out at the world through borrowed eyes. And she wondered whether the sorrow she felt was something Jamie had intended, something Allie herself had imagined, or such an intrinsic part of Maggie that it floated through the halls of this untried school like a sunken, dissatisfied ghost.

*C*am sat at the work station in the flower shop, watching Mia rewrap the wire around the eight bonsai trees. "Looks like it hurts," he said.

Mia smiled. "When was the last time you were wrapped with copper wire?"

Cam laughed. "Now, *there's* an idea."

It was his third night with Mia. With the exception of his mother, who had arrived the day before at an unfortunate time, no one would have suspected him of unlikely behavior. And even *she* had no proof. Cam had been acting the way he always did during the day, going into the station and checking the schedules and the court book and doing whatever needed to be done. But at six o'clock, he'd lock his office and tell Hannah that he was going to take Mia Townsend to dinner. That Allie had asked him to keep an eye on her.

He thought that telling half the truth might be better, in the long run, than lying.

Then he'd walk to the flower shop, stopping to chat with the old-timers in front of the coffee shop and on the steps of the post office, and he'd knock on the locked door. When Mia opened it, his senses would be assaulted by the fresh, sweet scent of the flowers she'd been working with that afternoon. She always looked as if she was surprised to see him, but she'd draw him into the shop and lock the door again and kiss him, her fingers kneading the short muscles of his lower back.

The first night had been something he would never be able to put into words. Making love with Mia was a bit like waking up one morning to discover the color green. You saw it in the grass and the trees and the road signs and you could not imagine that you had spent so many years of your life in the absence of this hue, which seemed to make the rest of the world fall into place.

Tonight he had been watching her work, knowing how swiftly and gently her hands could move and shape and heal. She began to dig around the roots of a Chinese juniper. "Tell me what you were like as a kid," she said. "I want to know what I've missed."

Cam grinned. "When I was six I plugged up the drain in my mother's bedroom shower. It was one of those glass stalls, you know, and I figured I could make my own swimming pool for the winter. It leaked through the floor and ruined the dining room table downstairs."

"Ah," Mia said, walking behind him and trailing her hand across the back of his neck. "That tells me quite a lot."

"I used to stick dimes between the black and white keys of the piano," Cam added.

"No doubt." She wrapped her arms around him.

"My mother used to tell me," he murmured, feeling Mia's lips run down his neck, "I had one foot on the road to hell."

She crossed in front of him and straddled him as he sat on the stool. Cam felt the heat from her skin through all the layers of clothing between them. "And," Mia said, kissing him, "now here you are."

He stood up and carried her with him to the couch. As he bent his head toward her, she touched her hand to his lips. "Tell me your darkest secret."

Cam laughed. "I wanted to be a travel writer," he admitted, his breath warm against her throat. "I wanted to go to the Yucatan, and Singapore, and Culebra, and Prague and tell the world what they'd been missing." His voice dropped to a whisper. "I would have been good at it. I know I would."

Mia pictured Cam on the steps of the white temple in Sagaing, walking along the gray ribbon of Burma's Irrawaddy River. She saw a pencil tucked behind his ear and a notepad in his back pocket. "Why didn't you do it?"

"I had to come back here. When my father died, I was supposed to be the clan chief. I couldn't do that without a permanent address."

"You could do it now," she said.

Cam closed his eyes and thought of Mia in white linen, barefoot and sunburnt beside him on a catamaran that wove its way through Sail Rock and Mustique and the other Windward Islands. He shrugged, pushing away what had not been meant to be, and touched Mia's cheek.

"What's *your* deep dark secret?" he asked.

Mia blinked at him. "I love you."

The words stunned him. They were simple ones, ones he knew had been coming, ones he had heard a million times before from his wife. It made no sense to him, but just as Cam knew that his soul belonged to Mia, this ordinary phrase belonged to Allie. He did not want to hear it from Mia, could not bear to hear it, because it reminded him of the colossal price he had to pay and the pain he would have to cause to take what should have always been his.

Cam rolled away from Mia and sat down on the floor. He rested his head on the heels of his hands and took a deep breath.

Mia scuttled to the corner of the couch, and when he turned she was huddled into a knot, as if she were trying to make herself smaller than was physically possible. "I shouldn't have said that," she murmured, picking at her cuticles. "I'm sorry."

Cam reached up behind him and squeezed her hand. "Don't be sorry." He hesitated, weighing the fences that his mind was already building against the fire that had crawled from his belly to his throat. "I love you too."

Mia became still. "You do?"

Cam nodded. He was feeling faint, and he did not know if this was because of the lilacs and the marigolds that seemed to fill every corner of the shop, or because—in the blink of an eye—he had turned into someone he no longer knew. "God help me," he said, "but I do."

Mia placed her hand, light and cool, on the back of his neck. "God has nothing to do with this."

Mornings at Sunny Side Up, the local coffee shop, were crowded, full of colorful locals who had implicit reservations and tacitly assigned seats and could order the usual just by nodding at the short-order cook. Every now and then Cam stopped in too. He was rarely hungry enough to take more than the coffee pushed at him, since Allie unfailingly made him a healthy breakfast; but it was a good place to sit if you wanted to know which teenager was most likely to set the bleachers on fire after graduation, or whose wife had been wearing sunglasses to hide a bruise on her face.

With Allie gone, though, there was nothing for breakfast but cold cereal. So Cam had driven into town, come into the restaurant, and ordered scrambled eggs with bacon. It was placed in front of him within two minutes, runny and malodorous.

Cam looked up at Vera, the morning waitress. "That's amazing," he said. "I've never seen someone cook an egg so fast."

She shrugged. "He's looking to impress you. Don't be shocked if you find shells mixed in."

Cam spread the paper napkin in his lap and lifted the first forkful to his mouth. The eggs were greasy, almost unfinished, the sort of thing Allie wouldn't have been caught dead serving. He lifted his coffee cup and scanned the restaurant, trying to match the puzzle-piece edges of names and faces as he nodded and smiled. In the rear of the establishment was Elizabeth Fraser, children's librarian, and Wheelock's newest citizen—her three-week-old baby. In the front window was Joshua Douglas, a nine-year-old kid who as far as Cam knew was on the straight and narrow, but all the same, shouldn't be sitting alone in a coffee shop having his breakfast. He made a mental note to check on the Douglas family as the man sitting to the left of him said goodbye and vacated his stool at the counter, leaving Cam an unobstructed view of Jamie MacDonald lowering a newspaper from his face.

Jamie stared at him levelly. "Chief MacDonald."

Cam snorted and turned back to his coffee.

"Enjoying your breakfast?" Jamie asked pleasantly.

Cam swallowed. "I *was,*" he said. He fixed his attention on his plate, wondering what it was about Jamie MacDonald that rubbed him the wrong way. He'd been around criminals before, some far more dangerous than Jamie was, but this one set him on edge. Even more so, now that things had started up with Mia. Cam could not look the man in the eye and know Jamie was being tried for murdering his wife, without feeling, somehow, that *he* was the one who should feel guilty.

If Jamie was telling the truth, he had done the one thing he least wanted to do, just because it was what his wife had wanted. Jamie, the felon. Whereas Cam, the upstanding police chief, could not get past what he *most* wanted to do: push thoughts of his wife aside and be with Mia Townsend.

Disgusted with his own absence of honor and the line of reasoning that was turning Jamie into a plaster saint, Cam clattered his fork against his plate. In his peripheral vision, he watched Jamie separate the folds of the newspaper and hold out a section to him. "Sports page?"

Cam grunted and took it from him. He stared blindly at the statistics for the regional high school teams and finally shoved the paper beneath his plate. Without looking at Jamie he rested his chin on his clenched fists. "Angus all right?" he asked.

He could sense Jamie's head swinging slowly toward him as he realized that Cam had taken the first stab at a civilized conversation. But before Jamie had a chance to answer, the door of the coffee shop flew open, crashing against its frame and ringing the sleigh bells that hung from its handle. A man in a black raincoat with wild yellow eyes was waving a Beretta.

He advanced on Jamie, who shrank back against his stool and paled. In the background, Elizabeth Fraser's baby had started to cry. "James MacDonald," the man hissed, "no one but God has the right to take a life." He released the safety on the gun.

Cam stood up and pulled his own gun from his holster in a swift motion. "Police," he said, in case the nut couldn't see for himself the badge and uniform that were as plain as day. "Drop your weapon."

The man's eyes didn't waver from Jamie. "No. I've been called to do this."

Cam glanced over his shoulder, motioning for the other patrons of the restaurant to file out slowly through the door. "Do what? Take Jamie's life? I thought that was only up to God."

"I'm an *agent* of God."

"Of course." Cam cleared his throat. "You can shoot him," he said, ignoring the shock on Jamie's face, "but then I'd have to shoot you."

If the man weighed that as a consequence, he didn't show it. He started running toward Jamie, screaming biblical proverbs and interjecting these with cries of "Murderer!" In the split second that lengthens with danger, Cam realized Jamie was doing nothing to defend himself. Jamie was looking at the man, waiting, really, for the lunatic to shoot at close range.

Cam leaped on the man, grabbing his wrist and yanking it up so that the gun fired into the ceiling, raining plaster down on Jamie. He wrestled the man down to the floor, pulling his wrists behind his back so that he could snap on the handcuffs and spit Miranda into his ear.

The short-order cook came out of the kitchen, visibly shaken, and pointed to his damaged ceiling. "What do I do about that?" he asked.

"Take it up with the mayor," Cam suggested, hauling his prisoner to his feet. "Come on."

Jamie stood up from his stool. The man pursed his cheeks and spat at Jamie, a glob of saliva landing on the left side of his neck. "I may have taken a life," Jamie said softly to the man. "But it wasn't much of one." Then he looked up at Cam. "Thank you."

Any compassion he'd felt for Jamie MacDonald five minutes ago had vanished, and Cam did not even remember trying to make polite conversation with him over the morning paper. He did not remember the moment when he realized that, amazingly, Jamie seemed to welcome an unprovoked attack. All he could see was the milling crowd outside the restaurant and the bent head of the sobbing psycho in front of him. All he could feel was his heart pumping out adrenaline in a rush that reminded him of making love to Mia. Cam glared at Jamie, redirecting the anger and the blame. "If this happens again in my town," he said heatedly, "I'll let him shoot."

*C*am sat in his boxers on the couch in the flower shop, reading a paper from three days ago that had been wrapped around a root ball. Mia had stepped out to get them some food—even Romeo and Juliet, she'd said, had stopped for dinner. The front page was missing, so he scanned the World Briefs, the tiny snippets of stories that always left you wondering what hadn't been said.

An oil tanker had sunk near Alaska; the IRA had confessed to setting a bomb at a Devonshire post office; and on a German army base in Fulda, a GI had beheaded the man who was having an affair with his wife.

Cam pulled the paper closer. The U.S. soldier had suspected his wife of adultery, had chopped off the head of his rival, and had placed it in a plastic bag beside his wife's hospital bed. His wife was being treated for complications in pregnancy.

The soldier had submitted quietly to the arrest. The headless body of the other man was found in a phone booth at an army airfield.

Cam stood up and walked away from the couch, stepping on the wrinkled paper that had fallen beneath his feet. "Fuck," he muttered. "Fuck."

He walked into the storeroom and stood in the bathroom in front of the tiny mirror. It was chipped in the corner and there was very little direct light, but Cam had no trouble making out the stark lines of his face.

He did not see a police chief, or a clan chief, or a husband. He did not see a family man, or a good citizen, or anyone else he could respect.

He recognized the anger in his eyes, the dare-me attitude that mocked anyone for criticizing his right to do something he wanted for once in his whole damn life. He saw a flush on his cheeks and a burn in his eyes that he remembered as signs of falling in love.

He knew that he would no more walk through the adjoining curtain and ask Mia to leave his life than he would relish cutting off his left arm. He told himself he could not change what had already been done.

Then Cam left the bathroom and glanced at the desk, where Allie had a framed photo of the two of them, kneeling in the sand dunes on Nantucket. He picked up the picture, rubbing his thumb over the glass, choosing not to look at Allie but instead at his own image. He frowned at the photo. Was it just his imagination, or did his smile seem forced?

He had not thought of Allie during these past three days; he had not allowed himself to do so. But she was coming home and he had never wanted to hurt her and he loved Mia and he could not have it all.

He did not want to put Mia through the inevitable confrontation that would come. He thought of the two of them as he had once before, on a catamaran in the hot sun, and knew that although he was chained to his town and his circumstances, Mia was free to fly.

It was what made her so attractive.

If you loved someone, really loved them, would you let them go?

Out of nowhere, Cam thought of Jamie MacDonald.

Feeling the room close in around him, Cam tossed the photograph back on Allie's desk, cracking the glass of its frame. He pulled his pants from the couch and stepped into them; he buttoned up his shirt. He was just tucking it in when Mia opened the door of the flower shop.

She brought winter with her, wrapped in loose, flighty threads around her thin parka. "I got ham and cheese and a meatball sub."

"I can't do this," Cam said.

Mia dropped the paper bag and took a step toward him.

He held up his hands. "I can't," he said, his voice breaking. He did not let himself touch her as he passed, but she followed him just a fraction of movement behind, like a shadow he could not shake.

Watchell Spitlick and his wife, Marie, had owned The Pickle Barrel, a mom-and-pop store in the center of Cummington.

When they retired last year, the Spitlicks had taken the trappings of their trade and resurrected the place they'd run for forty-five years in their own house.

Allie sat beside a huge white freezer that was not functional but still urged her in bold print to drink Moxie. She held a sweating glass of iced tea in her left hand; her right hand stroked a blind tabby cat that made its way from place to place by bumping into the furniture. Watchell was smiling at her from a cracked leather chair; Marie perched lightly on a stack of fabric bolts.

"This is quite a collection," Allie said politely.

"Well"—Watchell nodded—"you never know what people are going to need." He beamed at her.

Marie tapped his knee. "Now, Bud, Mrs. MacDonald didn't come to talk business." She frowned at Allie. "What *did* bring you here, dear?" Before Allie could answer, Marie smacked herself lightly on the forehead. "How stupid of me. You must be a relative of Jamie's, and he's not at home." She darted to a bookshelf stacked with Farina and health tonics and an assortment of pipe cleaners, and began to rummage behind the clutter. "I know Maggie left me a key, it's here somewhere . . . Remember, Bud, when we watered the plants for them last summer—"

"Mrs. Spitlick," Allie interrupted, "I have a key to the house." She set her tea down on a tremendous barrel that served as a coffee table. "I need to speak to you about Jamie and Maggie."

"Terrific kids," Watchell boomed.

"We love them like our own," Marie added.

Allie opened her mouth to break the unfortunate news, but then knotted her hands in her lap. "I wonder . . ." she said carefully. "I'm a distant cousin of Jamie's, and I haven't seen him in years." She offered her most ingenuous smile. "What's he like, now?"

"Oh," Marie said, fluttering back to her fabric seat. "You've never known the like. Jamie's got a good solid head on his shoulders. Works with computers or something or other, you know that fancy stuff I can't get into my head. Shovels our driveway out all winter because he doesn't want Watchell to exert himself."

Allie was smiling so hard her face was beginning to hurt. "And has he been married long?"

Marie and Watchell exchanged a look. "You haven't met Maggie, then?" Marie said.

Allie shook her head. "I— No. This is a surprise visit."

Marie pursed her lips. "There isn't another pair like those two. Joined at the hip, you'd think. Why, I remember when Maggie first moved into the house—Jamie had been a bachelor for a few years—they holed up in there for days at a time. Watchell and I would see the pizza delivery trucks coming and going, and every now and again I'd notice a flash across the upstairs windows, one of them chasing the other." She smiled, her eyes crinkling in the corners. "Don't think anyone ever told Jamie the honeymoon was supposed to end after a couple of weeks."

"You know them well, then."

"Oh, yes," Marie said.

"And Jamie's devoted to Maggie?"

"Like nothing I've ever seen."

Allie stood up. "I think I'll wait back at the house," she said, mentally checking the Spitlicks off as viable character witnesses.

Watchell peered out the window toward Jamie's house. "You been waiting long? Seems I don't recall seeing a car there for a couple of days."

"That's why I came to check with you," Allie improvised. "Jamie must have forgotten I was coming." She could feel the blush of her lies staining the collar of her turtleneck.

"Oh, I hope that's all it is." Marie looked at her husband. "You don't think anything's happened to Maggie?"

The words stopped Allie in the middle of shrugging into her coat. "What do you mean?"

"She's been ill," Marie said. *"Cancer."* She whispered the word as if it might creep over the threshold of her own house. She began to walk Allie to the front door. "It's a good thing you're here, if that's the case. Family's a blessing." She turned toward the living room. "Bud, you walk Mrs. MacDonald back."

"Oh, I'm fine," Allie protested.

"It's dark and I won't hear of anything else," Marie said.

Allie waited for Watchell Spitlick to zip up his jacket, then offer her his arm down the concrete front steps. Allie was several steps across the lawn when she realized that her escort had stopped moving. Watchell was staring at the bare curb in front of Jamie's house as if there was something there.

"Few months ago," he said, his words coming out in round puffs of cold breath, "Maggie took a bad turn in the middle of the night. Some kind of reaction to the medicine she was on, screwed up her lungs so's she couldn't breathe on her own. Ambulance came, must've been two in the morning, and when they brought Maggie out on this fold-up stretcher, Jamie was standing right next to her. He wasn't wearing a stitch, and he didn't seem to even notice. I can't look at that house anymore without seeing those flashing red lights all over the street, and Jamie, bare-ass naked, kissing Maggie as if he could breathe his own life into her."

Allie opened her mouth to speak, but could not find any words. Watchell ushered her across Jamie's front lawn. "There you go," he said, waiting until Allie had unlocked the door. "You make sure to call when Jamie gets home." He smiled. "We want to know everything's all right."

On Sunday, Cam had every intention of going to Mass. He put on his nicest suit and his red tartan tie and he parked in a spot that wasn't too ridiculously far from the church. He spoke to his great-aunt Chloe and he helped his dispatcher, who was nine months pregnant, waddle up the hill in the center of town. He explained to everyone who asked that Allie was out of town on a family errand, but he didn't go into any more detail. When he saw Jamie MacDonald himself helping Angus up the steps that led to the church, he even smiled.

He wanted to be cleansed. He could remember being forced, as a kid, into sitting through Sunday Mass. He had spent most of the time thinking about his new basketball, or about the pickup game of ice hockey over at Dundee Pond that started at noon, but he had always left the church feeling a little lighter, breathing a little easier. At the time, he had not given in to the spirituality of religion, but had simply seen the church itself as a wonderful machine in a Dr. Seuss book, the kind where you walked in one end and popped out the other, a whole different color or shape or set of beliefs in your mind.

Cam had not gone to confession this past Saturday. He hadn't wanted to. He felt that if he spoke of the feelings he had for Mia, they'd lessen in intensity, their color and vibrance growing paler and paler as the words diffused in the air.

He walked through the main double doors of the church and was handed a pamphlet detailing the order of the Mass. But there was a backlog of people waiting to get into the pews, and Cam stepped out of line, hoping for a few more minutes of the cool autumn air.

He stood at the top step, which was worn down in the center from years of piety. Spread at his feet was his town. *His,* as it had been his father's and his grandfather's. He knew every street in Wheelock and every resident. He knew which shopkeeper on Main Street was the first to shovel the walk after a snowstorm. He knew which kids he'd find drinking beer behind the bleachers of the high school on the longest, reddest night of the summer.

He let his eyes sweep from left to right, from the coffee shop to the post office to the station, where Zandy was just letting himself in. He looked down at the bottom of the church steps and saw Mia.

He had not known she was Catholic, a thought which pounded dully in his head. He knew that she was allergic to chocolate, that her skin was very sensitive to cold, that she had a small square birthmark on her right thigh, but he did not know her religion. He did not even know where she had been born, or her middle name.

In spite of his willpower, he started to walk down the steps of the church.

She was gone before he reached the bottom. Cam stretched his hand out, aware that people were watching and starting to whisper. He touched only the thin, chilly air. And he walked back to his car, thinking that he hadn't really wanted to go to Mass at all.

Mia felt awful, so she knew she was in love. Her head swam, her shoulders ached, her skin no longer seemed to fit. She spent hours making flower arrangements without a single splash of color. At the Inn she turned on the TV and watched reruns of "The Love Connection" with Kafka curled on her belly.

She wished she'd never come to Wheelock.

She could not believe she had wasted so many years before arriving.

Yet what she loved most about Cameron MacDonald was not the way he looked in the waving light of a candle, or the image of his straight red hair mixed and tumbled with her own. It was what he represented that was so attractive: a steady mortgage, a niche, unequivocal respect. Cam had a place in the world that was unshakable. Granted, it had been carved for him by his ancestors, and it involved a life that by definition excluded Mia herself, but it was very seductive to someone who had grown up never really knowing where she fit in.

She pictured each of his conditional titles as another string tethering Cam firmly to the ground: clan chief, police chief, friend, confidant. Ask anyone in the town who Cam was, and they'd be able to give you an answer: *He's my cousin. He's the laird of Carrymuir. He's my husband.*

Mia moved Kafka off her lap and curled into a ball. She closed her eyes, making certain that she could picture Cam as she had last seen him, standing in the doors of the church: his hair windblown, his tie flying back over his shoulder, his hands fisted at his sides as if he could actually fight what he was feeling.

There was no use in putting it off any longer. Mia stuffed her clothes into her knapsack, wrapping her old bonsai in a button-down oxford shirt and giving it room to breathe at the top. Then she turned off the television and the lights and drew the shades, so the room was completely dark. She listened intently to the sounds that came muffled through the carpet—the innkeeper's draw of a key from the cubbyhole, the whoosh of the heavy front door as it opened, the squeal of the lazy wheel on the bellboy's luggage cart. She waited for these noises to fall away into a background hum, so she could hear the subtle sounds of a world gone gray. Then, sitting down at the table with a piece of Inn stationery she could barely see, Mia began to write. And when she was satisfied that she had given him all that she could, she sealed the envelope, scooped up the cat, and locked the door behind her.

# PART II

Nothing emboldens sin so much as mercy.

—Shakespeare, *Timon of Athens*

Did you know that I have a picture of you? It's not one I took; it somehow made its way into my possession months later. You're in the background—someone was photographing something else and you just happened to be there. You're sitting under a tree, wearing a big sweatshirt, and your knees are drawn up to hold a book. But you're not reading, you're looking at the camera.

You're slightly blurry in the photo, but I like it anyway. You've got this little knowing smile on your face, like you realized you were going to be in someone else's photo, and you didn't give a damn. That smile—that's what gets me about the picture. It covers so many different things that I think of when I think of you. It shows that you're happy, that you're concentrating, that you're curious. I guess mostly it shows someone I loved.

I remember so much about you.

# NINE

When Allie told Pauline Cioffi that Maggie MacDonald was dead, Pauline closed her eyes tightly, as if blocking Allie out of her vision would also dispel the news. When she opened her eyes and Allie was still standing there, she sank her teeth into her bottom lip and nodded sharply before turning away. "Well," she said stoically, "that was to be expected."

Allie waited until she had been invited into the house to tell Pauline that Jamie was on trial for murdering his wife. She expected another denial, maybe even a burst of outrage, but Pauline only pulled a pair of socks out of a pristine pile of white laundry and knotted them together. "I suppose," she sighed, "that was to be expected too."

Pauline was Maggie's best friend, or so said the list that Jamie had written for Allie. They had met in an aerobics class given by the local church, the only three hours during the week that Pauline was away from her children. To prolong the holiday, she took Maggie out for coffee one morning, and it became a tradition.

She was built like an apple and her house was a tangle of toys, cloth diapers, and single shoes. She invited Allie to take a seat in the den, but did not offer her coffee. Instead, she plopped one damp, sticky toddler in a playpen, shooed the others out of the room, and listened as Allie related the circumstances of Maggie's death.

"It doesn't surprise you that Jamie's on trial for murder?" Allie said. "Did you know him very well?"

Pauline shrugged. "Well enough to know that when Maggie asked him to kill her, he would."

Allie leaned forward in her seat. "You *knew* that Maggie was going to ask him?"

Pauline nodded, as if the conversation she'd had with Maggie had been as mundane as a discussion of the weather, or brands of cereal. Allie's mind began to spin with the implications of putting Pauline on a witness stand for Jamie. Would her story uphold the confession Jamie had signed for Cam? Or would it only be dismissed as hearsay?

"Jamie MacDonald is a blessing and a curse."

Allie's head snapped up. "What do you mean by that?"

"Maggie says it to me all the time—" she said, and then corrected herself. *"Said* it to me." In the low light of the afternoon Allie could see the film of tears over Pauline's eyes. "I'm sorry. I thought I was ready for this. I mean, I knew that it was coming, and Maggie and I had talked about it, but when you get right down to it, preparing doesn't make it hurt any less." She took a deep breath and faced Allie again. "Tell me again why you're here. I'll help Maggie any way I can."

"You said that Jamie was a blessing and a curse," Allie prompted.

"Oh, yes. Maggie loved him to death." She stopped abruptly, realizing the implications of the idiom she'd used. "Maggie loved him to death," she repeated softly. "She knew that Jamie would have done anything for her, so she figured that if she pushed him hard enough, he'd make it easier when the time came." She looked up at Allie. "Did you know her? Maggie?"

Allie shook her head. "I wish I had. I wish I could."

Pauline walked over to the playpen and retrieved her youngest child, a little girl who began to chew on the long rope of her mother's braid. "It's impossible to tell you what Maggie was like unless you figure Jamie into the situation. They were inseparable, I swear. But not through any doing of Maggie's. I used to tell her I'd swap lives with her in a second—trade her all the dirty diapers and the school lunches and the carpooling for a man who was hanging on my every word, and Maggie said it wasn't the bliss that I thought it was. I think she felt bad because Jamie couldn't let go and she couldn't hold on as tight as he did."

She bounced the baby in her arms. "She told me that if it was the other way around—if Jamie had the cancer—she wouldn't be able to . . . you know. Said she'd worry too much about what was going to happen to her, after. She said it wasn't like that for Jamie, since he wouldn't imagine a future that didn't have Maggie in it too." Pauline glanced up. "What Maggie said to me—about the dying—was that she didn't have a choice anymore. She knew she'd be using Jamie horribly, but she didn't even care, if that was what it took to stop the pain."

Allie watched Pauline press a kiss to her daughter's tangled hair, and swallowed thickly. "How's Jamie doing?"

Allie took a deep breath. "He's angry. And frustrated. Lonely. I think he's starting to feel guilty."

Pauline nodded. "Just like Maggie." She waved her free arm around the room, encompassing the clutter and the discord that made up a family. "She was jealous of me. Me! She used to say that whatever else my marriage was, at least it was still equal between Frank and me. But with Jamie, well, no matter how hard he tried—no matter how much he gave—it would only make Maggie feel worse, more guilty for what she couldn't give." Pauline shook her head. "I told her she was crazy."

Allie thought of Jamie clutching Maggie's limp body in the cab of his truck, unwilling to let anyone else close enough to touch her. She thought of the way her heart lodged at the back of her throat every time she opened the door to the police station to visit Cam unannounced, hoping that he would say or do something to make her believe he had wanted her there in the first place. "Crazy," Allie repeated. "I don't think so."

Cam drove out of Wheelock with the windows rolled down, his car speeding down side roads in an effort to outrace his guilt. With the wind blinding him and the cold numbing his fingers and his cheeks, it was easier to forget about Mia. It was easier to concentrate on Allie.

The leaves were starting to fall—crimson and orange, they spiraled like tiny, stiff ballerinas across the windshield of the car. It was nearly time for fall colors, that three-week stretch of October when everyone and his brother decided to visit the Berkshires for the scenery. It was the only month of the year when the Wheelock Inn was filled to capacity; when the coffee shop in town had a line out the front door. Wheelock did not have the grandeur of Great Barrington or the charm of Lenox, but it was one of those towns off Route 8 that still seemed quaint and untouched. The reputation led to problems—tourists seemed to think it was a reconstructed village, like the Shaker town down in Pittsfield, a place too cute for people to really live in. He remembered once, as a child, someone had knocked on the door of the house. His mother had smiled politely at the man in his sleek Italian suit and wing-tip shoes, at the woman on his arm with a feathered cap and a muff made of rabbit fur. "We were wondering," the man had said in a tight Long Island lockjaw, "have you any antiques you'd be willing to sell?"

Cam pulled over to the side of the road and leaned his forehead against the steering wheel. It was impossible to think of the influx of hundreds of strangers into a town that no longer seemed big enough for Mia, Allie, and himself. And with this damned murder trial in the local papers, Wheelock was guaranteed to become a circus.

Cam stepped out of the car and slammed the door shut, realizing as he stretched to his full height that he was still wearing a tie and a jacket, the trappings of a morning at Mass. He hooked his finger into the knot at his neck and pulled, loosening his tie. He unbuttoned the top of his shirt. Then he took off his shoes and socks and set them on the hood of the car.

He went barefoot all the time in the house, in spite of Allie's warnings about drafts and colds, but the last time he'd run free outdoors had been seven years before. It was early October, just as it was now, and Allie had shown up at the station with a picnic. "Come on," she'd said. "No one's going to commit a crime on a day as beautiful as this."

They had been dating for a few months. Cam liked her enough and had become accustomed to spending Sunday afternoons at Allie's apartment, reading the newspaper. He knew that when she looked at him, she was seeing him at the altar of the church, holding out a gold band, but this did not bother him. If he wanted to get married, he would do so in his own time. He had been forced into coming back to Wheelock, forced into succeeding his father as police chief, but no one was going to make him sign the rest of his life away.

Allie had wanted to eat behind the football field at the high school—some misguided sense of nostalgia for their roots, he supposed—but Cam insisted that he'd only take time off for lunch if he got to pick the picnic site. Allie agreed, as he had known she would, and he had driven her in one of the cruisers toward Wee Loch at the northern end of town.

He remembered looking across at her when they came to a stoplight. He had wanted her to look up at him and smile—he'd silently *willed* this to happen—but Allie had been fixated on the dashboard of the car. Without glancing at Cam, she'd pointed to a button. "Are those the lights?" She gently traced the button with her finger.

Cam laughed and covered her hand with his own. "Go ahead," he said. "Now's your big chance."

Allie pushed the button for the flashing lights, and they sped toward the lake without the siren. When Cam pulled into the shade of the trees at the edge of the water, he put the cruiser into park and sat back, arms crossed, watching Allie. "Well?"

"I feel very privileged. Of course, I couldn't really see them from in here."

Cam grinned. "You'd rather be an observer than a part of the action?"

"Well," Allie said, "that depends on what's being observed."

Cam insisted they leave their shoes in the car—what was a picnic with shoes? He helped her carry the Playmate slowly across the stretch of grass, giving time for Allie's feet to feel out acorns and stones he did not notice. Allie had brought huge submarine sandwiches—pastrami on French bread, Italian salami and provolone, roast beef and boursin. She'd packed a thermos of peach iced tea and a small container of red potato salad. There were, for dessert, individual apple tarts. Allie told him that she'd just thrown this together on the spur of the moment, but Cam knew from the bruised skin beneath her eyes that she had been planning this for days and had stayed up late to cook for him.

To his surprise, he liked the idea of that very much.

He watched her kneel on the ground to open the Playmate cooler.

She unpacked half of the contents in an array to her left before she turned to Cam. "I forgot a blanket," she said, as if this was the worst thing in the world. "I cannot believe I forgot the stupid blanket."

She looked like she was going to cry, and that was just about the last thing Cam thought he'd be able to handle, so he jumped to his feet. "I ought to have something in the car," he said, and he ran back to the road, but only found emergency flares and a spare jack. When he walked back toward the lake, Allie was waiting, her hands in her lap and still filled with the apple tarts. He started to tell her they'd have to make do, but the trust in her eye stopped him. Cam had seen it before on the face of nearly every townsperson who'd attended his father's funeral and had, afterward, put himself blindly into Cam's care. Cam knew the expression, and the burden of responsibility that slogged in his chest whenever he faced it. But on Allie, trust looked different. Cam saw himself as Allie did, and for the first time he began to believe it was possible to be someone's everyday hero.

He did not remember what he said to her, or how he came to stick his knee into one of the tarts as he caught Allie up in his arms and fell with her onto a blanket nature loaned them, made of the brilliant gold of fallen maple leaves. It was not lust that overwhelmed Cam. It was the sense that this feeling of invincibility would fade unless he could somehow ensure its permanence. And the surest way was to take the person who made him feel like this, and make her a part of himself.

Cam had pulled at her clothes, frustrated by something as simple as buttons, until Allie gently pushed him back and freed them herself. As if it were perfectly natural to be lying half-naked in the middle of the day, she held out her arms to Cam, and he fell to her, tugging at her hair, pressing her back on the crinkling leaves, bruising her throat with his kisses. Even now, years later, when he closed his eyes and pictured Allie, it was with her eyes heavy and her face turned to the side, those vivid yellow leaves tangled in her hair as if she were backed by the sun itself.

When he came inside her he was so focused on how warm she was and how well they fit that he did not notice the leaves which fell from overhead to prick at his shoulders, or the quick rigidity of Allie beneath him, or the quiet cry she muffled against his neck.

There was a pressure, and a yielding, but Cam believed this was some internal barrier he'd constructed giving way as he accepted what he had always been meant to do.

He did not realize that Allie Gordon had been, at twenty-five, a virgin, until he rolled to his side and saw against the gold leaves the smear of red, bright as a sugar maple, between her thighs.

Cam jumped to his feet and began to pull on his clothes. He did not speak until he was fully dressed, and by this time Allie had curled up into a small ball, her arms around her knees, her clothes draped protectively about her. "Why didn't you tell me?" he demanded, standing over her.

"You didn't ask," Allie said.

With a curse, Cam stalked off toward the lake, kicking at the leaves. He stood there for several minutes, until he realized that Allie, now dressed, was standing behind him. "You're mad at me."

"Hell, yes," Cam said.

Allie shivered a little. "It doesn't change anything. It's the eighties. I wasn't trying to trap you into a relationship. And it probably would have happened eventually anyway."

"That isn't the point," Cam muttered. "The first time should have been different. In a bed, for God's sake. Slower."

Allie beamed. "Then you're *not* mad at me. You're mad at yourself."

She put her arms around him from behind and rested her cheek against his back. They stood that way for a while, watching the leaves chase each other across the lake like pixies. Finally, Cam disentangled Allie's hands from his waist and walked her to the car. "I'll get the cooler," he said, not wanting her to go back there.

He crossed the road again, barefoot. Before picking up the Playmate he kicked the leaves at the spot where they had been, covering up the evidence of Allie's pain. When he turned, he saw Allie standing in front of the police cruiser, her hands on her hips. She'd turned on the ignition and the flashing lights, and the circling blue beam caught her every few seconds, freezing her into something pale and still and lovely, like an angel.

Shelley Pass, the first town off Route 8 once you left Wheelock, suffered from the same fate as its neighbor: it too was a prototypical New England town set in the beauty of the Berkshires and overwhelmed by visitors when the leaves turned. But it had the added attraction of being the birthplace of the poet who'd penned the verse about Little Boy Blue, and in the town center, across from the church, was a bronze statue of the lazy pint-sized shepherd, clutching his horn and asleep beside a haystack. For reasons Cam could not fathom, people actually traveled to see this statue, to take photos beside it.

Cam drove through the little town, his shoes tucked into the passenger seat, his toes curled over the brake pedal at the rusted stop signs.

He did not know what he was looking for, exactly, but he did know that he was looking. He passed the landmarks of any small New England town: barber, fire station, post office. Cam leaned closer to the windshield, as if this might make some boutique appear. He would give it five more minutes, and then he'd just drive to the nearest flower shop that did not have Mia Townsend working in it and buy Allie a dozen roses.

He turned down a side road purely on a whim, and at the end of a dirty cul-de-sac was a prettily painted sign. *MEENA AND HEDDY'S,* it said, in purple script. *FINE ART AND OTHERWISE.* Cam smiled at that. What was unfine art? Hooked rugs and paint-by-numbers?

When he entered the shop, he had to duck his head to accommodate the low ceilings. There was no one in the shop but a small woman wearing a caftan that covered her from her neck to her ankles. "Hello. Can I help you?"

Cam grinned at her. She came up, maybe, to his ribs. "I'm looking for a gift for my wife," he said. "I think I'll just poke around."

The woman shrugged. "Suit yourself."

Cam walked around the clutter, remembering Allie telling him to shoot her with his Smith and Wesson if she ever let her shop get, as she called it, cute and kitschy. He fingered heart-shaped cut stones and hand-potted mugs with clay lizards as handles. There was a small collection of pet rocks and lampshades encrusted with seashells. He glanced at watercolor paintings of different spaniel breeds, sterling silver hanging earrings, embroidered vests. "Is this for a birthday?" the woman asked.

Cam spun around. *No,* he thought, *it's to soothe my conscience.* "She's a florist. Anything along that line?"

She led him to wreaths made of dried primroses, and raffia baskets spilling with ivy, but these were things that Allie had in her own shop. Resigned, he shook his head. "Thanks for your time," he began.

"Wait." For a tiny woman, her voice held the power of a drill sergeant. Cam stopped in his tracks. "My sister's out back working on something. Maybe we can come to an arrangement."

She was bent over a table, painstakingly cutting a sliver of blue. It was the last jigsaw piece in a stunning pane of stained-glass that depicted three graceful daffodils against a sapphire background. Their thin stems were a light gem green, their centers as red as fire. The daffodils themselves were the shade of the silver maple leaves that Cam would always associate with Allie. And the blue background was the color of Mia's eyes.

He realized that having this panel hang in his living room for the rest of his life would be penance enough.

"I'll take it," he said, knowing that price would not be a factor. He waited for the woman to wrap it in layers of gauze and tissue, and lay it with a last caress across the back seat of his car. There was a certain irony in buying something that was, by name, already considered stained. The whole way home Cam thought of blueberries and blood and other indelible things, and he wondered how long it took for a soul to come clean.

Graham MacPhee had lost the rhythm of sleep. He hadn't made it through a night since he'd accepted the police chief's offer to take on Jamie MacDonald as a client. And now that he'd officially entered a defense of temporary insanity at the hearing, he couldn't bed down for more than five minutes before waking in a cold sweat and wondering why he hadn't decided to try the case on the principles of euthanasia.

He stood in a pair of silk boxer shorts, staring out at the stars from the balcony of his apartment. The problem with a euthanasia defense was that he only wanted to win. He didn't want to set a precedent. And if he created a huge media circus with an unorthodox defense strategy, who the hell knew how it would affect a jury?

Not to mention the fact that for the rest of time, whenever someone killed someone else without eyewitnesses, he was going to try to claim the other person asked him to do it.

There were too many folds in a mercy killing defense; folds you could get trapped in at a trial and never make your way out of. Who would have to give consent, for example? Jamie had Maggie's permission to kill her, but what if she had been comatose, unable to speak her mind?

And who said Maggie's consent was all that was needed? What about her best friend? Her aunt Lou in Chicago? Her old college roommate? Anyone else who knew her, who was a part of her life, who wanted her around a little longer?

And if you had consent, did someone have to give approval? A doctor, who said the cause was past hope? What illnesses were past hope, anyway? Everyone knew the story of someone who'd come out of a fifteen-year coma. Did an illness have to be protracted? Painful? Fatal? Did a person have to be sick at all?

Then there were the mechanics of death. Smothering was okay, for example, but a gunshot to the head was out of the question.

Graham sat down in a cold metal deck chair and propped his feet on the railing of his balcony. There were a million stars out there, and just as many facets to a euthanasia defense. You couldn't possibly make a law or set a precedent, because the very next case would break it with hairline circumstances.

Jamie MacDonald might not appear to be insane, might not even have been temporarily insane when he murdered his wife, but this was something Graham could work around. Euthanasia . . . well, euthanasia was not a sure thing. He sighed and stood up, glancing over the roofs of the many houses of Wheelock, lit at simple intervals by hissing streetlights. He wondered if Jamie was staring into the night too.

When Cam arrived at the station the next day, it was late in the morning. He unlocked his office and set the stained-glass panel on the floor behind his desk—Allie was due back that afternoon, and he'd brought it in case she came to the office before stopping off at home. Then he shrugged out of his coat and hung it on the hook on the back of the door.

Sitting at his desk, he leaned back in his chair and let his mind wander. When there was a knock on the door, he jumped. He hollered to come in, and the door swung open to reveal Hannah, leading Jamie MacDonald. "Chief," she said, "it's noon."

Cam looked at his watch. It was actually 11:59. Damn Jamie; he'd followed Martha Sully's strictures to a tee—he had yet to arrive later than noon to check in with Cam. And it was always the same—Hannah knocked at the door, pulling Jamie behind her like a recalcitrant schoolboy. Jamie would ask him how he was doing that day, and Cam would only grunt and nod his head in dismissal.

"Chief MacDonald," Jamie said pleasantly, filling the door-frame. He always called Cam that, and for some reason, it always rankled. "How are you this morning?"

Cam looked up from his desk, a frown on his face. "I wanted to thank you," Jamie said quietly. "For loaning me your wife."

At the words, Cam's blood stopped running. He stared at Jamie with a fury banked in his eyes, uncomfortable with the inti-macy—however false—that the statement suggested. "Go away," he muttered, his voice as thin and sharp as the letter opener he had inadvertently picked up to brandish like a weapon in his left hand.

It took Cam most of the afternoon to calm himself down. He was still sitting in his darkened office, his head on his desk, taking deep, cleansing breaths, when Hannah walked in with the day's mail. "Good Lord," she said, stepping behind him to draw the cur-tains and crack open the window. "It's like a mausoleum." She tossed the packet of envelopes over Cam's bent head. "There's a phone bill in there," she added as she turned to leave. "One of the calls to Canada is a personal call I already docked from my pay."

Sighing, Cam began to sift through the mail. Junk mail, junk mail, a request from a lawyer, more junk mail, the phone bill. And a smaller envelope from the Wheelock Inn that had Cam's head throbbing before he even opened it.

*Cameron,* she said, *please give these keys to Allie and make my apolo-gies. The copper wire on the bonsais should be taken off completely sometime in February.*

*There isn't anything I can tell you, except that I cannot stay here. It's the coward's way out; I'm sorry about that.*

*The other thing I have to say is that I have cared about and slept with a number of men, but I've made love only with you.*

By the time Cam came to the end of the letter, tracing the imprint the heavy pencil had made as if it might hold some further clue to where Mia had gone, he was shaking. He ran out of his office without his coat, without a word to Hannah. Dashing across the street to the Wheelock Inn, he stormed through the front doors and demanded the key to Mia's old room. "But, Chief—" the clerk began, before Cam cut him off with a raised hand.

The room was empty. It did not smell of her, but of white, fresh sheets and cleaning fluids. The King James Bible was in its customary place in the nightstand, the television remote was balanced on top of the console. With the bellboy gaping in the doorway, Cam sank to his knees.

He had forced her out of his mind, and this was the consequence.

He considered for one lovely, irrational moment running back to the station and smashing the stained-glass pane, as if Mia's disappearance was linked to its physical existence and shattering it would bring her back.

Cam sat down on the edge of the bed and curled his knees up to his side, the way Mia had slept in his arms on the couch for three nights. He closed his eyes and tried to feel the slightest ridges in the mattress, adjusting himself where there may or may not have been an imprint of her body. He pretended he was lying just where she had lain, and he whispered this to himself until he believed it was true.

He sat up and swung his legs over the side of the bed. He straightened his tie in the mirror and glanced toward the doorway, but the bellboy had gone. He left the Inn and walked across the street as if he were in complete control. Then he opened the door to the police station.

Allie was standing in his office, holding in her hands the white-tissue-wrapped pane of glass. Her face was bright with a kind of joy that Cam associated with small children, who could find wonder in things they did not understand. "Cam!" she said, her eyes shining, "is this for me?"

\*   \*   \*

$S$he hung the stained-glass panel in the bedroom from a cast-iron hook that had been the former home of a lush, green wandering Jew. "I love it." Allie was sitting cross-legged on the bed beside him, holding her glass of Coke and balancing her dinner plate on her lap. She'd insisted on waiting for him for a late supper and serving it in the bedroom, so that she could look at her new gift as the sun set through it. "I'm going to go away more often," she said.

Cam smiled at his food. The stained-glass reflected itself in a puddle on the comforter that ran just over the edge of his foot. He scooted back a bit, but the color reached toward him again.

When she'd opened the pane in the police station, she had held it to the bright afternoon light, turning it this way and that. She'd gone on and on, trying to describe the color of blue in the panel—how the lighter parts were something beyond robin's-egg, like the color you imagined when you pictured summer; how the darker slices reminded her of a moonless sky. In the end she gave up trying to put the colors into words. They were blues that you had to see for yourself, she decided, and that was the very beauty.

But Cam knew she was wrong. The lighter shade of blue was the color of Mia's eyes the moment before he kissed her; the darker shade was the color of her eyes the moment he drew away.

The last minutes of sunlight burned through the stained-glass, and then left it curiously dull and flat. "I'm never going to get tired of looking at it," Allie announced. "Maybe I'll have it set right into a window."

"There's an idea." Cam shoveled a forkful of potatoes into his mouth and tried to swallow. He knew he was not being fair to Allie—since she'd been gone for the better part of a week, he should have been animated and interested and plying her with questions about her trip—but he could not put Mia from his mind. He was afraid to, thinking it would drive her even farther away than she was right now.

He was going to find her before that happened.

"I think I'm going to take up investigative work," Allie said lightly, and Cam blinked at her, wondering if she had been reading his mind. "I liked scouting around for Jamie." She set down her plate and stretched. "I'd tell you all about it, but"—she lowered her voice here—"it's *classified.*" Then she laughed. "I always wanted to say that. You know, like you're on a jury for a huge murder trial and you can't tell anyone what you know because you've been sworn to secrecy. This is almost as good."

"So you think you'll be able to help the defense?"

"Oh, I think Jamie's going to walk," she said, with unshakable conviction. "I can't tell you who I met with, but it's clear that the people of Cummington think his arrest is a mistake."

"That's not enough to sway a jury," Cam pointed out.

"No," Allie agreed, "but we've got proof that'll make them think twice about Jamie's motive."

"His objective was to kill Maggie. He told me so."

Allie snorted. "Sure, if you want to see it literally. But what if he wasn't himself?" Her eyes brightened, and in their reflection Cam could see the daffodils of the stained-glass pane. "Can you imagine loving someone so much that you completely lose the voice of reason?" Her mouth quirked up at the corners. "It's very romantic, I think."

No, Cam thought, it's a living hell. "I love you," he said thickly, "but I wouldn't murder you."

Allie stared at him. "I don't suppose you would." She was quiet, and when she spoke again, Cam had to strain forward to hear her. "But then, you and I aren't at all like Maggie and Jamie."

Cam had nothing to say to that. He set his plate down on the floor and stretched his hands behind his head, reclining on his pillow. "Nothing like a little light dinner conversation," he mused.

Allie grinned. "What do you want to talk about, then?"

Mia. Cam thought of the note in his back pocket, the keys he had yet to give to Allie. Maybe he would not tell her tonight. He'd let her get a good night's sleep and then break the news to her that her latest assistant had left town without a backward glance. But he found himself pulling the keys out of his pocket and rolling to face Allie. "Mia asked me to give you these," he said. "She had to leave town."

Allie frowned. "Is everything all right?"

No. "I guess so. Family emergency."

"Did she say when she was coming back? Did she leave a number?"

Cam fell onto his pillow. "She didn't say a hell of a lot of anything."

Allie lay down beside him, fitting her head into the crook of his arm. "I hope we didn't scare her away," she murmured.

Cam closed his eyes. He pictured Mia's curls, which stood out in a wild tumble after he'd buried his hands in them, proof of his passion.

Allie's fingers slipped between the buttons of his shirt and began to stroke his stomach.

He imagined the weight of Mia, damp and open on top of him as she cried out in the night.

Allie kissed his shoulder, her breath making a hot circle through the fabric.

He altered his breathing so that it was even and deep. He managed to produce a short snore.

Allie brushed her hand over his brow. "Tough week?" she whispered. She kissed the corner of his mouth and gently pulled away from him to lie on her side of the bed. Cam kept his eyes closed, but he could feel the moment when Allie's hand moved down between her own legs. The silverware on the empty dinner plates trembled. Cam clenched his jaw, thinking that this hurt more than sleeping with Allie would have, and he forced himself to endure the quiet rock of the mattress as she gave herself what he could not.

# TEN

*B*almoral Beene had been named after the English royal family's castle in Aberdeenshire; not because his parents were Scots or English or had ever even traveled across the Atlantic, but simply because his mother had seen a picture on a postcard and liked the way the word filled up her mouth, like a cheekful of rich sponge cake. It was almost poetic justice that he should wind up on the Rolodex of the Wheelock Police Department, quite possibly the only town in America where every resident was practically born knowing the name Balmoral. For that reason, or maybe in spite of it, he had taken to calling himself Bally several years before he became a private investigator-for-hire.

As far as Cam knew, the department—meaning himself, his father, or his grandfather—had never commissioned the help of Bally Beene. Sure, they got shorthanded, but whenever a case that big happened involving Wheelock, there was always a battalion of state troopers the DA would loan to help with an investigation. Nevertheless, Bally's number remained in the Rolodex.

Bally Beene had answered the phone himself, and had stalled over setting a time for an appointment, as if he was incredibly busy. But when Cam arrived at his Great Barrington office at the decided hour, Bally was sitting back in his chair, his feet on his desk, filing his nails. "Hey," he said when Cam walked through the

door, as if he'd known him his entire life. "You ever get a mani-
cure?"

Cam stopped, the door open behind him. "No," he said slowly.

"Damn me if it isn't the most relaxing thing in the world." He
grinned at Cam. "So how's your father?"

"Dead."

"I'd heard that," Bally admitted.

*Then why did you ask?* Cam thought. He looked around the
tiny room, which was located above a bakery and as a consequence
was laced with the most remarkable scents of cinnamon and fleshy
dinner rolls and chocolate babka.

"The answer is no," Bally said. "You can't put on weight just
breathing the stuff in." He tossed his emery board into a trash can
that had a picture of Larry Bird's smiling face and the exuberant
green number 33 on its side. "Come in, close the door." He gestured to a chair in front of the desk. "Stay awhile."

Cam tried to collect his thoughts enough to sound dispassion-
ate while he commissioned this man to find a woman he hardly
knew yet could not function without. He was startled by Bally's
laugh. "Look at what you've turned into. Your dad would have bust
a gut with pride."

"Have we met?"

"Not really," Bally said. "Not quite."

Cam shifted in his chair. "Maybe this is a good point for you to
tell me why you're in the files at the Wheelock station. What did
you do for us in the past?"

"I'm an investigator. I investigated."

"What case?"

Bally narrowed his eyes, and then sighed. "I don't give out information like that, but seeing as how the guy who hired me—
your dad—is dead, I expect it don't much matter." He smiled
beautifully, revealing even, white teeth that looked odd and out of
place among the crags and pits of his thin face. "I investigated
you."

Cam blinked. "You investigated me?"

"That's what I said."

"For my father?"

He nodded.

Cam shook his head, trying to sort the information. "Why?"

Bally sighed. "Investigate probably ain't the best word. I sort of kept an eye on you. When you were jet-setting all over the world." He grinned. "Never got myself over to Paris, not to mention Nepal. Shit, I ain't even been to California."

"My father paid you to follow me?"

"I didn't really follow you. I just kept tabs from here. You can do anything with a computer and a telephone line. I tracked where you got your money, who gave it to you, whose apartments you spent the night in." Bally paused. "It wasn't that he didn't trust you," he said. "It was just that he wanted to make sure you were safe."

Cam stared down at his hands, fisted in his lap. He wondered if his mother knew about this. He wondered what, in his character, had seemed so lacking that his father would feel a need to check up on him.

He was not certain at all that Bally Beene was the right man to find Mia.

He was on the verge of standing up and leaving, when Bally's voice rang out again. "Before you think you made a mistake coming here," he said, "let me remind you how good I am at being confidential. After all, it's been fifteen years since I started tailing you, and *you* didn't find out."

Cam forced himself to relax. He took deep breaths of anisette, fresh yeast, and icing. "I need to find someone who has disappeared. This has nothing to do with police business."

"A personal matter," Bally said, flicking a pen out of his shirt pocket and beginning to scribble on the back of a Dunkin' Donuts napkin.

"Very personal."

"She steal something of yours?"

"No." Cam stopped. "How do you know it's a she?"

"Lucky guess," Bally said, not glancing up.

For the next hour, Cam answered so many questions about Mia that she began to take shape before his eyes, as if she were sitting perched on the desk before him. He stared at the pale V of skin that rose above her cotton sweater, the willowy bow of her neck.

"No picture?"

"Not one you can hold on to," Cam murmured, and at that, Bally looked at him curiously. "Never mind."

Bally would not promise him anything but said he'd try to find Mia. She'd leave a paper trail of some kind—charge receipts, work applications, a driver's license—and since she hadn't been running away per se, she probably would not bother to alter her name. He said he would call Cam, not at home, and refer to himself as Albert Prince.

"Prince Albert? Like Victoria's consort?" Cam said, laughing.

Bally had shrugged. "Hey," he said. "Whatever."

He walked Cam the three feet to the door, urging him to try the napoleons the bakery made on his way out. "It's funny. What goes around comes around. The first case I did for your dad was to find some woman who ran away."

"Police?" Cam said, buttoning his coat.

"Personal. What did you call it? Oh, yeah—*very* personal."

Cam looked up. The image he had of his father was crumbling in bits and pieces. The man had had him tailed through Europe and Africa and Russia. The man had had some connection to a woman who had run away from him.

"Did you find her?"

Bally laughed. "If I didn't, you think your dad would have kept using me? Of course I found her."

Cam stared at Bally. He wouldn't know, of course, what Ian MacDonald had done after he'd handed him the address of this woman. Had he set her up in a house miles away from the one Cam had grown up in? Did he exist at home with Cam and his mother, but come to life with someone else?

"I wonder if he kept in touch with her," Cam said steadily.

Bally lifted his eyebrows. "I would think so. She's your mother."

The chimney of the house Cam had grown up in was covered from top to bottom with ivy, so recognizable from a distance that as a child Cam had believed it was a tall, furred, slumbering beast. He found Ellen in the backyard, poised at the base of the chimney, holding a pricey pair of L-shaped copper dowsing rods as she began to make her way slowly across the lawn. "Digging a new well?" Cam said, standing at the sliding door that led outside.

"Directing my inner vision," Ellen called out. Since Cam's father had died, she'd taken up the practice, joining the American Society of Dowsers and becoming so good at it that several years back, after locating accurately on a map the places where the Bosnian Serbs had been keeping their supply of missiles, she was named Dowser of the Year. She did it as a hobby now, finding water lines for the people who bought property in Wheelock, determining the sex of unborn children, hunting for lost pieces of antiquarian jewelry. "I think there's an electromagnetic field in the northwest corner here that's bothering Pepper."

Pepper was the fourteen-year-old cairn terrier, who was not bothered by doorbells or grease fires or anything else Cam could think of. "How do you know it's bugging him?"

Ellen smiled at her son over her shoulder. "He just ain't like he used to be."

Cam rolled his eyes and walked casually across the lawn to watch his mother in action. She held the copper rods at waist level, like a pair of six-shooters, closing her eyes periodically when one of them twitched toward the other. As Cam got closer, the rods began to shake and cross. "Cam," Ellen chided, "you're ruining this for me."

"Because I think it's a crock?"

Ellen sighed and transferred the rods so that they were both in one hand. "Because you've got too much energy around you. It's all I can tap into when you're so close."

He crossed his arms over his chest, and not for the first time Ellen MacDonald looked up at her son and remembered the day she had gone to spank him and realized he stood a foot taller than she. "What's the matter with you?" she asked.

"You tell me. You're the one with the sixth sense."

Ellen smirked at him. "That's no challenge. Any halfwit can tell when you're angry, Cam. There's a big black cloud that follows you around."

In spite of himself, Cam glanced over his shoulder. He turned back to the sweet rhythm of his mother's laughter. *Why had she run away?*

"I got some interesting news today. I met with a man named Balmoral Beene."

"Oh really?" Ellen said, starting back up to the house. "Do you want lunch or something?"

Cam followed her in. "Mom, you know who he is?"

"Of course, Cam." Ellen swiftly pulled a can of tuna from the shelf and opened it for Pepper, who liked Starkist more than any tabby cat Cam had ever seen. "He's a PI your father used from time to time. Is there something going on at the station?"

Cam froze, realizing too late that bringing up Bally's name would of course make his mother ask what he needed a PI for in the first place. "Some case," he said noncommittally. "Bally told me Dad used him to check up on me when I was traveling."

"Well, yes. I told him to."

Cam leaned forward. "*You* told him to?"

"Of course," she said easily. "I wanted to make sure you were all right."

"I was twenty. I wasn't a kid."

Ellen shrugged. "You'll *always* be my kid." She opened the refrigerator and picked out a Tupperware container full of something thick and brown. Dumping it onto a plate, she moved toward the microwave. "You sure you don't want some? Stroganoff. Made with tofu."

"How come you ran away?" Cam blurted out.

Ellen dropped the plate so it rang against the Formica. Little splats of gravy landed on her shirt. "Who told you that?"

"Bally," Cam pressed. "He said it was the first case Dad ever asked him to take."

Ellen stuffed the plate into the microwave and began to set the table. With slow, graceful movements she pulled two place mats from a rack on the counter and centered them in front of the kitchen chairs. She added napkins, forks, and knives. She had just picked two goblets off a shelf when she turned around to face Cam. "Well," she said, "for starters, I'm really fifty-two, not fifty-three."

Cam's jaw dropped. "Do you think I give a damn if you lie about your age? I find out this morning that my parents didn't trust me, and if that isn't enough, I've got all kinds of assumptions running through my head about you being forced to marry Dad—"

"Cam," Ellen said quietly, "think back. Do you really believe I didn't want to marry your father?"

Cam tried to remember his parents interacting in any way

whatsoever, and the first image that came to mind was once when, as a five-year-old, he had wakened from a nightmare and wandered into their bedroom in the middle of the night. Even in the dark, he could see the lump in the bed writhing and moaning. Frozen, he'd thought he heard his mother's cry, and that was when he realized the horrible thing was eating his parents alive.

He'd crept to the side of the bed, ready to scream down the house, and saw his father under the covers. It was some kind of game. He watched for a minute, then tapped the nearest limb beneath the sheet. "Can I play?" he asked, wondering why, as his parents began to laugh, he hadn't been invited to participate.

"Listen to me," Ellen said. "Why in the name of God would I go around telling people I was a year *older* than I really am?" She sat down in the chair that had been hers as long as Cam could remember. "And if you'd ever consider giving me a grandchild, you'd figure out that a baby born two months early is never, ever ten pounds."

Cam's hands fell to his sides. "You ran away because you got *pregnant?*"

"I ran away because I got pregnant and because your father thought I was eighteen. He was eleven years older; I didn't think he'd appreciate being shackled to someone like me, however entertaining I had been at the time. And we're talking about 1959, where men who weren't as honorable as Ian still did the honorable thing. So I figured I'd save him the trouble. Except he found me— thanks to Bally Beene. I turned seventeen on the day we got married. In Maryland, where we could fudge my age and didn't need my parents' consent."

Cam stared at his mother in a whole different light. "Dad didn't care?"

"Oh, he cared a great deal. He cared about me and he cared about the fact that, as tiny as you were at the time, you existed. He didn't speak to me for a week after the wedding because I'd been stupid enough not to confide in him."

The microwave beeped. Cam crossed toward it, removed the steaming plate, and set it down in front of his mother. "You hot little number," he said, grinning.

Ellen speared a piece of tofu and blew on it to cool it down.

"You going to tell me what you've got Bally working on?" she asked.

Cam shook his head, still smiling. "You'll have to hightail it down to the station and dowse the files to see if you can figure it out. Confidential police business."

"I married one chief and gave birth to another," Ellen said. "Don't give me this garbage."

"It's just some stuff," Cam hedged.

"As long as it has nothing to do with Jamie. He's got trouble enough."

"Digging up dirt on a murderer isn't my job. I'll leave that to the DA."

"Mercy killer," Ellen said, "not a murderer."

"Seventeen, eighteen," Cam murmured, "a matter of semantics."

Ellen glared at him.

"Sorry," Cam said.

She stood and began to bustle around the kitchen, rinsing her plate and her silverware and settling it into the dishwasher. Even the soft tap of her sneakers on the white floor was familiar, and Cam began to remember this room as a place of light and music, waffles burning black at the edges on a rainy Saturday morning while he clapped his hands to his parents' impromptu dance around the kitchen table. Even when the radio was turned off, he used to walk into the kitchen in his parents' house and hear its presence, its energy. Cam realized that he did not think of the kitchen of his own house this way, like it was a heart that pumped life out to the other rooms. When he and Allie were together in their kitchen— chopping vegetables, or making coffee, or even eating—he was mostly aware of the quiet.

"Allie back yet?"

Cam nodded.

His mother did not turn around, but that had never stopped her from being able to see him. "That must be nice for you."

"It was," Cam said. "It is." He started back to the table to pick up the untouched setting that his mother must have laid out for him.

"Oh," Ellen said over the stream of water in the sink. "You can just leave that."

"I told you I didn't want any. You didn't have to set a place."

Ellen shut off the water and wiped her hands on the dish towel. "It isn't for you," she said, a blush stealing over the bridge of her nose and her cheeks, taking away the lines and the history until Cam could clearly see what she had looked like as a girl of seventeen. "It's for your father."

Cam started. "Dad?" He glanced at his mother's copper dowsing rods, carefully packed back in their padded wooden carrying case. An interest in New Age phenomena was one thing; channeling was quite another. He opened his mouth to tell her not to get her hopes up too high.

"It's not what you think," Ellen said. "I just thought that if he was planning on returning for any period of time, it would probably be to me, and it would probably be during a meal. My guess is Thursdays, when I make chicken pot pie."

Cam fingered the fringed edge of the place mat, picturing his father's strong body filling the space that surrounded his chair. He remembered how his father would salt everything without even tasting it, until one day his mother cooked a chicken with an entire box of Morton's to teach him a lesson. He remembered his mother serving vegetables onto his father's plate, a cloud of steam curling the edges of Ellen's hair while Ian held her close with a hand slipped around her thighs.

"Has he come yet?" Cam heard himself ask.

"Not that I've noticed," Ellen admitted. She moved beside Cam and placed her hand over his, on top of the place mat's fringe. In the reflection of the plate, Cam could see their faces, and the slight distortion made by hope. "But that doesn't mean he's not on his way."

Graham opened the package with Jamie in his office. It had arrived beaten and battered. Jamie fiddled nervously with the arms of the chair while Graham attacked the yellowed tape and brown paper wrapping of the box. "You don't think it's a bomb, do you?" Jamie asked.

"It's not making any noise," Graham said, although the very idea—a *bomb,* delivered to him on behalf of a client—was so incredibly dramatic he couldn't help but revel in the thought for a mo-

ment. He grunted and ripped away the last of it to reveal an ordinary Bible, the kind found in hotel rooms. He handed it to Jamie.

As they passed it over the desk, a note fell from the fron-
tispiece. Jamie unfolded it and began to read it aloud.

*Repent*, it said. *Our loving God will forgive you. Remember Isaiah,
1:18—"Come now, and let us reason together, saith the Lord: though your
sins be as scarlet, they shall be as white as snow; though they be red like
crimson, they shall be as wool." I know you will pray for forgiveness during
your trial, may this Bible begin your salvation.*

Jamie crumpled the note in his fist. "I haven't forgiven God for
letting Maggie get sick," he said. "So why the hell should He
bother to forgive me?"

*D*uring the interminable night after Maggie asked Jamie to kill
her, he must have slept for at least five minutes. He did not
remember falling asleep—he thought he watched every digital flip
of the clock—but at one point Jamie opened his eyes and ran his
hand over Maggie's side of the bed and came up with nothing.

He'd shot upright, thinking, *She's already gone.* Then, as his reason returned, he got to his feet and wandered out of the bedroom. He
checked the bathroom first, but it was empty; then he went downstairs to the kitchen, where Maggie sometimes went to brew herself
some tea when the pain was getting worse. It too was deserted. Jamie
had stumbled through the dark house, hitting his shins and his elbows on unlikely pieces of furniture. He stuck his head outside and
whispered her name. Then he started back to the bedroom.

Jamie was coming upstairs when he noticed the line of light
ribboning from his study. He turned the knob and silently swung
open the door to find Maggie standing in front of his home computer terminal, dressed in her bathrobe, wearing the HMD and the
glove that were attached to the system.

He knew she would not be able to hear him with the HMD's
audio feedback in her ears, so he did not bother to call her name.
Instead he walked forward until he was standing just behind her,
watching her interact with one of his old programs.

It made absolutely no sense, but then again, nothing had that
night, starting with Maggie's request to be killed. She was not a
computer jock like he was—she wasn't even an aficionado. She

went so far as to refuse to dust in Jamie's office because she was afraid of crossing wires or upsetting the delicate technological balance. In the years they'd been married, Jamie could not ever remember seeing Maggie voluntarily enter his study, much less boot up one of his virtual reality programs.

He peered at the screen. What he was seeing was far different, of course, from what Maggie was seeing, since she had the HMD on. But even in two dimensions Jamie was able to tell that Maggie had found the disk for the program he'd written years ago, the architectural walk-through for which he'd digitized an image of her body. She was somewhere in the middle of an elementary school, determinedly stalking the halls. "Come on," she said softly, under her breath. "There has to be one around here somewhere."

Jamie frowned and watched her stretch out her gloved hand to open the door of a faculty bathroom. He had designed it with female professionals in mind, complete with a full-length mirror on the wall beside the paper towel dispenser. Maggie stepped in front of it, so that she had a clear picture of her own face and form. Except that her body was the one which had been digitized in 1993 before she'd gotten sick.

He heard her draw in her breath and, with her bare hand, untie the sash of her robe. Then, with her gloved hand, she began to stroke herself. Jamie knew what she was seeing, because the same mirror image he could make out on the small computer screen was what Maggie was visualizing through the HMD. But Maggie, who was also wearing all the trappings of a VR system, would not only *look* different to herself, but *feel* different as well.

Jamie stepped closer, until he was within arm's reach. Maggie's hand, in the specialized glove, hovered just centimeters from her own skin, yet he knew she was feeling the heat and resilience of a real body. Her hand skimmed over her ribs, toward her collarbone, cupping the air above her mastectomy scar. On the screen, in the mirror, she was holding her healthy breast.

Beneath the goggles of the HMD, Maggie was smiling.

Jamie felt the backs of his eyes burn. And he, who had dedicated a career to creating virtual environments that did not allow for intrusions, committed the cardinal sin of invading the periphery. He slid his arms around Maggie's waist and retied the sash of her robe. He reached for the glove and tugged it off her hand and laced his fingers with Maggie's; squeezing until there was pain, until she had no choice but to remember that out here, still waiting, was the real world.

Once, in the middle of a very boring meeting, I thought of what it would be like to see you again. I was nervous just imagining it. I started to sweat; I could not control myself. I actually had to leave.

I stood in the parking lot with all the attendants looking at me as if I was losing my mind, and I gulped in the air until I felt better. I went back into the meeting, thinking: I would kill to hold you again.

# ELEVEN

Audra Campbell, Assistant District Attorney, pretended to converse with one of the Pittsfield Superior Court clerks while instead focusing her concentration on the small but dedicated clot of media that was hovering outside the building. A grand jury hearing was not usually cause for much press—ninety-nine percent of the cases presented to an impaneled jury ended in indictment—but this one had attracted the papers and the local TV stations. A little ambition could go a long, long way, and Audra meant to ride Jamie MacDonald's filthy coattails all the way to a promotion.

"It's like this," she said, turning to the clerk whose name she had already filed away for a future favor. She balanced a pencil over the backs of her knuckles, hooking her middle finger over it. The clerk had been trying the stupid bar trick but could not seem to master it; Audra squeezed her fingers and the pencil snapped in two.

"Don't think about it as the power of your strength," Audra said. "It's all in the strength of your power." She smiled brilliantly at the young man and turned away, nodding at the grand jury she had helped select some weeks ago as they filed through the door of the small conference room.

There were twenty-three of them, all of whom had at least one distinguishing characteristic to fix them in Audra's mind: a handle-

bar mustache, a pregnant belly, shifty black badger eyes. The foreman sported a pug nose with uneven nostrils; she couldn't have forgotten that if she had tried. She grinned at him as he stepped
through the doorway.

The witnesses she had subpoenaed were sitting in a row outside the conference room. Hugo Huntley, the mortician, sat alone
doing a crossword puzzle. The police chief and the underling who
had investigated MacDonald's room at the Inn were bent together,
heads nearly touching and dressed alike, forming in tandem a mirror image.

The defendant, of course, and the defense attorney could be in
Bermuda or orbiting the moon, for all she knew. In a strange and—
for her side—wonderful twist of justice, the defendant had absolutely nothing to do with a grand jury proceeding. Even in a
crime where someone was unjustly accused, at a grand jury hearing
the defendant was not allowed to be present.

With the high surge of anticipation burning a patch down her
spine, Audra Campbell stepped into the conference room and
closed the door.

"They're going to indict me," Jamie said glumly, sitting on a
bag of Blue Seal dog food and watching Angus go about his
morning chores. Graham MacPhee, who had come over to offer emotional support on a day that was bound to be difficult, was leaning
against the garage, trying not to get dog shit on his expensive
Bally loafers.

"A grand jury indicts *everyone*. If the prosecution said a ham
sandwich had committed a murder, hell, they'd indict a ham sandwich," Graham said. "It isn't a personal thing, and it doesn't have
any bearing on the trial." He watched Angus move out of the way
of a mean black Rottweiler. "The best thing we can do is just take
the information Allie gave us, and start preparing your defense."

Angus had been given the dubious honor of being Wheelock's
dogcatcher. Cam had offered him the position to keep him busy
when he'd first dragged him all the way over from Scotland, and
Angus took to it eagerly, constructing a large wire kennel in his
backyard and diligently roaming the back roads of Wheelock to
find unlicensed, uncollared dogs.

Today, there were two mutts, the Rottweiler, a fluffy thing that looked to Jamie like a bichon frise, and a fat Dalmatian, all barking furiously to get Angus's attention as he calmly poured dog food into several large bowls. Angus locked up the gate of the kennel, pulled a small pouch of tobacco from his pocket, and lit his pipe, taking a deep draw before turning to Graham and Jamie. "Having a *cèilidh,* are ye?"

"No, not quite a party," Graham said. "Jamie's not in a festive mood."

"Aye, well, ye should have had your hearing at Carrymuir, laddie. Scots justice comes down to 'guilty,' 'not guilty'—but there's a third verdict, too—'not proven.' " He paused for a moment, then turned sharp eyes on Jamie. "Sort of means 'not guilty—but dinna do it again.' "

Jamie kicked at the dirt with the toe of his boot. "Not much chance of that."

"Jamie," Graham said, "we're going to get you off." He grinned. "Scot-free, if you'll pardon the expression. You won't have this hanging over your head for the rest of your life."

Jamie smiled ruefully. "Do you think it's as easy as that?"

"Oh, yeah," Graham said, pushing away from the garage and walking toward Jamie with the best image of confidence he could present. "Piece of cake."

Angus looked from Graham to Jamie and back again. "Clothead," he muttered. He straightened, stared at the whooping dogs, and started back to the house. "Would ye care for a wee dram, Graham?" he called over his shoulder. "No?" he said, not giving Graham a chance to answer. "Well, you'll have to come again sometime when you're no' due back at the office." The screen door slammed behind him, leaving Jamie and Graham alone.

"I'll let you know what I hear," Graham said, moving down the driveway.

Jamie walked into Angus's house and sat on the bottom step of the staircase. He rubbed his eyes with the heels of his hands and sighed.

"Blue-deviled, are ye?"

Jamie looked up to see Angus holding a bottle of whiskey and a small tumbler. Angus poured some liquor into the glass and handed it to him. "It's barely eleven in the morning," Jamie said.

"That's as good a reason as any." Angus tipped the bottle up to his mouth and sank down beside Jamie. "Is she with ye much today?"

"Who?" Jamie said warily.

"Maggie." He patted Jamie's arm. "Some days are stronger than others. Fee used to tell me when I got to looking like you do now that I'd best snap out of it and stop digging my own grave, since she fully intended to go before me."

"Fee?"

"Fiona. My wife. Died—just like she said she would—in '75."

Jamie's mouth dropped open. "I didn't know you were married."

"Oh, aye, well." Angus smiled. "She was scared to death of being left behind. I'd wake up from a doze in a chair to find her poking my side, or holding a mirror up under my nose." He laughed. "It got where if she wasn't trying something or other when I woke up, I figured I must be well and truly dead." His eyes stared through the screen of the door, unfocused. "In the end, 'twas I who found Fee, asleep too late in the morning for all to be right." Angus closed his eyes, remembering how, in that moment of stillness, her face had blurred at its edges, until he was left looking at the smile of the girl he'd met barefoot beside the river Dee.

Jamie took the bottle from Angus and poured him a drink in his own glass. He passed it wordlessly to his uncle and waited for him to drain it. "It all works out in the end, though, no?" Angus said, pulling himself up on the banister.

"What do you mean?"

Angus held the bottle of whiskey up to the light. Jamie watched his uncle through the amber liquid, which did not distort the old man's face, but made it take on darker and more somber shadows. "It willna matter, after a time, that Maggie and Fee have gone," Angus said softly. "What matters now and for always, Jamie, is that they went the way they wished."

*T*his case," said Audra, pinning all twenty-three jurors with her gaze, "is about murder. Murder One is legally defined as a murder with malice aforethought. If you find the defendant guilty, he has to be guilty of three separate processes: premeditation, deliberation, and willfulness. Premeditation means he formed a plan to kill. Deliberation means he considered the pluses and minuses of his plan—even if this consideration lasted only a couple of seconds. And willfulness means that he intentionally carried out what he planned to do.

"Now, as you know, Maggie MacDonald is, indeed, dead. We have a witness who heard the defendant confess to killing his wife. We have a statement signed by the defendant which indicates he actually drove all the way to a different town from the one in which he resided to commit the murder. You'll hear from the officer who investigated the crime scene, finding incontrovertible evidence that links the defendant to the scene of the crime. And you'll also hear from the medical examiner who performed the autopsy on the deceased." She stood up from her rigid plastic chair, her feet braced apart, her hands clasped behind her back. "I'll bring each witness in, and I'll question him. If there are any issues you need clarified, I'll turn to you afterward."

Audra opened the door and gestured down the hall to Hugo Huntley, who folded his crossword into his pocket and moved toward her reluctantly, as if he were being pulled slowly and inexorably into her web.

The foreman of the grand jury swore Hugo in. His hair was brushed asymmetrically back over his left ear, as if to conceal a bald spot. His hooked, bulbous nose reminded Audra of a pelican. "Would you please state your name and address for the record?"

"Hugo Huntley," he said. "Fourteen-fifty Braemar Way, Wheelock, Massachusetts."

"And Mr. Huntley, what is your profession?"

Hugo licked his lips. "I'm the owner of Huntley's Funeral Parlor in Wheelock. I also serve as the medical examiner for the local police."

Audra nodded. "Could you describe for these people what you saw on the afternoon of September nineteenth?"

"I was working when Zandy Monroe—he's a sergeant with the police station—asked me to come over to retrieve a body. So he brought me across the street, and showed me this woman in the front seat of a pickup truck who had been dead, at first glance, for several hours. We took—"

"We?" Audra pressed.

"We meaning me, and Zandy, and Allie MacDonald—she's the

chief's wife and she happened to be there at the time with Zandy. We took Maggie's body to the funeral parlor and I started to take care of her like I take care of all the funerals in Wheelock."

"But this wasn't an ordinary funeral," Audra prompted.

Hugo blinked at her. "It was very nice. Flowers and everything."

Audra set her teeth. "I was speaking in terms of the deceased. Can you describe the cause of death?"

"Asphyxiation," he said curtly. "Most likely by smothering, as there were no bruises on the neck that would indicate strangulation or any other kind of struggle." He stopped, removed his glasses, and wiped them on the lapel of his jacket.

"Was there anything else you found?"

Hugo thought for a moment. "Various evidence of chemotherapy and radiation treatments, and the radical mastectomy scar on her right breast."

Audra froze in her tracks, scanning the faces of the jury to sense the slightest confusion or leanings toward sympathy. "I meant anything out of the ordinary."

Hugo stared at her. "I don't know what you want me to say."

"Did you find evidence of the defendant's skin beneath the victim's fingernails?"

Hugo nodded.

"You'll have to speak up," Audra prompted.

"Yes," he said dutifully.

"Which would indicate what, exactly?"

He shrugged. "She scratched him. But that doesn't mean much. I mean, who's to say there was a fight? It could have been a back rub." He blushed. "Now, I certainly didn't know the two of them when the missus was alive, but I saw that man at her funeral. Believe me, I've seen plenty of mourners, but Jamie MacDonald is the only widower I've seen who couldn't stand because of the grief. He was . . . distraught. I guess that's the term."

"Thank you, Mr. Huntley," Audra smoothly interrupted, before he could go any farther to undermine her case. "I have nothing further."

Hugo left, closing the door behind him. Audra turned to the grand jury, smiling warmly. "Now," she said, "are there any questions?"

Cam walked around the small studio apartment, which was overfurnished in a country-kitchen way complete with an oxen yoke over the doorway and braided rag rugs. There was a staggering amount of bovine paraphernalia: Holstein-patterned spoon rests and salt and pepper shakers, a milk pitcher in the shape of a heifer, a black-and-white-spotted armchair, cow quilts and posters framed and tacked on the wall. It was a frowsy, overblown room and he never would have believed it was Mia's if he hadn't seen her bonsai, centered by itself on the kitchen table, a palm tree on an island in a storm.

Bally Beene had called him three weeks and one day after Mia left, to tell him she'd been under his nose the whole time. He had braced himself when he'd taken the call at the station, expecting to be given an address in the Texas Panhandle, or maybe Bombay, but Bally had only laughed. "You won't believe this," he said. "She's living over a family's garage in North Adams." For a nominal fee, Bally had been able to get Cam an extra key.

North Adams was fifteen minutes away from Wheelock, if you were driving very fast.

Cam told Allie he had a Drug Awareness and Resistance Education meeting that night; not to expect him for dinner. He had been planning to work the day and then set off for North Adams. But he had gone out on patrol and pulled over a drunk driver, only to find that he couldn't remember the words that made up the Miranda rights—something he could normally recite in his sleep. So after lunch, when he could not sit still behind his desk any longer, he drove to Mia's new address.

He parked his car down the street and just stared at the place where Mia had managed to exist for three weeks without him. He played the scene over and over in his mind, the one where she opened the door and found him standing on the other side. She was wearing a fluffy white robe and a towel over her wet hair; she held her hand to her throat as if she were seeing a ghost. Then she whispered his name and leaned forward, fitting herself to him.

The funny thing was, he did not picture hopping into bed with her. He imagined sitting down on the floor, his back to a corner, with Mia between his legs. He imagined pulling the towel from her head and combing the tangles from her hair. He imagined their voices weaving the house into a delicate net that could hold the night as it fell all around them.

When it became clear she was not there, Cam made himself at home in Mia's apartment. He ran his fingers over the familiar curled edges of the old bonsai tree and let Kafka rub up against his legs. He opened a can of salmon, gave half to the cat, and ate the other half himself. He would have liked a beer, but the only things in the refrigerator were mustard and a large vat of aloe vera juice, so he settled for a tall glass of water.

He was sitting in the dark on the cow armchair, Kafka curled on his shoulder, when he heard Mia coming up the stairs. She opened the door, slung her knapsack onto a small table, and flicked on the lights. When she saw Cam, her hands went up to her mouth, and then fluttered back to her sides. Her eyes narrowed. "Get out of my apartment."

"I will," Cam murmured, coming to his feet. "Soon."

Kafka ran between Mia's legs, meowing. She scooped him up in her arms, weighing him as if he could serve as a weapon. Mia turned her back on Cam, and for the first time he realized what she was wearing. The short red skirt barely covered her bottom, and her long legs were encased in crimson tights. A striped halter top with puffy sleeves and a hat that looked like a coxcomb completed the uniform. Bally had told him she was working at a Jolly Chicken fast-food place, but he hadn't remembered until now.

"You smell like french fries," he said.

Mia moved toward the kitchen. "Occupational hazard," she answered curtly.

He crossed the room to the counter which separated the kitchenette from the rest of the apartment. "Why'd you go?"

Mia looked up at him over a glass of water. "Why did you find me?"

Cam smiled. She was angry, she was being ridiculously belligerent, she looked like an idiot in the Jolly Chicken suit, but he could not tear his eyes away from her. He could feel every inch of the space he occupied, from the balls of his feet to the edges of his fingertips against the counter, and he thought that it was weeks since he'd been so patently in control of himself. "You answer my question," he bargained, "and then I'll answer yours."

Mia pulled off the floppy red cap and shook out her curls. "I already did. I left you that note." When Cam did not answer, she sighed. "I told you I couldn't stay."

"And I can't let you go. So I guess we're at an impasse."

Mia began to take a can of cat food out of the pantry. "I fed the cat," Cam said. He whispered the sentence again to himself, liking the sound of such mundane information being passed from him to Mia. He thought of being able to ask her where his belt was, how much money was in the checking account, whether he should buy milk on the way home—simple, open, married exchanges that could not belong to the two of them, and this hurt more than any physical constraint of their relationship.

"How did you find me?" Mia asked.

Cam shrugged. "I hired someone. I had to."

"I'm not coming back."

He sat down on the couch. "Is it Allie? I—"

"Don't even say it," Mia whispered. "Just don't." She sank down on the cow chair across from him, leaning forward with her arms braced against her knees. "You have everything," she said slowly, as if she were explaining the order of the world to a small child. "A family, a great job, a lot of people who look up to you. You've got a place to go home to." She smiled a little. "So go."

Cam shook his head. "Not without you."

Mia traced one of the black spots on the upholstery with her finger. "You can't make me come back."

Cam did not say anything for a moment, content to watch the play of her hands over the armchair, the sunset flushing one side of her face and her upper arm a faint seashell pink. He slid from the couch to the rag rug on the floor, kneeling before her like a supplicant. He touched the hand that was drawing circles on the armchair, the first contact he'd had with her in weeks. They stared down at their fingers, Cam unwilling to move and Mia unable, both paralyzed by their individual recollections. "You love me," Cam said.

Mia managed to slide her hand free. "That's why I left."

Cam reached up with one finger and traced the line of her mouth, stopping at the corners and the little divot of her top lip with a sureness and familiarity, as if it were he who had sculpted her. "Don't do me any favors," he whispered. Then he turned and walked out of her apartment, hearing Kafka's yowl and the stifled, soughing break of Mia's resistance.

C. J. MacDonald, a part-time police officer in Wheelock and part-time package store stockboy, slowly and methodically told the grand jury what he'd found at the scene of the murder of Maggie MacDonald. "There were fibers that matched the defendant's clothing," he said, "and fingerprints all over the room that matched both the defendant and his wife." He stopped for a second, counting on the fingers of one hand as if to see whether he'd left out something he had dutifully memorized. "I think that's it."

"From the disarray," Audra pressed, "could you tell us anything about the way the murder had been committed?"

C.J. frowned. People didn't usually ask his opinions on things like this; they asked the chief. He glanced up at the thin woman in the blue suit who reminded him of the nasty terrier that lived down the street. "There wasn't much disarray. The bed was made and everything, and the suitcases were all packed up like they were getting ready to go."

Audra turned around. "Like they were getting ready to go? As in, run from the scene of the crime?"

C. J. shrugged. "I guess, but I can't be sure of that."

"Of course not," Audra said. "Perhaps you can tell us what sort of scenario you *did* reconstruct, as one of the detectives that examined the crime scene."

Reluctantly—C.J. had nearly failed creative writing in high school—he began to weave the story of a murder. Audra leaned her shoulder against the wall and closed her eyes. She pictured Maggie MacDonald's face frozen a moment before her husband placed the pillow down, the split-second indecision that had made her claw at his wrist and his face. She wondered what, if anything, would have made Jamie MacDonald stop.

C am stood at the edge of the kitchen counter, shoveling Cheerios into his mouth at an astounding rate. He watched Allie bend to remove the silverware, now clean, from the dishwasher. Then she walked to the drawer where it belonged, setting like utensils into their spots with a jangle that grated on his nerves.

"You put too much soap in the dishwasher," he muttered. "It never gets clean that way. We're eating off a film."

Allie nodded and turned back to the dishwasher, now removing the plates. She set them one by one into the cupboard, making a long, scraping sound each time.

Cam slammed his bowl down on the counter. He waited for Allie to turn around and ask him what the hell his problem was—not that he planned to mention that it had been four days since he'd seen Mia and she still hadn't returned to Wheelock. He wanted Allie to glare at him and tell him to load the goddamned dishwasher himself. He wanted to get a rise out of her.

He wanted her to provoke him, so he could justify all the anger that was seeping from inside him.

Instead, like always, Allie just smiled. "Sorry," she said. "Got a headache?"

Cam turned away. If he admitted to the throbbing at his temples, she'd probably force him down on the couch and make him drink some crap brewed with dandelions. She wouldn't let him go to work until he was feeling better. Until she'd *made* everything better.

Cam did not like himself these days. He watched Allie bustle around the kitchen, getting the house "ready," as she called it, before they both disappeared off to work. He could find fault with nearly every move she made, from the way she twisted shut the faucets to the place she put the milk back in the refrigerator. He knew the problem was not Allie herself, or her ordinary routine—a routine he'd grown accustomed to, in which he was the primary beneficiary of her care and her attention to detail. It was simply that Allie was not someone else.

Allie walked up behind him and slipped one arm around his waist, leaning her cheek against his back. "Are you sure you're all right?" she asked, her voice steady and low, modulated to soothe. For some reason this only irritated him more.

*I'm sorry,* he wanted to say. *I don't mean to do this to you.* But the words wouldn't come, and this made him angry too. He pulled away from her. "Can't you just leave me alone?"

Allie flinched slightly, something he knew he was not supposed to see; and then using what must have been all of her strength, she summoned a wide, forgiving smile. Cam stared hard at her for a long moment before he grabbed his hat and his gun belt and fled out the door.

C am had been subpoenaed for Jamie's grand jury hearing. It was hardly a surprise, since he'd been the arresting officer, but that didn't make it any easier to publicly speak against his own cousin. He had never been more aware of the phrases he chose to string together for a testimony, of the two distinct definitions of a *sentence*.

"He came into the center of town," Cam said, in answer to Audra Campbell's question, "and he asked to speak to me. He wanted to tell me he'd killed his wife."

"Did the defendant say that *he* did it?"

Cam nodded. "Yes." In his mind, he saw Jamie sitting in his pickup truck, tension creating a blue fugue around his body, asking if Cam was indeed Cameron MacDonald, Laird of Carrymuir. He remembered that what he had noticed about Jamie was his height and the MacDonald red hair, plus the three parallel scratches on his left cheek. Cam had seen Jamie that very morning before driving out to Pittsfield for the grand jury hearing, as per the conditions of Jamie's bail. There were no scratches anymore, a full month later; there weren't even faint white lines. Cam thought that Jamie would have welcomed a scar.

"Chief MacDonald?"

Cam looked up and realized that the ADA had asked him a question he had missed. "I'm sorry," he said. "Could you repeat that?"

"I wanted to know about the confession the defendant signed." She waved a paper in her right hand, which Cam recognized as the voluntary confession statement of the Wheelock police.

He sighed. "I took the defendant into custody and he told me the circumstances leading up to the death of his wife, which involved a long and protracted illness—cancer, in several forms. He also said that his wife had asked him to kill her, although he didn't have any proof."

Audra smiled, and Cam was amazed at how predatory she could look. He fleetingly thought of Graham MacPhee, and hoped the attorney had been sharpening his pencils. "Did you advise the defendant of his right to counsel?"

"Of course."

"Was there any coercion used to get the confession?"

Cam scowled at her. "That's not a practice at the station."

"Did the defendant sign a statement to that effect?"

Cam sat up. "Look, you've got the damn thing in your hand." He stood up, glorying in the fact that Audra Campbell's face turned a deep shade of red. "I've given you all I can. He confessed. Period. And I've got other things to do."

Audra pinned him with a glare. "Mr. Foreman, could you direct the witness to answer questions only when asked?"

A short fellow with a nose turned so high Cam could see right up his nostrils smiled apologetically. "Chief MacDonald, please answer only when you're directed to do so."

Cam sat down and glared at Audra. She tossed him a glance over her shoulder. "No further questions," she said.

*U*sually, when Cam yelled at her, it was because Allie was the closest thing to him. In a way, she supposed it was an honor. She knew that he was not truly angry with her—it was a prisoner rubbing him the wrong way, or a case he was working on—he simply felt comfortable enough with her to let down his guard. So it wasn't the *things* he was saying that morning that had affected her, but the way he looked when he'd said them. He had been staring at Allie as if he really did not like her at all.

She glanced at her face in the bathroom mirror for another few minutes, searching for something that might justify Cam's change of heart. "You're being stupid," Allie said out loud. "You're reading into this."

She slipped out of her heavy terry-cloth robe—a navy one embroidered with metallic stars that Cam had given her for her birthday, with a cute note about being able to move the heavens and the earth for him. She did not have much lingerie—the entirety of her collection was courtesy of her bridal shower five years and seven pounds back. But she remembered that the emerald satin robe, which reached to the knee, had once been Cam's favorite. She remembered making love with it spread beneath them, cool and shifting under her skin.

She hadn't worn her lingerie since her honeymoon—it was sort of pointless to look sexy for the same man who saw you throwing up with the flu and picking up the trash that raccoons had scattered across the front lawn. The satin felt wonderful against her shoulders and back, clinging lightly with static and skimming over her hips. Allie picked up her spray bottle of perfume and put some on her wrists and behind her ears, and as an afterthought, behind her knees. She had always seen women do it in the movies, although she didn't really understand why. What man spent time sniffing around there?

With a sharp tug at the lapels of the robe, she covered her breasts and walked out of the bathroom. Cam was in bed, his legs drawn up, the latest issue of *Field and Stream* open in front of him. He glanced at her when she stepped into the bedroom, and rubbed his eyes with his thumb and forefinger to show he was tired.

Allie sat down on the edge of the bed. He hadn't spoken to her much, except for the necessities, since he'd stormed out of the house that morning. "Hi," she said.

Cam couldn't help it; he smiled. "Hi."

"I don't want to fight."

Cam looked at her. In the soft light of the reading lamp, Allie's eyes were deep and dark, and triangular shadows danced a pattern down the side of her neck and throat. "Neither do I." He reached for her hand, the one that nervously stroked the tie of her robe. Her fingers were strong and curled naturally into his own. "Come here," he said, patting the space beside him.

In a flash of leg, Allie crawled over his body. She fit herself neatly to him, her face in the curve of his neck, her arm stretched across his middle, one calf slipped between his own. How many times had they lain like this?

He felt himself stirring, blood rushing heavy into his center. He thought of Allie's body, spread in front of him like a banquet, and he grew harder. He wanted her to touch him. Now.

He wondered how someone so comfortable and familiar could make him as excited as someone mysterious and unknown.

Cam took Allie's hand and settled it over his boxer shorts, sucking in his breath when her fingers slipped through the opening to brush his skin. She moved her hand up and down, alternately stroking and cupping him.

There was a pattern to their lovemaking. He felt his balls

tighten and he rolled to his side, pushing Allie onto her back. He kissed his way up the insides of her thighs, moving her legs onto his shoulders, all the while thinking of unrelated matters—baseball, world news, duty rosters—to keep himself from going over the edge.

But when he came into her, he ceased thinking. His body reacted by itself, thrusting so hard Allie's head knocked against the headboard. He rubbed his cheek against the L of her neck. He spread his hands in her hair and pinned her to the bed.

He knew she did not feel any pain—no more than he noticed the bites and the scratches on his shoulders and back that Allie tried to soothe, like a mother cat, when it was over. It was always like this, always had been, with Allie. He considered the nights he had spent with Mia, where lovemaking had lasted hours and had been slow and gentle, a series of increasing, rippling shocks.

Within minutes he could feel the guilt, pressing up around him from the mattress like a featherbed that threatened to swallow him whole. He was guilty of thinking about Mia when he should have been thinking only of Allie; he was guilty of having sex with Allie when he knew he loved Mia; he was guilty of wanting them both.

"How come it isn't like this in the movies?" Allie murmured, her lips against his throat.

His arms tightened around her waist. "Like what?"

He could feel her smile. "Like they're trying to kill each other."

Cam thought of what he'd felt with Allie in the kitchen that morning. And he wondered if that hadn't been his very motive after all.

With a flourish, Audra Campbell opened the courthouse door, smiling with confidence at the collection of media representatives waiting for the outcome of the grand jury hearing.

"Ms. Campbell," a reporter called. "Can you tell us what happened in there?"

She turned a beaming smile in the direction of the nearest television camera, wondering how many channels she'd be able to videotape that night. "In the case of the State of Massachusetts versus James MacDonald, the grand jury has voted to indict the defendant."

A voice spiraled up through the crowd. "Was this something you expected?"

"Naturally," Audra said, "since he's charged with murder." She glanced around at the people gathered before her, hanging on her words and furiously writing them down for posterity in tiny white notepads. "And I'm very confident of a conviction when we go to trial." She waved—a dismissal—and stepped down several stairs, parting the crowd of reporters.

*I*f she had her choice, Allie would have picked a funeral any day over a wedding. When she did the floral arrangements for the foot and head of a casket, nobody complained, and she didn't have to worry about ruining someone's day with a wilted rose or drooping alstroemeria. On the other hand, a bride only got to do it once. If the stephanotis wasn't wired quite right, it could flop out of the trailing bouquet halfway down the aisle, and no one wanted that on their videotape. If the flowers didn't make it to the church on time, there would be no second chances.

Cam had dropped her off at the church with her buckets of flowers and raffia and Oasis and spools of florist's wire. The tall arrangements were in place on either side of the altar, but she still had to drape a flower garland down the pews that were reserved for family. Allie would have been able to do these ahead of time too, but she had been up all Saturday night doing the bouquets and boutonnieres for the ridiculously large bridal party.

She sat down in the quiet aisle of the church and wired a stem of mimosa. She had done this so often she did not have to be an active participant. For the thousandth time she wished that Mia had not gone off to her emergency, or that she'd come through the door now and roll up her sleeves and help.

The bride was going with a traditional white wedding, accented with some autumn lilies in rosy shades of crimson. Allie had talked her into this. It was a Halloween wedding—well, two days before—and the bride had wanted a garish black and orange. Worse, the guests had been invited to come in costume. In fact, Allie had met the brother of the bride on the front steps of the church, dressed as Napoleon.

Now he came through the door of the church and stood beside

her. Allie looked up and saw him—an unreasonably tall Napoleon, she thought—with his hand stuffed into his coat. "Doesn't bother you if I'm here, does it?" he asked.

Allie shook her head. "I can't chat, though. I'm pretty busy."

"I'm supposed to make sure the minister gets here." He smirked. "I thought they just lived under the pulpit when they weren't preaching."

Allie carefully wrapped a second stem of mimosa. Delicate white flowers, they trembled at her touch. "I take it the minister hasn't arrived yet?"

The man shook his head. "Nope."

Allie glanced up. "I can keep an eye out for him. What's he coming dressed as?"

He looked down at her as if she was crazy. "A minister," he said, "what else?"

At the sound of feet, Allie looked up, panicked. It was only eleven; she had two hours left before the ceremony, but there were guests. At least she assumed they were guests—a medievally dressed lady, a court jester, and Elvira, Queen of the Night. "Hey!" Napoleon shouted, waving. "Aunt Anne! You look great!"

He went to talk to his relatives for a few minutes—during which time Allie made one entire garland of ivy—but returned as if his presence was a help. "They're early," he announced to Allie. "They misjudged the traveling time from New York."

Allie nodded and plucked a lily out of one of her buckets. The lilies would be at the head of the garland, fastened to the top of the pew, and then the mimosas would be wired to cascade down in a soft, white fall.

"Nice flowers," Napoleon said. He crushed one of the mimosa flowers between his fingers, making Allie grimace. "Smells good."

"Mimosa always does. Watch." She picked the stem of the flower away before he could do any more damage and brushed her fingertip lightly against another bud. The petals retracted slightly, as if they were shy. "That's why it was traditionally used at weddings. People used to say if a girl passed this plant in a state of sin, it would shrink back like it was being touched by something evil."

Napoleon laughed. "So much for my sister's storybook wedding." He waved his hand over the half-finished garland. "The whole thing'll curl up and die. She's been living with Pete for a year now already."

Allie hung the first garland up as a terrorist, Shirley Temple, and a hippie came into the church. They sat down behind the other guests and began to talk quietly. "I'm never going to finish," Allie murmured to herself.

"Hey," Napoleon said, standing. "I heard a car. It must be Reverend Allsop." He started down the aisle, his Hessians muffled by the long white runner.

She gritted her teeth when she heard the man's voice again, pitched against a different voice, higher and soft. "I found someone who was looking for you," Napoleon said, and Allie glanced up to see Mia standing just behind him.

Her face broke into a smile. "You couldn't have staged a better entrance. Give me a hand, will you?"

Mia had already flung her knapsack, which was meowing, into a pew, and crouched beside Allie to wire a lily stem for the next garland.

Allie gestured to a completed garland and held the top of it against a pew, pulling a nail from her apron to peg it into place. "Just drape up the bottom half," she instructed.

Mia picked up the long chain and walked backward. She touched her fingers to one flower, which had become twisted in the process of movement. The mimosa's petals shrank away, as if it were embarrassed. And then the next one closed, and the one next to that, and so on, until all the buds had retreated, shaking and modest, and there was no beauty at all.

# TWELVE

Why is it that only in the very beginnings of a relationship are you aware of the heat coming from inside a person, of the number of inches you would have to move for your shoulders to brush as if it were an accident?

Cam kept his eyes on the road. Funny, how he could bump into Allie forty times a day—in front of the refrigerator, or near the bathroom sink—but he was never aware of her proximity, never felt as if all his nerves were reaching just a tiny bit farther. He wondered if, years ago, he had sat beside Allie in a car thinking of ways to press his leg up against hers and blame it on the frost heaves in the road.

On the other hand, Mia was sitting so close beside him he could smell the wool of her sweater. At red lights, from the corner of his eye, he could see the pulse beating behind her left ear.

He hadn't said much to her at all since he'd come to pick up Allie at the church and found Mia working beside her. It had shocked the hell out of him; seeing her bent over a bucket of tiny white daisies, her hair twisted on her head and knotted with a strategically speared pencil. Cam had stood in the aisle of the church, feeling something swell up inside him that might have simply been relief, but that felt like a rush of heat, an explosion of hope.

"Hey," he had blurted out. "You're back. How was your aunt?" The words tumbled out onto the bride's white runner before he realized that he had just fabricated a level of detail he should not have known.

Allie had been stuffing her floral wire and Swiss army knives back into the little red toolbox she used for transport. Her hands, chafed and green-stained, fiddled with the catch that closed the box. "How'd you know it was her aunt?" she asked, and then she stood and kissed his cheek.

He looped his arm around Allie's waist only because it was expected. "It's always an aunt," he said, looking to Mia for help.

"She's fine," Mia replied, and with her eyes she threw back the thread of the lie, knowing it would soon be a net as big as those on a shrimper's boat, and equally as easy to become entrapped in.

Allie's car was in the repair shop for a broken taillight, which was why Cam had dropped her off at the church in the first place, and why he was now driving her and Mia back to Glory in the Flower. But he'd had to take the unmarked car, whose trunk was full of boxes containing pamphlets and T-shirts and caps to promote the DARE program at the area schools. Which meant that the extra buckets of flowers and the mound of supplies had to ride in the back seat, while he and Allie and Mia shared the front.

Mia was doing her damnedest to stay on Allie's half of the front seat—Cam wondered how she had wound up in the middle, anyway—but every now and then a bump in the road would throw her up against him. Cam noticed the smell of Mia too, the woody pine of her hair and skin mixing with Allie's light apple perfume to make him slightly sick.

"Six-two-one to four," the radio crackled. Cam looked down to see it cutting into Mia's thigh. He reached down and pulled the unit free. "Four to six-two-one," Cam said, followed by a string of other letters and numbers. Finally he set the receiver back against Mia's leg. "I've got to go," he told Allie. He stepped on the gas so that the car raced a little faster, and pulled into the parking lot of the flower shop. "Can you handle this stuff?"

Allie nodded. "I'm an old pro." She slid out of the car and reached into the back seat to grab two buckets of flowers.

"I'll give you a hand." Mia reached in as well, refusing to meet Cam's eye. Allie started up the walk, juggling the buckets so she could reach into her pockets for a key.

"You came back," Cam said quietly.

Mia nodded. She tugged at Allie's toolbox, but it was stuck on some part of a seat belt and would not come free.

"When can I see you?" Cam asked.

Mia glanced up. "You can't." She tugged on the handle of the red box again.

Cam twisted from the driver's seat and covered Mia's hand with his own. With a sharp yank the toolbox came flying forward, opening its latch and spilling floral wire, Oasis, scissors, and knives all over the back seat. "Shit," Mia murmured, bending to retrieve a length of ribbon that had worked its way beneath the seat.

Cam's hand pulled her up again. He tugged her forward until she was kneeling in the back seat and then he kissed her. Right in the middle of Main Street, with Allie on the other side of an open door. His mouth moved over hers until her stomach knotted up and her sigh became Cam's next breath.

When Mia heard the first footstep, she pushed herself away. Cam's face was red and his mouth had a rough ring around it. Mia had no doubt she looked much the same. She bent her head so that her curls hid her cheeks and felt around the car's mealy carpeting for the spilled tools.

Allie opened the other rear door, the one behind Cam, and took one look at the paraphernalia which covered the back seat. She fished a spool of floral wire out of one of the remaining buckets of flowers. "What happened?"

She was too busy lugging a tub of lilies out of the car to see Mia and Cam exchange a look. "An accident," Mia said, and then she slammed the car door as if it could truly keep Cam in.

*T*he trial of the State of Massachusetts versus James MacDonald was set for January 16, which meant that Graham MacPhee had little more than two months to pull a rabbit out of a hat. He had been sleeping with a notepad beside his bed and scribbling down whatever entered his mind for Jamie's defense. He was still planning to use insanity, but he was going to throw a few wrenches into the prosecution's machine as well. For example, Allie had found some friend of Maggie's who could confirm that she had asked Jamie to kill her; that would take some of the deliberation out of the act. And Graham also planned to drum up sympathy by subtly playing a euthanasia card. He pictured himself in a grand courtroom, his voice echoing as he saved Jamie's pound of flesh, having rewritten his own speech on mercy.

Graham had been filing pretrial motions for a couple of weeks now—ordinary motions that would help delay the case a little. He had Audra Campbell served with a motion that she'd be expecting—one that said they'd be using an insanity defense, so she could come up with some state shrink to evaluate Jamie for twenty minutes and pass judgment. Then, just to piss her off, he filed a motion to review the prosecution's evidence. It wasn't that Jamie thought she had any aces up her sleeve, but it would take a while to get a copy of the confession, the lab results, et cetera, and he liked the idea of Audra Campbell using up valuable time she could have spent preparing a strategy for prosecution.

Today, though, he had come all the way back to Pittsfield in front of Judge Roarke, fighting a motion that Audra had handed down to *him,* which requested that the words "mercy killing" not be used in the trial at all. Jamie would be referred to as the defendant, or as Mr. MacDonald; the soft edges of the deed he had performed would be rendered in the prosecution's colors of black and white. Audra was smart enough, damn her, to know what aspects of the case Graham could use to his advantage. The first time he'd read the motion, Graham had doubled over in his chair, staggered by the image of a courtroom that was stripped of mercy. Judge Roarke, a big black bear of a man, upheld Audra's motion. "But Your Honor," Graham said, "we're not talking about cold-blooded killing here. We're talking about something that was done to spare someone else pain. What kind of defense *wouldn't* claim mercy?"

The judge leveled his gaze at Graham. "I imagine, Mr. MacPhee," he said, "that this is your problem, not mine." Out of the corner of his eye, Graham could see Audra's smile, white against the flushed blur of her face. "You will be aware that during the trial, you will not use the words 'mercy' or 'mercy killing' or . . . well, you get my drift. Not in your questioning, not in you cross-examination, not in your opening and closing arguments. And you will instruct your witnesses not to bring the term up, or I will consider you personally accountable and hold you in contempt. Do I make myself clear, Mr. MacPhee?"

"Crystal," Graham muttered, stuffing his folders into his briefcase and leaving the courtroom before Audra had a chance to gloat.

He got into his car and headed toward Wheelock. It was dark; in mid-November, nights came much earlier. He didn't know whether to drive to Angus's and meet with Jamie right away, or spare him a sleepless night and just wait till the morning.

Graham took the left-hand pass into Wheelock, the one that skirted the center of town and continued straight toward Angus's place. The road happened to pass the graveyard, too, which Graham never really noticed as he was driving by—except in the winter, when it was covered in snow, and Graham would wonder if that made death any colder or more claustrophobic, a train of thought that fairly convinced him he wanted to be cremated. As Graham drove by now, he noticed a thin green beam bobbing up and down somewhere in the rear of the cemetery.

It was past Halloween, so he didn't think any kids were playing pranks, but you never did know; and after all, Graham's own grandparents were buried somewhere in the northwest corner. He parked the car and cut the ignition. Then, following the single slice of light, he made his way between the worn headstones.

Pulling the lapels of his coat up to his ears, Graham wondered briefly what the hell the police force of Wheelock did to earn a living, if *he* was prowling a graveyard looking for trouble.

He turned at a huge Japanese maple, naked and bent like an old woman against the silver profile of the moon. Sitting on a folding deck chair in front of a grave was Jamie MacDonald.

His hurricane lamp was balanced precariously on Maggie's headstone, which was so new that Graham could see from this far away the deep crevices on the granite which spelled out her name.

Jamie was nodding to a voice Graham did not hear. "I know it. Angus tries to get me out; I just don't have much of a desire to go." Jamie stood up and paced the edge of the grave, careful not to step on the long run of matted earth where the coffin had been interred. "I've been thinking of you," he said softly. "I try to get one picture of you in my head and keep it all day long. Today I kept seeing you at the surprise party for my thirtieth birthday. I ruined it, remember?—I came home from work early because I wanted to call you and take you out to dinner, and there you were letting in my old college roommate at the front door. Christ, that was amazing. You actually convinced people to come from California, and Florida—guys I hadn't seen in years. But what got me the most about that party was some-time in the middle of it, when I came into the kitchen for another beer. You were stirring this big log of chop meat into a huge pot—I think you were making chili—and smiling up at me with the steam curling your hair all around your face. You were a vegetarian, but here you were grinning over this block of raw meat like it was the greatest thing in the world. And that's when I understood how much you loved me."

Jamie sank down into the deck chair again, which was just close enough to the stone for him to be able to touch it with his fingertips. Graham took a step backward, watching his client's hands caress the cold, smooth marker as if it were as vivid and resilient as a woman's skin.

She wouldn't see him. Cam had sent notes to the Wheelock Inn, had left messages at the front desk when Mia would not pick up the phone, had once even banged on her door when he was on the midnight to eight a.m. shift and he *knew* she was there, but she hadn't answered. He began to wonder why he had ever asked her to come back. Having her in the same town and noticeably distant was twice as hard as having her far away.

He began to drop into Allie's shop twice a day, just in the hopes of seeing Mia.

Most of the time, she was in the back arranging something. Cam watched her while trying to carry on a conversation with Allie. He noticed that she favored strange shapes and textures, using these for patterns instead of color. He also noticed that she had either a sixth sense or a canny knack of hearing—she always looked up when Allie took a step toward him, no matter how silent; twice he had seen her answer the phone before he or Allie heard it ring.

One day when he walked in Allie was pulling on her coat. "Bad timing," she said. "I'm on my way to Graham's office." She threw Mia a glance. "Think about it. You can bring your aunt."

"Bring her where?"

"Thanksgiving." Allie reached up on her toes to kiss Cam's cheek as he held the door open for her and followed her to the parking lot. "I want Mia to come, but she says she's got plans with her aunt."

"The sick one?"

"Well," Allie said, swinging into her car, "now she's better."

Cam bent down and smiled at her. "Put on your seat belt." He waited until she had fastened it, then he adjusted the strap so it lay flat over her shoulder and between her breasts, disappearing in the folds of her coat. "Have a good time."

He crossed to his black-and-white and sat down, fiddling with the radio for a minute until he knew that Allie had driven out of sight. Then he got out of the car and walked back into the flower shop.

Mia was waiting for him, perched on the overstuffed arm of one of the couches. "You're working on Thanksgiving."

"I always do," Cam answered. "You don't have an aunt."

Mia stood up and walked to the cooler, plucking out sprigs of Saint-John's-wort and tickseed. "I have an aunt," she said belligerently. "She lives in Seattle." She glanced up. "The Wheelock police must have remarkably little to do."

Cam hooked his thumbs in his pockets. "Why are you avoiding me?"

Mia turned away. "I'm not avoiding you."

Cam came up behind her, his hand gently clasping her shoulder. "I'm glad to hear that." He turned her around and pulled her to the front of the shop, where he locked the door.

"What are you doing?" Mia said, reaching past him toward the dead bolt. When Cam blocked it with his body, she crossed her arms over her chest.

Cam's eyes widened. "Mia." He grinned. "What kind of man do you think I am?" He reached for her hand again, and rubbed it until he could feel the resistance rush out of her body. "I want you to take a walk with me."

Mia narrowed her eyes. "A walk?"

"Just walking. One foot, then the other. I'll bet you're an expert by now."

"Ten minutes," she said, and she followed Cam out the back door.

He led her up the incline behind the shop that ran right into the Berkshire Mountains. As they climbed, Mia's feet tangled on roots and brush and her shoes slipped on fallen, wet leaves. Her breath came in faster spurts, and she was not sure if this was because of the exertion or because of Cam's steady motions ahead of her.

Finally he stopped and pulled her up onto a level plateau that overlooked the parking lot of the shop and the rest of Main Street from behind a wall of narrow brush pines. The flat of the area was covered with fallen needles. "Pretty," Mia said, peeking out from the thin trunk of one tree. "I didn't know it was here."

"There's a lot of things you can't see if you aren't looking." Cam dropped down to the ground and leaned back on his elbows. "What made you come back?"

Mia sat down beside him, her legs crossed Indian style. "The pay was better."

Cam chuckled. "Not to mention the uniform. Jolly Chicken ought to be brought up on sexual harassment charges."

She waited for him to say something more, something like: *Was there anything else?* or, *What about me?* When he didn't, she took a deep breath. "I didn't have nearly as much talent when it came to flipping chicken patties, either."

"No," Cam agreed. "Although you probably met a more interesting class of customer."

Mia laughed, thinking of the pimply teenagers who would dig money out of their jeans, the coins sticky and covered with lint. "Not nearly as interesting as the people you meet," she said. She lay down on the ground, closing her eyes, unaware of the way Cam's breath stopped at her movement. "What are some of the strangest cases you've ever had?"

It felt so lovely, lying beside him again like it was the quiet after and they were letting their words get as close as their bodies had been. She imagined her sentence as a physical thing, a spider's thread that roped about Cam and drew him closer. And she pictured his response, wrapping her tight and binding her to him. *This* was what she had missed the most, not the sex or the forbidden excitement.

Cam forced himself to lie down without touching her. "The first year I worked as an officer—before I went over to Europe—I was the first on site at a motor vehicle accident over on Route 8. The guy who cracked up his car against a telephone pole was forty-six, sober as a judge, and just fell asleep at the wheel. When I pulled him out, he started speaking French, and then crying like a baby, and then he'd speak French again. Turned out he'd never left the Berkshires his entire life and had never studied any other languages. I guess it went away after a couple of weeks, but he was written up in the medical journals.

"And there was the time a swarm of bees got into the hardware store and attacked every single customer. It turned out that a neighbor had started up his lawn mower near their hive and they went crazy, flying in the back windows and loading doors. Thirty people all stung, some having allergic reactions."

Mia propped herself up on an elbow. "They called the police for that?"

Cam groaned. "They call the police for *everything.*"

"What you wouldn't give for a high-speed car chase," she laughed.

"We have those, too. Wheelock's not as sleepy as it looks." He frowned. "Two years ago on Halloween someone dug up a body at the cemetery and took the head and the right arm of a corpse that had been buried thirty years back."

"Ugh."

"Tell me about it. There are some things you never get used to when you work in law enforcement." He rolled to his side, so that he was facing Mia directly. "Like telling a parent that his only kid's been killed in a motorcycle crash. Or throwing open a door and knowing someone on the other side is going to try to shoot you. There are some weapons you can't protect yourself against."

Mia thought of Cam vulnerable and under attack. "But that doesn't happen often," she whispered.

Cam stared at Mia, who knew nothing of Berettas or calibers or bullet gauges, but who could drive him to his knees with a smile. "You'd be surprised," he said.

*Dear Mr. MacPhee,*
*I read about you in the* Boston Globe, *and I feel that I have to write.*

*Three years ago my brother was in a motorcycle accident that forced an amputation of his legs. He fractured his back in several places too and was in pain for over a year, at which point he shot himself in the head. I heard the shot and went running to his room. He was moaning, moving around, half his face blown off. Without even thinking twice about it I picked up the gun and shot him a second time.*

*I went through the same sort of procedure I imagine your client is going through now. After six months of investigations and an*

*awful media circus, a medical examiner decided that the first shot
would have killed Jeff anyway.*

*Please show this letter to your client. I hope the jury has heart.*

A ngus woke up from the nap he'd been taking on Allie's living
room sofa. He'd fallen asleep sometime during the second quarter and now it was already past halftime. Squinting, he peered at the
television, trying to remember which college teams were playing.

Ellen MacDonald walked out of the kitchen bearing a casserole
of yams. "Fancy that," she said, glancing at Angus. "We'd taken you
for dead."

"Aye, well. Dinna give up on me yet."

He rubbed his hand over his face and got to his feet, wandering
toward the kitchen. Allie backed out carrying a turkey that looked
nearly half her size. "Watch out," she called, the steam waving in
front of her face like a billowing curtain.

Angus sat down at his seat—which was actually Cam's seat,
but Cam was working this Thanksgiving as he had every Thanksgiving for the past eight years. It was a fair trade; this way he was
sure to get Christmas off. For reasons Angus had never understood,
Allie always insisted on making Thanksgiving dinner, and then
proceeded to invite Cam's entire family. It seemed to Angus that
since she was the one left alone, she should have been the one
picked up by someone else.

He supposed he'd just keep his mouth shut and enjoy the meal.

Allie leaned over Angus's shoulder and adjusted a bright orange
flower in the centerpiece she'd made. It was a hollowed-out pumpkin, jammed with Oasis and a combination of strawflowers, spindle,
snowberries, and Chinese lanterns. In another minute the Brussels
sprouts would be done; the salad and the stuffing were already on the
table. "Jamie," she called, "dinner."

He walked listlessly to the table and slid into the chair beside
Angus. "So what do you think? Do they give you turkey on Thanksgiving when you're in jail?"

"Ye ken, I believe that they do. Seems I remember—"

"Stop," Allie said. "This is not polite dinner conversation."

"Then again," Jamie added, "I'm not polite company."

Ellen reached across the table and plopped a spoonful of yams onto Jamie's plate. "Eat."

Allie walked around the perimeter of the table, pouring white wine into everyone's glass. When she passed Angus, he grabbed at her sweater. "And what about me?"

"You have grape juice. You can't have any alcohol with your heart medication."

"I would ha' rather skipped the pills," he muttered.

She set the decanter down next to the turkey and raised her glass. "Well," she said, smiling around the table. "On behalf of Cam, we're very glad you all could come here this year for another Thanksgiving. And for those of us who—who could not be with us this year, our thoughts are with you." She turned to Jamie. "I thought you might like to carve."

Jamie took the sterling utensils Allie offered. He could hear the gravy bubbling on the stove in the kitchen, the chatter at the table, and the drone of the sports announcers on the television. He glanced down at the turkey, already skinned by Allie for nutritional purposes, its pale white breast beneath his outstretched hand. He dropped the fork and touched his fingers to the curve, thinking of Maggie's skin, Maggie's throat. Then he dropped the knife and bolted up the stairs.

Allie found him sitting on the edge of the bathtub. He felt her take a seat beside him. She reached for his hand and pressed something greasy and slippery into it. He looked down to see the wishbone. "Ellen carved," she said. "But I thought you might appreciate this."

He smiled, feeling better than he had all day. She was something, this little cousin-by-marriage. "Maggie liked the wishbone, but we used to decide together on the wish. She said we both had to wish for the same thing, so that no matter who won, it would be guaranteed to come true."

"Should I guess?" Allie asked. "World peace? Winning the lottery?"

"We used to wish for kids," Jamie said, glancing up at her. "So I guess neither of us won." He traced the shape of the wishbone with his finger. "How come Cam doesn't take Thanksgiving off?"

"It's that or Christmas."

"He could take both days and dock his pay."

"But who'd watch the town?" Allie grinned. "It's like being married to a doctor. When someone's having a baby, it isn't going to wait for Thanksgiving to be over. Same for robberies and car accidents and the rest."

"All the same, he ought to be watching *you.*"

Allie turned a shade of pink. She took the wishbone from Jamie. "Name your poison," she said, gripping her fist around one tine.

Jamie thought for a moment. Then he wrapped his hand around the other fork of the wishbone, flexing it slightly to gauge the tension. "Let's hope that the people we're crazy about come back to us," he said. "Soon."

*I*n his black-and-white, Cam turned the volume down on the radio so that he could hear the pebbles catching in the tires as he patrolled his town. He didn't have to worry about missing a call; his code leaped out at him no matter how low the dispatcher's voice was. He drove by his house for the third time that night, seeing the lights on in the dining room and the glow of the television through a picture window.

Thanksgiving wasn't a bad one. Christmas got depressing; all those old folks setting fires in their kitchens or locking themselves out of their houses so they'd have someone to talk to, even if it was only a police officer. That was what he hated most about his job: he could not pretend, like the other citizens of Wheelock, that it was a quiet little New England town. He knew who abused his children, who beat his wife, who pushed drugs in front of the middle school, and who was most likely to be drunk at ten a.m. on a Wednesday. He knew his town like a mother knows her child.

When he got tired of prowling Main Street, Cam pulled into the lot of the Wheelock Inn and turned on his radar. He thought of Mia and wondered if she was upstairs, if she was with Kafka, if she was doing anything special for the holiday.

If she was thinking of him.

When the radio crackled, he automatically set the car into drive. The sound of static translated into a coded language he understood effortlessly. A robbery, in progress, at the minimart.

It didn't become any easier with time. Cam floored the gas pedal and went speeding down Main to the gas station on the edge of town, wondering if he'd catch the bastards before they lit out. The problem was, these were always the assholes who shot first and thought about it later.

He'd responded silently for obvious reasons, and shut off his reds as he came within a mile of the minimart. Through the plate glass Cam could see Gordo Stuckey, the teenager who worked there most afternoons, prone on the floor, his hands jerking spasmodically with his sobs.

Where the hell was his backup? C.J. was on, somewhere, and Wheelock wasn't that big a town.

Pulling his Smith and Wesson from its leather casing, he held it arm's length in front of him and slunk along the front of the building. There were two men inside, one overweight and eating a Twinkie while he pinned Gordo to the floor with his gun, the other shoveling money out of the cash register into a Friends of the Wheelock Library tote bag.

Pointing his gun at the guy standing over Gordo, Cam eased his way in through the door. *There are two of them,* some voice in his head said. *There are two of them, but you don't know if the second one has a gun, and C.J. is coming.*

"Put down your weapon," Cam said.

The man laughed. "I don't fucking think so."

As Cam took a step forward, the man who had been emptying the register raised another pistol and leveled it at Cam's head. "Maybe you should listen to him, no?"

Cam raised his hands as the one at the register came forward to relieve him of his own weapon. *Fuck fuck fuck,* he thought. And then a non sequitur: *But it's Thanksgiving.*

The man walked around the counter, past the coffee machine with the Styrofoam cups and lids and the milk decanter that always leaked onto Cam's regulation black boots. He slipped and landed on his back, and the gun went sailing under the metal shelving that held the rolls and bread.

"Drop it," Cam yelled, pointing his gun at the second man. On the floor, Gordo was whimpering.

He felt, rather than saw, the moment when the man went to pull the trigger. There was a displacement of the air around him, then an alteration of pressure that compressed his chest and burst upon his eardrums.

His own shot landed in the man's shoulder and sent the robber's bullet wild, shattering the tempered glass window of the minimart into a conflagration of spiderwebs. "Don't move," Cam shouted, as the accomplice inched toward the rolls.

By the time C.J. arrived, Cam had them sitting back to back, cuffed to the newspaper rack. "Shit," C.J. said. He looked Cam up and down. "Shit," he said again.

"There's a gun under the bread aisle." Cam wearily rubbed the back of his neck. "Ambulance is on its way." He nodded to the back storeroom. "I'll impound the car. Gordo Stuckey'll come down to the station to give a report after he changes."

"Pissed himself?"

Cam nodded. C.J. walked toward the two prisoners. "I'll take them to the lockup." He knelt in front of the wounded man, who spat. Then he looked up at Cam. "Were you aiming for the shoulder, or did you miss?"

Cam snorted and walked out to the black-and-white. It had been all of seven minutes.

He was still dazed as he pulled into the station. He had to file a report, he had to account for the discharge of his gun, he had a million and one things to do now that these two lowlifes had decided to infiltrate his town on Thanksgiving. But instead, he called into the dispatcher and announced that he was going home, that C.J. would be back with the prisoners shortly. He suggested calling one of the part-time cops in for the rest of the night, just in case these guys had friends.

Then Cam walked out to his car, which was parked behind the station. He sat down and gripped his hands to the wheel as his entire body started to shake. His vision bobbed and his shoulders grew rigid. He briefly thought of his house, overrun with people he had no desire to see, bright and holiday-happy. With great care, he drove less than fifteen miles an hour down the road to the Wheelock Inn.

Mia opened the door and the cat slipped from her arms. As she reached across the threshold to grab Kafka back, she noticed that Cam was trembling, a violent, frantic shaking that she had never seen before on a grown man.

She dropped the cat, who ran down the hall toward the ice machine. "What happened?" she asked, drawing Cam into the room. She was expecting the worst: *My mother died. I have cancer. Allie knows.*

Cam sank down on the bed and Mia crawled behind him,

cradling him as best she could in spite of his size. He told her about the dispatcher's call, about how he'd been sitting in the parking lot just below her window, about the robber with the braided tail of hair and the way Gordo had shivered on the floor and the spill of milk which had ruined his shoes and now had saved his life.

When there were no more words, Cam opened his eyes. Mia was lying on the bed facing him, curled into a fetal position just as he was. Her arms were tangled with his, her feet were caught behind his ankles. He was reminded of those Chinese ring puzzles that you would work on for hours to pull free. *Just try,* he thought. *You just try.*

With the fear gone, his body seemed too big for his skin. He was bursting. He rolled Mia onto her back and kissed her, crushing himself against her and driving his tongue into her mouth. It was not the gentle lovemaking he was used to with her; it was the quickness and fury he'd always had with Allie, and somewhere in the back of his mind he noticed how easily, in certain dangers, the lines could be crossed.

He never took off his shirt. Mia tightened herself around him, stroking his hair and squirreling closer until the rhythm became a slow rock. At the last moment, he pulled out of her, spilling across the neat white sheets of the bed.

"I'm sorry," he said.

Mia smiled at him. "Imagine. A cop who's just no good at protection."

He brushed her curls off her face. "I missed you." He leaned down to kiss her neck, and shifted slightly away from her. His finger reached down to trace an angry mark over her breast, a welt left by the badge that had been on his shirt, digging into her skin.

Mia curled her way off the bed and walked into the bathroom. She stared at the welt. "It doesn't hurt," she assured him. "It'll go away." But it remained livid and red for the three hours Cam stayed in her room, through the second time they made love and a long, hot soak in the tub. In the end, before he left, she pulled on her thick, gray sweatshirt again; as if that might hide it, as if either of them might forget that she had been branded his.

I once heard someone on a bus say that this guy had gotten under her skin. And it struck me as a remarkable thought—that someone would affect you so deeply they'd always be a part of you.

There's an image that goes with that phrase: something fluid and warm that starts at your heart and spreads all the way out to your fingertips and your toes, carried by the blood.

This girl on the bus, she said she couldn't stop dreaming about this man. She said she wouldn't be the person she was now if she hadn't met him.

Under the skin, she said.

And I started thinking.

# THIRTEEN

*I*t had taken Graham MacPhee over ten minutes to get up the nerve to call the Chief of Police. Ten minutes of rubbing his palms against his expensive trousers and getting Hannah's voice on the phone and then hanging up. He now had less than two months left before trial, during which he'd be interviewing witnesses. Cam would be called by the prosecution—there was no doubt about that—but Graham wasn't leaving anything to chance. If he could just get a foot in the door, he could feel Cam out about his cousin. Every good defense attorney knew that even when you cross-examined, you never asked a question you didn't already know the answer to.

"MacDonald." Cam's voice was as blunt and abrupt as the rest of him.

"Chief, this is Graham MacPhee." He took a deep breath. "I was wondering if you'd have the time to meet me for a few minutes."

Cam was silent for a second. "Is this about what I think it is?"

Graham nodded before he remembered that Cam wasn't able to see him do it. "Jamie's case."

"Not in this lifetime," Cam said, and he hung up the phone.

Well, that was no surprise. Graham sighed and tipped his chair back, propping his feet on his desk. The police and the DA were always in each other's pockets in situations like this.

Normally, that wouldn't have bothered him. The truth was he had a copy of Cam's arrest report and the notes the chief had made on Jamie's arrival in town. He had all the statements of the evidence taken at the crime scene. Hell, he'd been given a duplicate of the Wheelock police file, courtesy of Audra Campbell.

He remembered being in high school, when Cam had busted him for partying at the construction site. "Fuck you," he had said over and over as Cam cuffed him, pushed him into the station, and opened the door to the lockup. "Fuck you, fuck you, fuck you." Cam had only laughed at Graham. "Believe me, you can find someone you'd consider a lot more pleasurable."

Cam had known that Graham fully understood he'd done something wrong. He didn't feel that Graham had to be punished, really; he just had to be reminded of it, scared by it.

Graham thought of this as a strange kind of justice, but an honest one. And now, years later, Cam had come into Graham's office to hire him for his cousin, a man he'd booked for murder hours before. Yet Cam had asked for anonymity. Maybe because he truly thought a public defender wouldn't do a polished job; maybe because he was rooting for the underdog in spite of his support for the DA's office. Either way, it meant that no matter how stiff-necked and uppity Cam got when it came to this case, he had to have some sympathy for Jamie; he had to care how this all turned out in the end.

That's what Graham had to do: show the jury that Cam was just as worried about Jamie as they ought to be.

Graham stared at the black modular phone on his desk. He glanced out the window toward the police station. If he kept careful watch, he could arrange to accidentally bump into Cam when he went to the coffee shop for a late lunch; he could happen to be on the street when Cam arrived at the station in the morning.

Or he could simply use the best weapon in his arsenal. With a triumphant smile, Graham picked up the phone and dialed the number of Glory in the Flower.

Allie unwound a long length of copper wire from her bonsai tree, letting it straggle from the branches in an uneven kink. "Look at that," she cried, tugging at Cam's shirt. "It's taking hold!"

Cam glanced at the little tree. "That's something," he said noncommittally, "if you like that kind of stuff."

Allie carefully began to rewrap the wire over parts of the trunk and branches that hadn't rubbed raw from the last placement. "Well, as a matter of fact, I do. Mia's going to be very proud of me."

"Mia's going to be very proud of you for what?" The voice came through the back door of the flower shop, and then Mia herself came around the corner, carrying an armful of holly and ivy and pine boughs. She let her eyes dart to Cam and slide back to the worktable. Then she dropped her bushel onto the floor, brushing the needles off her jacket. "I hate Christmas," she said. "I hate all the sap."

Allie nodded. "You can't get if off your hands, and you have to work with it all the time." She put her hand on Cam's shoulder and with her other hand executed a flourish. "Check out my maple."

Mia ran her fingers over the line of the branch. "Very nice." Out of the corner of her eye she saw Allie's palm brush the back of Cam's neck, and she forced herself to walk away.

Cam took Allie's hand away under the pretense of holding it, and then stood up and stepped back. He did not understand how he had come to this—being parceled up between the two women, so that Allie had a hold on certain things—like his name and his house—and Mia had a hold on others—his mood, the memories of this shop, the spot on the back of his neck that Allie had been rubbing a moment before.

He did not like coming to the flower shop, but he did it at least once a day so that he could see Mia. He had started telling Allie that he was doubling up on shifts, working eight hours Wednesday and then midnight-to-eight the next morning as well because one of the part-timers had moved and he was forced to fill in; but he spent that time instead with Mia, making love in her hotel bed with Kafka watching them from a perch on the television console, his eyes wide and yellow with knowledge.

Often he went to bed after an early dinner on Wednesday, waking up at eleven to find Allie pressed closed to him and those stained-glass daffodils dull and flat in the window before him. He'd dress quietly and drive to the Wheelock Inn, but he'd park on the side and take an employees' staircase up to the second floor, where Mia's room was. He did this so seamlessly that after several weeks, his duplicity was second nature, and it did not seem possible that his life had ever been any other way.

Allie began to sort through the holly that Mia had dumped onto the floor. She made two piles, one for greens and one for greens with berries. "Wreaths," she sighed. "I'm going to be doing wreaths all day."

She glanced up at Cam. Graham had called her a few days ago and asked for her help again, but this wasn't nearly as simple as rounding up the details of Jamie's life in Cummington. He had explained to her how he was questioning prospective witnesses, and how she couldn't really be one since she didn't have firsthand knowledge of the incident or of Jamie's character before the incident. But, he had said, she knew Cam better than anyone else. And if she could get a bead on how, exactly, Cam was feeling about Jamie in the days leading up to the trial, it would make the defense a lot smoother.

"You're asking me to spy," she had said, laughing.

Graham cleared his throat. "No, I'm asking you to infiltrate."

He did not tell her why it was important that she barrage Cam with reminders about Jamie, only that it was necessary to Graham's line of questioning at the trial. Still, Allie wasn't stupid; she assumed it had something to do with guilt. And it wouldn't be difficult to work Jamie into their dinner conversations.

She took a sprig of holly, complete with three berries, and tucked it into the buttonhole of Cam's breast pocket. "There. Very dapper."

Cam looked down at it. "I've got to go now."

"Oh," she said, tapping her finger to her lips. "I remember what I was supposed to ask you. Jamie wanted to know if you have one of those adjustable ratchet sets."

"*Jamie* wanted to know that?" He frowned. "Is something broken at Angus's, then?"

Allie shook her head. "Not that I know of. He's just trying to come up with Christmas gifts, I think." She set herself to the task of pulling the lower leaves from several bunches of holly. "He was really set on getting you something you need."

"I don't need anything from him. I don't *want* anything from him." Cam pulled the holly out from his buttonhole and rolled the stem between his fingers.

"Scrooge," Allie chided. "He's your cousin."

He set his cap on his head and pulled the brim down to his eyebrows. "I don't know if I'll see you later," he said, deliberately changing the subject. From the corner of his eye, he noticed Mia outside on the front porch of the shop, battling with several long whips of curly willow as she twisted them into a tidy circle. "It's Thursday."

Allie nodded and turned to the ivy, spread at her feet. She began to gather it up. "I'll probably be here until four in the morning myself," she said. "You don't know how many orders I already have for next week."

Cam knew next week was Christmas, which wouldn't have ordinarily been a problem, but Allie would be going off with Graham for several day trips to Cummington, to meet with the witnesses she'd dug up on Jamie's behalf. Which meant Mia would be left here all alone to make up over fifty different wreaths and centerpieces and holiday baskets. Which meant that Mia would be left here all alone.

Feeling much better, Cam put his hand on the doorknob. Mia was still outside; he could see her breath steaming on the cold air. He turned his attention to his wife. "You'd better get something for Jamie. I mean, I don't want to be caught empty-handed."

He had already turned his back, so he did not see Allie's bright, wide smile. "I'll take care of it," she said. "Don't you worry."

*H*ugo Huntley led Graham into a chamber filled with caskets. "I'm sorry," he said for the fifth time, "but we have very little room when there's a wake going on."

Graham would have gladly postponed his interview with the funeral director/medical examiner if he'd known there was going to be a wake in progress. However, overwhelmed by details, Hugo hadn't called to cancel the meeting, and so Graham had found himself offering his condolences to a tiny weeping woman. Now he was in the selection room. At twenty-six, Graham hadn't given much thought to dying, not even considering Jamie MacDonald's case. It was something that happened to you when you were much older and much more finished with living. He had never contemplated securing a family plot in the cemetery; he had never even realized that coffins came in different shapes and sizes and colors, as individually suited to the deceased as the clothes in which they were buried.

"Mr. Huntley," Graham began, "I'm trying to get a bigger picture of the events leading up to Maggie MacDonald's death. And I understand that you provided the autopsy report for the DA's office."

"Oh." Hugo leaned against one of the coffins. "I'd be happy to tell you anything I can."

Graham breathed a sigh of relief: a witness for the prosecution who was going to be cooperative under cross-examination. "What can you tell me about the cause of Maggie MacDonald's death?"

Hugo pursed his lips and pushed his glasses higher on his nose. "She was smothered, in layman's terms. Probably had been dead for about five or six hours when I first saw her. He most likely used a pillow; there were fibers on her lips and in her hair that matched up with the police lab reports, although that might have just meant she liked to sleep on her belly."

"Anything else?"

From the other room came the high sob of a mourner. "You know, of course, that she was in the advanced stages of cancer."

Graham nodded. "I'll be speaking to her doctor in a few days. But you found . . . ?" He let his question trail off.

"A radical mastectomy of both the breast and the lymph nodes. Evidence of radiation for a tumor affecting the optic nerve. Bone lesions all over her body that had been present for some time." He shrugged and looked up. "She wasn't in great shape."

"You mentioned in your report evidence of skin beneath her fingernails."

"Her husband's," Hugo said. "But as I've told Miss Campbell, I don't think it necessarily means there was a struggle. There was no other indication of that—no bruises or contusions, and from what I've heard, the room was in pretty good condition too, although I suppose it could have been picked up clean after the fact . . ." He smiled ruefully. "You get into my line of work, Mr. MacPhee, and you start to get a sixth sense about things. I'm no expert about police business or matters of the heart, either, but I have a connection with the people I lay out for a burial. I would have been able to tell if Maggie was fighting him. People who are shot or stabbed always die with their eyes wide and scared, their mouths still screaming. Maggie looked like she'd gone off to sleep."

"Well," Graham said, forcing a smile. "How about that." He realized he had been sitting on the foot of a mahogany casket and leaped to his feet.

Graham remembered that Maggie's casket had been closed, and white, and delicate. He wondered if Jamie had picked it after he'd been released on bail. He tried to imagine having to do such a thing. Did you proceed automatically, the way you might select a kitchen cabinet or a color to paint your house: the sandy one, no, the black with gold trim? How could you go about choosing something that would hold the half of your heart you had to bury?

*I*t had taken Angus nearly three full days to get in touch with the branch of the Scottish National Trust that took care of Carrymuir and to convince them that he was indeed a former custodian of the estate, but a week later he presented a package to Allie still bearing the marks of overnight international airmail. "Ye canna possibly thank me for all the trouble I've gone to, lassie," he said, "so dinna fash yourself trying."

Allie fell in love with the picture, which was still in a cracked obsidian frame and faded with age. It showed two little boys on the front steps at Carrymuir. One was crouching over a game of marbles, the other had his hand on the broad back of a wolfhound. The two boys were about five, and a stranger would have guessed they were brothers, so alike were their rangy builds, their Beatles haircuts, and the shadow of their coloring.

As far as she knew, Cam had never seen the picture of himself with his cousin Jamie, taken in 1965.

She had removed the photograph when she got home from the shop, and Krazy Glued the frame back together. It wouldn't be dry till tomorrow, but she slipped the picture back behind the glass so that Cam could get the overall effect.

He came in, clearly exhausted, unhooked his belt and holster and kicked off his boots. Then he flopped down on the couch, barely noticing Allie at the dining room table. "Rough day?"

"I was a traffic light for rush hour," he mumbled.

Allie smiled. "Is that like being a goblin for Halloween?"

Cam groaned and sat up, hugging a throw pillow to his chest. "I want to know why the DPW has programmed the only god-damned light in Wheelock to go on the blitz at four-thirty."

Allie rubbed the corner of the frame with her sleeve, making it shine. "Do they really need someone to direct traffic? What happened before there was a light?"

"People got into accidents." Cam glanced over at her. "What are you up to?"

She walked into the living room. "I got Jamie's Christmas gift," she said, presenting the frame with a flourish.

Cam looked at it dispassionately, a word of praise hovering at his lips, and then his eyes flew open. "That's me."

"And Jamie."

He grabbed the frame out of her hand. "That's Carrymuir. Where the hell did you get this?"

His eyes were poring over the picture, as if sheer scrutiny could force the blurry edges of the background into focus, or make the years that had gone between come flying back. "Angus had it," she said, bending the truth just a little.

Cam looked up at her. For a moment, a play of light from a passing car froze her features, then she again became someone familiar. "Angus owns one picture. It's the one the National Trust made into a postcard."

"Well, he must have forgotten about this one."

Cam set the picture down on the couch beside him and shook his head. "You aren't giving this to Jamie."

Allie smiled. "I knew you were going to want one too. I had a duplicate made up. It should be ready on—"

"You are *not* giving this to Jamie," Cam said again. "I don't want him coming up to me and thinking, 'Shit, we used to play with marbles together, he must owe me something now.' "

Allie crossed her arms over her chest. "You're being ridiculous. Give me that."

"No," Cam said, coming to his feet. He towered over her, and she had to crane her neck to be able to maintain eye contact. "I'm sick of hearing about Jamie MacDonald from you and from my mother and from the newspapers. I don't want to know that we used to play together in Scotland. I don't want us to have any history whatsoever."

A cord was pulsing erratically in his neck, and his eyes had darkened to a shade just shy of black. Allie took a step back, recognizing this part of the argument. Here was the point where she usually backed down. Here was the point where she smiled at Cam and told him whatever he wanted to hear.

"You can't change something that's already been done," she heard herself say.

He didn't know, never would know, what put him over the edge. He wasn't even thinking about Jamie anymore when Allie decided to take a stand and impart that piece of wisdom. He was thinking of Mia, and what he was guilty of. Cam looked at his wife, beautiful and fierce, and realized that he had finally succeeded in doing what he'd set out to do months before. He had provoked Allie. And now he was overcome by his anger—at himself, for falling in love with Mia; at Allie, for finding this photo which was sure to make its way to the local paper; at Jamie, who had so usurped Allie's thoughts that she hadn't been there to stop Cam from tangling up his life to the point where getting free was only possible with a painful, irrevocable cut.

"Wanna bet?" he said, his voice silkily quiet, and he took the photo from the couch. The healing frame gave under the pressure of his fingers, and the glass shattered around their feet. Cam pulled the yellowed strip of photo out and tore it in half, so that he and the wolfhound landed a good three feet away from Jamie's image.

Allie shoved him, catching him so off guard he landed back on the couch staring up at her. He watched her throat shake as she tried to control her words. "You bastard. Did you ever once think that what *you* want and what *you* need is not necessarily what's best for everyone else?"

She grabbed her purse from the low parson's bench in front of the window and started for the front door. She kept hearing her words in her head, and wondered at what point the argument had gone from a silly squabble about a Christmas present to a question about her whole life with Cam.

Everything about her was in some way connected to him. The

location of Glory in the Flower had been chosen for its proximity to the police station. She had adjusted her mealtimes so that they coincided with the shifts that Cam was working on a given week. In the past five years she had learned how to fish, how to target-shoot, how to tell time by the height of the sun, how to clear her mind in the aching cold. She was rarely Allie; instead, she had become the police chief's wife, the clan chief's wife. She had wanted Cam so badly eight years ago that she hadn't realized the price would be giving up herself.

It was liberating to be furious; it took her twice the distance in half the time. She would give Jamie a hundred of those pictures if it struck her fancy. She'd let Cam flounder in the unnatural confines of his own home, trying to remember where she kept the receipts for his dry-cleaned uniforms and how to cook beyond boiling water.

She thought about staying with Mia at the Wheelock Inn, but that seemed to be an imposition. Graham MacPhee had instigated this, but she didn't know him past the level of acquaintance. And Angus didn't have the room for both Jamie and her. So she walked all the way to the center of town, to the pay phone beside the police station. Then she called Cam's mother, and asked her if she'd like an overnight guest.

Allie was chopping celery with a passion. "He's a jerk," she said. "I'm not putting up with this anymore."

Ellen lifted the circles of cucumber off her eyes. She was lying on the kitchen floor so that she'd be able to talk to Allie while she chopped. They had already eaten, but there was a negative aura about Allie that had to be worked off before she could transcend into sleep, and since Ellen didn't own a punching bag or something equivalent, she'd emptied her vegetable drawer. "He's also my son," she pointed out.

Allie glanced over her shoulder. "I know," she apologized, as if this were too much of a cross for Ellen to bear. "At least *I* can walk away."

Ellen laughed and stood up, the caftan falling gracefully down to pool around her bare feet. "I can't, and neither can you, dear." She took Allie's wrist, shaking free the sharp knife and turning it up so that a pale silver scar showed under the fluorescent lights. "He's gotten under your skin."

Ellen had a scar too. Most couples who'd been married in Wheelock did; it was the pagan ending to the church wedding ceremony. Years ago Scottish marriages had been sealed with a blood vow, and the tradition had been carried over the ocean with the residents of the town. There was a joke once about a woman who'd divorced and remarried a number of times—something about her having more notches up her arm than a yardstick.

Ellen had fainted when Ian took the *sgian dhu* from his boot and sliced both their wrists neatly, wrapping them close with a handkerchief to stanch the blood. They had been standing on the front steps of the justice of the peace's office, and all of a sudden the sun had seemed too white to be real and she had awakened with her head in her new husband's lap and a low, dull throbbing in her arm. If Ellen remembered correctly, Allie had taken the blood vow quite well. It was Cam who had looked a little sick.

Allie wrapped her free hand around her wrist as if, five years later, it was still sore. She walked to the kitchen table and sat down. "This trial is going to kill us. We won't be speaking at all by the time it's over."

Ellen nodded sympathetically. "Guilt," she said flatly. "Why else would he flare up every time you mention some little kindness?" She paused. "I suppose you could get a bit less involved with Jamie's case. You could let Graham go to Cummington by himself this time."

Allie shook her head. "He can't keep me from doing something I want to do. This is Cam's problem, not mine."

"Yes, but you learn to pick your fights. If it's more important to you to be an integral part of the defense strategy, then concede a little battle. Tell Cam you won't give Jamie the photo for Christmas."

Allie sighed and rested her cheek on the cool wooden table. It was a full moon. She could hear the faint strains of a dog barking somewhere down the block, and the whistle of the wind through the fireplace in the adjoining room. "I'm supposed to leave tomorrow," she murmured.

"Cam mentioned that."

"I don't want to leave if things are like this." She sat up abruptly and rubbed her face with her hands. She absently rubbed her wrist, as if she wanted to feel the scar made the day of her wedding. What else had they promised each other? She remembered

Cam looking down at her, his voice steady and firm as it fell around her shoulders like a protective cap. *With all that I have, and all that I am, I thee endow.*

She had said the same words to him. Had they been true, they should have traded bits and pieces of their selves the same way they had shared blood: Cam might have taken her calmness, she might have inherited his quick temper; and so on, swapping emotions and attributes until they were no longer opposites but two of a kind.

They probably would never have had this fight.

She looked up at Ellen and smiled a little. "You're always on his side," she said.

The older woman laughed. "Force of habit." She handed Allie her own car keys. "Take the Accord. Cam can follow you here in the morning when you drop it back off."

Allie walked to the sink, washing the residue of the celery off her hands. "How did you know I was going to leave?"

"Because I know you, and I know my son, and you're the bigger person."

Allie sighed. "You'll check in on him when I'm in Cummington?" she asked, kissing Ellen's cheek. Ellen nodded, and opened the door to let her daughter-in-law pass by.

It had begun to snow, a fine moonlit dusting that turned the world into a ghost's playground. Allie tipped her face back and let the snow land on her eyelashes. She snaked out her tongue to catch several flakes, and she let them melt in her mouth with her pride.

She knew Cam wasn't asleep the moment she stepped into the bedroom. She flicked on the light. "I'm back."

Cam rolled toward her and blinked. Allie sat down on the edge of the bed and slipped off her shoes. "Look," Cam said thickly, as if the word were lodged in his throat.

"I don't want to fight. I'm going away tomorrow for three days and I just want to sleep in my own bed." She glanced over at him. "Does it bother you that I'm going away? That I want to do this for Jamie?"

"You can do whatever you want, Allie."

She frowned at him. "That isn't what I asked you."

"You can do whatever you want. I just wish you wouldn't drag his name up all the time. I don't want any part of it." When Allie didn't say anything, Cam peeked up at her. "You can give him the goddamned picture if it means so much to you," he muttered.

Allie ran the edge of the comforter through her fingers. "No, you've made yourself clear about that. I'll buy him a sweater."

"Give him the picture."

"He could probably use a sweater anyway—"

"Allie," Cam interrupted. "Give him the stupid picture."

She stretched out on the bed and crossed her arms over her chest. "We're fighting about it again. We can't do anything right."

She wondered what had happened between yesterday and today, since that was all the time it had taken for her to lose control of herself. The old Allie would have welcomed Cam's apology, would have helped him through it because she knew how difficult it was for him to say it. The old Allie would have settled in happily for the night at this point, knowing she'd managed to lighten the mood and restore the peace. That was why, after all, she had come home. But instead, Allie remained still and withdrawn on her own side of the bed, trying to breathe in spite of the stone that had settled on her chest.

The trees swayed outside the window, blocking the moonlight and Cam's view of his wife. "We can do certain things right," he said suggestively. He did not question his motives—something any good police chief should have done—he simply shifted toward Allie and pulled her into his arms. He closed his eyes and tried to think about the comfortable set of her shoulders against his chest, the twitch of her feet feeling out cool spots under the covers. Something rushed through him like a nicotine draw, but warmer and similar to relief. He brushed his lips behind her ear.

For a moment, Allie seemed to melt underneath Cam and realign herself closer to the source of his heat. He heard her skin sigh where his fingers touched her. But then, to his surprise, and for the first time in his life, Allie Gordon MacDonald drew herself away.

Watchell Spitlick told Graham that after they were done with their little talk-to, he'd show him a crate of hair pomade he had left over from business days. "You use that fancy gel stuff," he said, "but it isn't any different. You pay what, four bucks a pop? I'll let you have the whole crate for four bucks."

If it was anything like what Watchell himself wore on his hair, which plastered the white strands down on his pink head like yarn on a baby's bottom, Graham wanted no part of it. Still, he had a better deal than Allie, who was in the kitchen with Marie Spitlick, looking at a photo album of the poodle they'd just had put to sleep. He was having second thoughts about these two. He knew, at the most, he'd put one of them on the stand; but it was a toss-up as to which one was more credible.

"I wish Mrs. MacDonald—Allie—had told us last time," Bud said, shaking his head. "I would have felt better if I'd gone to the funeral."

Graham smiled. "By the time Allie met you, the funeral had already passed. Things were a little hectic back then."

The older man nodded. "I can't imagine what Jamie's been going through. He could have called, you know. Collect. I would have listened."

"I'm sure you would have." Graham shifted slightly so that a tower of eight-track cartridges would not jab into his hip.

"Well," Bud sighed, lifting a glass of carrot juice in a silent toast. "Maggie's better off this way."

Graham sat up, freshly alert. "You knew about Maggie's illness?"

"Hell, yes," Bud said. "Didn't Mrs. MacDonald—Allie—"

"Let's just assume that when you say Mrs. MacDonald," Graham interrupted smoothly, "you mean Allie."

"Well, didn't she tell you what I mentioned last time?" If she had, it was months ago, and Graham couldn't really remember. "About the night the ambulance came for Maggie when she stopped breathing. Damn near broke our hearts to see those kids going through that. And Maggie the way she was."

"Weak, you mean?"

Bud laughed. "Maggie? Weak? No, I mean helpless. She couldn't stand anybody doing for her. Told me flat out when I was going through the same thing with my sister that she'd rather be dead than hooked up to the mercy of machines."

"Can you tell me about that?"

The man leaned back and set his glass on a coaster made of shellacked beer-bottle caps. "It wasn't a real good time for me. My sister had a stroke and she never came out of it. For a few months there, Marie and me were up at the hospital almost all day long. Maggie took some vacation time off work and ran the store for us, and she got Jamie to clean our house on the weekends. She used to bring those cookies with M & M's in them and big loaves of pound cake, right to the hospital, because she said we needed to keep up our own strength.

"Anyhow," he continued, sighing, "one night when Marie went off for the call of nature, Maggie came closer to the hospital bed than she ever had. She'd come into the room before, but she'd always run away like she was afraid of catching some disease. She looked right down into Frances's face, which was still frowning on the side that got took by the stroke, and touched her cheek. 'That isn't a way to live,' she told me."

Graham whipped a notepad out of his breast pocket and began to scribble down what Watchell Spitlick said. "Anything else?" He tried to keep the excitement out of his voice.

"I told her that Frances would go when God wanted her. And"—he shook his head—"Maggie said to me that if it was her, she'd want someone to wake God up and ask Him what the heck was keeping Him."

Graham leaned forward, balancing his elbows on his knees. He knocked over the eight-tracks, David Cassidy and Joni Mitchell and the Bee Gees spilling over his black loafers. "Mr. Spitlick, would you be willing to testify to all this in court?"

Bud smiled sadly, looking out the window at the empty Mac-Donald house. "I'd do anything for those two." He stood up and Graham stood with him, then he clapped Graham around the shoulders with a big, work-rough hand. "I figure she's an angel now," he said, his voice sounding oddly thin.

Graham glanced toward Jamie's house, where a bronze wind chime cried on the overhang of the porch. "I figure she is."

*D*r. Roanoke Martin was thinking more about his secretary than about the man in front of him. As a psychologist on call for the state of Massachusetts, he had seen his share of deadbeats and schizophrenics and borderline psychotics. Once he'd even interviewed a guy who believed he had been given a transplant of the left side—mind you, only the *left* side—of Charles Manson's brain. Roanoke Martin had no reason to believe that James MacDonald would be any different, any more or any less than ten minutes he could be putting to better use with a lunchtime fuck.

He had asked the standard questions: Did he know his name? The year? The president? Could he talk a bit about his childhood, his family? The man who sat before him was calm and soft-spoken, although he had a good eight inches on Roanoke, which made the doctor a little nervous—you couldn't be around mentally ill people who flew off the handle without prejudging someone strictly on their size.

"Can you tell me what happened on September nineteenth?" Roanoke asked. He tipped up his thin black watch so that its LED display reflected on his glasses. Angela would be swinging back and forth in his swivel chair by now, her feet propped up on the desk, her skirt hiked to midthigh.

"I killed my wife," Jamie said. "I put a pillow over her face and I smothered her like she'd asked me to."

In spite of himself, the doctor leaned forward. "And are you sorry you did this?"

Jamie made a noise that sounded suspiciously like a snort, but Roanoke knew it wouldn't be that, it *couldn't*—defendants always knew they were supposed to impress the State, and even the truly crazy ones managed to behave accordingly. "Sorry? That's a loaded word, Doctor."

Roanoke tapped his fingers on the conference room's table. "What does it mean to you?"

"The same thing I imagine it means to everyone else who speaks English," Jamie snapped. He pushed a hand through his hair. "Am I sorry I killed Maggie? No. Am I sorry that I had to? Yes. Am I sorry that she's not here anymore? More than you could possibly know by talking to me for ten fucking minutes."

Roanoke was silent for a moment. "You seem to have a great deal of anger in you."

Jamie laughed. "You went to school for this?"

The doctor shuffled around the papers that comprised the file of James MacDonald. He already knew what he'd write in his report. The defendant was articulate, hostile, and perfectly sane. He was capable of standing trial. He had a full comprehension of what he had done to his wife three months before.

And no remorse.

With a sigh he pulled out the morality test he always gave to the state patients pending trial. Kohlberg had created it; it was controversial in his field—something about the scoring that was disadvantageous to women, but Roanoke tended to simply listen to the responses of the patients rather than rating them on a scale of scrupulousness. It involved a hypothetical situation: someone is suffering from a very rare and painful disease. All the medicine in the world to treat this disease is located in a drugstore in Switzerland, kept under lock and key, and is outrageously expensive. Without the medicine, this person will die. Would you steal the medicine?

Morality was judged, supposedly, by the criteria a patient used to make a decision. Some inflexibly refused to break the law. Others said that exceptions could be made. Still others suggested trying to bargain with the owner of the drugstore.

But then you tried to change their answer by giving a name to the person who was ill. What if it was not a stranger, but your friend? Your pet? Your mother?

Roanoke cleared his throat. "I'm going to present a situation to you, I'd like you to tell me what you'd do in the circumstances." He raised the paper to scan it in the original situational form, as Kohlberg had designed it. " 'Your wife,' " he read, " 'is dying of a very rare and painful disease.' "

He stopped when he realized something was casting a shadow on the page. Jamie MacDonald was standing, all six feet four inches of him towering over Roanoke Martin and effectively ending the interview. "You'll forgive me," Jamie said quietly, turning to leave, "but I think we've already covered this."

Was she joking when she said it?" Graham asked. "You know, a funny ha-ha kind of comment you'd make to your best friend?"

He and Allie were sitting on one side of a red plastic booth at the Cummington Taco Bell; Pauline Cioffi was on the other side.

She had come with her children, apologetically saying she really didn't have a choice in the matter; they seemed to be parasitically attached until they got their learner's permits for driving.

"Maggie had a sense of humor," Pauline said, "but she also had taste. You don't say, 'I'm going to ask Jamie to kill me,' in the same breath you'd say you were going to ask him to take the luggage down from the attic and then fix the back sprinkler."

"Those were the words she used?" Allie asked. "Exactly?"

Pauline shook her head. "I can't be entirely sure, but it was close."

"And what did *you* say?" Graham pressed.

"I offered her the use of my kids for a week," Pauline said. "That would do in Mother Teresa."

Graham scrunched down slightly on the banquette. "So you did make a joke out of it."

"*I* did, but when I said that, she grabbed my hand. That wasn't something she did a lot—you have to understand, she wasn't one of these touchy-feely friends who hug all the time. Anyway, so she grabbed my hand and she made me look right at her and she said, 'I mean it.'"

From the indoor playground at the back of the restaurant, one of Pauline's children started wailing. "What made her think Jamie would do it?" Allie asked.

Pauline turned her head in the direction of her crying son. "You're all right," she called out. "Now what was that? Why would Jamie do it?" She shrugged. "Jamie would have slit his own throat if it made Maggie happy, and thought about the consequences after the fact."

Graham made a low, strangled noise. Allie glanced at him, but his fingers were steepled together in front of his face and she could not read him well enough to know what he was thinking. "You'd call their relationship a close one, then?"

Pauline smiled sadly. "Apparently too close for comfort."

Graham's eyebrows drew together. "So you think what Jamie did was wrong?"

For a long moment, she did not speak. She let her eyes wander over to her children, who were climbing onto an oversized plastic tortilla shell. "No," Pauline said finally. "I don't think what he did was wrong. I think what *Maggie* did was wrong." She turned back to Graham and Allie, her tired brown eyes rounding softly in a way that almost made her beautiful. "The way I see it, love is just a bigger, stickier form of trust. Maggie promised him it would be all right, and Jamie never thought twice about believing her. But it didn't work out that way, did it? She was my best friend, God help me, but she's the one who ought to be on trial. She took advantage of the fact that her husband was crazy about her, and now he's being called a murderer."

Pauline reached down and blindly found her Coke, taking a long sip before she released it and leaned back against the seat. She closed her eyes, but she was smiling. "Maggie and I used to say that for my fortieth birthday—mine would come three years before hers—we'd go to Hawaii. Just the two of us, she said, and Jamie stowing away in a forty-inch suitcase, since he wouldn't know what to do with himself if she went away." She blinked at Allie and Graham then; her eyes bright, her smile brittle. "Well," she said. "You know what they say about the best-laid plans."

*H*ow come doctors," Graham hissed across the waiting room to Allie, "only subscribe to magazines no one wants to read, and even those are from the year one?"

Allie smiled at him. He was a good man; he always offered to pay for lunch and he never complained about the times Allie started questioning the witnesses more than she was supposed to. "It's a conspiracy," she suggested. "They know it pisses you off."

Graham tossed down the magazine—some tiny little thing printed by a Catholic Charities organization—and stretched his legs out in front of him. "Maybe this is how he gets his patients," he mused. "He keeps them waiting until their bodily functions fail from old age."

"I'm sure he'll call us soon. You wouldn't have wanted to go before that little boy, would you?"

Actually, Graham *would* have preferred it, since that would have meant that he and Allie were through with Cummington after three grueling day trips for interviews. He let his eyes wander over Allie MacDonald. She was only a few years older than he was, and there was a lot to find appealing. She always looked put together, even when she was wearing clunky L.L. Bean boots with a silk shirtwaist so that she could trudge through the snow and the mud. She was a very good copilot when it came to finding shortcuts on a map. And she was remarkably tenacious.

"The doctor will see you now."

At the words, Graham bolted to his feet. Allie followed him into the private office where she'd met Dr. Dascomb Wharton more than two months before. He was not eating this time, but his bulk seemed to seep out of the armholes of his swivel chair like poured batter.

Graham extended his hand. "Good afternoon, sir. I'm Graham MacPhee, defense counsel for James MacDonald."

"Cut to the chase," Dr. Wharton said. "I'm a busy man." He sifted through several files on his desk and opened one with a heavy sigh. "Before you ask, the answer is yes, I'll testify, and here's what you want to know. It was a ductal carcinoma, first diagnosed in 1993, although the secondary site was discovered before the lump in the breast." He read through his notes, his florid face rising and falling with the efforts of his lips as he meticulously detailed Maggie's deterioration.

When the doctor finished, Graham shifted slightly. "Did Maggie MacDonald ask you to kill her?"

"Of course not."

"But she asked for pain medication? For radiation treatment?"

The doctor furrowed his brow. "I offered it. It's standard, in cases like hers, to do whatever you can."

"Dr. Wharton," Graham said, "do you believe in euthanasia?"

"I took the Hippocratic oath, Mr. MacPhee. I'm always going to favor living."

Allie let her eyes dart over the doctor's diplomas, wondering where Graham was going with this. He sounded like he was practicing for the real thing, although she didn't really see the point of antagonizing a defense witness.

"You've never upped a morphine dosage for an elderly patient? You've never, well, speeded things along?"

"Excuse me," the doctor said. "I didn't realize I was the one being prosecuted."

Graham had the grace to blush. It was a lovely thing, in Allie's opinion, the way the dull red worked its way from his collar to the middle of his ears. Cam never blushed.

"I'm just trying to figure out what was going on in Maggie's head," Graham explained. "Why she picked this particular option, versus another more orthodox one."

"I don't imagine there was much going on in her mind at all at that point," Wharton said. "She was in a considerable amount of pain; she was living with the fact that she was going to die, but not knowing how or when it was going to happen. Doesn't leave a lot of room for extraneous thought."

"Maggie knew she was going to die?" Graham asked.

Wharton looked at him strangely. "I would think that was obvious."

"But did she ever come out and tell you she knew that she was going to die? For that matter, did you tell *her* that it was going to happen by a certain date?"

The doctor removed his glasses and began to polish the lenses on the front of his white smock. "We talked about it the last time I saw her. You have to understand that her system was just shutting off, bit by bit. And I mean what I say when I tell you that I'll fight to keep someone alive, no matter what, but that doesn't mean I don't see gradients in the quality of life. What I said to Maggie, specifically, was that nobody knew the answer. The cancer was going to surface again, but it was anybody's guess where and when. It could have been that afternoon; it could have been three months from then." He glanced up. "I imagine it was a bit like being locked in the dark with a rattlesnake you could hear but never see."

Allie winced. Graham reached over instinctively and knotted his bony fingers around her hand. "When was the last time you saw Maggie MacDonald?"

Wharton looked down at the file. "September fifteenth," he said. "She had the last appointment of the day."

Allie and Graham glanced at each other. "That gave her three days," Allie murmured. "Three days to make it happen."

*I*t was the longest period of time they had spent together with their clothes on.

Mia arrived two hours after Allie had gone off for the third day in Graham MacPhee's car, headed to Cummington overnight. She didn't carry a suitcase—that would have been presumptuous and obvious to the neighbors. But Kafka was in her knapsack, and a change of underwear.

She was giddy with the idea of playing house. She was going to cook for Cam and sleep next to him the whole night long and sit in front of a fire with him, their feet tangled together on the floor while they read Cam's travel magazines.

"I love this," she said on Sunday morning. There were waffles cooking in a Belgian waffle maker that had been stashed behind a broken Mr. Coffee in one of the kitchen cupboards. "I may never move out."

Cam wrapped his hand around his mug of hot chocolate. "Now that would prove interesting."

He hadn't left the house all weekend. There was something about seeing Mia in his own bathrobe, his own shower, his own bed, that made him feel like a teenager doing something illicit. The house was beginning to smell of her, and instead of wondering if Allie would notice the difference, he found himself questioning how long it would last for him to enjoy.

She had her nose stuck into a cookbook now. Both of them were admittedly inept when it came to cooking, so they'd had to rely on the arsenal of texts Allie kept on a shelf beside the microwave. "We're going to burn these," she said, sniffing.

Cam stared down at the machine, a big black thing that was emitting smoke at a frightening rate. "We should have stuck to eggs."

Mia turned in his arms and locked her wrists behind his neck. She grinned at him, "Oh, I don't know. When you dream, you're supposed to dream big."

Cam wrapped his hands around her bottom and boosted her up onto the kitchen counter. "If you could go anywhere, where would you go?"

Mia smiled down at him. It was warming up outside, and the sun was melting the snow on the roof, sending it in a steady drip past the kitchen window. "Are you coming too?"

"I might," he said. "Depends on the destination."

"Okay, then . . . Turkey." She closed her eyes, remembering the little villa on the sea that she had rented for the month she could stand being a paid escort for visiting Arab oil magnates. It had been white; everything had been white, except for the bright poppies on the front stoop and the remarkable blue of the sea, which faded so seamlessly into the sky it was difficult to see where one ended and the other began. "You'd wear baggy pajama bottoms and drink iced coffee on the lanai."

"I wear boxers to bed and I don't like iced coffee," Cam said.

Mia jumped off the counter and slid down the length of him. "It's my fantasy. Don't spoil it." She cocked her head. "Where would you go?"

He thought about it for a moment. He pictured Mia on the Italian Alps, her skis dangling from a gondola. He pictured her in Tokyo, surrounded by giggling Japanese schoolchildren who pointed to her bright blue eyes. He pictured her being tugged by his own hand through the halls of Carrymuir.

"Eight years back," he said simply. "That's where I'd want to go."

He did not know if what he was implying was true; if, given the chance, he would have done things differently. Even with Mia in his arms, he could not completely forget Allie, who held the spatula a different way and who had spackled the splashboard tiles behind the sink herself while sashaying around the kitchen to a Motown CD. It was difficult to imagine a life that hadn't been shaped by Allie; it was equally impossible to consider how he had survived all this time without Mia.

He looked at her, wondering what might have been set into motion if he had stopped at The Devil's Hand for a *latte*. What if he'd brought her back to Wheelock when his father died, and had married her instead of Allie? Somewhere in the back of his mind he knew that it would not have happened; that part of his attraction to Mia was the fact that she moved as freely as she pleased. She would not have been the same woman if he had created her boundaries.

He was overcome with a desire to keep her with him for a little while. His eyes darkened at the edges and Mia's mouth quirked as he bullied her down to the floor—not gracefully, like in the movies, but heavily, falling hard the last foot so that their breath came out in a collective whoosh.

Cam's face lowered toward hers. "We're going to ruin the waf-fles," she murmured, and then she buried her fingers in his hair and pulled him close.

He was amazed anew at the image of her body. Her skin seemed to glow. His hand spanned the distance from her breasts to her hips. He told her he loved her, and it was not a confession, but a prayer.

Mia was on top of him, her head thrown back and her unruly hair making spiral shadows on his chest, when the back door that led directly into the kitchen opened. She had heard it somewhere in the back of her mind, along with Kafka's paws padding along on the carpet upstairs and the temperature rising a degree outside. But, as with these other things, when Cam was filling the rest of her senses she was not inclined to pay attention.

Ellen MacDonald stood three feet away, a spare key in one hand and a plate in the other. Her cheeks were as pale as the angel food cake she had brought for Cam. A treat, because Allie was not there.

"Something's burning," Ellen said, and then she threw the cake down on the counter and left without another word.

*B*ecause he didn't want anyone around who was liable to eaves-drop, Graham asked Jamie to meet him at the foot of the pass in the Berkshires that made Wheelock so picture-perfect. There was a path there that eventually fed into the Mohawk Trail, but for a good ten miles before that it was just a dirt road used by ambi-tious teenagers on neon-painted mountain bikes. With the few inches of snow that had fallen over the past week, Graham knew he'd be assured of privacy, and it was finally time for his client to tell him the truth.

Jamie knew why he was there; knew he was going to have to talk about it with Graham sooner or later and in much more detail than he'd gone into for his voluntary confession. The two men walked in silence for half a mile, their heads bent against the wind, their hands buried deep in their parkas.

"When did she ask you?" Graham said.

"First? In January. We were in Quebec. It was after the chemotherapy, but before the radiation treatments for the eye. I sort of laughed it off."

"And then?"

Jamie bent down to pick a twig out of the snow. He traced the footprint of a rabbit, white on white. "After her doctor's appointment that week in September. She went on a Friday—she always scheduled the last appointment of the day, because she wanted to put in a full day of work before hearing bad news. So she usually got home about six.

"She didn't get home until after nine o'clock at night." Jamie smiled faintly, caught in a memory. "Of course by then I'd called every local hospital and police station looking for car accidents and hit-and-runs. She was carrying a box—a big one, I think it was a Stolichnaya box she must have gotten from the liquor store. She didn't say anything to me. She walked upstairs and started putting all her clothes inside it."

W*hat are you doing?" he asked. "What did the doctor say?"*

*But Maggie continued to fold her clothes. She put the shorts in first, and he thought maybe she was going through her drawers and sorting them for the winter. But when she packed her underwear away, and the nightgown she had worn the evening before, he knelt down beside her and grabbed her shoulders, forcing her to look at him.*

*"Jamie," she said, "I'm not going to do this anymore."*

*Do what? His mind grasped at straws. Fold clothes? Talk to him? He pulled at her hands until she came to sit beside him on the bed. "I don't so much mind the dying," she said. "It's not knowing what's coming next that's killing me."*

*She asked him, flat out, to take her life. He told her he absolutely wouldn't do it. She said he was being selfish. He said she was being selfish too. She told him she had every right to be.*

*She wanted him to do it then; he wanted to have one more weekend with her. She wanted to get everything in order so that he would not be cleaning up after she was gone; he forced her to put her clothes back in the drawer, saying a shadow and a memory of her were better than nothing at all. He told her he would pick the place, since he could not continue to live in Cummington if he always remembered it as the town where he had suffocated Maggie.*

*On Saturday they slept late so that Jamie could wake up with Maggie's hair twined over his hands and his face. They had a picnic on the roof of their house, from which they could see nearly twenty miles. They went to a movie they did not watch and kissed and stroked each other in the silence of the very last row.*

*On Saturday night they went to the very expensive restaurant where eleven years before, Jamie had asked her to marry him. They ordered the priciest entrees on the menu and they ate with their hands, holding ripped pieces of tenderloin and lobster to each other's mouths. They crashed a wedding party at the Red Lion Inn in Lenox and danced until the swing band went off to bed.*

*On Sunday, they watched the sun creep over the Berkshires like an unfolding fan. They spent the day looking for the richest colors—the blues of a brilliant sky, the yellowest dandelion, the reddest fire engine—so that Maggie would be able to take them with her. They held each other on a black night when the moon was too embarrassed to appear, and gave names to the children they'd never had.*

*On Monday morning they drove to Wheelock and checked into the Inn. Jamie bought a bottle of champagne from the bartender downstairs and they drank this and ate pizza and discussed how it would be done.*

*They made love Monday night, passed out in exhaustion, and woke up still joined together.*

*On Tuesday morning, Maggie kissed him goodbye.*

I t took less than five minutes," Jamie said, shuffling his boots in the snow. "I used a pillow. She scratched at me in the middle of it, but this was something we'd talked about, and I wasn't supposed to stop. So I just leaned closer and whispered to her—you know, things I knew she would want to be thinking, and then she stopped moving completely."

Without a word, Graham started back down the incline to the foot of the hills. He looked behind him when they reached the main roads of Wheelock Center. Jamie's face was red and chapped, his nose was running. Graham imagined he looked the same. It was another reason Graham had chosen this place for their interview. In December, coming back from the pass, you would never be able to tell if a man's face was raw with the cold, or if he had been crying.

"Jamie," Graham said, turning to face his client. "I know

you would do it over again. But would you do anything differently?"

He watched Jamie's face fold in upon itself as he struggled with control. "I'd like to say that this time I'd kill myself, too," Jamie answered quietly, "but I've never had that kind of courage."

# FOURTEEN

When her son Cameron was sixteen, Ellen MacDonald had walked in on him with a girl. She had knocked on his bedroom door, like she always did, but it was a quick one-two, and then open. And on the bed, kneeling before each other, were Cam and a girl she had never seen.

Cam's shirt was off, but then again so was the girl's. His hands were fastened on the girl's breasts, and for a moment, that claimed all of Ellen's attention—with a middle-aged jealousy, she focused on those high, round globes that looked a way hers never would again. She must have made a noise, because the girl looked up and squeaked. Cam whirled to face his mother, his lips soundlessly moving over syllables he couldn't utter.

For a long time after that, Ellen could not look Cam in the eye. It was not his shame, or her embarrassment, that strained their relationship. It was what she never would have believed secondhand; what, after all these years, still stood out in her mind like a red flag: that in a matter of seconds, she had watched her child turn into a man.

Ellen had not stayed at Cam's house after finding him with Mia. She didn't trust herself. When this happened before, she had consigned the episode to a teenager's raging glands. This time was entirely different. And where she had once been silent, she now felt as if she was volcanic, ready to explode in her indignation.

If she had known where Allie was, she would have called her. Instead, Ellen spent two whole hours trying to restore herself to a state of peace. Then, giving in to her anger, she took out her dowsing rods. She held them at hip level, comfortably setting her wrists so that they acted as shock absorbers. With the dog following her, Ellen walked from room to room—starting in her bedroom, where Cam had been conceived, moving to the room that had been the nursery before it became Ian's office, then down the hall to the room that would always be Cam's.

She stood in its center, her rods quivering. She glanced from the wallpaper—big clipper ships with unlikely, topheavy masts—to the narrow bed, which Cam's feet had hung off of from eighth grade on. Glancing down at her rods, she cursed. They were shaking a bit, but they weren't crossing. In fact, she could not be sure that the shivers which ran down the sleek copper weren't coming from her own internal imbalance.

But she would be damned if she'd stop trying. She walked back to her bedroom and retraced her path to the nursery and then Cam's room. Ellen sniffed at the air, catching only a trace of Lemon Pledge when there should have been something rank and strong; surely something that had festered for so long would be dark and deep and malodorous. She crawled on her knees to look beneath the radiator; she checked the spot beside the fireplace where there had once been dry rot. She would not give up, she told herself, until she found the puddle of immorality which must have seeped into her own child's soul.

Damn his mother. Cam followed Mia around the house as she dumped the burned waffles into the sink and picked her socks up from the crevices in the couch and collected her toothbrush from the bathroom. He had a hard-on like he couldn't believe because of what they hadn't been able to finish, and he wanted to speak to her, but all he could think of to say was that they still had twenty-one hours left.

"Where are you going?" he asked.

Mia tossed Kafka into her knapsack. "Where do you think?"

Cam rubbed a rough spot on the hardwood floor with his bare toe. "I'll come by later, then. After I strangle my mother."

"Don't." Mia slipped the knapsack over her shoulder. The vinyl made a faint zipping noise against her down jacket that sounded terribly final to Cam. "I have things to do."

"You were going to do them with me," he said. "You planned to spend the whole day here."

"That was before," Mia said. She brushed her hair back from her eyes, and her cuff fell over her hand, obscuring it like a small child's.

He took the knapsack off her shoulder and slid the sleeve of the coat up her arm so that her fingers peeked out again. He curled his hand over hers and kissed her knuckles. "She won't say anything," he promised.

"It doesn't matter if she does or if she doesn't. She knows."

Cam knew he couldn't stop her, so he followed her down the stairs. At the door, when she would have walked out without saying goodbye, he put a hand on her shoulder and spun her around. "Do you know what it's like," she said, "to know that the only way you can be happy is if you make everyone else's life miserable?"

Cam watched his hand cup Mia's cheek. When he drew it away, his palm was crossed with fine wet lines. He thought of his mother's pinched face, and then he thought of Allie. "I have a fairly good idea," he said.

*I*n her hurry, Mia had left half her clothes behind. A bracelet, which Cam pocketed, a clean pair of underwear that had tumbled out of her knapsack during her hasty packing, and a Minnie Mouse T-shirt marked with a day-camp-style label that said *Mia Townsend*. These things Cam stuffed into a drawer with his boxers and socks. Then he dressed in a St. Andrew's sweatshirt and a pair of jeans and drove to his mother's.

The front door was open; his mother was nowhere in sight. Her dowsing rods were lying on the kitchen table, crossed, which was a better sign to Cam of her emotional distress than any amount of yelling could have been. You *never* crossed dowsing rods; how many times had she told him that? Carefully, he picked up the copper sticks, surprised at the hum that rang through his forearms, and set the rods into their protective wooden box.

He glanced up to find his mother standing three feet in front of him. "Damn," he said, trying to smile. "You're good at sneaking up on a person."

Ellen folded her arms across her chest.

"Are you going to tell Allie?" Cam asked.

She looked directly into his eyes. "That's *your* punishment," she said.

He could hear the house settling around them, creaks and groans that had once made Cam run from his room in the middle of the night to sleep in the solid protection of his mother's embrace. "Are we going to talk about it?" Cam said quietly.

Ellen shook her head. "I don't know you. I didn't raise you to do this."

Implicit in her statement were the words *Neither did your father.* How many times had he heard the lecture? MacDonalds don't cheat and they don't steal. They honor their word. And they never, ever break a vow that has been sealed.

If you were a MacDonald and you made a promise, you took it to the grave.

An image of Jamie flashed across Cam's mind. *What had he sworn to his wife?*

For that matter, what had Cam sworn to his own?

He thought of Allie and visibly became smaller, his shoulders rounding and his head ducking down with the weight of his impetuousness. Then he remembered that this had nothing to do with her. Falling for Mia had not been something born out of spite for his wife, or out of dissatisfaction in his solid, stable marriage. It was a selfish act. And it was probably the only thing Cam had done in his life strictly because he had wanted to.

He had wanted to wear cutoff jeans and faded khaki T-shirts and to be a travel writer; instead he was a uniformed police chief. He had wanted to skim the surface of the world, touching down like a dragonfly where he chose to; instead he was bound and tied to Wheelock. He had wanted to become a faceless individual in the crowds that thronged the Riviera and the running of the bulls; instead he was the titular head of a clan and completely unmistakable to its members.

He had wanted Mia so strongly it shook the faith of his convictions; and in a moment he could not have stopped even if he'd wanted to, he had grabbed hold before the opportunity passed him by.

Ellen took a step closer. Cam was reminded of how, seconds before the sting of her hand flashed across his bottom when he was a child, she had always seemed to grow in size. It had taken him years to figure out that this was simply a matter of perspective as he cowered beneath her fury.

He forced himself to stand tall, towering over his mother. She looked up at him, and for a moment he didn't have the courage to meet her eye. However, when he finally glanced down, she was not glaring at him at all. Her eyes were soft and sloe, the color of the belly of the sea. *I married her because of her eyes,* Ian MacDonald had liked to say. *I fell the whole damn way into them, and I couldn't find my way out.*

"I don't understand you," she said quietly, and she walked out of the room, leaving between them the faint and glowing image of Cam's father, the memory of his parents kissing behind a half-closed pantry door, and the looming question of why something that felt so incredibly right could be undeniably wrong.

In his left hand, Graham held the magazine article that had led him way the hell to Boston to visit Dr. Harrison Harding, psychiatrist. In his right hand was the report of the State psychologist's findings from his aborted interview with Jamie: *Mr. MacDonald presented no clinical evidence during his examination to indicate any psychopathology. He does not exhibit signs of psychosis, neurosis, or aberrations in personality. His affect was appropriate and his answers were lucid and reasonable. From a legal aspect, it is clear that he knew the nature and quality of his acts.*

Jamie was sitting next to Graham, his feet nervously tapping on the floor. He had agreed, out of desperation, to take a battery of tests: Rorschach, IQ, WAIS, Graphic Projectives. But he spent the three-hour car ride telling Graham that since he wasn't crazy, a psychiatrist wasn't going to say that he was. It was his opinion that Dr. Harding would be no different than the asshole the State had sent him to.

Graham had other ideas. "If Harding doesn't think you were disturbed enough to affect your judgment," he said, "we'll find someone else who does."

But he didn't think he was going to have to look much farther than this finely fashioned, austere office. According to the *Time* article he clutched like a lifeline, Dr. Harrison Harding ardently supported euthanasia. Not that he'd acted on his impulses; he was just a sort of well-mannered, gray-templed spokesman for assisted suicide. He had been interviewed in conjunction with a feature story on Kevorkian, some reporter's way of showing that more than one educated man of science believed in mercy killing.

Harding himself came to the outer office. "Mr. MacPhee," he said, extending a hand. He raked Jamie with his gaze. "Mr. MacDonald."

Graham turned to Jamie. "Stay here," he said, feeling like a mother. "I want to talk to him alone for a minute."

Jamie grunted, but he sat down and opened an *Omni* magazine. Graham followed the psychiatrist into his inner sanctum. Unlike the neat waiting room, this chamber was warm and full of sunlight. Bowls of Chex Mix sat on small Formica cubes that served as coffee tables, refreshments for an upcoming session. Dr. Harding sat down on a plump couch and gestured to a matching one across from him. "Quite a case you've got."

Graham had spoken to him when he called to make the appointment, so they had hashed through all of the particulars. Now, briefly, he told Dr. Harding about Jamie's view of events leading up to Maggie's death, about his own impressions of Jamie. "Sometimes you look at him and you think, How the hell could he do something like that? And sometimes you look at him and he just breaks your heart." Graham finished speaking, took a deep breath, and glanced at the psychiatrist, trying to read his face for a clue as to how his words had been received.

Psychiatrists must learn during med school not to give anything away. Harding rested his head on his folded hands and nodded shortly. "You've entered an insanity plea," he said conversationally. "Why not euthanasia?"

Graham didn't bat an eye. "Because America isn't ready for that yet, especially not in the Berkshires, where half our jury will be farmers with eighth-grade educations and machine workers who think in terms of what circle gets welded to what square."

"Mr. MacPhee," the psychiatrist said, "what brings you to me?"

Graham swallowed. "I need you to determine if Jamie knew the nature and the quality of the act he committed. Basically, if he understood the consequences of smothering his wife, if he knew it was wrong, that sort of thing."

"I don't know if I can fit my evaluation into your legal standards."

Graham felt his face burning a dull red. He had no doubt that if he'd breezed in here and said he was changing the plea, Harrison Harding would have done cartwheels to get his name connected with the case. "You thought I was coming to ask you advice about a euthanasia defense."

The doctor nodded, then sighed. "Let me tell you about myself," he said. "My wife and three-year-old daughter were shot by a sniper who went berserk at a Kentucky Fried Chicken in Chicago. My daughter died immediately; my wife lasted on life support for over three years, fed through a nose tube and wearing a diaper, shrinking away until she was so unrecognizable I could not be entirely sure she was the same person. Out of this came my need to be able to control death."

Graham sat forward, transfixed. "You didn't kill her."

"That doesn't mean I didn't want to. Or that I don't think other people should have that right."

Graham picked a Rice Chex out of the mix on the table and ran his finger around its rough edges. "Then you should have quite a lot to discuss with Jamie."

For a long moment, neither man said anything. Finally the psychiatrist stood up and walked to the window. "I can't promise you anything, and I can't make judgments without having seen Mr. MacDonald," he said. "On the other hand, there are things you might consider. Impulsive behavior in Jamie's past, for instance. Is he the kind of man who packs up a suitcase and flies standby to Fiji for the hell of it? Or would he buy his tickets six months in advance for the price break? And there's also the psychiatric concept of regression, which suggests that under a period of extreme pressure the mind would revert to the state of a child."

Graham dug his notebook out of his jacket pocket and began to write down these terms. "There's a theory that suggests Jamie's personality may have been so fragile he would mentally bind himself to someone else," Harding said. "It's called a fusion fantasy. He was actually, in his mind, feeling the same pain that was affecting his wife. By killing her to end her suffering, he was ending his own suffering as well."

"That's probably right on the head," Graham said, "but I don't think it will hold up in court."

The doctor turned around, lost in thought. "In extreme cases, undue stress can lead to a psychotic episode. Think of the Vietnam vets who came back with PTSD—post-traumatic stress disorder. Some of them relive battles regularly. There have been a few instances of murder, when afflicted patients killed someone close by who, in their minds at the time, was VC."

Graham's eyebrows raised. "Will you see Jamie?"

Harding nodded. "I assumed you'd brought him for more than company on a long drive." He crossed to the door and opened it, gesturing to Jamie, who leaped to his feet like a puppy too long confined. "Mr. MacDonald," Harding said, shaking his hand. "I've been following your case."

Jamie glanced from Graham to Harding and back to Graham again. He sat down and belligerently crossed his arms over his chest. "I suppose you're going to want me to lie down and talk about my mother."

"No," Harding replied. He sat on the corner of his desk and reached for a small tape recorder, which he held out to Jamie for inspection. "You don't mind?" He pushed the record button, and let the dead air fill the room. Then he looked at Jamie. "I'm going to ask you some questions, yes," he said. "But first I'd like to tell you about my wife."

Cam was flipping through the past repair receipts of the Wheelock police cruisers when his mother walked into the station. He had not seen her since that unfortunate intrusion a week before, and he knew she had spoken to Allie since and had kept her silence. Allie had told him a few nights before that Ellen had called to say she wouldn't be able to make it to Christmas dinner; an old friend from a Vermont commune had invited her for a country celebration. "I can't say I'm not disappointed," Allie had said, "but how can we possibly compete with horse-drawn sleighs and a séance?"

Ellen stood in the doorway of his office, carrying two festively wrapped gifts. "Merry Christmas," she said, her mouth turned down at the corners.

"Merry Christmas," he murmured, keeping his eyes glued to his desk. He cleared his throat and stood up, jamming his hands into his pockets. "I heard you're going away for Christmas."

She nodded. "To the Peace of $\pi$ Living Community. A woman I met in a shiatsu class a year ago set it up on her eighty-acre farm when her husband passed away." She dumped the gifts onto the desk unceremoniously. "I invited myself. I couldn't possibly look Allie in the eye," she said. "God only knows how you do it day after day."

Cam forced himself to look directly at her. "I'm going to tell her. I am. But I'm not giving Mia up, either."

"And has anyone told Mia how foolish it is to run away with a man who's run away from somebody else?" She shook her head. "History repeats."

Ellen straightened her spine and touched the two gifts sitting on Cam's desk. "The skinny one is yours," she said. "I think you should open it while I'm here."

Cam slowly ripped the jolly green paper and the circus of ribbons that garnished its top. Inside was a handmade broom with a woven thatch of straw on one end and a carved face at the top of its sassafras wood handle. "A broom?" he said.

Ellen touched the leather thong that had been punched through its neck as a loop. "You're supposed to give a broom to a new couple for luck," she said. "Well, that's fitting, because even if I wish it wasn't happening quite this way, I still want you to be happy, Cam." She pointed to the face, the tiny image of a wizened, grizzled old man. "That's a tree spirit. It guides your spiritual cleansing."

She laid a hand on her son's arm. "If God had wanted us to act on instinct, we wouldn't have the power of reason." She drew him down and took him into an embrace, so that Cam could smell the familiar curl of peppermint drops and Fantastik and Chanel No. 5 that had laced through his childhood. He gave in to the urge to sink against his mother. "Promise me," Ellen said, "that this time you'll think twice."

M ia opened the gift box to find a wool scarf bright with the Carrymuir MacDonald tartan. "Thanks," she said, looping it around her wrist. She glanced at Allie and smiled, thinking, *What is this supposed to mean? Does she know?*

"I didn't get you anything," Mia said. "I'm sorry."

Allie grinned. "I certainly wasn't expecting anything. If it makes you feel better, consider this a Christmas bonus for taking over while I was helping out with Jamie's defense. I would have had to close the shop, otherwise."

Mia laughed nervously. It was the day after Christmas, a slow day they would use to reorganize the stock and tidy up the shop, which had been strewn with velvet ribbon and overturned boxes of votives in the mad rush to do over sixty holiday arrangements.

She had not seen Cam on Christmas Day. Only briefly, on Christmas Eve, when he'd come to pick up Allie. They were supposed to be celebrating tonight. She did not know what excuse he was planning to use.

Allie began to move around the shop, picking up spools of

French-wired ribbon and a few floating disks of Oasis that had managed to get overlooked by a broom. She was wearing an obviously new Christmas outfit—pale pink pants and an oversized sweater in shades of gray and white and pink. Her hands kept coming up to her ears, fiddling with a pair of twinkling sapphires. She glanced up at Mia. "Aren't they beautiful?" she said, clearly not expecting an answer. "Cam got them for me."

"Very pretty." Mia tried to keep her voice steady. "What did you get him?"

"Oh, things." Allie reached for a broom and leaned her elbow on the handle. "Some casual shirts, a portable CD player, a guitar."

Mia glanced up. "A guitar? Does he play?"

Allie smiled. "Not yet. I got him lessons, too. I always wanted a guy who would sing love songs to me."

Mia walked to the low table that held the bonsai trees they had started together several months before. She ran her fingers over the lines of the trees, bending sideways and down in all sorts of carefully wired, unnatural positions. "You have to trim these buds," she told Allie absently. Then she walked to the cooler and took out her yogurt. She thought of herself in the shower of Allie's master bathroom, pressed against Cam and loudly laughing through rondos of "Row Row Row Your Boat." "I didn't know Cam could sing," she said.

"He can't," Allie admitted. "But I couldn't change that on my Christmas budget."

Mia had had a difficult time finding a Christmas present for Cam. She would have loved to buy him a sweater or a faded old chambray shirt, so that when she undressed him she would finally be removing something chosen for him by her own hand, but she'd realized this was impossible. How could he explain to his wife a new item in his wardrobe that Allie knew nothing about? Cam wasn't the type to do casual shopping in a mall; he would tell Allie he needed a pair of jeans and scribble down his waist size and inseam.

The same went for pieces of art, or things electronic. Mia couldn't buy him tickets to a Bruins game because she herself was a beggar for his time, and she couldn't presume to steal any more of it. She had worked herself into a fury over choosing a gift, to the point where one morning she had called in sick to the flower shop and spent the day sifting through catalogs that she'd spread over the bed at the Inn like a bright-colored quilt.

"So Jamie's trial is coming up," Mia said.

Allie stopped sweeping for a fraction of a second. "In less than a month. It's hard to believe."

"That it came so soon?"

"No," Allie said. "That it's coming at *all*." She set the broom against the worktable and put her hands on her hips. "I'm probably going to be out most of the time between now and New Year's. Graham asked me to do some kind of telephone survey."

"A survey?" Mia spooned up the last of her yogurt and rested the cup on the large waxy leaf of a plantain. "For what?"

"For the jury. I think he's trying to outsmart the process. I'm supposed to meet with some university guy today who's going to explain it all to me."

*And then I'll go home to Cam.* The words were unspoken, because they were routine for Allie. Mia looked down at the table, following the whorls in the wood. She wanted what this woman had. She wanted to be able to take Cam's exits and entries so easily that her heart would not beat at the back of her throat and her palms would not itch with anticipation.

*Six more hours,* she told herself. *Six more hours and he belongs to you again.* She looked up to find Allie watching her, a strange expression written across her face. "You don't mind?" Allie asked, and for a moment Mia froze, wondering how important the question she had missed was.

"Mind?" she repeated.

"Running the shop alone." Allie smiled a little. "Being your own boss. Again."

Mia stood up and dumped her empty yogurt container down the hole in the worktable that was centered over a thirty-two-gallon trash can. "Of course not," she said. "I'd be happy to take your place."

As a personal rule, Graham MacPhee did not believe in blind dates. He thought they revealed a flaw as deep as a mountain fissure, as if simply agreeing to one meant you were branding your forehead with the word *DESPERATE*. He went out when he felt like it, which was not often in this tiny town. In the back of his mind was the niggling suspicion that his mother believed he was gay.

His mother was a dental hygienist, and was always offering up the daughter or niece of one of her patients. "Lovely," she'd say over

Sunday dinner. "Magna cum laude from Skidmore." Graham had once picked up girls at a country-western bar two towns south of Wheelock, but it was a half-hour drive and one of his excursions had left him with a raging case of crabs, so he had been single and celibate for some time. For his last birthday, his mother had enrolled him in a video dating service. He had never been to their office; he threw out their newsletter.

Then his mother found Veronica Daws. She had come in with an emergency cavity. She taught third grade. She had curly blond hair and a figure, his mother said, to die for. She was willing to go out with Graham.

"That's fine," he had said, "but you don't have *my* consent."

So his mother had started making Veronica Daws her personal crusade. She somehow procured a picture of the girl, who was passably attractive, and mailed it to Graham return receipt requested. She brought up the girl's name during every phone conversation and meal until Graham realized it would be easier to simply go out on one blind date than have his mother on his back for the rest of his natural life.

"I heard about your trial," Veronica Daws said, playing with her Caesar salad. Through an entire appetizer and now the salad course, she had managed to shuffle her food into unlikely configurations, but Graham had yet to see her put a bite into her mouth. "It sounds pretty heavy."

*Heavy?* He scowled, then tried to cut the woman a little slack. How else would she be able to reduce the mass of roiling emotions that made up Jamie MacDonald's defense to a third-grader's level?

"Did he do it?" she asked.

She was looking up at him with these baby-blue eyes, raking her fork over her plate, flawlessly acting out the suggestions in whatever universal women's dating manual said that you were supposed to get the guy talking about himself. "Yes," Graham said.

Veronica shuddered. "Eww. How can you be in the same room as him?"

Graham glanced over her shoulder at the clock. "It's not like he's Charlie Manson," he said. "I don't exactly have to fear for my life."

"But still," Veronica pressed. "He *killed* her. I mean, I know she was dying and all, but that doesn't mean he has the right to play God."

Graham flashed her a smile. "Would you excuse me?" He

walked to the rest room and stepped inside, mentally taking note of the fact that the only window was too high off the floor for him to reach and too narrow for him to ever escape through. Sighing, he sat down on a toilet seat in a stall, still wearing his trousers.

Sure, Jamie had been playing God. But then again, he'd assumed the position at Maggie's request. Graham could rationalize a hundred different ways—a life spent as a vegetable was not a life; a person in pain has the right to end that pain; an act of mercy precludes an act of murder. In the abstract, most people would agree to those statements. We were all programmed to think the best, weren't we? But that didn't cancel out the fact that Jamie MacDonald had held a pillow over his wife's face until she stopped breathing. Whatever he had believed he was doing, he had believed strongly, and these emotions were so real that he had killed another person.

In the long run, it didn't matter what label Graham pinned on these feelings. Call it love, call it fear, call it desperation, call it mercy. It could have been all or none of these. And still, Jamie MacDonald had felt it and had done the thing that the overwhelming majority of us wouldn't do.

Graham knew why Veronica Daws didn't buy it. Why the waiter had looked at him sideways when he'd first given his name at the reservations desk. It was difficult to see past the reality of a victim's body into the shady areas of motivation and controlling passions. It was tough to admit to yourself that someone else had more courage than you would in the same situation, or that it was possible to love someone in a way that you had not personally experienced.

And because it was so hard for outsiders to understand, Graham knew the only chance he had of getting Jamie off was to make him look like he'd gone crazy.

Graham flushed the toilet twice, as if this would help to clear his mind. He washed his hands and patted them dry against his thighs and decided he would use the rest of the dinner as a mock trial, trying to sway Veronica over to his side. She was young and impressionable; she could have been a member of a jury. *You know,* he would say when he sat down again, *in law there's often a lot that does not meet the eye.*

Graham mentally reviewed a hasty opening statement and walked out of the bathroom. Veronica Daws, fluffed and bubbly and waiting, immediately gave a tiny wave. Graham straightened his tie and wondered if in matters of love, he'd ever be as lucky as Jamie.

*F*yvel Adams, professor of sociology at the University of Massa-chusetts in Amherst, worked out of a closet. He said he didn't need a lot of light and space to collect and shape data.

Allie and Graham stood out in the hall. It was lit by fluorescent balls strategically hung every three feet, which gave Graham dark shadows beneath his eyes and a five o'clock beard. Allie wondered if it was just the dungeon offices, or if he'd been having trouble sleeping.

Graham had explained the principle of a jury survey on the long ride to Amherst. The final list of jurors for Jamie's case would come from a list of three hundred names, pulled from a random sampling of citizens in Berkshire County. The survey she'd be working on with Fyvel Adams would involve questioning their own sampling of citizens. Then, personality attributes of respondents who had been sympathetic would be computer-matched to demographics such as age, sex, occupation, political affiliation. Based on the results of the computer run, the characteristics of the perfect juror for Jamie's case could be outlined, and these would be used as a benchmark when it came time for Graham to select a jury.

Fyvel Adams was of a height such that his Adam's apple bobbed directly in front of Allie's eyes. He seemed all throat—he was skinny and his head seemed to recede to a point at the top. He had two students working with him, thesis candidates who were happy to volunteer their services to Allie.

He spread out several papers on the floor so that Allie and Graham could read them. "We've got the basics," he said, running his fingertip down the first page. "Age, sex, religion, nationality, what have you." He flipped this over and began making a graph that neither Allie nor Graham could decipher. "Then you get the fuzzy gray statements."

Allie knelt down and read the poorly typed second page. The instructions asked respondents to rate their answers, *1* being strong agreement, *4* being strong disagreement. She glanced at the first statement: *In certain circumstances, a person should be allowed to break the law.* She glanced at Graham.

*Success can be measured directly from how hard you work at it.*

*God created man; science had little to do with it.*

*If a person is pronounced brain-dead, he or his family should be able to ask a doctor to turn off the life-support machines.*

"Well," she said, taking a deep breath. "This ought to be fun."

She pulled out of her pocketbook the Berkshire County voter registry, marked off with a red dot at every ninety-seventh name. "How long do we have to finish this?"

Graham rubbed his hand over his face. "A week," he said. "You can call from my office; the kids will take the last half of the registry pages and call from the sociology department phones."

He smiled at Adams, thanked him for his cooperation, and gently turned Allie away by the elbow. "Who the hell am I kidding?"

Allie smiled up at him. "You get a gold star for effort."

Graham smirked. "In this case, I need to have the highest grades in the whole goddamned class."

They drove in near silence back to the law offices of MacPhee and MacPhee, where Allie spent the remainder of the afternoon with a tub of chicken salad from the coffee shop and a headset she'd taken from Graham's secretary which allowed her to talk on the phone without holding a receiver. She had just made her fortieth call when Graham walked into the room.

"Any luck?" he asked, flipping through the pile of completed surveys.

Allie shrugged. "Incredibly inflexible people. I think everyone I've called moonlights for the KKK," she said. "Except for those few who told me they didn't have time to talk to a telemarketer, and how would I like it if they called *me* at home?"

Graham laughed. "I hope you gave out your number." He stuck a spoon into the chicken salad and took a bite. "I'm going out. I have my own hunches about jury surveys."

Allie glanced up at him. "Bring me coffee. It's going to be a rough night."

When he reached his car, Graham opened his briefcase and pulled out his copy of the voter registration list. The first name on it was Arlene Abbot, 59 Cheshire Road, Wheelock.

He drove down Main Street, making only one wrong turn on his way to find a vaguely familiar street. The Abbot house was a tiny ranch, with a huge American flag hanging from a pole in the front yard. He noted this next to her name.

Two more Wheelock residents had what Graham considered symbols of inflexibility: chain-link fences, German shepherds, manicured hedges. With a sinking feeling in his gut, he wrote down these details.

The next name he picked was Lawrence Alban, 7572 Groundhog Path, Hancock. It was a bit of a drive to the bordering town, but he found the house with the help of a local map. Hubcaps in the yard, house painted shocking green, homemade bird feeders. He smiled, and scrawled a big star next to this first glimmer of nonconformity.

For Christmas, Mia had given him the world. Cam turned the tiny globe around in his hands, letting the tissue paper from the box fall to the floor. There was no axis; it was speared in place by a strange magnetic attraction, or maybe by magic.

"Brush up on your geography," she said, spinning the globe and offering one of those lies that always seem just within reach when it is Christmas. "We're going to go, someday."

"This is great," he said, delighted. He kissed her. "This is perfect." He thought of Allie, who had bought him a guitar that he didn't know how to play. Mia hadn't purchased something *she* wanted him to have; she had read his mind and given him what *he* wanted. "Where did you get it?"

Mia couldn't stop smiling. He liked it; he really liked it. "A catalog. One of those stores that have presents for the man who already has everything."

"I don't have everything," Cam said. *I don't have you.*

"Oh, I don't know." Mia slid an arm around his waist. "You've got a toehold on the American dream."

Cam thought about that. The house, the cars, the backyard. The wife and the shadows of kids who would someday arrive. It made a pretty, colorful painting, but it was frightening to think of Mia standing somewhere outside the frame.

"I thought you should have something you could keep at the office," Mia said quietly. "Small enough to stuff in a bottom drawer."

Cam brushed her hair away from her face. "I'm not hiding this. I'd just spend the whole day taking it out and playing with it, anyway."

They lay on their bellies on the bed at the Inn, the globe at arm's length. Like blind men, they shirred their fingers over the relief map that covered the ball, trailing up the Himalayas and into the Sahara and through the Mediterranean Sea.

"Well," Cam said finally, pulling an envelope out of his breast pocket. "It's not nearly as exotic. But Merry Christmas."

Mia tore the envelope open. Inside was a brochure, carefully hand-lettered, announcing the presence of Braebury House, a bed-and-breakfast in the White Mountains of New Hampshire. Her hair spilled over her face as she sat up, glancing at the photographs of a wing chair before a glowing fire, a four-poster bed, a comfortable clutter of antiques.

"Two weekends from now," Cam said, his eyes pleading. "I'm going to say there's a training session in New Braintree. Your aunt could get sick again."

Mia considered having Cam for a weekend, a whole weekend, in a place where nobody would judge her as the other woman and no one would know his name. She tried to imagine being part of a two-some like her parents, so close they would be able to think for each other. She considered what it might feel like not to be the odd one out.

He pressed a kiss against the side of her neck, as if he thought she was hesitating; as if he thought she could truly tell him no. "Please," Cam whispered. "Let me try again."

Christmas was not nearly so much of a celebration in Wheelock as Hogmanay, which was known to the rest of Massachusetts as New Year's Eve. As in Scotland, most of the town got roaring drunk. After midnight, neighbors went first-footing, going from house to house to wish each other a good new year, bearing shortbread or bottles of wine or fine whiskey.

Since Cam was always working New Year's Eve, it was much the same as any other night for Allie, except for all the noise outside—it was difficult to ignore the drunken, off-key renditions of "Auld Lang Syne" and the spit and pop of firecrackers the teenagers set off in the wet, cold streets. She had tried to convince Angus and Jamie to spend the night at her house watching the Times Square ball drop, but Angus had simply grunted and said if he'd lived another year, he was damn well going to celebrate it by sleeping in.

Jamie—well, Jamie just hadn't felt like celebrating. "Come by then, after twelve," she had said. "They say the perfect first-footer is a tall, dark-haired man who brings lots of food."

Jamie had laughed at that. "Cam's just as tall. And I can't imagine he'll be happy to shoot the breeze with me after a night of locking up drunks."

So Allie had found herself celebrating alone. At eleven o'clock she took out a bottle of Glenfiddich, which she never drank, and tossed back a shot. She did two more before eleven-thirty. By the time it was midnight, she was feeling charged and festive, her stomach burning pleasantly, her power enough to conquer the world.

She watched Dick Clark for a little while and then went upstairs. On Hogmanay, Cam usually made it home around two in the morning. She could shower, change the sheets, and hope he wasn't exhausted when he got in.

It was just after one when she finished. The bedroom was lovely; lit with candles she'd kept out from Christmas and smelling of the rose infusion she added to her detergent when she washed the sheets. She was still wearing plaid pajamas and oversized slippers in the shape of elephants, but she had plenty of time to change. Sighing, she glanced around, looking for something to do.

She didn't want to straighten Cam's drawers, but she was feeling generous. It had always amazed her how someone who looked so starched and perfectly pressed during the day in a police officer's uniform could unwittingly wrinkle everything else he owned. Allie had once teased him, saying that he'd joined the force because he couldn't keep any other work clothes in decent shape. And Cam had said that when he was a kid, Ellen had ironed his underwear, so maybe this was just his way of rebelling.

Allie opened his shirt drawer, riffling through the rainbow of fabrics. She couldn't imagine Ellen ironing boxer shorts; ironing anything. It would go against her principles now—she said ironing took all the creativity out of the fabric's personality. She had even taken Allie to task for her bonsai project at the shop. How could she justify chaining with copper wire something that was meant to grow wild and free?

Absently, Allie began to organize Cam's T-shirts according to color. She knew it wouldn't stay that way for more than a day, but she had nothing better to do, and with all that whiskey in her, if she lay down and closed her eyes just for a minute she'd be out like a light. Reds on top, blues on the bottom, whites and decals on a side all their own.

She opened Cam's underwear drawer and began linking the socks. *"Dahlink,"* she drawled, pulling one long gray sock from the tangle, "have I got a match for *you!"* She fingered the rest of the pile for its mate, rolled them into a ball, and set them on the top of the dresser. She did this until all the socks were lined up. "Like Noah's Ark," she murmured, and then she heard Cam coming up the stairs.

She turned around to face him, her eyes glowing and her cheeks on fire. "Figures," she said. "Redheaded first-footers are the worst kind of luck." She took an unsteady step toward him, pulling on the front of his shirt.

Cam smelled the whiskey; he could have smelled it from downstairs. It was overpowering the fresh floral scent of the turned-down bed. "Well, Jesus," he said, grinning so hard a dimple appeared in his cheek. "You, Allie MacDonald, are drunk."

"I am nothing of the kind," Allie said indignantly. "You're just sober."

"As a judge," Cam laughed. "Exactly what I wanted to come home to."

He sat down on the bed and pulled off his boots, looking at the row of socks on the top of his dresser. "I hope you weren't doing this for me. It's hopeless."

Allie shrugged. "I was bored." She took a step toward him, swaying suggestively and nearly falling in the process. "I was waiting for you."

Cam smiled. "You'll have to wait a little longer. I need to take a shower."

"That's okay," Allie said. "I'll attack some more drawers." She turned back to the dresser and pulled out Cam's boxer shorts. There were some white ones, but most were printed with the images of tropical fish or moose or traffic signs—Allie always stuffed a new pair into his Christmas stocking. She lifted the boxers on top—lipstick kisses—and something tumbled to the floor.

It was a T-shirt, rolled tight into a ball around a pair of women's bikini underwear, nothing at all like the ones Allie wore. "Look at this," she said, holding them up to the light.

Cam had just pulled his shirt over his head. He turned to see Allie holding the clothes Mia had left behind the weekend before Christmas; the clothes that he, like an idiot, had forgotten to bring back to her.

The moment of reckoning hit him like a sucker punch, driving him to sit down on the bed with a sharp intake of breath. *Not yet, not yet, not yet,* he thought. *I don't want to let her go.* He did not let himself wonder which woman he meant.

Allie brought the T-shirt closer and noticed the little label in the neck. "Mia's," she said matter-of-factly. "I should have known." She folded the shirt and placed it on the bed beside Cam. "God, have we had them all this time? She must have left them months ago when she first stayed overnight."

Cam felt his mouth moving woodenly around words that seemed to have no edges. "Maybe you washed them. Maybe you stuck them in there by mistake."

Allie nodded. "I probably wasn't thinking. I do the laundry on automatic pilot. If it's soft, it must be a pair of boxers."

Cam stuffed the shirt and panties beneath the bed, where he wouldn't have to think about it. He had never loved Allie more than he did in that incredible, guileless moment; the feeling flooded him in tandem with a hot swell of relief, so that he became full and heavy, immobile.

He looked at his wife, hiccuping behind her hand, her hair straggling out of its braid and down the back of her plaid pajamas. Her teeth bit into her bottom lip as she folded his underwear; her conversation tumbled along in a giddy rush.

Innocence looked lovely on her.

Your hair was wild around your face, and your thumbs were pressed up close against each other in front of your lips where they held the top of the acorn. "Like this," you said, but you were laughing too hard; you couldn't show me how you made those little wedges with your thumbs on the wooden cap and blew through your knuckles to make an unholy whistle.

You had been wearing those little flat black shoes, like a ballerina, but you didn't mind walking through the woods. I remember that the wet leaves wrapped around your ankles like leeches and I am pretty sure that a bramble nicked your skirt, leaving a hole the size of a dime.

I was hopelessly bad at whistling through an acorn top; you kept at it for hours, holding your hands over mine and telling me to get another damn acorn when the first cap shattered under the pressure of my clumsy thumbs.

Do you know how you love people more on certain days? It wasn't the way that your hair looked when the sun was painting the curls, or the feeling of your hands locked around mine, willing them to move a certain way.

It was because on that day, at least, you didn't give up.

# FIFTEEN

Allie and Cam usually celebrated Valentine's Day on January 14, because the shop claimed too much of her attention the following month for her to enjoy the holiday herself. It had been a tradition for six years now. Allie would wake up in the morning and pull a card for Cam and a gift out of her nightstand, and Cam would stare at her, his mouth opening and closing like a trout's, as he realized he'd forgotten yet again.

It wasn't like she was buying him something extraordinary— usually she went to an outdoorsman shop and picked up a couple of off-season flies—but she could not keep herself from thinking, the night before, that this year was going to be the year Cam remembered all by himself. And she supposed she could have stacked the odds, too, by mentioning Valentine's Day in passing a week or so before, but that would have defeated the purpose.

To Cam's credit, he always bounced back. He'd return after work with a box of chocolates and a card, *I love you* scribbled in pencil and slightly shaky, as if he had written it while his car was still moving.

This year, they were celebrating two days earlier, January 12, because Cam would be away on business that weekend. The sun was high and still when Allie woke up, but she screwed her eyes shut and willed herself to go back to sleep. She pretended that she could smell something dizzy and sweet—the perfume of, say, a half-dozen calla lilies that Cam had stowed beneath his side of the bed in the middle of the night. She slid her eyes to her right, but Cam was snoring lightly. One arm was tossed up over his head, one foot peaked out from the quilt.

*I am going to count to ten,* she told herself. *And then he's going to wake up and surprise me.*

One. Two, three . . .

She didn't know why this year seemed to matter more than the other years. Maybe it was because they had been fighting so much during the holidays. Maybe it was because she had seen so little of him while conducting Graham's jury survey. Maybe it was because she was getting tired of doing all the work.

Seven, eight . . .

With a sigh she rolled toward Cam. The stained-glass panel he'd given her months before cast half of his face into a blue shadow, making him look otherworldly. The glass heart of one daffodil, a bright red shard, reflected on his cheek like a scar.

She dug in her nightstand for the card and the tiny box. Then she poked him in the ribs. "Happy Valentine's Day," she said.

Cam's eyes shot open. "No," he groaned. He rolled his face into his pillow. "Shit."

Allie ran her hand over the muscular line of his shoulder, down the ridges of his spine. "Let me guess."

Cam propped himself up on his elbows and offered her a smile that would have charmed a snake. "I've been preoccupied with this stupid training," he said. "You know, getting things set at the station so that I can leave today. Besides, I've got till midnight," he reminded her.

"That's what you always say."

"That's because it's always true." He rolled onto his back. "If you were smart, you'd wait until dinnertime to give me a card."

He was already tearing it open. "If I did that," Allie said dispassionately, "I'd *never* get anything in return."

Cam sat up and read the card, grinned, and kissed her cheek. "Look at it this way—since I'm leaving at noon, you're sure to get something by then." He stripped away the wrapping paper on the tiny gift and lifted two woolly boogers out of the box. Laughing, he placed them on the sheet between him and Allie. "These are great. I love getting fly-fishing stuff when there's a foot of snow on the ground."

Allie swung her legs out of bed. "Makes spring come that much faster," she said, and padded to the bathroom.

When she'd closed the door behind her, Cam exhaled slowly and held his hands up to his face. They were trembling. He was planning to meet Mia in Shelburne Falls at one, and leave her car at a Stop & Shop so they could drive the bulk of the way to New Hampshire together.

Allie came out of the bathroom while he was stuffing clothes into a duffel bag. She watched him fold jeans, a turtleneck and a sweatshirt, a pair of long underwear. Then he put his heavy snow boots right on top. "Aren't you forgetting a uniform?" she asked.

He jumped, zipped the bag, and turned around. "Christ," he said. "You scared the hell out of me." He gestured at the bag. "It's a casual seminar. No uniforms."

Allie arched an eyebrow. "Are they holding it indoors?"

"In the middle of January? What do you think?"

She moved to her dresser and pulled out a pair of stockings. "Then what's the long underwear for?"

"Oh, that. They're doing some kind of survival thing. A bi-athlon. Skiing, shooting. You know."

He wondered when he had become so good at distorting the truth.

He watched Allie struggle into a pair of panty hose. It was not a graceful thing, in spite of what you imagined when you were a teenage boy. He turned abruptly, picked up his bag, and left the bedroom.

Graham sat on the floor in a pair of rumpled khaki pants, his shirt wrinkled and buttoned incorrectly so that one flap hung longer than the other. He dipped a doughnut into the sludge he'd made that was passing for coffee and stared at the dry-erase board in front of him.

He'd appropriated it from the MacPhee and MacPhee conference room. It was set up like a grid. On the left-hand side, in green ink, were the days: September 15, 16, 17, 18, 19. At the top, under the fifteenth, Graham had written: *APPOINTMENT, 4:45 P.M., DR. DASCOMB WHARTON.* At the bottom, underneath the nineteenth, he'd written: *MAGGIE, ESTIMATED TIME OF DEATH, 7 A.M.—10 A.M., HUGO HUNTLEY.*

In the middle, the chart looked like a crossword puzzle. He'd tried to re-create the days as Jamie had described them during their walk a few weeks earlier, and with Allie diligently working on the jury survey, he'd taken time to prepare his witnesses and to corroborate Jamie's story. In many cases, to his astonishment, there had been someone to witness Jamie and Maggie as they celebrated their last weekend alone. Bud Spitlick remembered seeing them up on the roof of the house eating something or other; he said he'd yelled at them to be careful up there. And an usher at the Loew's multiplex cinema remembered Jamie and Maggie from that Saturday night; he blushed when he told Graham he'd had to shine his flashlight on them as they were making out and tell them to keep it down a little.

American Express had a credit card receipt with Jamie's signature at The Rooster's Comb, the swanky restaurant where they'd had dinner Saturday night. The manager of the Red Lion Inn directed Graham to the newlywed couple whose wedding Maggie and Jamie had crashed, who of course remembered them, and were surprised to hear that the couple who could jitterbug like professionals were not friends of either of the families.

Graham had had a difficult time finding eyewitnesses for Sunday, the day Jamie had taken his wife out to memorize the world. A hot dog vendor who had a spot at the park near the mountains where Jamie said they had been *might* have seen them, but he couldn't truly remember. Bud Spitlick had been mowing his lawn when the MacDonalds returned to their house at about five o'clock that night.

On Monday, a gas station attendant in Cummington had filled up the tank with unleaded and had chatted with Jamie as he wiped the windshield. He remembered Mr. MacDonald saying they were taking an impromptu vacation—remembered, in particular, the word "impromptu" because he hadn't known what it meant. The Wheelock Inn register had Maggie's signature, on behalf of Mr. And Mrs., entered at 11:15 A.M. The bartender in the lounge broke down when Graham asked if he remembered selling Jamie the champagne, saying he couldn't help but wonder if he'd sort of aided things along in the murder by getting Jamie drunk.

The owner of the pizzeria did not remember seeing Jamie Mac-Donald that Monday night, but then again he did not speak much English, so he might not have understood Graham's question.

On Tuesday afternoon Jamie had driven to the police station, as the police chief and Allie and any number of town eyewitnesses could verify.

But from Monday night to Tuesday afternoon, Graham's board was a blank.

He stuffed the remainder of the doughnut into his mouth and traced his finger over those gaping white holes on the dry-erase board. There was no telling what exactly had gone on in the room at the Wheelock Inn between eight-thirty Monday night and one p.m. Tuesday afternoon. Jamie and Maggie could have had a vicious, sniping fight. Jamie's mind could have snapped. Or Jamie might have simply been saying goodbye.

Graham hung his head and rubbed his hand over his hair, making it stand up in unruly tufts. He knew that, like his own, the jury's collective eye would be drawn not to the tangle of proof scribbled all over the board, but to those glaring white spaces. More than any tale he could weave as a defense, those blank spots invited interpretation. Everyone loved a mystery; everyone loved to be involved in the process of writing the story.

He pictured the unknown faces of the jurors, inventing their own versions of the last night of Maggie's life, and he wondered if even one of them would approximate the truth.

*C*am had had every intention of taking his time at the card store to find something just right for Allie, but the DUI Zandy brought in for booking started throwing things off the counters and shoving Zandy and the other officer on duty, until it took all three men to physically restrain the asshole and get him into a lockup.

"I can't fucking believe this," Cam said to Zandy. "How come the crazy ones get arrested on the weekends when we can't ship them out for a bail hearing?"

The other officer, MacIver, was a middle-aged, part-time cop who'd worked for years with Cam's father. "Same reason your kids get sick when the doctor's office is closed," he said. "Just to piss you off."

The prisoner began to hurl his body hard against the door of the cell. "Hey!" Cam yelled. "You want to take it easy?" He glanced at the custody report and turned to Zandy and MacIver. "You two okay here, or do you want me to call in a backup?"

"The National Guard would be nice," Zandy muttered as a gob of spit hit the inside surface of the Flexon. "Or a few sacrificial natives to feed him for dinner."

The prisoner was as tall as Cam himself and twice as meaty. Cam wasn't worried about the man getting out of the cell, but he'd certainly be a pain in the ass. "I can call the courthouse," he suggested. "Maybe we can get someone out here to set bail and ask the sheriff to ship him to the county lockup."

Zandy shot Cam an appreciative look. "Whatever. Just make sure you leave in time to get down to New Braintree."

Cam had told Hannah and the other officers that he was attending a training seminar. He knew no one would doubt his word if he said there was a special weekend meeting for police chiefs on gun safety. With a nod, he went to his office and sat down.

He called the courthouse and got a court clerk to round up a bail officer; then he set the phone back in its receiver. He had meant to call Mia to finalize plans, but time had gotten away from him this morning, and by now she'd be at the flower shop—or even on her way. With a sigh, he stood up and walked out of his office and locked the door behind him. "They say they'll send someone out by the end of the day," Cam said to Zandy. "You want me to call from the road?"

Zandy shook his head. "Contrary to what you believe, Chief, we *can* function without you here." He grinned and nodded toward the door. "Go on."

Cam almost drove to Allie's shop, until he remembered her Valentine's Day gift. Making a U-turn in the middle of Main, he headed for the card store on the other side of town. He turned on the radio and sang along with Van Morrison. As he pulled into the parking lot, the midday news was coming on in the announcer's nasal drone.

Cam glanced at the clock on the dashboard. Noon. Shit.

He ran into the card store, grabbed a box of candy, pulled the first card with a heart off the shelf, and drove fifteen miles over the speed limit back to Glory in the Flower.

Allie was bent over her bonsai tree, carefully rewrapping the painstakingly twisted limbs. "Hi," she said, her eyes fixed right on the bag in his hands.

"Where's Mia?" he asked, the way he had practiced a hundred times that morning.

Allie shrugged, wiping her hands on her jeans and moving closer to Cam, her hands hovering about the paper bag like honeybees. "She asked for some time off. Her aunt's sick again."

Cam nodded in sympathy. "That means you'll be all alone this weekend. You gonna be okay?"

She smiled. "I can function quite well without you, thank you very much," she said, and she reached into the bag.

Cam sat down on one of the work stools. "That's the second time someone's said that to me today."

Allie ran her thumb beneath the sealed edge of the envelope. "And what does that tell you?" She pulled the card out of the envelope, red with a big pink heart on the front. *HAPPY VALENTINE'S DAY, DAD*, she read. She opened the card. *I MAY BE DIFFICULT, BUT AT LEAST I'M CUTE.*

He had signed it *Love, Cam*. Thinking she must have been mistaken, Allie closed the card again. *HAPPY VALENTINE'S DAY, DAD*. "Is this a joke?" she asked, smiling tentatively.

Cam stared at her. "What are you talking about?"

She waved the card beneath his nose. "Happy Valentine's Day, *Dad*?"

Cam snatched the card from her hand. He scowled at the front and passed a hand down his face, rubbing his eyes. "I'm sorry. I wasn't thinking."

Allie blinked at him. He wasn't thinking? He couldn't even read a stupid card to see what it said before he bought it for her?

She looked down at her hands, still stained with soil and scratched by sharp ends of copper wire. She didn't want him to leave in the middle of an argument. She bent over the bonsai tree so that Cam would not be able to see the thoughts skittering across her features. Maybe she was making too much of this. Maybe he had other things on his mind.

She just wished she were one of those things.

"Well." She set the card and candy on the worktable beside the bonsai tree. She picked up a pair of wire cutters. "You probably want to get going."

"Yeah," Cam agreed, coming to his feet. "You never know what kind of traffic you'll hit."

They both came toward each other, awkwardly hugging around Cam's gun belt and Allie's wire cutters. Cam kissed the top of her head. "Happy Valentine's Day," she said brightly.

"Happy Valentine's Day," he murmured. His chin was tucked over Allie's shoulder, and he could see out the big picture window in front of the store. He knew it faced north. He wondered how many miles it was to New Hampshire.

Mia watched the smooth slide of snow run by, curved and white like the lines of a woman. She sat in the passenger seat, her legs tucked beneath her, her back turned to Cam. He was driving with one hand; the other was laced with her own fingers on the inches of seat between them.

They were in Braebury, New Hampshire, a town that ran over the Connecticut River and into Vermont when you least expected it. It was close enough to the ski areas to be renowned, but distant enough to keep the crowds at bay.

Cam pulled the dark blue Ford sedan into the driveway of a gingerbread Victorian, riddled with cornices and turrets and painted the slightest hue of pink, so that it stood against the snow as if it were ashamed. Stuck into the piles of snow in the front yard was a sign, *BRAEBURY HOUSE B & B,* and a carved wooden gull whose wings spun in the wind.

"Oh," Mia exclaimed, staring at the winding, circular porch. "It's terrific."

Cam laughed. "It could have been a cave, and it would have been terrific." He squeezed her hand. "Let's go in."

He carried her knapsack for her—complete with Kafka and tins of Fancy Feast dinners—and his own duffel bag. Mia walked in the path he cut through the snow, and thought that this, more than anything else, signified their relationship. Her bag and his bag, unmatched, clasped by the same unrelenting hand.

The innkeepers, Alice and Horvath Kingsley, were waiting at the front door. "Come in, come in," Horvath said, his voice heavily accented.

Alice fussed over the snow that had caught on the edges of Mia's big jacket. "You made good time getting up here?"

Cam smiled. "Not a soul on the roads."

Mia stamped the slush from her boots. "I should take these off," she said, bending down to untie the laces. She tucked down her chin, oddly self-conscious around this old man and his wife, who did not know her or Cam, yet around whom she felt like a horrible imposter. She was wriggling her toes in their thick ragg socks when she felt Cam's hand on the back of her neck, heavy as a yoke.

"You've come to ski?" Horvath asked. His belly hung over the lip of his suspendered pants in odd juxtaposition to his wife—thin as a stick, all angles and elbows.

"Among other things," Cam said easily. "We're newlyweds."

Mia's mouth dropped open, and she forced herself to close it and smile as she turned to Cam.

Alice Kingsley beamed at her, looking rather like a hawk. "How wonderful!" she cried, and touched Mia's arm. "How long has it been?"

Mia's mouth felt full of stones. "Three—" she said, her voice cracking on the single word. "Three weeks," she repeated, at the same time Cam interrupted and said, "Three months."

Cam looked at Mia and laughed. "It *feels* like three months."

Over the icy white acres came the soft moan of a cello, joined by the dance of a piccolo and a lively violin. Mia turned her head to the breezeway door, thinking this was something she must have imagined. "Is that what I think it is?" she asked.

Alice nodded. "We're a mile away from a musician's colony," she explained. "Members of the BSO come for a couple of weeks at a time, and when the wind's blowing right, well, you can hear it all. Of course, it's much more pleasant when the strings come than, say, the percussion. But it's lovely in the summertime. They do little quartets sometimes, right on the front lawn."

She slipped an arm around Mia's shoulders and pulled her into the main room of the house, a den with a cavernous ceiling and a fireplace that could seat six. "Come, dear," she urged. "You'll have to sign our register." She glanced at Horvath, who was talking with Cam about the bird feeders dotting the snowy back lawn like tiny telephone booths. "Why don't you show Mr. MacDonald to his room?"

Mia picked up the pencil and looked at the neat loops and curves of the names of the people registered before her. Her hand started trembling. It wasn't right, she knew it wasn't right, but then again, Cam had said they were married.

*Mr. and Mrs. Cameron MacDonald,* she scrawled unsteadily. *Wheelock, Mass.*

She stared at it for a moment, feeling better and better as the sloppy, scratchy words came into focus. It was her weekend after all, her present, and didn't she have a right to pretend?

Cam came up behind Mia and pulled her against him, the pad of his thumb just brushing her breast. He looked at what she'd written in the register, his name in Mia's shaky handwriting.

Cam wound his fingers with hers. He understood for the first time how if you believed you belonged to someone, no piece of paper or priest's benediction could make it any more real. "Not bad for a beginner."

Mia turned in his arms to face him. "Well," she said, "practice makes perfect."

## PSYCHIATRIC REPORT

### SUBJECT: James MacDonald
### BY: Harrison Harding, M.D.

*In my initial session with Jamie, he was reserved and guarded. He repeatedly told me that since he wasn't crazy, he didn't understand what a psychiatrist could do for him in court. I explained that, court procedure notwithstanding, it made sense for someone who had experienced the trauma he'd experienced to discuss his feelings with a trained professional. To which he said that no one else, with the possible exception of his attorney, thought he'd been through a trauma.*

I asked him to tell me about his background, his current living situation, and his relationship with his wife, all in an effort to understand what he was like when his wife died. I said that eventually we would discuss the days leading up to Maggie's death, but that did not necessarily have to be today.

He spent most of the time discussing his wife, Maggie. He said that he believed you fell in love once, and he was lucky enough to have experienced that for eleven years. If pressed, he could describe details of his wife, from the arch of an eyebrow to the length of her fingernails and the location of beauty marks. When speaking of Maggie, Jamie smiled quite often, and he would stand and walk to the window occasionally, as if he was expecting to see her.

He indicated several times that the woman he fell in love with was not the same woman he had killed. I asked him to elaborate. He said, "Everyone says I killed Maggie, but they don't remember what she used to be like. There was very little of her left by the time we got to Wheelock." He told me graphic stories of the pain she experienced, from hallucinations during the night to violent vomiting after chemotherapy. He said the last of her ailments was the cancer spreading to the optic nerve, and he relayed how he had sat pressing the sides of her skull in his hands because she was convinced the bright flurry of colors would send it flying apart.

It seems that in spite of the reports from physicians, Jamie's awareness of the pain his wife was undergoing came from Maggie herself. Moreover, the nature and strength of their relationship indicates that Jamie may have indeed felt emotionally the same anguish his wife was physically suffering.

When I asked him if there was anything he hadn't had a chance to tell Maggie, he nodded. "That she was wrong," he said. "When we talked about it, she said it would be better to remember her as the woman she was than the woman she had become. But the truth is, now I have neither."

Jamie views his relationship with his late wife as something fine and sacred. His actions in the past seem to have

*been calculated to please Maggie, which led to his agreement
and involvement in her death.*

*NOTE TO GRAHAM MACPHEE: I know what you're look-
ing for from me, but the truth is Jamie was well-spoken and
calm. He seems to feel remorse—not over the fact that he committed murder, but because at the very end, the woman he'd
idolized betrayed him about the ramifications to his own life.
It's not his mind that was broken. It was his heart.*

*D*emocrats rated the highest. People under thirty scored five
points, while senior citizens received only one point. Jews
were worth six points; Protestants, three; Catholics, one. Graduate
degrees were each worth an extra point.

According to Fyvel Adams, who'd run the computer analyses
of the jury survey, sex made no difference in determining the ideal
juror for Jamie's trial. Neither did nationality. The best juror for
Jamie would receive, in total, twenty points. Anyone who rated less
than fifteen points shouldn't be allowed to serve.

Graham and Audra Campbell had met with Judge Roarke
an hour before, agreeing to select fourteen jurors, which included
the two alternates. Roarke reminded Graham about the verbal-
prohibition motion Audra had filed. "Oh," Graham said under his
breath, sneering at the ADA, "you mean the 'M' word?"

When Roarke gave him a dirty look, Graham had realized
something crucial to his client's case. Judge Roarke wanted a conviction. Which meant he would not make mistakes that could lead
to an appeal.

On Friday afternoon, Graham, Allie, Jamie, and Fyvel Adams
sat at the defense bench as the veniremen were called up individually. Jamie's left leg tapped nervously until Allie, cool and prepared
in a smart plum wool dress, stilled it with a touch. Graham smiled
at her. He saw her take Jamie's hand and clasp it on the defense
table between her own.

The first prospective juror was Alexander Grant, a retired
colonel, who'd made a career of the Army. Graham rolled his eyes.
"Great way to start," he whispered, and he used one of his twenty
peremptory challenges to excuse the juror.

Grant was replaced by Roberta Cavendish, forty-seven, Catholic, high school diploma, mother of five. "Seven points," Fyvel murmured, leaning toward Graham. "That won't do." Graham scanned his own list of yard checks, and saw that he had passed by the Cavendish home. *Mangy dog,* he had written. *House only half painted. Christmas lights everywhere.* "She stays," Graham murmured.

The next potential juror, a young woman who taught music at the elementary school in Wheelock, winked at Graham as she sat down to answer questions. Audra Campbell folded her arms across her chest and used one of her peremptory challenges.

Graham challenged a sixty-five-year-old farmer with a sixth-grade education. Audra challenged a twenty-five-year-old black social worker.

A woman with limpid eyes and badly dyed orange hair waddled her way up to the stand. Obese, tentative; she knotted and unknotted her fingers every time Audra or Graham fired a question at her. Beside him, Fyvel was furiously circling the number he'd totaled up on his scale for her: 8. He shook his head and mouthed the word "No." But Graham looked her in the eye, and thought he noticed the yellow spark that compassion sometimes leaves in its wake. He nodded to the judge.

The jurors that were called got worse and worse, as if the lottery itself had been fixed. After a quick recess in the late morning, everyone seemed to be over the age of sixty; everyone was Catholic; everyone had done some time in the service. Graham began to ignore Fyvel's tugs at his trouser leg and violent scribbling on his legal pad. He whispered instead with Allie: *I like the way she blinks too much. Her mouth looks kind. A Mickey Mouse tie is a sure sign of nonconformity.*

Audra challenged a young woman with a shaved head, as well as a Japanese computer technician. Graham objected to a lady who ran the local organization of right-to-lifers.

When there were fourteen potential jurors, Graham turned around to the jury box and took a deep breath. Of the fourteen, Fyvel had accepted only two: a self-professed starving artist and a nursery school teacher's aide. Allie felt strongly about the man with the Mickey Mouse tie and the fat lady with the dyed hair. Jamie said the woman with the kind mouth had smiled at him.

Most of the jurors could go either way, but even Graham had to admit it did not look good. The average age of the jurors assembled thus far was fifty-two. The majority were Catholic, Republican, fairly uneducated. Fyvel threw his pencil down; it rolled off and under the defense table.

Graham looked at the veniremen who had yet to be called for questioning. A sea of blank, old faces; no one who overtly possessed any of the characteristics that would have guaranteed a 20 on Fyvel's scale. Not, of course, that you could pick a Democrat or a Jew by just looking—but Graham had no reason to believe that the remaining prospective jurors would suddenly take a turn for the liberal.

He had five peremptory challenges left. If he used one of them, he gave Audra the chance to get rid of one of the jurors they really liked, such as the artist or the aide. With the way his luck had been running, the replacement would be a White House Chief of Staff from the Reagan era.

He glanced at Audra Campbell before turning to Judge Roarke to tell him that the defense accepted the jury.

*H*oecht Lake sat like a cherrystone in the middle of Braebury, ensconced in a valley that rose on all sides to become the town. It was enchanting. Cam laced Mia's skates for her and tugged her around the oval once until she felt steady enough to keep her own balance. The people that circled around laughed and bobbed in her field of vision like a sea of balloons. A little girl offered to take their picture with a Polaroid Mia had bought. Instantly the picture developed: Cam with the sun shining to rival his hair, his arms around Mia, a wide smile splitting her face.

But when you don't know how to skate, you quickly get tired of falling down. "There's something genetically wrong with my ankles," Mia said, grabbing Cam's hand for support as she stumbled over a piece of straw stuck into the ice. "They turn in."

"There's nothing wrong with your ankles. They're just not used to this."

Cam gently detached Mia's fingers and skated ahead of her, turning in a sharp curve on his hockey skates to send a spray of snow into her face.

"Show-off," Mia said.

"Now *that* is genetic." Cam did a little loop around her and locked his hands on her hips. "Just glide."

Mia felt her feet coming out from under her. "Let go," she said, pushing at Cam's palms. "I don't like going fast."

"Mia, the *trees* are moving faster than you."

He moved away, and Mia stumbled over another piece of straw sticking out of the ice. Cam straddled her and pulled her up from her armpits. "I knew that going away with you would be dangerous," she muttered. "I just didn't figure it would be quite like this."

Cam hauled her to her feet. "If you're very nice to me, I'll let you sit the next round out."

Mia clutched his elbow and smiled gratefully. He propelled her to one of the Adirondack benches. "I'll be back," he said, and he took off toward the separate hockey oval at a breakneck pace.

She watched Cam dart and weave between the three hockey games in progress, leaving a thin white line on the ice where each skate had been. Suddenly, this grace of movement was not beautiful but upsetting. Mia would never skate like that. She'd never fit seamlessly into the harsh New England winters like everyone else up here; like Cam. It was just one more difference to add to the mountain between them.

By the time Cam skated back to her, bright-eyed and panting, Mia was curled into a ball on the Adirondack bench, her toe picks digging into the scarred wood and her arms hugging her knees. She lifted her face at his approach, knowing her nose was running and her eyes were red and her skin was mottled with the cold.

Cam's chest constricted when he saw her. All he could think was that she had hurt something when she fell and he had been stupid enough to leave her alone. "Mia?" He gathered her close. "What's the matter?"

Her voice, hitched, was little more than a whisper. "I don't want to go skiing."

Cam blinked. "You *what?*"

She pulled back. "I don't want to go skiing. Tomorrow." Sniffling, she wiped her sleeve across her nose. "I don't want you to see something else I do terribly."

Cam kissed her ear. His lips were at least ten degrees warmer. "We don't have to go skiing," he said, slipping his arm around her shoulders. He thought of the grammar of Gaelic, in which you did not say you were in love with someone, but that you "had love toward" her, as if it were a physical thing you could present and hold—a bundle of tulips, a golden ring, a parcel of tenderness. "I'd love you if you just sat in a chair all day."

They sat in companionable silence, staring at an ice sculpture some burgeoning local artist had created at the juncture of the two skating ponds. It was a bird—a phoenix, Cam supposed—rising out of the pond with its wings spread.

Something at the back of his mind burned a little, and he recalled Jamie MacDonald's voluntary confession, which he'd read again on behalf of the ADA for trial preparation. He remembered Jamie talking about an ice sculpture he'd seen somewhere on vacation with his wife, how it had been nothing but a shell with the life gone out of its eyes, how it had been like Maggie.

Mia laced her gloved fingers through his bare ones. "You're not thinking about skiing anymore," she said.

Cam shook his head. "Jamie," he stated, as if this would explain it all. He turned to Mia and stared into her eyes. "Do you think he was wrong to kill his wife, if he knew she was dying anyway?"

Mia glanced away. "The papers say she *asked* him." Cam nodded. "Well, in my book that makes a difference."

"I know," Cam agreed. "I'm not talking about placing the blame. I'm asking what you would have done if you were Jamie."

Mia looked at Cam, his cheeks rough with beard stubble and his breath quick with health. She squeezed his fingers just to feel him squeeze back. She of all people knew that what you thought you would do in a given situation didn't mean a thing until you found yourself actually facing it.

Would she kill Cam if he asked her to, for a good reason? Probably not. She was too selfish for that. She always had been. Her parents would have done what Jamie had done, in a heartbeat. Of course, they wouldn't have stopped there.

Which brought her to the question she really thought everyone should be asking Jamie MacDonald. How could he not have killed himself, too?

"Do you think he was right?" Cam repeated.

Mia bit her lip. "I think love makes you lose yourself," she said carefully. "My mother used to start kitchen fires all the time because she'd get to teasing or kissing my father and forget anything was on the stove." She paused. "And I don't think my parents would have left me alone nearly as much as they did, but they were so wrapped up in being husband and wife they forgot about being a father and mother."

She leaned close enough for her words to fall directly on Cam's lips. "I don't know about Jamie, but I understand doing something you know you shouldn't be doing, and knowing at the same time it's not wrong."

Turning her head, she nestled closer to Cam. A single drip ran down the side of the ice sculpture, boring a hole in the snow at the side of the pond. Cam buried his face in Mia's curls, and he wondered how much time was left.

*I*'m not making any promises," Graham said, picking at his BLT. "I'm just telling you what's at stake."

Jamie stared dejectedly at a turkey sandwich. The mayonnaise was seeping through the white bread, which hadn't been cut thick enough to begin with. He pushed the center with his finger and watched the dressing ooze up. "Never thought I'd hear you say that." He glanced up. "What's it been? Three, four months? 'You're gonna walk, Jamie,' " he mimicked in falsetto.

Graham shook his head. "Who knows?" he said. "You may walk."

"And I may get twenty to life."

Graham went to protest, but shut his mouth and took a bite of sandwich. Jamie wasn't a fool, and he'd seen the jury selection process that day. He had watched Graham bow his head when it was all over, as if the weight on his shoulders had suddenly become too much to bear. He had noticed the way Judge Roarke's eyes trapped him, like a scientist inspecting a rare insect, when he thought that Jamie wasn't looking.

Jamie pushed his sandwich away and took a drink of water. He thought about the snow, which lay knee-deep over Maggie's raw grave. He would miss the outdoors, he thought. He would miss seeing the sky.

Other than that, he didn't much see how the punishment

would differ: a life sentence that made the limits of your world a prison, or the prison your world became when your sentence was simply to live.

On Saturday, Allie drove Jamie all the way to Pittsfield to buy a suit for the trial. He had several at home, but he refused to wear them. "She picked them out," he told Allie, who understood exactly what he was saying.

The men's shop was called Lou's, and Lou himself came forward to offer his assistance. "You're a big one," he said, glancing up at Jamie. "What, forty-four, forty-six long?"

Allie stepped up to the man. "We're looking for something sedate. Something tasteful but not flashy."

"Tasteful," Lou said, trying the word on his lips as if he had never quite heard it put that way before. "Tasteful."

Allie pushed past the proprietor to a rack marked *44 Long*. "You like blue, Jamie, or gray?"

Jamie followed her. "I don't know. Blue, I guess." He ran a hand down the rack of jackets, making the hangers clack and sing. "Does Cam buy his suits here?"

Allie laughed. "Cam buys his suits through a public safety catalog. He owns one sports jacket. His mother bought it for him when he was twenty-two."

She deftly pulled a couple of suits from the rack. "You've got the height to carry double-breasted," she mused, "but I don't want the jury to think you're slick."

"I'm going to wear the same suit through the whole trial?" He stuck his finger through a buttonhole.

"Graham says that you don't have to wear a suit every day. Just during the opening and closing arguments, when you're making the biggest impression on the jurors. He suggests V-necked sweaters and ties with Wall Street dots."

"Wall Street dots?"

Allie nodded. "You know, yellow or red with those little divots in neat little rows. Like you have no imagination at all." She glanced up. "Come over here."

She held a suit up to Jamie's chest, as high as she could reach. "I think I like this one best. Go try on the pants." When Jamie stood there, just staring, she laughed at him. "Go on," she said, pushing him off. "I'm not going with you."

Jamie looked around for the fitting rooms and finally realized they were hidden away behind the row of mirrors to the left. He stepped inside one and hung the three suits Allie had chosen on the tiny hook in the wall. Then he stripped out of his clothes and pulled on the first pair of trousers.

Allie had forgotten to give him a shirt. He stood there for a moment, staring at his bare chest. The hair ran down in an arrow to disappear beneath the baggy waist of the pleated trousers. He looked like a kid dressing up in his father's clothes.

He remembered once when Maggie had dragged him bathing suit shopping. She said it was the worst thing a woman could possibly do to herself, and she'd really appreciate having someone there who loved her no matter how flawed her shape was. The dressing room had been big, so he came inside while his wife tried on one maillot after another. He thought they all looked good and he told her so, but she wasn't considering the bathing suits at all. She'd poke at her stomach and suck in her breath and slap at her thighs with each suit she tried on, until Jamie realized that in spite of each shiny scrap of red and aqua and purple, she was only seeing herself.

Maggie had not much liked mirrors after the mastectomy. She'd shower in the morning and wrap a towel around herself in the steamy stall so that she wouldn't have to see. As far as he could remember, after the operation she had always gotten dressed in her walk-in closet.

Suddenly, Jamie was sweating. He stripped out of the trousers and hurriedly got dressed. When he opened the dressing room door, Allie was waiting for him. She held up two shirts.

He thrust the suits into her hands, a smooth spill of herringbone and subtle checks and dark wool. "Any one," he said, pushing past her toward the clear, cold outside. "I don't care."

*I*t wasn't nearly enough time. They would be driving the following afternoon to Shelburne Falls, picking up Mia's car, and Cam would go home to Allie while Mia would return to the Wheelock Inn. A day of skating, a morning when he could wake up with Mia beside him, and then Cam would have to go back to the way it always was, as if this weekend had not occurred at all.

While the water was running in the bathroom, Cam laid a fire in the bedroom grate. He turned off the lights so that the four-poster bed was bathed in a red, smoky glow, and pulled the towel away from his waist.

Mia came out of the bathroom with a towel turbaned over her head, her skin still dripping. "Feel better?" he asked.

She walked closer to the fire and huddled in front of it. "Warmer," she said. Cam put his hands behind her thighs and drew her near. He unwound her towel and rubbed his palms from her bottom to her calves. "Much warmer," she said, smiling.

He knelt on the hearth, ignoring the cut of the stones into his knees as he kissed his way down the front of Mia's body, following a shifting line that the fire made as it crackled. He felt the heat against his back, and the heat that was gathering between his legs as he closed his mouth over her breast. Mia's breath came out in a rush, and it seemed to him a symphony.

When she finally straddled him on the thick braided rug in front of the hearth, he stared at her. Her hair was outlined crimson. Her head was tossed back, so that he could not see her features, only shadows.

Cam forced himself to close his eyes. Mia had taught him how to listen. So over the pulse of the winter, he heard the cry of a saxophone making love to a flute in the musician's colony a mile away. He heard the soft snore of Mia's sleeping cat. He heard the sound of snow striking snow as it fell outside the window. And afterward, when he fell asleep in Mia's arms, he dreamed this was the last night of the world.

*M*ia did not wake until nearly noon, letting reality slowly wrap itself around her. She started considering an idea she wanted to bring up to Allie. A personalized Flower-of-the-Month club, much like the Fruit-of-the-Month organizations that ran out of Florida, except instead of oranges and persimmons you'd receive calyx and corolla . . .

"I've been thinking," Cam said, a disembodied voice from the warmer side of the bed. "Maybe we don't have to go back."

Mia rolled toward him and smiled. "It's Sunday," she said. "This afternoon the coach becomes a pumpkin again."

He reached out for her. Cam felt full of Mia, ripe to bursting with her, and he did not know how he could ever go back to living halfway. "I'm serious. You'd come away with me, wouldn't you?"

Mia felt her breath return to her. This was familiar, this was their game. "To Turkey. To Greenland. You name it," she said.

Cam shook his head. "I mean I'm going to leave—" Mia reached out to cover his mouth, but he said the word anyway, and it tangled obscenely in her fingers. "Allie."

Mia sat up, pulling the sheet with her so it left Cam bare and flaccid, exposed. "Don't say that," she murmured.

He rolled toward her, placing a hand on her leg. "What else could you possibly want?"

*You,* she thought, *the way you are. The life you have.* She thought of Cam traveling with her in her rental car, Kafka sleeping in his lap during the long stretches of driving. She tried to picture him working as a hired hand on big farms in the South, or dispatching delivery trucks in the cities, just to make ends meet. She tried to picture him without a name, without a position, without a family. She tried to picture him and she saw herself.

If Cam packed up his duffel bag and went home to Wheelock and filed for divorce, he would not be the man she had fallen in love with. If people passed him in the street without calling a greeting; if he slept beneath the stars with her and ate Chef Boy-ardee for three weeks because it was all he could afford, he would not be the man she'd fallen in love with. And how long would it take before he turned against her for taking away the criteria by which he'd always defined himself?

What she had always wished, she realized, was simply to turn back the clock. To meet Cam before Allie had come into his life and to take the place she occupied so smoothly beside him. And in one of those blind, white moments of insight, Mia realized that what she had wanted all along was not necessarily what Cam could offer, but what Allie MacDonald had.

Cam turned Mia toward him and wiped a tear from her cheek with his finger. "You don't want to leave either."

Mia smiled halfheartedly. "That must be it."

But she knew it was more. If she really loved Cam, and she did, she would spare him the pain of feeling like there was no place you could call home.

She stared out the window at the spotless run of snow. Cam was sitting on the edge of the bed, pulling on his boxers. She watched his triceps flex and relax. She thought of how, in a moment or two, he'd ask her what she wanted to do today instead of skiing, and how she would want to say, *Stay here. Make love. Remember you.*

He came to her side of the bed and pulled her into his arms, mistaking her silence. Mia allowed herself the luxury of leaning against someone she would have trusted with her life. She kissed the base of his throat, letting her tongue dart out and make a small, wet mark that was already vanishing when she left it. Then she straightened imperceptibly, just enough for the muscles and the marrow in her bones to realize she had taken the first step toward separation.

# SIXTEEN

At 8:05 on Monday morning, Mia Townsend took the clothes she'd neatly arranged in the dresser of the Wheelock Inn and rolled them into sausages, which she'd always found to be the best method for traveling. She stuffed her belongings into her knapsack and scooped up her cat with her free hand.

Setting Kafka on her stomach, she lay down on a bed that still smelled of her and Cam from the afternoon before. She had arrived in Wheelock before him, and he'd come to the Inn instead of going home. Cam had undressed her so tenderly she thought he must have guessed her decision. But then she realized that it was simply his way of marking something that, in his mind, was not an end but a beginning.

Her body could not let go quite so easily, and had sung to him a lullaby orchestrated by her skin moving against his, until he fell into a deep sleep at her side. Then Mia had closed her eyes and concentrated on the sounds that pushed through the walls and the windows, family sounds and leisure sounds, the hum of a weekend as it shuddered to a close.

She turned her face into the pillow that had been Cam's. She didn't think she'd ever quite forget the scent of him, but when he'd gone to the bathroom she had stolen one of the sweatshirts he'd brought to New Hampshire, just in case. That was what she was taking this time, her keepsake of Wheelock.

Kafka mewed and scratched at her ribs. She absently stroked his neck, and she tried to imagine every line of Cameron MacDonald's face.

Mia took a last look through the drawers and the bathroom to check that she was not leaving a piece of herself behind. With a gentle hand, she ran her fingers down the twisted trunk of her ancient bonsai, the one that had accompanied her everywhere. This she placed on the middle of the bed, where Cam would be certain to find it.

She locked the door to the room that had been hers for a little while. She walked downstairs and settled her bill and returned her key. Then she stepped outside.

It was unseasonably warm for January. Fifty degrees, at least, and it was early in the morning. The snow had melted down to the bare ground in some spots, leaving the grass weak and yellow, looking violated.

Mia took a deep breath and kept her chin held high on the way to her car, carefully avoiding a glimpse into puddles that would only show her herself.

At 8:05 on Monday morning, Allie was rounding up the dirty laundry for dry cleaning. She took it in to Mr. Soong's place every other week, or else Cam would run out of uniforms. He had left early this morning—*another* meeting out of town, this one for some kind of task force. And since he'd returned after ten the previous night, he hadn't had a chance to unpack.

Allie could remember him saying that the gun safety seminar in New Braintree had been casual, but she wasn't sure if he'd packed anything other than a uniform which might merit dry cleaning. He had several cotton sweaters that couldn't be laundered in any other way.

She bent down to rummage through the duffel bag that was lying on its side, pulling out a pair of jeans and a wet musty set of polypropylene long underwear. She was absently thinking that the yellow sweatshirt he'd left town in was missing, when the pictures tumbled into her lap.

They were very bad Polaroids, that was the first thing she noticed. The images were filmy and the colors a bit too awkward, so it was almost possible to believe that she was not seeing clearly as she recognized Cam and Mia standing together in front of a pond full of skaters.

They had red eyes, like people in Polaroids always do.

His arms were around her.

She, Allie, had been so stupid.

As if the images were whirling by in a carnival ride, she remembered Mia standing beside Cam in the kitchen, Mia's toothbrush in their bathroom, Mia and Cam making conversation in the flower shop with her in the back room.

Mia's underwear in Cam's dresser drawer.

Allie felt her spine give way. She lay on her side on the bedroom floor, holding on to those pictures, wondering why she wasn't starting to cry.

It was what she had thought she would do, if this situation ever came about. And she supposed she'd imagined it—didn't everyone who was married consider the worst that could happen? She read *Glamour* and *Cosmo;* she knew the stories. The magazines advocated strong, ballsy women, but Allie believed that when push came to shove, if her husband was cheating on her, she would shut down her systems and retreat into her shell.

As if the idea spurred her to action, she tore at the duffel bag with such a vengeance she broke the zipper. She ripped the pictures as best she could given the resilient Polaroid film. She found condoms in Cam's shaving kit and woodenly moved herself to the toilet, where she opened each foil pack and flushed them, one by one.

She still wasn't crying.

She wasn't thinking, *What did I do to deserve this?* She was wondering instead, *What did you do to deserve me?*

She dressed quickly, because she had a great deal to do. Then she sat on the edge of the bed, hugging the information she'd unearthed to herself until it became a small, hot knot of pain as hard as unmined coal, and lodged just as soundly.

At 8:05 on Monday morning, Jamie MacDonald was running with the wolves. At least, that was what he was pretending.

He'd stepped barefoot into the melting snow and had walked through Darby Mac's cornfield slowly until the soles of his feet grew numb. In the winter, the field was nothing but a square of stubble sticking out above the snow. Jamie made his way between the rows, darting back and forth, stumbling to his hands and knees and going up to his elbows in snow.

He hoped he'd get pneumonia.

He pushed himself on, back and forth across the acreage, until his breath was burning in his lungs and his eyes were tearing with effort. Then Jamie sat back on his heels and threw back his head and howled in the direction of the sun. He yelled until his voice gave out. He yelled until there was nothing left inside.

He stood up and walked back, like a man again, to the side of Angus's little house. In the dogcatcher's mesh cage were two mutts and a purebred spaniel. They jumped and yipped at him as he drew close. They pushed their hot, wet muzzles into the shell of his hand.

Without thinking twice, Jamie unlatched the cage. He watched the dogs take off down the road, their tails twitching, their feet picking up speed as they caught the faint scent of freedom.

A t 8:05 on Monday morning, Graham MacPhee was asleep on top of a collection of dusty law books. The spine of one had carved a thick line down his cheek, and his eyes, when they started to open, were red and gritty. He had been up most of the night preparing his opening statement. Although it was Monday, it was Martin Luther King Day, and the courts weren't in session. It gave him, Jamie, everyone involved, a day of grace.

He sat up and took a swig of Coke from a two-liter bottle, hoping to wipe out the metallic taste in his mouth. No one who could see him this morning—shoeless, disheveled, sallow—would recognize him tomorrow at the defense table.

A woman was walking in front of his dry-erase board. "Hey," he said, wondering how the hell she'd gotten in when he hadn't yet unlocked his office door. "Mind telling me who you are?"

At his voice, she simply touched the board where the three days before Jamie's arrest were chronicled. Her hand went straight through it. More gently this time, she reached a fingertip to one of the empty white squares that marked the night Jamie and his wife had last been alone together.

With his heart pounding, Graham scrambled to his feet. He took a step closer to the woman as she turned to face him.

He had seen the Polaroids taken by the medical examiner. He had seen pictures Allie had stolen from Jamie's house in Cummington. He was staring at Maggie MacDonald.

When Graham tried to speak, nothing came out of his throat. He rubbed his eyes, but she didn't disappear. He thought of Dr. Harrison Harding, and wondered if this was a psychotic episode.

Maggie rubbed her hand against the gaping hole in Graham's defense theory, the only period of time he could not account for before the death. And as quickly as she had appeared, she was suddenly gone.

Graham stepped up to the board. He stretched a hand out to touch the place Maggie had touched. Instead of a bare white box there was a spot, a fingerprint. It was an unmistakable mark pressed in dark red ink, or maybe blood.

*E*llen MacDonald was out for her daily constitutional at 8:35, Monday morning. If she took off south from her house and looped around the park and the library, past the Wheelock Inn, she could get a good two-mile track. If she was feeling particularly lively, she could make it briskly in a half hour.

She had on her Walkman, playing an Enya tape. Her jogging suit was made of natural fibers. Her sneakers allowed her feet to breathe.

One of her shoelaces became untied at the Wheelock Inn. She crouched down to fix it, unintentionally hiding herself behind a melting drift of snow. It was from this vantage point that she saw the unmarked cruiser Cam usually drove pull into the Inn's parking lot.

Ellen turned around and headed home before she could bear witness to anything else.

*A*t 8:45, Cam was informed that Mia Townsend was no longer a guest at the Wheelock Inn. Stifling an urge to grab the manager by the throat and shake an explanation out of him, he calmly asked the man to check his records a second time. "You must be mistaken," he said. "She must have said something else."

When Cam entered the lobby, the manager—who'd been bribed weeks ago to ensure discretion—had called out to him. Ms. Townsend had settled her bill and left early this morning, the manager said, pulling her checkout slip from a small pile. Cam recognized Mia's signature, the same spiky hand that days ago had registered them as husband and wife at a secluded bed-and-breakfast.

As Cam jogged up the stairs, he told himself he didn't have time for this crap today. He was going to a legitimate seminar, this one on breaking and entering, so he had to be in Pittsfield by ten o'clock. He had come to tell Mia that he hadn't told Allie anything because it had been too late. That he was going to see a lawyer when the seminar was over, and speak to Allie tonight. He had come to see her smile at him and to hold her close, so the attraction could come like a shock between them and he could carry the after-effects with him all day.

He opened the door to the tiny room beside the closet with the key Mia had given him. The space was neat and markedly empty of personal effects. Except for the mussed bed, which still smelled of sex, and the bonsai tree in the middle of it.

It was propped between two pillows so that the soil would not spill out. The image hit him more strongly than any note could have, which must have been why she left it.

Left it.

As he watched, the tree began to twist. It was no longer wrapped in copper wire, but gnarled through time into its unnatural shape. Cam's mouth dropped open as the trunk split and expanded. The branch that dipped horizontally and then toward the ground flexed like a bicep and redirected itself toward the sun. The exposed roots burrowed deep into the soil and the snipped, pinched buds began to flower with waxy green leaves.

No longer a bonsai, the tree began to grow the way nature had intended.

Cam leaned against the wall of the room where he had fallen in love, and realized that this time, there would be no visit to Bally Beene, no tracking Mia across the country.

The tree festooned in a burst of pink blossoms.

This time, there was no going back.

At 9:05, at Glory in the Flower, Allie stood in front of the parson's bench that held the bonsai trees and watched, transfixed, as they burst free of their copper wire. As if they were hatching, their branches tussled and stretched, breaking the coils that bound them, until they looked like they had months before when Mia and Allie brought them home from the nursery.

Allie had come to make sure that her assistant was not around; would never come around again. She had played the scenarios out in her mind driving to the center of town. She would storm in and scream at Mia and tell her to get the hell out of her life. She would be extra sweet and go about business as usual and then, when Mia least expected it, drop the bomb that she *knew*. She would offer her a week's extra salary and simply dismiss her.

Her rage had not lessened. In fact, Allie felt more in control of herself than she had in a long, long while.

But the bonsais beneath the window had distracted her. They had claimed her attention so completely that she'd missed seeing the geraniums which Mia had toppled from their pots to carpet the floor, the worktable, the counter.

The petals were blue and mauve and purple, pink and red and white. They caught on the bottom of Allie's shoes and stuck to the ankles of her slacks. Geraniums meant: *I shall never see him.*

By the time she had hung the Closed sign on the door and visited the liquor store for spare boxes, the snow had nearly melted. The lawn was virtually clear; there were only a few white spots left to remind Allie it was winter. With great deliberation she spent the morning sifting through her husband's belongings, removing every trace of him from the house. She set his shoes and his books and his fishing poles and power tools out on overturned cartons that lined her driveway; she sat with a strongbox beneath a makeshift clothesline hung with his uniforms and casual wear and his one sports jacket.

Good weather drew people to garage sales.

Allie bartered and bargained, her objective to clear the tables rather than to make any given amount of money. She told shoppers to send their friends along. She made deals: two-for-one on sports equipment. Buy a uniform, get a pair of shoes for free. She watched the evidence that her husband existed disappear in the arms of neighbors who had simply been passing by. She felt the winter sun, just as unexpected and hot as her anger.

And she waited for Cam to come home.

# PART III

If you forgive people enough, you belong
    to them,
and they to you, whether either person
    likes it or
not—squatter's rights of the heart.

—James Hilton, *Time and Time Again*

I think you sent me a postcard once. It was just a post-card, addressed to me in unidentifiable block lettering, with nothing at all written on the message side. It was about two years after the fact.

On the front was a picture of a pig and a heifer dressed in fancy hats and polka-dot dresses. I'M SWINE, the head-line said. COW ARE YOU? It was exactly the kind of thing you would never in a million years pick off a postcard rack, and so that's why I thought it was from you; yet an-other layer to hide behind.

It was postmarked from Edinburgh.

It is not true, what they say, about writing being the next best thing to being there. For days I stared at that post-card and touched it in all the places I imagined you had, when you wrote the address and affixed the stamp and what have you, but never once did I feel like I'd found you again.

# SEVENTEEN

*A*llie remembered once hearing a song that said the first person you fell in love with stole your heart. The first person you made love with stole your soul. And if these were one and the same, you were damned.

She was huddled over her stool at the country-western bar in Shelburne Falls, watching people whose lives had not hit rock bottom line dancing to the lively strains of a fiddle. She had left Cam standing in front of the cartons from which she had sold his possessions, left him standing right in front of the house, and had walked into the center of town. From there, she'd hitched rides until she was far enough away from Wheelock to breathe again. The only reason she'd come to Rodeo Joe's was because it was the first place she'd found in Shelburne Falls with a liquor license, and she planned to get rip-roaring drunk.

She fingered the napkin beneath her glass—a straight shot of tequila, her sixth. Rodeo Joe's motto promised her, personally, a shit-kickin' good time. Allie wondered if she could get her money back. After all, you never could get drunk when you most needed to.

A man in a red western shirt hooked a leg over the stool beside hers like it was a horse. He nodded a greeting, then gestured to the bartender. "Rexie, the lady's next one's on me."

She stared at him. How long had it been since someone had bought her a drink? "That's very nice, but I'm not going to be good company."

"Draw a bad one today?" he asked. His voice had that wide western sound, and he was talking with rodeo lingo, as if he ranched in the middle of Massachusetts. Allie bent down over her drink, trying not to smile. Country-western did that to people— made them wear big hats and say things they wouldn't otherwise be caught dead saying. The man beside her was probably a tax accountant on State Street in Boston.

"Cowboy," she said, "I should never have climbed into the chute."

He was not as tall as Cam, and his body was not as muscular, but he was in good physical shape. Rangy—like he played racquetball instead of working out at Gold's. The features of his face were sharp, almost to the point of discord, but came together in a way that made him look honest and rough. His hair was darker than Cam's. And he didn't have a dimple in his chin.

Allie pushed her drink away, disgusted. When would she stop measuring everything by that benchmark?

"The name's O'Malley," he said.

Allie glanced up. "Just O'Malley?"

He nodded. "It's all I'll answer to, at any rate."

She laughed and traced the beads of condensation on her glass. "I'm Allie."

"Just Allie?" The man was grinning; it softened him.

Allie smiled back. "It's all I'll answer to," she repeated. "Do you live around here?"

O'Malley nodded. "A fair ways west. I'm the foreman on the Double K."

Allie's eyes widened. "You mean there's actually a ranch around here?"

"Of sorts," he said. He leaned forward conspiratorially. "Bet you five bucks no one on that dance floor could tell the nose of a horse from its ass."

Allie laughed again. It felt good, lessening the tightness in her chest and shoulders. "So you really are a cowboy."

O'Malley shrugged. "For lack of a better word. We actually breed bison out at the Double K."

"Bison? You mean buffalo?"

"None other."

Allie took a deep drink of tequila. "What for?"

"Mostly meat. You'd be surprised how many fancy restaurants in Boston place standing orders."

Allie raised her eyebrows. "I've never eaten buffalo."

O'Malley reached over and covered her hand with his. "You ain't missing a hell of a lot." Then he smiled, his teeth even and white, like a line of light. "Let's dance, Allie," he said, and before she could remember to resist, he'd taken her into the center of the crowd.

He held her left hand close between them, pressed against her breasts. From time to time he fiddled with her wedding ring, but he didn't say a thing about it. He didn't say much of anything, really. He hummed in time to the quiet ballad, moving his hips in a rhythm Allie suspected had been bred from a saddle, and he took her with him.

She couldn't breathe, at first. But she forced herself to relax. She closed her eyes so that the strobe lights were only pricks against her lids, and she made herself lean into the long, easy body before her. It was hard to be this close to another man, but she reminded herself that getting over the strangeness would be half the battle.

The music caught them like a whirlwind and drew them tighter, so that O'Malley's cheek was pressed against her own. Allie heard him murmuring the words of a song she did not know, and she sang her own lyrics to the same rhythm: *Cam did it; Cam did it; so can you.*

*T*he only items left were the things Cam assumed no one had wanted, and that included himself. On the overturned cartons on the driveway were a few spare pairs of socks and boxer shorts, a sweatshirt he had splattered bleach on several years before, a drill that did not work.

He left them sitting where they were and went into the house again. It was strange to see the empty spots on the wall where Carrymuir paraphernalia had been, cleared rings on dusty shelves that had once been home to mugs he'd brought back from Munich and Stuttgart. He wondered what Allie had said to the people who asked questions. He wondered if she'd lied to them, or if she'd told them the truth. He wasn't certain which one he preferred.

The house still looked furnished, but it was a woman's house. Allie's quilts were draped over the chair and the couch. Allie's curtains were pulled back to let in the dying sun. Allie's cookbooks stood in height order on the bookshelf.

He sank down on the couch—his favorite chair was God only knew where—and let it come. The frustration, the fury, the embarrassment. "Damn you," he yelled, and it felt so good that he did it again. "How could you do this to me?"

His voice was pitched so loud he could hear the echo of his outrage settling in the braided rug, the upholstered furniture. "Why did you leave me?" he said more softly, and that was when he knew that he hadn't been angry at Allie at all.

He wondered if Mia was thinking about him.

With a deep sigh, Cam stood up and dug his hands into his pockets. He moved through the house to get the full effect of his infidelity: the half-empty bathroom vanity, which housed no razors but a festival of lotions and bath gels and rose-colored soaps; the basement workshop, as bare as it had been on the day they'd moved in; the ridiculously tiny bedroom closet, now cavernous and spacious, littered with dust balls on the floor.

She'd even sold his fucking pillows.

He went into the bathroom again to take a leak, and noticed something wrapped in newspaper hidden in the dank area behind the toilet. Bending down, he drew it out. It was last Thursday's newspaper, and although he didn't think it had been intended, there was a big article about Jamie MacDonald's upcoming trial splashed across the page.

He knew what it was before he unwrapped it. Lying on the bathroom floor, with no incoming light, the stained-glass panel had no life or color. Cam sat down and stared at it. He did not know why it had not been placed in a carton with the other gifts he had given Allie; he would never know.

Cam could remember giving it to Allie. He'd told her to be careful with it. He'd given it to her and the whole time he'd still been thinking of Mia.

But he supposed it was going to be that way for a while. Regardless of what had happened to Allie and when she would resurface, another part of Cam had died. It was only reasonable to expect that he would need time to properly mourn.

Only he wouldn't let it show. He owed his wife that much.

*Wife.* The word congealed on his tongue. With great care he took a swath of toilet paper and cleaned the stained-glass panel. He wiped down the bright glass shards and dusted the lead panes. Then he walked with it into the bedroom and hung it again on its cast-iron hook, back where it belonged.

Cam stood before the stained-glass image until the moon rose behind it, and resigned himself to this day, the next one, and the next.

When you are married to a person for a long time and you make love, you know how long and when your husband will kiss you. You know that he'll start at your right breast, and then concentrate on your left. You know that he will move his mouth down your belly and bring you to the edge, then slide up to your mouth again and let you taste your own excitement.

With somebody new, you lose this rhythm.

Allie lay naked on her back in a room at the Green Gate Motel, O'Malley heavy on top of her. They had bumped noses when they kissed and scraped the enamel off their teeth and being drunk was not the only excuse for such mismatch. Allie felt nervous, but not about the act itself. She didn't know what he was going to do next, and the very newness of it, the *difference,* made it seem wrong.

O'Malley had spent an inordinate amount of time licking around and inside her ear, which she did not find erotic at all. He had a tendency to whisper things that made her want to clamp her legs shut: *Want to ride a cowboy, honey? I can stay in the saddle a long, long time.*

But to her surprise, she could feel her nipples tightening and her lower body going soft. She realized with a shock that this man she did not know and did not like was going to make her come.

*It's just sex,* she told herself as he slipped on a condom and drove into her. *It was that way for Cam; it's that way for me. It's not the same as a marriage.*

She started to cry, all the tears that hadn't fallen that morning or that afternoon on the way to Shelburne. She cried quietly at first, then loud sobs that made O'Malley pull himself from her with a bewildered look. She didn't explain to him. She didn't want to, didn't have to. She rolled to her side and curled into a ball, trying to remember the quickest way home.

Angus and Ellen left a spot between them for Allie when they entered the courtroom in Pittsfield, but ten minutes before the jury was set to convene, she still had not appeared. "I don't know what's keeping her," Ellen said, looking at her watch.

Graham, bouncing with nervous energy on the balls of his feet, shook his head. "She wouldn't miss opening arguments."

"A flat tire," Angus pronounced. "I canna imagine anything else."

Graham nodded, staring at the door Jamie would enter in a few minutes' time. "I hope she shows," he murmured. "It's going to kill him if she doesn't."

Graham leaned against the defense table, inadvertently scattering his notes. He wondered what Jamie was thinking, ensconced for a minute of quiet in a bathroom stall. He wondered how he'd be holding up by the end of the day, the first of many.

The defendant was the least important person in the courtroom. He wasn't involved in the case. He wouldn't be arguing his innocence. The only purpose he served was as a visual aid for the jurors while they heard testimony from others.

Graham also knew that this case was not going to be like the civil suits he had tired. The prosecutors had their evidence. The defense wasn't going to refute it or offer any other vindicating evidence. In fact, most of Graham's own witnesses were going to say things that corroborated the State's case. But he'd try to shape the facts with their attitudes and impressions of Jamie too. In essence, Graham's role was to tell the jury. *Yes, here's a body. But you've got to look at it in a different context.*

Not that Graham believed you could ever tell what the hell was going on in a juror's mind.

Jamie came back into the courtroom looking pale and tight, and slipped into a seat beside Graham almost at exactly the same time the jury filed in and the bailiff requested that everyone rise for the Honorable Judge Juno Roarke.

Audra Campbell was on her feet for an opening statement on the heels of Roarke's pronouncement that court was now in session. "Ladies and gentlemen of the jury," she said, "on September 19, 1995, Margaret MacDonald was murdered by her own husband. He drove her to a nearby town, checked into an inn, held a pillow to her face, and cut off her supply of oxygen so that she died of asphyxiation. The State will show that the defendant turned himself in to the local police and voluntarily confessed to these actions."

The prosecutor was wearing a black wool suit that stood out from her shoulders like a linebacker's gear. She stepped around the table and crossed to stand in front of the jury, smiling benignly. "I remind you all of the oath you've taken to uphold the law, and to bring the victim's murderer to justice." Then her eyebrows furrowed together to meet in the middle of her high forehead. "No one, myself included, will dispute that the circumstances surrounding this case are heartrending and pathetic. That it could not have been an easy time for anyone involved. However," she said, her voice strengthening, "the fact remains that the defendant committed a deliberate, willful, premeditated murder—and admitted so *himself*. As you, the jury, listen to the facts, remember that this is a case about breaking the law. Not about compassion, not about sympathy. It is the law you have been called here to consider, and it is the law which dictates conviction."

She sat down.

Jamie leaned close to Graham, who was halfway out of his chair. "Where's Allie?" he whispered.

Graham shook his head and glanced at Angus and Ellen and the space between them. Then he turned toward the jury. He didn't say anything for a moment. He walked back and forth in front of the jury box, as if he was embittered about something and still trying to come up with the words to voice his protest.

"Ladies and gentlemen, I'll tell you the same thing that the prosecution just did. Yes, Maggie MacDonald was killed on September 19, 1995. Yes, Jamie MacDonald, her devoted husband, admitted to this. However, unlike the prosecution, I'm going to put these facts into the proper emotional setting. On the day that Maggie died, Jamie was suffering from an exorbitant amount of stress and grief brought about by months of dealing with his wife's terminal illness. The latest news of her condition and her prognosis had reached a new low." Graham paused and looked directly at the juror with the badly dyed orange hair. "You'll hear testimony about how this prolonged grief and depression was affecting Jamie, to the point where his capacity to tell right from wrong was diminished. On the morning of his wife's death, he was not in control of himself."

The orange-haired woman looked into her lap. She didn't buy it.

Graham took a step back and hammered home his points. "One day, Jamie was deliberately making appointments with Maggie's physician to discuss a new form of treatment he'd heard about that might help the cancer. The next day, he'd be overwhelmed by the futility of putting his wife through more pain without guaranteed results."

The orange-haired juror looked up.

"This is not your average murder trial," Graham said. "Most criminals are driven by greed. Jamie was motivated by grief. Most criminals commit an act out of hate. Jamie committed an act out of love." He moved closer to the defense table, so that the jury would see Jamie out of the corners of their eyes. "You can't judge the deed unless you consider the context in which it was acted out. You can't consider reason and consequence unless you also figure in emotions and morality. Nobody lives, or acts, in a vacuum."

He glanced at Audra. "The prosecution would have you believe that this case is open-and-shut, a question of black or white. Well, look around you, ladies and gentlemen. In the real world, there's color. Lots of different kinds. Maggie MacDonald's death did not occur in a textbook, but in the real world. And Jamie's trial will take place there." He paused. "The evidence will show that in the real world, not everything is black and white. At the very least, there are infinite shades of gray."

Cam took a personal day off from work. He spent the morning going around to the houses of people he barely knew, asking them what it would cost to buy back a uniform, a fishing rod, a needlepoint MacDonald crest. He endured subtle ribbing from men in his father's generation about being in the doghouse, and outright smirks from his own contemporaries. It seemed that Allie had only let slip that they'd had an argument—she hadn't given the particulars. For that, he supposed, he was thankful. But it was still enraging to think that people saw his situation as same kind of childish prank on the part of his wife.

He drove to Glory in the Flower, thinking Allie had spent the night at her shop, but there was a sign that said the store would be closed for the duration of the MacDonald trial. For a moment he panicked, thinking of a greedy divorce lawyer bleeding him for his house, his possessions, his money. Then he realized she must have been talking about Jamie's court appearance.

The ADA said Cam would probably go on the stand tomorrow, which of course would be an impossibility if he didn't find a goddamn uniform before the day was out. Part of the deal in being the expert witness for the prosecution was coming in with all the trappings.

He wondered if Allie was watching the trial, or if, in the light of the past day, she'd forgotten too.

He managed to buy back some of his power tools and fishing equipment and he physically tore a uniform from a four-year-old who was playing dress-up in the nursery school make-believe corner. He ate lunch in his car and went into his office to find several more of his personal effects strewn across his desk: his sports jacket, a dress uniform, a pair of Sorrel boots, skis. Hannah came to stand in the doorway. "I did a little calling around, and I got some people to feel bad," she said quietly. "I'm not going to ask what happened."

He thanked her and locked the door when she left. He put his head down on the desk.

Seven times that day he turned to look out the window at the Wheelock Inn. But he did not go over there to check again, and because of this simple thing he went home with his hands curled around a glowing, growing grain of pride.

*T*he first witness for the prosecution was Hugo Huntley.

Audra smiled at him as he settled himself on the hard chair inside the witness box. She patiently waited for him to wipe his glasses on the spare material of his shirt. "Can you state your name and address for the record?" she asked.

"Hugo Huntley." His voice screeched into the microphone, so he leaned back a bit. "Fourteen-fifty Braemer Way, Wheelock, Massachusetts."

"And Mr. Huntley, what do you do for a living?"

"I run the only funeral parlor in Wheelock. I also serve as the medical examiner for the local police."

Audra asked him to recite his credentials: college, medical school, certification by a board of medical examiners.

"What do your duties as the medical examiner of Wheelock entail?"

Hugo puffed out his chest. "I investigate deaths where the cause is unknown, or needs to be verified. I perform autopsies when it's necessary."

"About how many autopsies have you performed?"

Hugo smiled. "I've done a lot of autopsies, I guess. A few hundred. Sometimes the families just want to know what gave out at the end."

"Did you perform an autopsy on the deceased last September?"

Hugo nodded. "Yes, ma'am," he said.

"And what did you determine as the cause of death?"

"Asphyxiation." He leaned forward and took a deep breath. "In layman's terms, a lack of oxygen to the brain, which eventually caused a massive cardiac arrest."

"I see. Were you able to determine the time at which the victim died?"

"Roughly," Hugo admitted. "In my opinion, it was between seven and ten in the morning."

Audra prowled in front of the witness box. "Did you do an external examination as well, Mr. Huntley?"

The little man nodded. "Of course. It's part of any autopsy," he said.

"And what were your findings?"

Hugo glanced down at his lap, as if he had a script there. "Other than a scar from a recent radical mastectomy, there were no visible contusions or lacerations, no burn marks, nothing out of the ordinary."

Audra sucked in her breath. You couldn't lead a witness on direct questioning, and Huntley was forgetting the most important piece of physical evidence. "Did you examine her hands?"

Hugo's eyes shot up and caught the prosecutor's. "Oh, yes," he said. "Yes, I did. There was skin underneath her fingernails that matched up with samples taken from Jamie MacDonald."

"Did you also have a chance to see the defendant shortly after he confessed to the police?"

Hugo swallowed. "I did."

"Was there anything extraordinary about his face?"

"There were scratches on his cheek. His right cheek."

"And what did you conclude in your report?"

Hugo glanced at Jamie and then let his gaze slide away. "That this was a possible sign of a struggle."

Audra tossed her French braid back. "Your witness," she said, and she tapped her fingers on the defense table on the way back to her seat.

Graham remained sitting, like he had all the time in the world and he was just shooting the shit with Hugo on the back porch. "Mr. Huntley," he said, his legs crossed, his arm thrown over the back of the empty chair to his right, "have you ever testified at other trials?"

"One. It turned out to be a suicide."

Graham stood up gracefully. "So you aren't often called as a witness to murder trials?"

"No, oh, absolutely not. Things like that don't happen all the time in Wheelock."

"For which I'm sure we're all grateful," Graham said, and in the background he heard a stifled titter from the jury box. "How many funerals do you see a year?"

Hugo raised his eyebrows. "Oh, a good number. We have a decent reputation, so people from other towns come to us too. Fifty, I suppose. Maybe more."

"And how many years have you run the funeral parlor?"

"Fifteen."

Graham nodded slowly. "So that's seven hundred and fifty funerals you've seen." He whistled. "Would you consider yourself an expert on grief?"

"Objection!" Audra Campbell stood up. "Maybe defense could tell us what the criteria are for a grief expert?"

"I'll allow it," Roarke said.

"Let me rephrase." Graham leaned on the railing beside Hugo, like he was a buddy, a pal. "Do you think you have a familiarity with grief?"

Hugo nodded. "I see a lot of it, sure. There are certain things you notice over and over—the same things you'd expect—you know, crying, and shock, and that sort of thing."

"Mr. Huntley, did you attend Maggie's funeral?"

Hugo brightened visibly. "Yes, and it was lovely. I arranged it, you know. There were flowers and the priest gave a very moving service, and a good number of people turned out considering she had been an outsider from another town."

"Did you observe Jamie at his wife's funeral?"

Hugo cleared his throat. "I did. He was crying so much I don't think he even knew he was doing it, and he physically could not stand up. He actually didn't make it through the whole service. To tell you the truth, I've never seen the like."

"Did he happen to say anything at the funeral in Gaelic?"

Hugo smiled. "Yes," he said. "When they started to lower the casket, he said the words '*Mo chridhe.*' "

"Can you translate for us?"

"It means 'my heart.' "

Graham nodded. "One last point, Mr. Huntley. You say you saw scratches on Jamie's cheek?"

"Yes, sir."

"Did you see them being put there?"

Hugo shook his head. "I didn't see a fight, or anything, if that's what you mean."

"So it's possible that Maggie MacDonald was not the one to put those scratches on his cheek."

"I suppose so."

Graham started to walk toward the jury. "And those skin cells you found beneath Maggie's fingernails—is it possible they were *not* the sign of a struggle?"

Hugo tipped his head. "I guess."

"Is it possible, for instance, they were a leftover from, say, a hot night of passion between a husband and wife who were very much in love?"

This time, Graham could hear the guffaws coming from the jury. He smiled. Hugo nodded, his eyes black and huge behind his glasses. "It's possible."

Graham flashed a neat grin at his client. "Nothing further," he said.

Cam was sitting alone in the dark living room, nursing the third of a six-pack of beer, when he heard the front door open and close. He did not stand or go to greet her, but he set the bottle down at his feet.

Allie was silhouetted in the doorway. With her right hand she reached for the light switch, flooding the room garishly and making Cam blink like an owl at her, as if she were something he was not accustomed to seeing.

She tilted her head and stared at him, wishing that he did not look the way he always did when she pictured him in her mind. It would have been so much easier if, after all this, he had a scar across his face, or a visible brand that made her remember. She put down on the floor the strongbox she'd carried from the garage sale.

Cam gazed at it. "How much did you make off me?"

"Not nearly enough," Allie said.

Cam nodded. He had not known exactly what to expect. The Allie he remembered, the one he had married, would have never sold his belongings. She would have assumed his infidelity was a reflection of something *she* had done wrong and she'd beg him to give her another chance, and because he'd be so guilt-ridden, he would. This new woman, the one who had a mind of her own that he could not predict, might say and do just about anything at all.

He wanted the old Allie back. Not because he wanted that measure of power over her, but because he was hurting and he was tired and the one steady thing in his life—her unstinting comfort—was what he needed the most.

He closed his eyes, dizzy with the truth, and wondered how he had so quickly gone from holding everything he wanted in the palm of his hand to having absolutely nothing at all. He wondered how he could have been so blinded by something shiny and new and elusive that he couldn't at least give equal credit for the strength of something stable, and strong, and *his*.

"I guess you'll want a—" He tried, he really did, but the word would not come.

"Divorce," Allie finished.

Cam nodded.

"I don't," she said softly, and his eyes flew up to hers. He was surprised to realize he was not wishing that she was Mia. He looked at his wife and wished in that moment that none of this had ever happened.

Allie's eyes filled with tears that she would not let spill, at any cost. She notched her chin up when she spoke. "You hurt me," she accused, "but *you* were the one who made the mistake. It's not like I stopped loving you the minute I found out. I just stopped trusting you."

She started up the steps, leaving Cam on the couch holding the words she had tossed him like fluttering, nested birds. He glanced up the dark stairwell, but he could not see his future.

# EIGHTEEN

When Cam took the witness stand the following morning, he was staring at Allie. She sat almost directly behind Jamie, so that watching her meant watching his cousin as well.

Jamie looked good, for someone who was on trial for murder. He wore an olive suit that hung nicely from his shoulders and a red tie that was quiet and conservative. People who hadn't been trained like Cam to look quite so closely might never have noticed the beads of sweat on the hair at the back of Jamie's neck, or the way his ears burned red at the top every time Audra Campbell asked a question.

Cam had been sworn in and he'd entered into evidence the arrest report and the voluntary confession. He smiled at Audra when she crossed in front of him; he'd worked with her before. He didn't particularly like her, but he had an obligation to the DA's office. The police—the police chief, in particular—were key witnesses for the prosecution. By definition the police commanded respect. The jury naturally trusted a policeman to safeguard people like themselves, their property, their lives. Whatever Cam said most jurors would accept as fact.

He stated his name and his occupation for the record. "How many years have you been on the force?" Audra asked.

"Eight," Cam said. "Plus three years of part-time duty before I was made chief."

"And how many arrests do you make in a week?"

Cam frowned a little. "Me, personally? Or the department?"

"You, Chief MacDonald."

Cam shifted in his chair. "Six or seven. Ten on a busy week. Overall, an average of three people get taken into custody each day by one of our officers for some criminal activity or another."

"Were you on duty on September nineteenth?"

Cam nodded. "I was. I had actually just gone out to lunch when the defendant drove up to the station, asking to see me. One of my sergeants tracked me down."

Graham listened carefully and made notes on a yellow pad that he could barely read. Cam spoke clearly and dispassionately; relating the horrible facts of a horrible case without the benefit of emotion.

"The defendant arrived in a red Ford pickup truck," he said. "The victim was in the passenger seat, although at the time of arrival on the scene it was not obvious that she was deceased. He asked if I was the police chief, and when I answered affirmatively, he stated his own name and said that he had killed her."

"Do you remember the exact words the defendant used?"

Cam looked at Jamie. "He said, 'My wife, Maggie, is dead, and I'm the one who killed her.' "

Audra stood in front of the jury, as if she were just another interested member. "And then what happened?"

"There was a crowd that had gathered when the defendant drove up to the station. A couple of women fainted and one of the men in the group took a swing at the defendant."

"Was there anything else?"

Cam straightened his regulation tie. He stared at a juror who was busy resetting the buttons on his watch. "Yes. I motioned for my sergeant to check on the status of the victim, and the defendant began to fight. At that point I informed him that I would be putting him under arrest."

"Did you read the defendant his Miranda rights?"

"Yes," Cam said. He watched Allie lean over the railing that separated the viewers from the players of the court, to touch Jamie's shoulder in a gesture of support. "He waived the right to a lawyer and asked to make a voluntary confession."

"What are your standard procedures regarding voluntary confessions?"

"We go through Miranda again, and ask specifically a third time if the prisoner would like a lawyer to be present. Then we tape-record the confession, which is transcribed by the police secretary, and after verifying what has been typed, the prisoner signs it."

Audra walked toward the court reporter. "Let the record show that this voluntary statement has been entered into evidence as exhibit S-three." She turned back to Cam. "Chief MacDonald, can you paraphrase for us what the defendant said in his confession?"

"He said that his wife had been diagnosed with several types of cancer, and that her illness had been terminal. After a doctor's visit on the previous Friday, she had come home in a very depressed state. The defendant indicated that his wife asked him to kill her. He said that on Monday, they drove to Wheelock from their hometown of Cummington and rented a room at the Wheelock Inn. It was there, on Tuesday morning, that he covered his wife's face with a pillow and smothered her."

"How was the defendant acting when he gave his confession?"

"He wasn't crying, if that's what you mean. He spoke clearly and concisely, like he knew what he was going to say."

"Objection," Graham said. "Witness can't know what was going on in Jamie's mind."

Roarke nodded. "The jury will disregard that part of the witness's statement."

Audra continued, unfazed. "Based on the confession you heard from the defendant, Chief MacDonald, do you believe this killing was premeditated?"

"Yes."

"Do you think the defendant deliberated over killing his wife, even if only for a span of several minutes?"

"Yes."

"Do you think the defendant willfully suffocated his wife?"

"I do."

Audra stepped out of Cam's field of vision, so that he could see Allie, her eyes dark and sharp, supremely cold. From a long distance, he could hear the prosecutor's heels clicking on the speckled tile floor. "Nothing further," she said.

*D*uring the short recess the judge called after Cam's initial testimony, Graham told Allie that Jamie wanted to see her. He led her to a small conference cubicle down the hall from the courtroom, protected on the outside by an armed security guard.

Allie opened the door and then closed it quickly, shutting out the bustle and the accusations in the hallway. Jamie was sitting down, his head bent to the table as if the wood offered something fascinating. "I'm sorry," she said immediately.

Jamie looked up and grinned. "Did I lose already?"

Allie shook her head. "I mean about yesterday. I should have been here. I wanted to be here." She paused. "I just wasn't thinking."

He laughed. "I know that defense. You're not gonna get off with *that.*" His face realigned itself into a bitter line. "Unless I set a precedent."

Allie sat down across from him. "You look like you're doing all right."

Jamie glanced at her. "So do you." He leaned forward. "And what does that tell you?"

She knew that if she sat there for another thirty seconds, she was going to be crying, and she wasn't about to burden Jamie with her own problems. "I have to go."

"Tell me," Jamie said quietly. "It would be nice not to think about myself for a change."

Allie let herself sink back into the hard metal chair. Her skirt billowed around her ankles. "All right," she murmured. And she started to talk.

Once she began, she could not stop. Each sentence tugged another out of her heart in an unbroken line. Allie started by saying that Cam had been having an affair. That she had been too stupid to see that it was with Mia, her own assistant. That she found out after they'd gone away somewhere cold and snowy for a weekend. That Cam had lied.

She told Jamie about the garage sale, and the strongbox, and how she had hitched rides to Shelburne Falls. She told him about the buffalo cowboy and the awful night at the motel. She told him that, like an idiot, she couldn't keep herself from going back, but she didn't know if she could give Cam what he wanted.

"And what's that?" Jamie asked.

Allie let all her breath out in a rush. "Everything back to normal. Me, before it happened. Him, before he met her."

Jamie stared at Allie, taking in the circles beneath her eyes and the way her hands played nervously along the lap of her skirt. He had listened to Cam's testimony, of course, but what had struck him was who Cam appeared to be talking to. Graham had told Jamie that most of the witnesses for the prosecution, especially their so-called experts, would completely ignore Jamie and speak directly to Audra or to the jury. Well, Cam had ignored Jamie, but he had been focused on his wife.

He'd recognized that look. *Please,* it said. *You're all I've got.*

And it occurred to him that Allie MacDonald had brought about something unlikely that Jamie himself had not been able to bring about by giving his wife her final wish. Instead of doing what Cam had expected—crying, Jamie supposed, and carrying on and begging—Allie had pulled the rug out from beneath him. All this time, Jamie had believed the way to Maggie's devotion lay in doing whatever she asked and being whatever she wanted. Allie had proven differently.

She'd done it when she wasn't even trying. She'd shifted the balance between them. All of a sudden, instead of Allie trailing behind Cam, Cam was clinging to whatever Allie was willing to offer.

"Forty-sixty," he said, looking at Allie with a newfound admiration. "Who would have guessed?"

Cam took the stand again just after lunch, and Graham moved directly in front of him. He knew what his job was going to be, and he had to admit, it was going to be a pleasure to do it. You couldn't discredit a policeman's testimony, especially a police chief. Everyone on that jury saw Cam as a good guy just a few notches down from God and the President; a solid, helpful public figure. If he bullied Cam, the jury would judge Graham harshly. You didn't destroy the lawman; you destroyed the jury's blind acceptance of him.

"Chief MacDonald," Graham said pleasantly. "Are there a lot of murder cases in Wheelock?"

Cam shook his head. "This is a first for me." He smiled. "Thank God."

"Have you ever been involved in another case where the victim was terminally ill?"

"I don't think so."

"You don't *think* so?"

"No," Cam said, "I haven't."

Graham made an indiscriminate noise and crossed toward the jury. "Would you say, given your training, that this case is different from other murder cases?"

"In some respects."

"Such as?"

"Well, the perpetrator of the crime knew the victim in this case. He—"

"Yes," Graham interrupted. "He did. And isn't it true that in most other murder cases, the victim doesn't give her consent?"

"Objection." Audra waved from her table.

"I'll rephrase. In the majority of murder cases, does the victim give consent?"

"Of course not," Cam said.

"Chief, how did Jamie seem when he was confessing?"

"Objection." This time the prosecutor got to her feet. "Asked and answered."

"Sustained." Judge Roarke gave Graham a measured look.

"Chief MacDonald, you said earlier that Jamie was clear and concise, I believe, during his voluntary confession. Is that correct?"

"It is." Cam rested his elbow on the railing, as if he was beginning to enjoy this.

"Was Jamie clear and concise from the time you first saw him in front of the police station all the way through to the time you secured his confession?"

Cam shook his head. "There was an incident when my sergeant went to check on the status of the victim. The defendant pulled out of a restraining hold and pushed the officer out of the way. He kept mumbling incoherently, something about nobody else touching his wife."

"Was he crying then?"

"Yes, he was."

"So within an hour, in your opinion, Jamie went from being somewhat violent and upset to speaking clearly and concisely?"

"That's correct."

From the corner of his eye, Graham saw a fly buzzing around Jamie's head at the defense table. He swatted at it a few times and then trapped it against the table with a cupped palm. Graham noticed several of the jurors watching. He held his breath, and Jamie flattened his palm down, then removed the evidence with a napkin.

*Shit.* That set back all the ground he had covered. "Chief Mac-Donald, did you know Jamie before he showed up at the police station on September nineteenth?"

Cam's head jerked up. "Yes," he said. "The defendant is my cousin."

"That's fairly common in Wheelock, isn't it? Can you explain the origins of your town?"

Audra raised a pen into the air. "Objection, Your Honor," she said. "Relevance?"

Graham turned to the judge. "Give me a little leeway, here," he pleaded.

"I'll allow it." Roarke turned to Cam. "You may answer the question."

For fifteen minutes, Cam wove a tale of a displaced Highland clan that his ancestral namesake had shipped out piecemeal to Massachusetts two hundred and fifty years before. He explained that he was still technically the chief of the clan, although it was only an honorary title.

"But as clan chief," Graham said, "you might have even more of a sense of responsibility to the citizens of Wheelock than an ordinary police chief, is that right?"

Cam shrugged. "I'd like to think so."

"Is it possible that Jamie's decision to kill his wife in Wheelock had something to do with the fact that you were there?"

"Objection, " Audra said. "My witness is not on trial. "

"Counselor," Roarke admonished, "you're on thin ice."

"Chief MacDonald," Graham continued, doggedly driving toward his point, "as a member of the MacDonald clan, wouldn't Jamie have looked to you for advice?"

"In theory."

"Is it possible that he might have come to Wheelock for your support?"

Cam leaned forward and pinned Graham with a glare. "Then why didn't he get in touch with me *before* he killed her?"

For a moment, Graham was speechless. A dull red flush worked its way up from the collar of his shirt. "Do you consider yourself an honorable man?" he asked finally.

Cam looked at his wife. He was under oath. He shifted nervously, but Allie's gaze did not waver. "Most of the time."

"Can you recite the town motto of Wheelock?"

"*Ex uno disce omnes.* It means, 'From one, judge of the rest.' " He hesitated. "It's also the original motto of the clan from Carrymuir, over in Scotland."

Graham nodded. "So your motto involves judging, too." He glanced up at a water spot on the ceiling. "If Jamie MacDonald is a bad seed, what would it say about your clan and yourself, Chief?"

Cam scowled. "I don't see the real point—"

"Just answer the question, please."

Graham looked quickly at the jury, to see if anyone seemed to feel he was pushing the policeman a little too hard. Most of them were leaning forward in their seats.

Cam stared directly at his wife. "I think there are extenuating circumstances you have to consider," he said slowly, "anytime you judge a man."

Judge Roarke, who had a known penchant for Oreo cookies, called for a half-hour afternoon recess after Cam's cross-examination. Cam checked his watch. It was just after three. By the time the court reconvened, it would almost be time to go home. Allie had brought her own car this morning, but maybe he could convince her to talk over coffee or even dinner. He just wanted to make peace.

The worst part was being with her in the same house and not knowing what the hell was running through her mind. She'd go about doing things like always—emptying the dishwasher, watching the "Today" show—but she had this knack of looking right through him. She said she didn't want to get rid of him, but he was beginning to feel that the only reason she wanted him around was to punish him.

He told himself that he was the one who had been the asshole, and she had a right to her distance. He told himself that if he wanted to put Mia into a beautiful, frozen memory and not let the past months disturb anything else about his life, he had to show some signs of humility. He just wasn't very good at walking around with his tail between his legs.

Allie had said she loved him. She'd come around.

He was bent over the water fountain when he felt a hand on the collar of his shirt which pulled him up and slammed him hard against the wall. "If I didn't think I'd be booked on assault and battery," Jamie said through clenched teeth, "I'd break your nose."

He released Cam as suddenly as he'd grabbed him, leaving the bystanders and the security guards to wonder if they had imagined the confrontation. "I guess Allie told you," Cam said, embarrassed that this man would know so much about him.

"You're an idiot. You don't know what you've lost."

Cam stared at Jamie, thinking of what he had *not* mentioned during his testimony—Jamie's story about his wife's illness, the trip to Quebec, the gentleness with which he had touched the corpse after he'd pushed Zandy out of the way. And he realized that strangely enough, this man might be the one person to understand. "You don't know what I *had,*" Cam said quietly.

At his cousin's tone, Jamie took a step back. "Temporary insanity?"

"I guess that's what some people would call it."

Jamie stared at him. He did not speak, but his message was clear: *Or were you only doing something that you knew had to be done? Even if it broke all the rules?*

Cam nodded down the hall, to a spot that was less crowded, and they walked there in silence. Then Cam leaned against the brick surface, one leg bent at the knee with his foot against the wall, and tilted his head back. "How did you do it?" he asked, his voice thick. "How did you make yourself let her go?"

Jamie wouldn't meet his eye. "I just sort of accepted the fact that it would kill me a little bit every day for the rest of my life."

Cam considered Mia, her hair bouncing over the collar of her oversized coat, and wondered if she was feeling that, wherever she'd gone.

"I don't think I've given you enough credit," Cam said.

Jamie looked at his cousin, at the pristine cuffs and corners of his regulation shirt and the brass and buttons that winked from it. He thought of what Cam had just admitted, and then of Allie; and he knew that even if it all worked out in the end, her heart was still the one that would be broken.

Jamie turned away. "I think I gave you too much."

*E*llen and Allie sat across from each other in an empty room upstairs from the court. They were sipping cups of coffee bought from a noisy vending machine.

"I think the jury likes Jamie," Allie said, hoping to keep the conversation away from Cam.

"I think the woman with the beads in her hair does," Ellen agreed. "The art teacher, right?"

"Nursery school aide," Allie corrected. "But she was on our side to begin with."

Ellen looked intrigued. "How can you tell?"

"Hang around Graham and it becomes an instinct," she said.

She had her face turned toward the window. It was raining, and between yesterday's thaw and today's downpour practically all the snow was gone. The world looked completely different than it had just days before.

Ellen wrung her napkin in her lap. She had heard about Allie's garage sale; who hadn't? In fact, along with Hannah at the station, she'd been responsible for finding who had what of Cam's. Hannah had used the phone; Ellen had dowsed. "Cam did well today," she said, and she saw Allie visibly flinch.

The rain reflected on Allie's cheeks in hideous boils and spots that ran together. When she turned, Ellen was taken aback by the distortion. "Allie," she confessed softly, "I knew."

"You *knew*," Allie repeated, "or you *know?*"

"Does it make a difference?"

Allie turned away again. "I'm not sure."

There was so much negative energy burrowed into the girl that

Ellen thought she could dig and dig and maybe never unearth its core. And she had to try; people had burned up from the inside because of this kind of thing.

"I don't want to talk about it," Allie said tightly, but then she looked at her mother-in-law and sighed. "You can't blame yourself. He's your son."

Ellen did not hesitate. "Every bit as much as you're my daughter. And I wouldn't have taken well to a substitute."

Allie tried to smile, but instead she turned back to the rain and tried to count the drops that were chasing each other to the edges of the windowpane, as if there were some kind of censure in standing alone.

Ellen dropped her coffee all over her own lap. "Oh, Lord. I can't believe I did that." She began to mop ineffectually at the runny brown puddle with her single, drenched napkin.

Allie jumped up. "Did you hurt yourself? I'll get some more napkins." As she ran out of the room toward the ladies' lounge, Ellen quickly opened her purse and drew out a small vial of ground ignatia. This cure she had made without Allie, but she hoped that her teaching had rubbed off. It was the remedy for grief, for anger, and for disappointment that your own soul could not shake.

By the time Allie came back, the ignatia had been stirred into her coffee. She helped Ellen pat the mess on the front of her dress and clucked over the damage. "I'll be fine," Ellen said. "What's a little dry cleaning?" She spread her legs a few inches and waved the filmy material in the air, hoping to dry off before court went back into session.

She watched her daughter-in-law take a sip of her coffee. "Finish it," she urged when Allie pushed it aside. "God knows you need to replenish your energy."

Finally, Allie turned the cup upside down. One tiny drip rolled onto the conference table. Ellen smiled at her. She wondered how long it would be before the herb took effect. "How much did you get for Ian's old fly rod?"

Allie's mouth dropped open in disbelief. "Sixty bucks."

Her mother-in-law nodded. "All in all," she said, "I couldn't have done better myself."

\* \* \*

*T*he prosecution rested. Court was adjourned until the following morning. Ellen told Angus she would not take him home until he buttoned his entire coat, and Jamie and Graham left the courtroom with their heads bent together, discussing the strategy of the day.

"Want a cup of coffee?" Cam said to Allie.

"I just had one with your mother."

She started to walk out of the courtroom but Cam was only a step behind. "Dinner," he pressed. "You've got to eat sometime."

"But not at four-thirty." She flipped her hair over the collar of her coat; Cam watched it spill over her shoulders. "Begging doesn't suit you."

"I'm negotiating."

Allie ignored him. "I'll catch up with you later at home."

She started to walk toward her car, but was stopped by Cam's carrying voice. "No, you won't. You'll be there, and I'll be there, but we most certainly will not be together."

He had yelled across the parking lot, and although she thought that the people they knew were all gone by now, she could not be entirely sure. She walked toward him again quickly, stopping just a foot away, her face turned up to his in anger. "It has been *two* days," she hissed. "Two lousy days. How dare you."

A raindrop caught her in the eye, making her vision blur without the heat of a tear. Until then, she hadn't noticed it was still raining.

It had rained every single day of their honeymoon. In Aruba, where it never rained.

"I know what you're thinking of," Cam said, a smile spreading across his face, a big shit-eating grin that she wanted to slap right off him. "I always think about it, too, when it rains this hard."

"I don't remember."

Cam caught her upper arm. "You remember. You may be mad as hell at me but you can't just throw out everything that led up to the last few months."

Allie blinked the moisture from her eyes. "Why not?" she asked. *"You* did."

Do you remember me saying I wanted to be a travel writer? How some nights we would sit in the dark, feeling for each other with our voices, and we'd trade memories of places like it was part of an elaborate board game: your Acropolis to my mustachioed artist in Montmartre, your high-stepping calf in the streets of Bombay versus my vision of the Serengeti from a biplane, with the tall grass running left and then right like a school of silver fish.

It occurred to me that in the months after you left, I did become a travel writer after all. I wrote of Sicily and Haifa and the Yorkshire moors, about the Orient and the Mediterranean Sea, about anywhere I thought you might be. Except my destinations were imagined, and I never set foot on another shore.

At first this upset me. And then, as time passed, I remembered that I have always hated to fly.

# NINETEEN

*T*he first motion Graham made was a general one for dismissal.
He and Audra stood hip to hip in front of Judge Roarke's
bench, jockeying for better position like two cubs aiming for the
same teat. Roarke pulled off his eyeglasses and rubbed the corners
of his eyes with his thumb and forefinger. It was only nine in the
morning. "Why, Counselor?"

"Insufficient evidence."

Audra laughed.

Graham had told himself it wasn't going to work; that the
only reason he was even throwing motions at the judge before the
defense testimonies began was because it was standard procedure.
Insufficient evidence? Well, maybe it didn't really apply to this
case, but it was the most common grounds for dismissal.

"Motion denied," Judge Roarke said. "Is that all, or do you
want to waste more of my time?"

Graham squared his shoulders. He could feel Jamie's gaze from
the defense table, burning a small warm spot in his back. "It's es-
sentially wrong to try James MacDonald the same way you'd try a
sniper who goes nuts and shoots thirty people at a fast-food restaurant. This is a completely different sort of case."

Audra's lips drew back in a poor imitation of a condescending
smile. She had put on her blush badly this morning; to Graham it

seemed as if she had clown dots on her cheeks. "Tell that to your elected official," she said. "As of right now, murder is murder. It happens to be the law."

Graham looked back at the judge. "A common-law crime suggests the absence of consent of the victim."

Roarke nodded. "Yes, but unfortunately that's the way the statute still reads. You aren't planning to overturn the foundations of the legal system in this little courtroom, are you, Mr. MacPhee?"

Graham took a deep breath, his last-ditch attempt. "This case involves the right to die, not the taking of a life."

Audra smirked. "That's touching, Graham, but it isn't a legal defense."

Judge Roarke rapped his gavel with more force than he intended. "Enough. All motions denied. Trial will resume after a ten-minute recess."

Graham walked back to the defense table, reminding himself that motions for dismissal were a technicality, and that a denial was what he had expected all along. But as he raised his eyes to Jamie's hopeful face, he realized what it truly meant. *You made motions for dismissal so that you could cover your ass in the event of an appeal.* Which meant that on some level, Graham had already accepted the fact of defeat.

*H*e was an idiot to bring her flowers. Not only had Cam bought them from one of her competitors, but seeing so many blooms covering her dresser and the vanity and the bedroom floor made Allie think of her shop, which made Allie think of Mia.

There were mums and daisies and gladioli, amaryllis and gentians and fuchsia. There were lilies and cyclamen and a big bunch of pearly everlasting. Cam seemed to have gone to the trouble of finding every color in the rainbow, and bringing it into her room.

She had awakened while he was sneaking in with another vase to set beside her hairbrush. "What are you doing in here?" she asked, sitting up abruptly.

Cam smiled at her, and instead of placing the flowers on the dresser, held them out like a presentation bouquet. "Isn't that obvious?"

He had slept on the couch again last night, she supposed, because she wasn't about to let him into the bedroom. "It's not my birthday."

Cam sat on the edge of the bed, and Allie instinctively moved an inch away. "I know."

She glared at him. "You can't buy a clean conscience."

A flash of black flared in his eyes for a second, but disappeared behind a set mask of self-control. He forced a smile.

Allie knew she was being spiteful. She had told Cam to stay, but she knew that if she'd had to put up with the bullshit she was tossing Cam's way she would have left long ago. And yet, she couldn't help it. She'd open her mouth to declare a truce and this horrible thing that had taken up residence inside her would spew out a reel of its hate.

She wondered how long it would take her brain to convince her heart that this was no longer a contest. Cam had won, hands down. No matter what verbal weapon she used, Allie could not even begin to hurt Cam as badly as he had hurt her.

"Do you know where she is?"

Allie heard the question fall from her own lips, shocked she had uttered it. Cam's face reddened, then drained. "No," he said. "And if I did, it wouldn't matter."

"How can you say that? That didn't stop you before."

Cam stared at a spot just to the left of Allie's shoulder. There was a mark on the wallpaper. It had been a mosquito last summer; one night he had swatted it in the dark, mashing it up against the wall. He had been making love with Allie, and it had landed on her shoulder, drawing blood. "This is where I'm supposed to be," Cam said simply. "With you."

"Where would you rather be?"

*I don't know.* Cam stood up, took the flowers from Allie, and set them on her nightstand. "Look. You have to give me some credit. You have to give me a break."

Allie folded her arms across her chest. "I don't have to give you anything," she said, but her voice broke over the words.

Cam left the room a minute later. Allie could hear the water running in the shower, the quick zip of cotton as he pulled a T-shirt over his head and skimmed out of his shorts. She got out of bed and wrapped her big bathrobe around herself and padded down the stairs.

Cam had folded the blanket and sheets and stacked them on one end of the couch. His equipment belt was draped, as always, across the dining room table. His boots were sitting beside the TV.

His wallet and pocket change were on top of the VCR. Allie touched the leather billfold with one finger. Then she opened it, feeling her heart pound, listening with half an ear to the sound of water still running through the pipes upstairs.

Seventeen dollars. A driver's license. An organ donor card. She fiddled with the tight pockets, pulling out a CPR certificate, a Visa card, and an American Express Card. Some bank receipts; a charge slip from a restaurant in Pittsfield. An ATM card.

There were no hidey-holes in the wallet; she knew, because she had bought it for him two Christmases ago. She did not come up with a scrap of paper that had an unfamiliar address on it, or a note with a telephone number and a scrawled "M" beside it. There was no condom tucked into the back pocket of the wallet, no picture of Mia creased and weathered from handling. There was no evidence that Cam had lied about anything he'd just said.

She knew how you went about falling in love; she did not know how you went about falling into trust. Disgusted with her own curiosity, she snapped the wallet shut.

During the ten-minute recess, Judge Roarke's daughter broke her leg falling from a jungle gym. Frazzled and hurried, he dismissed the jury with an apology and stated that the trial would resume at nine o'clock the following morning. Jamie grinned from ear to ear. "This is good," he said to Graham. "Don't you think this is good?"

Graham glanced at him over the files he was shoving into his briefcase. "How so?"

"I figure if the jury has a whole day away from this courtroom, whatever the prosecution said won't be fresh in their minds."

"Jamie," Graham said, "never prejudge a jury."

Allie leaned over the rail that separated the spectators from the rest of the court. "Well, I think Jamie's right. The longer the trial drags out, the further away all the prosecution's testimony is."

Graham smiled. "You forget, Audra gets to do a closing statement, too." He clasped his briefcase and checked his watch. "You going back to Wheelock, Allie? I have a plea bargain I've got to work on; I think I'll head to the law library."

Allie nodded. "I'll take Jamie."

Jamie turned toward Graham. "You have other cases besides mine?" he said, smiling a little.

Graham grinned. "A good lawyer makes you feel like you're the only one on his docket. Of course, in your case, it's pretty close to the truth." He started off down the aisle of the courtroom, holding up a hand in a half-wave.

Allie took a deep breath and smoothed her hands down the front of her wool coat. "Well. Are you hungry?"

Jamie shook his head. "Graham won't let me outside the town lines until I've had a good breakfast." He took Allie's elbow and guided her out of the courtroom, ducking past the growing throng of local media. "I'm up for a quiet ride," he said. "I'll try to get some sleep this afternoon."

Allie unlocked Jamie's side of the car first, and watched him fold himself into the tiny space and then push back the passenger seat so that his legs could stretch out. She started the ignition; a thick blast from the heater blew her bangs from her forehead. "It's hard to believe that yesterday it was fifty degrees."

Jamie made a noise at the back of his throat. "It's getting hard to predict anything these days."

Allie glanced at him before making the right-hand turn out of the superior court. His eyes were bloodshot and the skin beneath them looked puffy and tender. Jamie felt her staring and turned her way. "I know. I look three shades shy of dead."

"Not sleeping much?"

Jamie shook his head. "I slept better than this after I killed Maggie," he said wryly. "If I knew the way the jury was going to fall, I think I could take anything that bitch Campbell dished out at the trial. Even if they said I was going to jail for the next five forevers. It's the not knowing that's driving me crazy."

Allie nodded. "It's like that for me, too. I can't imagine having Cam walk out of my life, but I have nothing to say to him when he's there. I wish someone would hold up one of those little photo key chains you used to get at amusement parks and say, 'Here, look. This is your future. This is the way it's going to be.'"

Jamie turned his face out the passenger window and watched a bird—who knew what kind, since it was late January—keeping pace with the car. "You're not getting along with Cam, then?" he asked quietly.

"That would be a nice way of saying it."

"Him, or you?"

*Me,* Allie thought. *A horrible piece of myself that I can't cut away.* "I can't help it," she said. "I say things I don't even want to say. I don't recognize myself anymore when I'm in the same room as him."

*But I recognize* him. The thought came to her, and she blushed. She noticed Jamie watching, and she fiddled with the air vents, pretending it was the heat. "You know," he said slowly, "Graham's making a big deal about whether or not I thought killing Maggie was wrong."

Allie nodded, trying to follow the shift in conversation. "It's his defense, Jamie. You shouldn't take it personally."

"No, I don't. It's just that my answer now wouldn't be the same as it was back then."

Allie slammed her foot on the brakes. *Remorse.* She remembered Graham saying something once about this trial: Remorse was the one stipulation for mercy. An absence of regret was what sanctioned punishment. "Did you tell Graham that?"

Jamie shook his head. "I'm only just thinking it now, and I don't believe it would have quite the same effect for him as it will for you."

"What do you mean?"

"Having been through it, I'd think twice about killing what's between you and Cam. You don't get it back, you know."

Allie pulled over to the curb and put her hand on Jamie's arm. "This is an entirely different situation. What you and Maggie had was being ruined by something out of your power. What Cam and I had was ruined by something he did."

Jamie drew up one knee and braced it against the glove compartment. "I'll tell you something else I haven't told my attorney," he said. "You know why I'm not sleeping? Because I'm dreaming about Maggie. Not about the dying, not like it was at first. I've been thinking what would happen—what *will* happen—when I see her again. Forget all the shit about her being sick, and her being the one who asked to die—what it boils down to, and any member of the jury can tell you this, is that *I did it*. I killed her. And I can't help but wonder if she's going to forgive me for that."

He turned to Allie and laced his fingers through her own, squeezing nearly to the point of pain. "Three months ago, if you asked me, I would have told you that if you really loved someone, you'd let them go. But now I look at you, and I dream about Maggie, and I see that I've been wrong. If you really love someone, Allie, I think you have to take them back."

She dropped Jamie off at Angus's house and then drove through the tangled streets of Wheelock, past her house, past the police station, to Glory in the Flower.

Allie left the Closed sign prominently displayed on the door and went to the cooler, where most of the flowers she'd bought were wilting and in various stages of dying. She hadn't come, however, to clean house. With a cursory glance she took some of the dead lily stalks from their buckets and dropped them into the trash. Then she pulled the thirty-three-gallon bag from the big metal drum and knotted it; set it outside the back door.

She knew she was going to panic the neighbors, so she opened all the windows, letting in the bite of winter and the fresh, unsuspecting air. She rummaged through her dried floral collection, pulling every strand of laurel leaves she could find. She tugged a few out of arrangements that already hung on the walls for purchase. She sifted through the rotting greens in the cooler and found the fresh laurel, the thick, ropy vines twisting around her wrists. She dropped all of these into the metal drum, added a few crumpled sheets of newspaper, and created a fire.

Legend had it that maidens who wanted to win back the attentions of errant lovers would burn laurel leaves.

The smoke rose high around her face as she leaned over the drum, making her choke and leaving a sweet, ashy scent in her hair and her coat that would not disappear for several weeks.

Allie closed her eyes, which is why she did not see the prickled vine of morning glory that had caught on her sleeve, its bell-shaped flowers closing as they fell into the flames. And it was only a long shot to think she would have remembered that morning glory, too, was part of a myth about burning; that the sputtering greens had once been a forewarning that somebody close was going to die.

When Allie went back to the house, she found Cam sitting in the living room watching the six o'clock news. He had heated up a can of soup; he had left at least half for her.

She shrugged out of her coat and left it draped over a dining room chair, so that the sleeve trailed over Cam's gun belt. "Hi," he said. "How was the trial?"

"Postponed," she answered. She picked up the mail Cam had left on the table and sifted through the bills and catalogs. "The judge's daughter broke her leg."

Cam glanced at Allie. "Well, that was lucky."

She lifted a shoulder. "Jamie seems to think so. Graham isn't saying anything."

"Did you see the soup?"

Allie nodded. She sank down on the couch and slipped off her shoes, tucking her stockinged feet into the crack between two cushions.

"You want me to get you some?"

She shook her head.

Cam set his bowl on the floor and sat down across from her on the opposite end of the couch. He glanced wistfully at the spot where his armchair had been. "Who bought the leather wing chair?"

"Darby Mac. For his wife."

"You think he'll sell it back?"

Allie tilted her head, as if she could still see it in its previous spot. "I don't know." She glanced at Cam. "You should have thought of that."

They sat for a moment in silence. "What did you do all day?" Cam asked.

Allie stared at him. She could not remember the last time Cam had asked her that question. She had always asked it of *him*. "Tell me something. What did we used to talk about before?"

"Before what?"

Allie gestured with her hand. "Before."

Cam leaned his head back. "Well, I think the difference was that you actually participated in the conversations."

Allie dug her feet deeper in the sofa. She could feel something with her toes: a dime? a pretzel? "You don't want me to talk," she said. "Believe me."

Cam stared at her. "Let's get it over with, Allie. Just say what you have to say and then let's start again."

"There isn't anything I *can* say," Allie muttered. "I haven't read up on Miss Manners for this." She turned away, feeling tears burn the back of her eyes, and she cursed herself. She didn't want weakness; she didn't need weakness, not now. She watched the chandelier hanging over the dining room table waver as she refused to blink. It was made of wrought iron; a bunch of running, wiry Keith Haring–style stick figures reaching to the center to hold a fat sconce which housed the light. When Mia had come home with her, that very first day, she had said that she liked it.

"Do you think about her?" Allie whispered, her voice so low Cam had to ask her to repeat her question. "Do you think about her," she said flatly.

He didn't answer. At first, the day Mia had left, he could think of nothing else, to the point where he had left his B & E seminar early to find out what had happened. Then he had come home, and found all his possessions missing, and he had been so wrapped up in thinking about Mia that he wasn't able to focus on getting anything back until the following morning.

But now, it had been several days. He'd been in close proximity to Allie. He'd bumped into her when they misjudged distance, and had rubbed against the raw edge of her pain. And he started to think a little less about what he had lost, and to concentrate instead on what could be salvaged.

He reached out until his hand was an inch away from Allie's ankle. "I still think about her," he said. "Not as much, but I do."

Allie turned away and tucked her legs beneath her.

"Why didn't you sell the stained-glass?" Cam asked.

"Because I'm an idiot. I should have." Allie glanced up at Cam. "Did she pick it out with you? Did she help you wrap it?"

"Stop," Cam said, reaching for her.

But Allie was already running up the stairs. He made it to the bedroom just as she'd pulled the panel from its hook on the wall. "You told me to be careful when you gave it to me," Allie said, her voice shrill. "You said it couldn't take pressure."

She let it drop to the floor.

A ngus had not gone to Pittsfield that day because he'd awakened blind. Of course, he hadn't told this to Jamie, who'd
come into his bedroom in the morning and then again when Allie
dropped him off. He only said that he had one of his wee migraine
headaches, and he thought it best he didn't make that long a drive.

Jamie had understood, he was a good lad. He'd asked if Angus
wanted something—aspirin, a cold cloth for his forehead, soup—
but Angus waved him away. *A good night's rest,* he told him. *We both
will be better in the morning.*

If you wanted to split hairs about it, Angus wasn't exactly
blind. He just wasn't seeing anything the way it was supposed to
look. He'd been in that bedroom for eight years now and knew the
exact location of the door, the placement of the bureau to the left of
the bed, the window and the hang of the curtains. But when Angus
had opened his eyes that morning, all he could see was the Great
Hall at Carrymuir.

It was disconcerting, to say the least, to watch Jamie come to
the door and lean against a crested shield that was over three hundred years old, and to see at the foot of what had once been his bed
the scarred wooden table that could seat thirty. Several times during the day Angus tried to close his eyes and rub them clear, or put
some Visine drops in to bring back his house, but his efforts were
to no avail.

That night, Angus dreamed. The walls of his room fell away
and his house became as round as the world and he saw three
globes of light coming down from where the moon should be. The
street rolled back and the asphalt gave way and below all this was a
moor. He watched two armies assemble themselves on his left and
his right. One wore blue and stood beneath a Scottish flag. The
other, in winking red, held fast to a Union Jack. The red army
charged at the blue two times, and two times the blue pushed them
back. The third time the Scots ran the English through with their
swords, scattering those who did not fall.

Angus watched the belch of the cannons and the gleam of the
singing swords, he saw the standards snapping in the sleet, but he
did not hear a single sound. That is, not until a man dressed in
blue came toward him. He held out his hand. The man was as tall
as Angus had once been and his hair was brighter than fire. Angus
reached out and realized he was handing the man a sword, hilt

first; and at this gesture, he realized how very tired he was of fighting. He smiled and sat up, feeling the ache and knot in his bones melt away and the sluggish set of his muscles firm and tone. "Come," the man said, as Angus fell into step beside him. "You're with us."

# TWENTY

Audra Campbell stared at the empty defense table and wondered what Graham MacPhee had up his sleeve. No defendant, no attorney, and the row behind their table that was usually packed with supportive MacDonalds was conspicuously empty.

She narrowed her eyes and tapped her pen against her legal pad.

Graham came dashing down the central aisle of the courtroom as the jury was filing in. He remained standing, straightening his tie, while the judge entered the room.

"Your Honor," he said immediately. "Permission to approach the bench."

Roarke waved both Audra and Graham forward. "The defense requests a temporary adjournment," Graham said quietly. "Angus MacDonald, Jamie's great-uncle, died in his sleep last night. Jamie had been living with Angus as per the conditions of his bail."

Roarke nodded. Even Audra remained silent. "How long will you need, Mr. MacPhee?"

"Till Monday? That's just after the funeral."

Roarke banged his gavel. "Court is temporarily adjourned until Monday morning at nine."

Audra leaned close to Graham as they stepped from the bench and made their way back to their respective tables. "If I didn't know better—"

"Don't even say it," Graham interrupted. Then he smiled. "But I'll admit that Angus's timing might be yet another act of mercy."

*T*he jury liked Bud Spitlick. He sat all around the witness stand, shifting his chair and hemming and hawing his way through Graham's questions. He was wearing gray slacks and a white dress shirt over a decaled T-shirt, whose message could easily be read through the thin fabric of the button-down: *GOD BLESS AMER-ICA*. Graham couldn't have picked out anything more fitting.

"Have you lived in Cummington long, sir?"

"Oh, I'd say." Bud smiled, showing his gold fillings. "Me and the missus have been there since we were born. We're sort of an institution in Cummington. Used to run the general store—" He turned to the jury, drumming up business. "Some of you may have heard of it? Spitlick's? We were done up in a special article in the *Globe* once, '89 I think. Anyhow, we got to the point where we wanted to retire, but not really, you know, so's now we sell our merchandise from our very own home."

"Your own home? Can you elaborate?" Graham knew damn well it had nothing to do with the case. But even the most cynical juror would believe this man. A little more couldn't hurt.

Bud flushed, which made his nose stand out in relief. "Well, we got the bolts of fabric in the living room, with the dry goods. And we stock a fair selection of children's hockey skates; we'll even do trade-ins on used ones, so we get a lot of parents coming in. We got penny candy for the little ones, and some best-seller paperbacks, and a few board games. I guess we got a little of everything and a lot of nothing."

"How do you know Jamie, Mr. Spitlick?"

Bud glanced at Jamie and gave him a big, honest smile. Graham hoped everyone on the jury had seen that. It was the first time Bud had seen Jamie since Maggie's death, and he wasn't going to be allowed to talk to him until after his testimony, so this was the only way to make a connection. "Jamie bought the house next to mine twelve or so years back."

"And you knew his wife Maggie, too?"

"Sure. Cutest little thing. He married her about ten years ago. My wife and I went to the wedding."

Graham leaned against the witness stand. "Can you tell us about Jamie and Maggie?"

Bud whistled through his teeth. "If a neighbor don't know you, you tell me who does. Jamie and Maggie, as I recall, went off on a honeymoon after they were married and just never stopped. They weren't the kind who'd be throwing pots and pans and yelling at each other about the checkbook every night. More often we'd hear 'em chasing each other around the house and laughing."

Graham looked at Jamie. For the first time during the trial, he was smiling.

"Crazy in love," Bud Spitlick said. "I cared for them like my own son and daughter." Then he cleared his throat. " 'Course, when Maggie got sick, it was just awful. I think it was easier for Maggie to handle than Jamie, since he was watching her hurt and knew he couldn't do anything about it."

"Can you give us an example?"

"Well, last spring—real early, I'd say March—something happened to Maggie in the middle of the night. She was on some new kind of medicine; she was always trying some new kind of medicine; and I guess her lungs stopped working. The siren from the ambulance woke me up. It woke up near everyone on the street, I figure, and most of us were outside in our bathrobes watching the paramedics run up the front stairs and bring Maggie back down on a stretcher. And there comes Jamie, naked as a jaybird, huddled over the stretcher, his mouth over Maggie's doing that artificial restoration. The paramedics pulled him away, told him to put on some clothes, but he just stood there like he was in shock. I don't think I'll ever forget the way Jamie looked, with those flashy red lights all over his skin, watching the ambulance take Maggie away."

Graham nodded, giving the jury a minute to let down their sympathy. "Can you tell us a little bit more about Maggie?"

"Objection," Audra said. "The deceased is not on trial."

"I'd like a little leeway, Your Honor," Graham countered.

Roarke nodded. He looked moved by the ambulance story too. "I'll advise counsel not to go too far with this." He turned to Bud Spitlick. "You may proceed."

Bud shook his head. He was becoming visibly choked up, so Graham handed him a box of Kleenex from the railing of the witness stand. "Well," Bud said, pausing to blow his nose. "Maggie was real sick. She wasn't getting any better, and we all knew it."

Graham waited for Bud to continue, then realized he was lost in his own memories. "Did Maggie ever speak to you about the right to die?"

"Objection!" Audra yelled. "This is absolutely irrelevant."

"This is completely relevant," Graham said, moving closer to Judge Roarke in tandem with Audra. "It goes to Jamie's state of mind, and the nature and quality of his act."

Roarke glanced from Audra to Graham and back again, as if he was trying to make a decision about which fool lawyer to throw out on his ass first. "Objection sustained," he said. "Watch yourself, Counselor."

Graham turned away, smiling inside. He hadn't expected Audra to be overruled, but now he'd managed to plant the idea of euthanasia in the jury's collective mind. Without mentioning the word *mercy*.

"Mr. Spitlick, what were your conversations with Maggie regarding her health?"

Bud was beginning to sweat; big patches stood out against the armpits of his white shirt. He tugged at his tie. "She was very concerned," he said. "She was nervous in general around people who were sick."

"And how do you know this?"

"Some time ago, I guess about five years back, my own sister had a stroke. Maggie was an angel; she ran the store while we were at the hospital and she brought us dinner at home or up at County General. My sister was pronounced brain-dead, you see, but she was living on those fancy machines, and this went on for a while. From time to time Maggie would come to the hospital to pick my wife up and give her a ride home, or to leave us sandwiches. Still, Maggie wouldn't much come past the doorway. She said people who were that sick scared her to death.

"One night, she came all the way into the room and looked down at my sister. She said that wasn't a way to live."

"What did you say?"

Bud had started to cry. "I told her," he said, his voice thick with emotion, "that God would take Frances when he was ready. And Maggie said that if it was her, she'd want someone to tap God on the shoulder and wake Him up." He wiped his nose with a ball of Kleenex. "I'm sorry. I'm real sorry about this."

"That's all right, Mr. Spitlick." Graham looked at Jamie, who was staring at his neighbor with obvious pain in his eyes. "Take your time." He waited until Bud glanced up at Jamie and received a short nod and a genuine smile. Then he turned to Audra. "Your witness."

Audra knew better than to antagonize a witness the jury not only liked but felt sorry for. Bud Spitlick was the real thing; he was too rough around the edges to have put on so fine a performance. She smiled at him and walked close to the witness stand. "Mr. Spitlick, I've got a hypothetical question for you. Thirty years ago, would you have guessed you'd be running a general store right out of your living room?"

Bud grinned. "No, ma'am, I would not. We were the toast of the town, back then. It was before Wal-Mart and Woolworth got to Cummington, so everyone came to us first."

"So you'd agree that what you say in answer to a hypothetical question isn't always the way things work out when you're faced with the actual situation?"

She could see the wheels turning as he sorted out the words. God preserve her from stupid people. "Yes," Bud said, "I guess that's true."

"Then what the deceased said in the context of your sister's unfortunate situation might not have been what she wished for when she actually found herself in similar straits?"

Bud's face went dull red. "I can't say," he mumbled. "I can't be sure."

"Mr. Spitlick, when your sister was terminally ill and comatose, were you under a lot of stress?" She started pacing, her back to the witness.

"Oh, yes," Bud said, relieved to be talking about a topic he could firmly grasp.

Audra turned to face him and pinned her cold blue gaze to his. "Why didn't you kill her?"

Graham jumped up. "Objection."

"Sustained."

Audra smiled at the defendant. "Withdrawn."

Allie could hear the water running, so she knew Cam was taking a shower. He had come home from work in the middle of the day because he had been on the midnight shift, and this was his usual procedure: he'd eat everything in the refrigerator that did not require heavy cooking, he'd shower, and then he'd crawl into bed and sleep like a log for six hours.

He had left the door ajar. Allie watched the steam slip out of the bathroom in a long, thick curl and come to lie on the Oriental runner in the hall. He was singing, and he must have been washing his hair, because every few words came out gurgled. His eyes were probably screwed shut.

She cracked the door a smidgen more and put her face up to the opening.

She told herself that she was still angry at him; that she didn't want to be looking, so it didn't matter if it was her business or not. Through the smoky glass stall she saw the length of his legs, his arms raised overhead to soap his back, the muted outline of his buttocks.

It wasn't until she had run back down to the kitchen and waited for the fire to leave her cheeks and the shaking to stop that she realized her agitation had nothing to do with voyeurism. It had to do with the fact that in spite of her best intentions, she could not help wanting something she knew she should not have.

Dascomb Wharton almost did not fit into the witness box. Graham saw several jurors hiding smiles behind their hands as the bailiff helped the doctor settle himself across the seat of the witness chair and a second one that was placed inside for his comfort. *Great,* Graham thought. *Our one expert witness is a laughingstock.*

But Wharton's answers were clear and clipped, very professional. When he listed his credentials, which included Harvard Medical School and a residency at Massachusetts General Hospital, even Judge Roarke looked impressed.

"How long have you practiced in Cummington, Doctor?" Graham asked.

"Twenty-one years," Wharton said.

"And what kinds of cases do you see?"

"I'm a general practitioner. I deliver babies, I take care of those babies when they have whooping cough, I get them through the chicken pox and give them school physicals and physicals for the Army, I help some of them give birth to their own children. I also see a wide range of emergent cases: appendectomies, gallstones, cancers of various kinds."

"When did you first see Maggie?"

Wharton shifted; the floor of the witness stand creaked. "Maggie started coming to my office when she moved to Cummington, which was in 1984. I was quite familiar with her medical history."

Graham nodded. "Can you tell us how you diagnosed her cancer?"

He did not listen to Wharton's story of how Maggie had come to him with a broken ankle, a skating accident, and how X-rays had revealed not only the best way to set the bone, but lesions which indicated a tumor had insinuated its way into her body. Instead, Graham watched the jury. For the first time during the trial, some of them were taking notes. Most of them perched on the edge of their seats.

Wharton explained in layman's terms the type of breast cancer Maggie had; the decision to do a radical mastectomy that would also remove the lymph nodes; the meaning of finding the secondary site—the bone lesions—before the primary one. He chronicled her forays into chemotherapy and radiation, as well as the side effects she experienced.

Jamie did not look at the doctor. He stared into his lap.

"Can you tell us, given the various cancers Maggie had, what the prognosis was?"

Wharton sighed. "She was going to die. It wasn't a matter of *if,* but of *when.*"

"In your experience, was there any hope for improvement in her condition?"

"I haven't seen it, no."

Graham stood beside Jamie. "Did you tell Jamie and Maggie this?"

"Yes, of course."

"And what were their reactions?"

"Maggie was very stoic about it. I believe that she had known what I was going to say. Jamie didn't take it quite as well. He held her hand the entire time I was speaking, but when I was finished, he told me I was out of my mind. He suggested that I had mixed up her results, and that they would get a second opinion."

"Did they, to your knowledge?"

"Yes," Wharton said. "The doctor's findings confirmed mine. He sent along a diagnosis to stick in her file."

"Did you ever meet with Jamie alone?"

The doctor nodded. "He came to see me several times with new cures he'd heard about. Once it was something to do with Chinese ginseng, I believe, and another time it was some sort of chiropractic nonsense that supposedly broke up the cancer. He said that he liked to meet with me alone because he didn't want to give his wife false hope, but he would then explain the latest theory that he'd found. It was evident he did a great deal of research on ductal melanomas and the different therapies that they'd responded to in other cases. However, even the more reasonable treatments he brought to my attention would not have made a difference for Maggie."

"Would you say he was a devoted husband?"

For the first time since he had taken the stand, Wharton looked at Jamie. "I've rarely seen the like."

Graham sat down again. "Dr. Wharton, when did you last see Maggie?"

"She came to my office for a 4:45 appointment on September fifteenth. Friday, I believe it was."

"What did you tell her on that date?"

"She was complaining of flashing in her eyes and temporary blindness, which I explained was a result of the tumor pressing down on her optic nerve. At that point, the cancer was spreading through the brain. I told her that I was not sure what part of her would be affected next. Depending on the direction the tumor took in its growth, it could have depressed her respirations. It could have led to seizures, or a stroke. It could have resulted in permanent blindness. I told her I just did not know."

"Can you tell the court what Maggie's state of mind was like when she left your office?"

"Objection," Audra said. "Witness cannot know what was going on in the deceased's mind."

"I'll rephrase. Can you tell me how she was acting before she left?"

Wharton shook his head. "She was very subdued. She thanked me and she shook my hand." He paused, as if remembering something. "She forgot her coat; my secretary had to call after her as she walked down the hall." He pursed his lips. "She already knew she was going to die; she was told that day that her body systems would be shutting down in a Russian roulette order; I don't imagine she was feeling very spirited."

Graham thanked the doctor. "Nothing further."

Audra stood up before Graham had even made it back to his chair. "One question, Dr. Wharton. In your expert opinion, can you tell the court what the chances would have been of the victim dying of natural causes by the morning of September 19, 1995?"

Wharton let out his breath slowly. "It would not have been very probable."

Audra smiled. "Nothing further."

Graham stood immediately. "I'll redirect. He walked in front of the witness stand. "Dr. Wharton, if Maggie had lived through September 19, 1995, would the quality of life she was experiencing have been equal to the quality of life she enjoyed before the onset of her cancer?"

Wharton glanced at the jury. "Absolutely not."

*C*am told Hannah he was going to be reviewing the log sheets for the officers who'd been on the night shift the previous few days, and then he went into his office and locked the door behind him. He sat down at his desk and picked up the small clock in the corner. He'd gotten it for opening up his first joint savings account with Allie five years back. For a thousand bucks, they could have gotten a hot-air corn popper. They'd only had two hundred and fifty at the time.

He opened the bottom drawer of his desk, the one that held the swinging green files with the mimeographed sheets of blank arrest reports, transfer-of-custody forms, voluntary confessions, cruiser logs. He'd tucked the globe Mia had given him for Christmas into the back.

He pulled it into his hands and spun it on its magnetic axis. "Where are you?" he said aloud. He pointed to Turkey, which they had talked about, and walked his fingertips all the way across to North America. He spun the globe again until all the colors and countries ran together in an indistinguishable rainbow.

Then he put the globe into the garbage can beneath his desk, and covered it with crumpled blank arrest reports so it would be thrown away with the trash.

*P*auline Cioffi should have been a stand-up comedienne. When Graham asked her to state her name and address and occupation for the record, she said she was Martha Stewart's stunt double, and that she'd be happy to be a witness for any other trials they had coming up since it got her away from her kids.

She wore a loud, flouncy dress with purple flowers all over it and she sat in the witness box as if she were a queen. She made lots of eye contact with the jury, and when she wasn't looking at them, she was staring directly at Jamie with compassion.

Graham thought he'd like to hire her.

"Mrs. Cioffi," he said, "how long did you know Maggie?"

She rolled her eyes upward. "Let me see. It was before Alexandra and Justin, but I'd already had the twins and I was pregnant with Chris." She beamed at Graham. "Eight years."

"How did you meet?"

"We were taking an aerobics class together given at the town church. Like I said, I was pregnant, so I tried to stay in the back where no one could see how stupid I looked in a maternity leotard. Maggie stayed in the back because she said she was motor-dyslexic and always went right when the rest of the class went left. We just hit it off, and we went out for coffee after the first class." She glanced at the jury. "Of course, I had decaf."

"How often did you two get together?"

"Twice a week, at first; after every aerobics class. Then I got to the point where I had too many kids for a sitter to take care of, so I dropped the class. Maggie would come over to my house a couple of times a week, sometimes on a weekend."

"Were you aware of Maggie's illness?"

"Yeah, I was. First of all, she couldn't get around as well as she used to. She popped pain pills all the time, and you could see her eyes glaze over sometimes when there was an ache the medicine couldn't get rid of. She was a very different woman from the one I met eight years back." Pauline paused. "She talked about the cancer a lot with me. She said she needed to get it off her chest, and she didn't want to upset Jamie."

"Can you describe for us the nature of Maggie's marriage?"

Audra raised her hand. "She's not a therapist, Your Honor."

"No," Pauline said cheerfully. "Just a household guru. I do therapy, but it comes awfully cheap."

"Rephrased. How did Jamie and Maggie act around you?"

Pauline sobered. "Jamie was very attached to her, and she was very much in love with him. They were the sort of couple that could have whole conversations by just looking at each other and raising their eyebrows and shrugging, you know? You always sort of felt like you were intruding around them." She smiled. "I was extremely jealous. My husband's idea of devotion is picking up his underwear from the bathroom floor." The jury laughed, and Judge Roarke shot Pauline a quelling look. "Well, I can't think of a time she came over that his name didn't come up. She told me that the worst part about dying would be leaving him behind."

"Did Maggie know that she was dying?"

"Yes, but she didn't know when. She told me once that what she really wanted was some control over it. And the same day, she said that she was going to ask Jamie to kill her."

Graham glanced at Audra, trying to circumvent an objection. "To the best of your knowledge, Mrs. Cioffi, and at the time that Maggie told you this, did you think Jamie would be capable of doing it?"

Audra remained quiet. For a moment, so did Pauline. She stared at Jamie, as if she was speaking to him with her gaze the same way his wife had. "I don't know," she said finally. "He would have done anything Maggie asked, but he never would have hurt her. I guess if he thought that killing her would cause her less pain than what she was already suffering every day, he would have done it."

Graham stood in front of Pauline. "Was Maggie your best friend?"

"She was the sister I never had."

"Are you angry at Jamie for killing your best friend?"

Pauline's eyes slid from Graham's face, over his shoulder, to rest on Jamie. She smiled at him, and Jamie's shoulders relaxed. A benediction. "No," she said. "Absolutely not."

For the cross-examination, Audra stood up and paced between Jamie and Pauline. "How very interesting. You wished your best friend dead?"

Pauline glared at Audra. She didn't like her, not her tight-ass little designer suit or her scraped-back hair or the way she talked through her nose. Well, hell, the prosecutor had yet to see the loyalty that was part and parcel of Pauline Cioffi. When a bully beat on her little son, Pauline had gone to the kid's house and slapped his mother. If this prosecutor bitch started to shred Pauline's relationship with Maggie—something sacred and fine, one of the bright spots in Pauline's life—she was going to get equal treatment.

"No," Pauline said. "Of course not. You don't know what she was going through."

"Yet you feel that she was better off dead. What if, Mrs. Cioffi, they found a cure for her cancer this month? Or this year?"

Pauline leaned to the edge of her seat and fixed Audra Campbell with a stare. "But they haven't, have they?"

Audra turned around, bested. "Nothing further," she said.

When the storm had blown over, and she came back to me, I tried not to think about you. This was my marriage; this was what mattered.

But sometimes I found myself wondering: If it had been the other way around—if she had been the one to run in and then out of my life—would she have invaded my thoughts in the months that followed, like a red herring, like a threading refrain, like you?

# TWENTY-ONE

*I*t wasn't until Jamie lost a dollar in the soda machine outside the courtroom that he realized he didn't believe in the legal system. It was not right that twelve people he'd never laid eyes on in his life were going to have a chance to determine his future. It was not right that they would get to hear the details of his relationship with his wife that Jamie wanted to hoard, so they wouldn't lose their intensity and shine. In a perfect world, there might be justice. But in a perfect world, nothing ever went wrong. The people you loved didn't get cancer. The issue of euthanasia wasn't up for debate. The money you put into a Coke machine actually produced a Coke.

The buttons of his shirt were pressing into his flesh. He realized he'd put it on inside out this morning; he wasn't thinking clearly. Through the tiny Plexiglas square in the swinging courtroom door he could see the American flag. He remembered being a little kid, trying to say the Pledge of Allegiance, and getting the words wrong. *One nation, under God. Invisible. With livery and justice for all.* But this was hardly a classroom.

He considered the first few days after Maggie's death, when the only thing that had seemed important was finding someone who would punish him. He remembered wanting to go to jail as quickly as possible. He did not know how he had come to change his mind so radically, so that the very thought of being locked away where he could not walk with the grass beneath his feet and the sky stretching all around him made him feel sick.

He realized he thought of jail and of dying the same way: you were just gone. It didn't really matter exactly where you went.

Through the Plexiglas, he saw Graham make a motion with his hand. Jamie MacDonald walked through the swinging doors and swallowed the bitter taste of his future.

Allie shifted on the hard wooden bench. They had just called Jamie to the stand; he was being escorted up to the tiny witness box. He was wearing the olive suit she had bought with him, and with his height and his wide shoulders, he looked like a man hunched over a grade-school desk.

She glanced around. Ellen was sitting next to her, grasping her hand and pressing a small round black stone between them. Yesterday she had given Jamie a mantra, a word to take home with him and up to the witness stand and anywhere else he thought he'd need to pull himself to center.

Angus, God rest his soul, was a few feet away from Ian in the Wheelock cemetery. But Allie knew he was watching. She could tell by the way she had sensed him sitting in the passenger seat of the car he hadn't used in years but which Jamie had unearthed and had taken to driving to the trial.

The rest of the spectators in the courtroom were people who had heard about the case, or reporters. Maybe there were court groupies. People who loved a mystery, who sat in on criminal cases and tried to guess the outcome.

She was beginning to turn her attention to the stand, where Jamie was being sworn in, when the flash of a badge caught her eye. Cam slipped quietly through the aisle and the back of the courtroom, taking a seat several rows behind her.

He had started coming to the trial the day they put Maggie's doctor on the stand. He said nothing about it, and they never discussed the case at home, but then they didn't discuss much of anything at all.

Allie liked to imagine the configuration of the courtroom spectators like guests at a wedding. Bride's family, groom's family—prosecutor's, or defendant's. Every day since the trial began she had counted the number of people on the prosecutor's side, and the number of people on the defendant's. Jamie usually lost out by a handful.

Allie realized that the people watching a trial would choose a side without considering the psychological statement that they were making, and that she was reading into it. But she glanced back at Cam, caught his eye, and smiled. Today was the first day since he'd started coming that he'd sat in support of his cousin.

*G*raham loved it. He absolutely loved it. He turned to Jamie, then looked surreptitiously at the members of the jury, who kept glancing at his client's shirt and letting their eyes slide away. "Jamie," he said, "since a lot of people are wondering, could you tell us why your shirt is on inside out?"

Jamie cleared his throat and flushed. "My uncle Angus told me it's an old Scottish custom: if you put on a piece of clothing inside out, you're not supposed to turn it around because your luck will turn with it. I wasn't taking any chances today."

The juror with the Mickey Mouse tie laughed out loud. A couple of spectators tittered. Graham walked up to the witness stand. "Jamie, on behalf of the court, let me offer my condolences on the loss of your uncle."

"Thank you," Jamie murmured.

"Can you tell the court what your occupation is?"

Jamie cleared his throat. As much as he'd practiced with Graham, he was still nervous. "I run my own computer company," he said. "A conceptual design firm. We create virtual worlds."

"Virtual worlds? As in virtual reality? Sci-fi gloves and headsets and all that?"

"Pretty much."

Graham whistled. "Sounds awfully high-tech. Could you define virtual reality, Jamie?"

Jamie shifted a little. He wondered, not for the first time, why Graham was bothering with questions like these. No one in the jury had a problem with Jamie's business contract with Nintendo. "Virtual reality is the willing suspension of disbelief," he said. "It can take the form of a dream, a book, a movie. The reason people associate the term with computers is because computer technology exists to actually place someone in willing suspension."

"What does that mean?"

"That there are no distractions—the real world isn't visible anymore. The artificial world becomes all you can see, or hear, or feel." He paused, pulled by the implications and ironies of his own definition. Jamie MacDonald, who had been on the cutting edge of virtual reality theme parks and toys, who had designed the Mega-Stick for Sega, and who had reconstructed reality on a ten-inch monitor screen, had never been able to truly dismiss the real world. Not for his wife, and now, not for himself. Whatever he and Maggie had chosen to believe about their actions, it was not enough. Like a conceptually designed toy, once the HMD came off, once the glove and bodysuit were removed, once you shut off the computer, you were only back where you'd started.

Jamie covered his face with his hands. Alarmed, Graham stepped forward, anxious to recapture his client's focus. "I'd like to talk a little about Maggie," Graham said, letting the light that came into Jamie's eyes stand for itself before he pressed on with a question. "How long were you married?"

"Eleven years."

"How did you meet her?"

Jamie smiled. "She was cleaning out a man-made duck pond at the park near my house with a mop. I couldn't take my eyes off her, and I didn't really know what to say, so I picked up one of the scrub brushes lying on the grass and pitched in."

"Why was she cleaning out a duck pond?"

"She said nobody else did it, and she was thinking of the ducks. That was the kind of person she was."

On a yellow pad in front of her, Audra Campbell scrawled, *Saint Maggie*.

"Did you have a happy marriage?"

"I think so. I think *she* thought so. I mean, we fought about things—how much money we had, whose turn it was to clean the bathroom—but I guess every couple does that." He glanced at Pauline Cioffi, sitting in the gallery with the other spectators. "She was my best friend, too. After I married Maggie, I didn't understand how I'd lasted twenty-five years without her."

Graham leaned casually against the jury box. "What were your plans for the future?"

Jamie's eyes clouded. "It became fairly clear about a year ago that we didn't have a lot of future left," he said. "But before Maggie got sick, we talked a lot about moving to a bigger house, maybe out of Cummington. Our goal was to have more than one bathroom. And we wanted kids. God, did we want them. We were trying; we had been trying for five years. But Maggie lost one baby, and she couldn't conceive, and then we found out that probably had something to do with the cancer too."

Allie shifted uncomfortably. She remembered the stack of ovulation-predictor tests in the linen closet of Jamie's house. With a child in the picture, Jamie might never have agreed to Maggie's request. With a child, all sorts of outcomes might have been changed. Ducking her head a little, she peered at Cam. If she and Cam had had a baby, would he still have betrayed her?

"Jamie, how did you find out about Maggie's illness?"

For a moment, Jamie didn't speak. Then he closed his eyes and leaned against the witness chair and let words fall from his mouth. They were spoken slowly and without emotion, but his hands were clenched on the wooden railing so tightly that the fingers and knuckles were white. He was telling a story, and even juror number 11, who seemed to have been nodding off, was alert and listening. Jamie created before everyone's eyes a skating pond, a snapped bone, a doctor's solemn conference.

Cam thought of Braebury, of the double skating oval, of Mia. He remembered the ice sculpture. By the time they left the pond, it had grown so warm outside that when he glanced at the melting phoenix before slinging his skates over his shoulder, it did not look at all the way he had remembered.

Graham waited a moment after Jamie fell silent. "When Dr. Wharton told you Maggie's bone lesions were a sign of cancer, how did you feel?"

Jamie shook his head. "I told him he was wrong. I mean, you've seen X-rays, right? How could they possibly pick out a lesion? I suppose it was the word 'cancer' that scared me to death. You hear it, and all of a sudden you aren't breathing anymore." He looked up at Graham. "It didn't much matter that the doctor was telling me it was in Maggie's body, and not mine. It would have hit me the same, either way."

"Did you get a second opinion?"

"Yes, from a doctor in Boston. He said that Maggie's bone lesions were the secondary site of a tumor too." Jamie looked down at his lap.

"How did the news affect Maggie?"

"She was afraid. She drew into a shell for a couple of days and didn't say anything, didn't really let me inside. But then she bounced back, and said she wanted to schedule an operation as quickly as possible. She said she wanted that thing out of her body."

Graham nodded. "What did you decide to do then?"

"She had a mastectomy. That terrified her too—you know, she was still so young, and she thought I would consider her deformed in some way. I kept telling her that it didn't matter, that she could have reconstructive surgery in a year, or whatever, but I think part of the reason that she kept talking about how she would look afterward was because it kept her from facing the fact that even getting rid of a breast wasn't going to take care of a cancer that had already spread."

"Can you describe the treatments Maggie underwent?"

Tenderly, as if they were layers of blankets he was peeling off to reveal his wife, Jamie began to outline the course of Maggie's cancer. He described her lying on the living room couch, doing reaching exercises to build up the muscles beneath her arm and in her chest wall that the mastectomy had severed. He listed the names of the drugs she'd had during chemotherapy as if they were old friends. He talked of driving Maggie home from these treatments, and pulling over to the curb so that she could push open the door and vomit. He described the waiting room of the radiology lab, with bald smiling children and sallow women who wrapped their heads with scarves. He described watching the laser of light, a red knife, spearing the center of Maggie's eye.

"Was there ever a time when your wife was in remission?"

"No," Jamie said. "It got to the point where the cancer became both of our jobs. We couldn't concentrate on anything else, and we didn't have room for anything else. We worked as a team to get rid of what was hurting her. We learned all the back roads to the hospital. The goal for each day was just to get through it."

"When did Maggie know she was going to die?"

Jamie glanced away from Graham. "The doctor told her the tumor was in her brain. She'd been having dizzy spells and then explosions, she called it, behind her eyes. This was in June of '95. We were in his office after a checkup—we always went in after a checkup—and she asked him flat-out. Wharton told her *everyone* was going to die, and Maggie got very angry. She said, 'Don't patronize me,' and she stood up to walk out of the room but she fainted." Jamie looked up. "Like I said, that was the problem at the time. When she came to, Wharton told her yes, but he didn't know exactly when."

"Did she say anything about it to you then?"

Jamie nodded. "In the car, she didn't say a word until we pulled into our driveway. But she didn't unhook her seat belt or make a move to leave the car. And then she looked at me and asked me if I knew what cancer looked like. I shook my head, and she started to cry. 'He's a big, fat, ugly puppeteer,' she told me, 'and he's holding all the strings.' "

Graham scanned the jury. Sympathy on many of the faces; some were leaning forward. A couple of women caught Graham's eye and turned away, as if they knew they were being monitored. He took a deep breath. "Did Maggie ask you to kill her before September of 1995?"

"Yes," Jamie said. "In January. We were on vacation in Quebec."

"What was your response at the time?"

"I told her to stop talking like that." He shook his head. "I knew it was bad for her, but I didn't think it was as bad as all that." He looked to the corner of the courtroom, to the American flag, dusty and still. "I didn't know it was going to get worse."

Allie sat across from Cam at an Armenian diner just around the corner from the superior court. Spread between them were platters of lamb and saffron rice, tabouli, hummus, and a basket of pita. Most of the food remained untouched.

"Do you think we should bring something back for Jamie?" Allie asked.

"I'm sure his lawyer will take care of it," Cam said. He leaned against the banquette and watched his wife. He couldn't quite believe how easily she'd agreed to go out to lunch with him. He must have caught her at a vulnerable moment, worn down from the sharp emotion of Jamie's morning testimony.

"Do you think he's doing okay? How he's talking, and the way he looks up there?"

Cam nodded. "I've been watching the jury. Some of the women on the left side were crying a little when he mentioned the treatments. That has to be a decent sign."

"Graham says you can't trust a jury. They'll act one way one minute and turn around and stab you in the back. Besides, the trial isn't about whether or not Jamie and Maggie were in a difficult, horrible situation. It's about whether or not he was crazy when he killed her."

"Which he wasn't," Cam said.

Allie shot him a look. "Thank God *you* weren't called to serve."

Cam pushed a wedge of pita bread toward her. "You've got to eat something. You look like you'll keel over if the wind picks up."

Allie stuffed the pita into her mouth. "Thanks a lot," she said sarcastically. She stared at Cam, in full uniform, his heavy gun belt riding high on his hips and his badge catching the reflected light from the window. "You know," she said, smiling shyly, "I always feel awfully safe going places with you when you're dressed like that."

Cam laughed. "You wouldn't believe how many people at the court have asked me where the bathroom is. They think I'm a security guard."

Allie leaned across the table and adjusted his collar. The brush of her fingers beneath his chin sent a chill down his spine. "I don't know if it's the uniform that does it for me. Maybe it's the gun. Maybe it's just you." *Maybe it's because when he's dressed like that, it is hard to believe he would lie.*

She sank against the seat, and Cam instinctively leaned forward, trying to pull her back and knowing that he'd already lost her. "You realize they came to town the same day," Allie said quietly. "Jamie and Mia."

"I know. I remember asking her if she knew him." His heart was racing again, simply because of the topic. But this time, Allie wasn't yelling at him. She was in a public place and she was speaking softly and holding out a little sliver of trust, just large enough to fit on the small saucer that the waitress had dropped off with their bill.

"Did you laugh at me?" she whispered. "I think of you two, laughing at me."

Cam had listened to heartrending stories all morning, and he didn't think any of Jamie's testimony had cut him as deeply and as painfully as what Allie had just said.

He thought of Mia; of how, when they were together, there was simply no room for anyone else. "No," Cam said. He kept his eyes locked to Allie's as he reached across the table and took her hand. For the first time, she did not pull away. Her fingers fluttered against his palm, then came to rest.

"No," he repeated, smiling from the inside out. "Never that."

A fter lunch, Jamie sat in the witness box and conjured Maggie. Graham asked questions from time to time, but it was only to guide Jamie in the right direction. He began on the night of January fifteenth, when Maggie returned from the doctor; he would finish when he drove up to the Wheelock police and asked for his cousin.

She had been grasping a red polo shirt when she asked him to kill her. The box she was using to store her clothes was about three-quarters full. On the top were the bras she had been able to wear before the operation. He was holding her hands. "I want you to kill me," she said.

"You've got to be kidding," Jamie answered. "Absolutely not."

Maggie pulled away from him, letting the shirt fall between them like a puddle of blood. "Jamie, let me go. You're being selfish."

He watched her frail shoulders tremble with the strength of her certainty and he sat on their bed and realized he was about to say the most awful words he could. "No," he told her. *"You* are."

She turned around and sank to the edge of the bed on the opposite side. They sat like studied figurines, their hands clasped in their laps, their heads bowed. "I have a right to be selfish," Maggie said bitterly. "It's one of the few privileges my body has left me in possession of."

Jamie picked up the red shirt and threw it back into her drawer. He reached into the liquor box for the bras, which slipped through his fingers like a skein of silken ribbons. He put these back in Maggie's dresser too.

They went to bed and fell asleep the way they were most comfortable: with Maggie's back to his front, one of his arms beneath the pillow, the other cupping her remaining breast. Sometime in the middle of the night, when his fingers relaxed, his hand brushed over the flat plane of her chest. He woke up feeling for her scar.

She drew in a sharp breath.

"Am I hurting you?"

Maggie turned in his arms. "On what level?" she asked, looking directly into his eyes.

She had looked at him before like that. Jamie liked to think of it as her Medusa look, the one that froze him in his tracks and rendered him incapable of thinking. But this time, in the middle of her gaze, her eyes widened just the slightest bit. And he knew that she couldn't even plead with him because of the pain.

He did not know what it would be like to go to sleep each night wondering if you would wake up in the morning. To stare into the bathroom mirror and see the sunken eyes, the bald patches on your scalp, to look at the jagged scar across what used to be your breast—and to thank God you could still stand on your own two feet and see your face clearly.

Jamie did know what it was like, however, to kiss your wife each night in bed and put behind the pressure of your lips a silent, last goodbye, just in case, a sentiment you'd never verbalize because it would feed her fear. He knew how he woke up sometimes to check her breathing. He knew how very tired he was, how he forced himself to drag up just a little more energy.

He was the one who spoke first. "Why can't you take pills? I'll get them for you. I won't call 911."

In the black night, with the sounds of their house settling around them, even this talk of death had a comfort zone. Maggie touched her hand to his chest. It was a stab in the dark, but her palm landed just over his heart, as if she knew she'd held it all along. "I want you touching me," she said. "I want your hands on me the minute I go."

She rolled onto her stomach and propped up on her elbows. The prospect of finally controlling this nightmare had her eyes gleaming, her smile sincere. "Do it now," she begged. "Do it before you lose your nerve."

Jamie turned onto his side, where he wouldn't see her. "Sure," he muttered. "Let me just grab my gun and I'll blow off the back of your head. Or I can put my hands around your throat and shake you back and forth until your neck snaps."

He was being crude; he knew it. But he didn't see any other way to shock her back to reality. He felt Maggie slip her arms under his and embrace him. "A pillow. It wouldn't hurt."

He was silent for so long she believed he had fallen asleep. The morning was just unraveling when Jamie turned and drew her close. "I want this weekend with you," he said, slightly nauseated by the nature of the bargain. "I pick the time and I pick the place."

Maggie agreed. Jamie pushed her away, ran into the bathroom, and threw up.

Late Saturday morning, they took everything they could eat from the refrigerator and had a picnic for breakfast. They climbed to the top of the roof, to the big dormer out back that kept the upstairs from having narrow, sloped ceilings. Bud Spitlick saw them when he came out for his paper and told them they'd better watch it or they'd fall. Jamie had instinctively tightened his arms around Maggie, where she sat in the nest of his lap. "I could break my neck," she whispered to him, and she started to giggle. "Think of all the trouble I would save you."

They both laughed then, until they realized exactly what they were laughing at, and then they just fell quiet and held each other.

Jamie asked her what she wanted to do next. Maggie said she should pack up her clothes; he argued that that wasn't the way she should spend her last few days. "Let's do something I've never done," she said, and he wondered what that would be: renting an X-rated film? jumping from an airplane? driving to Florida?

She wanted to go to a movie theater and make out in the back row like a teenager. Jamie couldn't remember the name of the film they picked; it didn't much matter. He unbuttoned her shirt and slipped his fingers into the waist of her jeans and in the end came into Maggie's hand while the movie glowed green and blue on her skin.

They had a fancy dinner that night and drove around Lenox, following the moon. On a whim, since they were dressed nicely, they infiltrated a wedding reception of people they had never met. Maggie laughed when Jamie had a ten-minute conversation with the father of the bride. They danced a jitterbug they'd learned one summer at a community dance class Maggie had signed them up for, spinning and twisting until a line of sweat made a T down the back of Maggie's dress, and only then did they notice that everyone was clapping.

They drove the car to one of the Berkshire passes and slept there, waking when the sun poured itself into the valley like a rich blush wine. Still dressed in a suit and a silk dress, they took off their shoes and socks and stockings and walked through the crabgrass at the base of the hills, looking for four-leaf clovers and winking primroses and flat, smooth stones for skipping. They drove home, faces flushed with color, and showered together. Then they sat in the middle of the bed and watched the stars come out.

On Monday, they were nearly out the front door when Maggie pulled Jamie's arm and dragged him back to the bedroom and ripped at his clothes until he fell back on the bed with her and loved her with a fury that at any other time might have promised more.

He drove her to Wheelock, stopping in front of his cousin's address, which he'd picked out from the phone book and located on a map he bought at the local gas station. "He'll take care of me," he said to Maggie, as they sat parked across the street. "He's family."

For the first time, Maggie seemed to consider that Jamie would be left to face the consequences. "What's going to happen?" she asked.

Jamie smiled at her. "Who cares? I don't have any immediate plans without you."

Maggie was tired. All the activity, in spite of her Percoset, was taking its toll. They spent most of the day in their room at the Inn. That night, while they drank champagne from a bottle and Maggie picked pieces of pepperoni from the pizza, she told him what she wanted of him. "You ought to get married," she said. "You'd be a terrific father."

The thought of anyone other than Maggie was ridiculous, but he did not tell her this.

"I *want* you to get married again," she pressed.

Jamie glanced at her. "I think you've asked me to do enough."

"You'll fall in love again," Maggie said smugly. "And you'll be happy we had this conversation."

Jamie stood up and walked to the window, where Wheelock was shutting down for the night. "There won't be anyone like you."

"I should hope not," Maggie laughed. "I was one of a kind."

"You were," Jamie said, turning around and looking at her. He realized they were already speaking in the past tense. "You are."

They made love again, so slowly that Maggie cried. Jamie woke in the night when her legs twitched against his. "Do you want to know when?" he whispered in her hair. "Should it be while you're asleep?"

"Oh, no," Maggie murmured, her lips against the pulse at the bottom of his throat. "I have to say goodbye."

In the moments before, she had kissed him. She wove her fingers into his hair and pulled so hard it brought tears to his eyes. *I would do it for you,* Maggie said fiercely, and Jamie nodded. But he knew he never would have asked. He never would have been able to leave her.

She lay on the pillow she'd slept on the night before. He placed the pillow he'd used over her face at 7:32 a.m. She put a hand on his wrist and lifted the corner of the cotton pillowcase from her mouth. "It smells like you," she said, and she smiled.

It was over at 7:38 a.m.

Jamie stopped speaking. The air in the courtroom seemed dry and stiff, and he was afraid to shift his position for fear the atmosphere would actually shatter. Graham had his hand on Jamie's arm. "You okay?" he whispered.

Jamie nodded.

"Did she try to fight you?" Graham asked.

"Yes," Jamie said. "She tried once."

"Why didn't you stop?"

*No matter what,* she had said. "She told me not to," Jamie answered. "We had talked about it."

"You say you killed her at about seven-thirty in the morning. Why didn't you go to the police until the early afternoon?"

Jamie thought of Maggie, lying still on the bed, and the way he had pulled the covers to her chin. He remembered watching her from a chair across the room, bent over, his elbows on his knees, waiting. "She looked like she was sleeping." He raised his eyes to Graham. "I kept thinking that maybe, if I gave her a little more time, she might wake up."

*T*hat night Allie dreamed of the day she'd lost her virginity. But because it was a dream, she let herself rewrite it, until her own history played the way she had wanted it to in the first place. In this recollection, Cam had realized before the fact, and left the decision up to her. It was almost as treasured a commodity—that rough rasp, *Are you sure?*—as the heat of his hands and the whisper of his mouth. With the power of one word, she had made time stop for both of them, something she had never been able to quite do again. *Yes,* she had said, when Cam touched her. She said it over and over. *Yes.*

Allie woke up hugging her arms to herself and shivering. She did not want to be dreaming of Cam; she did not want to think about him at all. Although she had hoped it might have gone away by now, she could not forget the image of him in another woman's arms.

She wondered if forgiving was any easier than forgetting.

She sat up in bed, letting the covers fall away. Then she got up and went down the stairs.

Cam, startled, felt her presence before he saw her standing in the dark; a few steps up from the bottom, her white nightgown gleaming with the moon.

"You can come upstairs," she said. She began to walk back. "If you want," she added over her shoulder.

She did not think she had ever heard anything quite as lovely as the groan of the mattress when Cam eased into his side of the bed. She sagged toward him a little, her arms still folded across her chest. They stared at the ceiling, as if they could see through it to the cold, constricting night.

He could not read the signs. She had invited him back upstairs but he didn't know if he was supposed to touch her or to beg forgiveness or to simply accept this small concession and lie in the dark, the heat from her body snaking across the extra foot of space to warm his side.

"Couldn't you sleep?" he asked.

"No. Could you?"

"I was asleep when you came downstairs."

He heard Allie shift a little. "I didn't know. I wouldn't have gotten you up."

Cam felt his erection tenting the material of his boxer shorts, a natural consequence of being this close and able to smell her skin and her shampoo, and he smiled at her choice of words. "It's okay," he said. "I'd rather be here."

She rolled to her side. In the faint light, Cam could make out the tight lines of her mouth, the unsettled flicker of her eyes. "I have to know. Was she here? In this bed?"

Cam thought of the weekend they had spent together when Allie was in Cummington. He had a flash of Mia, a towel wrapped around her wet hair, sitting on Allie's side of the bed. And he realized that in this one instance honesty was not going to serve any purpose. "No," he lied.

Allie flopped onto her back again. She crept to the edge of the bed, crowded out by Mia, who seemed to have taken up all the room between herself and Cam. He was thinking of her; she knew this as well as she knew her own name; and she had been stupid enough to plant the idea in his head. Mia's laugh, Mia's bright blue eyes, Mia's skilled and shaping hands. Allie clutched the mattress so that she would not fall off. She could not breathe for the lack of space.

She thought of her buffalo cowboy. It was right there on the tip of her tongue. She would look at Cam and say, *Guess what? I fucked someone else too*. She would watch his features freeze in shock and she would say, *How does that make you feel? . . . Oh, really? Now you know*.

He would not be able to tell what had happened, unless she let him know. And she realized she would not speak of it just to hurt Cam. This was something she would keep hidden within herself, maybe in place of the knot of pain and anger she had been carrying under her breastbone for more than a week. A security blanket, an ace up her sleeve. She might never use it, but she would always feel its presence like a swelling, secret stone, and that way when she let go of the rage, she would not feel nearly as empty.

A heady rush of power coursed through her as she realized that she was not giving in. She had watched Cam taking unsteady steps to come halfway for the first time, and she was simply allowing herself to meet him.

She moved a fraction closer to her husband and slipped her hand beneath his T-shirt.

He was leaning over her in a minute, pressing her against her pillow with his hands bracketing her head, strands of hair caught between his fingers. He kissed her on the lips, on the throat, on her closed eyes. He felt as if he'd been granted an audience with a king, as if he'd been welcomed to a sanctioned inner circle.

His body could think only of sinking into Allie, but for the first time in months his mind was in control. He could feel his desire physically being pushed to the background, and he slid down Allie's body to tuck his head against her chest. Instinctively, she cradled him, running her fingers through his hair and rocking him as the fear of what had almost happened to his life struck him full force. He did not want to lose her. If he did, he would no longer know who he was.

"I'm sorry," he whispered, his nose running and his tears scalding Allie's skin like individual brands. "I'm so sorry."

A udra Campbell had been waiting for days. She looked bright and refreshed first thing in the morning. Jamie followed her warily with his eyes as she crossed the width of the courtroom.

"If I asked you, Mr. MacDonald, would you kill me now?"

Jamie glanced at Graham, who nodded imperceptibly, as if to remind him he had to answer the question, no matter how ridiculous it seemed, no matter what fantasies it created in his mind.

"Of course not," he said.

"Why not?"

He spread his hands, a gesture of concession. "I don't know you."

"Ah," Audra said. "You only kill people you know?"

Jamie frowned at her. "There was a whole situation attached to Maggie's death. I did it because I loved her."

"Oh." Audra drew out the syllable, a discovery. "You only kill people you *love.*" She stopped pacing and faced him. "Let's go back to the doctor's visit on January fifteenth. When Maggie came home, that's when you first decided to kill her?"

"No."

"Isn't it true you were planning to kill her six months ago?"

"No," Jamie repeated.

"Had your wife's condition deteriorated?"

Jamie blinked at the abrupt change of subject. Graham had warned him about this. Campbell would try to get him flustered, confused, so that he'd say something she could use against him. "Yes," he said. "Maggie's condition had deteriorated very much."

"How?"

"She was having bouts of temporary blindness, and there was the mastectomy, of course. She was in a great deal of pain— headaches and hip problems and things like that. She got winded very easily. She'd lost about twenty-five pounds since the beginning of the illness."

"Isn't it a fact that your medical bills had increased astronomically?"

"Of course," Jamie said. "Treatment doesn't come free. But we had insurance."

"Speaking of insurance, Mr. MacDonald, did your wife have life insurance?"

"Yes," Jamie said, quietly.

"For how much?"

"It was a sixty-thousand-dollar policy."

"And who was the primary beneficiary of her life insurance?"

Jamie looked up at the prosecutor. He would *not* let himself seem guilty. "I was."

Audra started to move in for the kill. "Isn't it true that the woman your wife had become when she was ill wasn't the same woman you fell in love with—not someone you wanted to be around anymore?"

Jamie's mouth dropped open. He was stunned; he wondered if this was something everyone could see when they shook his hand or met him on the street, or if Audra Campbell had the power to read a sinner's mind. "No," he said, a little too late. "Of course not."

"You took your wife out to dinner two nights before the murder. Is that when you decided to kill her?"

"No," Jamie said firmly.

"Was it when you were picking flowers in the park?"

"No."

"It was before you got to Wheelock, though, right?"

*"No!"* Jamie thundered. He was still sitting in his chair, but his hands were gripping the railing of the witness box with the last shred of his self-control. He gritted out the rest of his response through his teeth. "I did *not* decide to kill her. Not before we got to Wheelock, not after. *Never.* She made the decision."

He did not want to look at Graham. The one thing his attorney had coached him about was keeping his cool. *She wants to make you look violent,* he had said. *She wants the jury to think you lost it that night.* Jamie peered up at Graham. He was sitting at the defense table, his head bowed to a blank pad, his forehead braced by his hand as if he was very tired.

Audra smiled condescendingly at Jamie. "Assuming the deceased was going along with this, isn't it true that she changed her mind in the moments before she died?"

"I don't know what you mean."

"Didn't she scratch you repeatedly on the face?"

"Yes, but—"

"Surely that was a clear enough sign for someone who couldn't speak at the moment," Audra smoothly interrupted. "Why didn't you stop, Mr. MacDonald?"

Jamie looked at the bobbing faces of the jury, as if he might be able to locate a friend. "She asked me not to. She didn't trust herself, but she trusted me. And I'd made a promise to her."

"A promise," Audra said slowly, rolling the word in her mouth like an all-day candy. "And didn't you promise in your wedding vows to care for her in sickness and in health?" She stalked back to the prosecutor's table as Graham was coming to his feet to object. "Nothing further."

# TWENTY-TWO

When Cam woke up in the morning he felt across the bed for Allie, but found only smooth sheets. He sat up and rubbed his hands through his hair, making it stand on end. She was probably downstairs making him breakfast. He sniffed at the air, but caught only the traces of the rose oil Allie used on the sheets.

He went to the bathroom and brushed his teeth. She'd hear the pipes run, and know that he was up. He stared at himself in the mirror.

He had slept with his wife last night. An act that was sanctioned by God and by law, an act that should have put things to rights. But he had not awakened relieved. He had a stunning headache, created by the two opposing thoughts he could not reconcile: he knew that he would love Mia a little for the rest of his life; he knew that he would live with Allie forever. The two ideas seemed to overlap, jagged edges he was forcing that would never fit in the way of a puzzle.

He had committed himself to saving his marriage because he knew he would never have Mia, and because—truth be told—he had never stopped loving Allie. In a way, he even looked forward to putting the whole thing behind him, and going back to the way his life had been. But as he'd touched Allie last night, Cam had realized that his wife was now a stranger. She'd looked the same and felt the same but gave off a heady wave of confidence and competence that made Cam unsure of his footing.

It floored him. Allie had always been the constant in his life. And although he was in no position to make demands, he wanted the old Allie back. He wanted to see her look up at him as if he'd created the sun, so he could watch her for clues and see what she still found within him of value.

He pulled on a pair of sweatpants and went downstairs. He would shower after breakfast. Maybe he could convince Allie to join him, but he had a feeling it would be more difficult to create a peace in the light of day than at night, when it was easier to forget that you were still hurting. "Allie," he called. He looked in the living room and the kitchen. Her pocketbook was gone; so were the keys to her car.

She hadn't left him a note.

He remembered that when they were first married, she would scribble down wherever she was, however ridiculous, just in case he needed to find her. "This is stupid," he had said. "When I come home, if you're not in the house, of course I'll look for you in the backyard. You don't have to bother to tell me." But Allie had done it anyway. *It's what I would want of you,* she told him.

He had never, to his knowledge, left a note about where he was going or when he would be back. He was a policeman, invincible, so nothing bad could happen to him. There were times Allie had called the dispatcher to ask if she knew where he was; times he'd been off-duty at four and had decided to walk the perimeter of the lake to take the edge off a harrowing day, or to drive through the pass of the mountains toward New York. Allie had been concerned for his safety; he'd sniped that she worried too much.

He wished she had left him a note.

Cam walked upstairs and turned on the shower. He let the steam fill the bathroom until he could not see even his own hand in front of him.

While Harrison Harding was waiting outside the courtroom that afternoon to be called, he scribbled down a thumbnail sketch of the jury for Graham. He passed this to him minutes before he was called to take the stand as a psychiatric expert for the defense.

Graham stared at it as the doctor was being sworn in. *Juror #2, staid, a problem. Juror #3, nervous tic in left eye, conservative, guarded. Juror #5, tie-dyed blouse, possibly the best. Juror #7, dreadlocks, fair and very involved. Juror #11, red dye job, grossly neurotic, unpredictable.*

Graham patiently walked Dr. Harding through the pedantic exercise of stating his credentials, done only to impress upon the jury that this in fact was someone who was an expert in his field. "How many years have you been in practice, Doctor?" he asked, his first real question since Jamie had left the stand.

"Seventeen years."

Graham let the jury file the information away. They were a bit off-kilter today. From time to time, one member or another would glance at Jamie, either in accusation or to see how he was standing up after yesterday's cross.

"Have you ever testified in court, Doctor?"

"Many times," Harding said. He folded his hands neatly in his lap.

"Can you describe your meetings with Jamie?"

Harding looked directly at Jamie, as if he needed to see into his head to remember what had passed between them. "Jamie is a reserved man, not one who opens up easily. He spent most of the time during our sessions speaking of his wife Maggie. It is clear from the depth of his detail and his affect when discussing her that their relationship was a powerful one, one that helped to establish his own sense of self. I believe that Jamie was suffering from a two-fold psychological problem. One involved a building fusion fantasy, in which a person's personality is so fragile that he physically connects himself to someone else. In Jamie's case, this would have been Maggie. Seeing Maggie in pain would have brought pain to Jamie himself, not sympathy as you or I might feel, but a true physical empathy. Likewise, ending Maggie's suffering would have ended his suffering as well.

"In addition, he suffered from a temporary psychotic reaction brought about by prolonged stress."

"Can you describe that for us?"

"It's a short period of time during which a person behaves in a way that is clearly strange and clearly different from his usual lifestyle. It often includes memory loss, periods of amnesia, and distortions of reality. In other words, a person might not be aware of what is happening, even if he's the one making it happen."

"In your professional opinion, Doctor, is Jamie aware of the difference between right and wrong today?"

"Yes."

"And at the time of his wife's death?"

"No."

"Why not?"

Harding crossed his legs. "Jamie was suffering from tremendous amounts of pressure, which impaired his ability to think clearly and to objectively weigh a statement made to him by his wife. People who live with a deteriorating spouse are often struck by prolonged grief that can lead to a more severe depression and a blurring of judgment. In layman's terms, Jamie went over the edge. In my opinion, he was unconsciously aware of the scope of his actions on the night of his wife's death."

Graham thanked Dr. Harding and turned the witness over to Audra Campbell. She stood up, put her finger to her lips, and then peered at him a little more closely. Then a smile broke across her face. "Dr. Harding!" she cried, as if she were seeing an old friend. "Haven't I seen your name before? In *Time* magazine? The Kevorkian case?"

Harding puffed up visibly, his shoulders becoming three inches taller and his chest expanding with a deep, indrawn breath. "That's right," he said. "November 1995."

Audra nodded at him like she was clearly impressed. "Isn't it true, Dr. Harding, that you've testified at numerous cases advocating the right to die?"

"Yes, I have."

"Isn't it possible that your interpretation of the defendant's understanding of right and wrong is actually your own personal justification for his act?"

Graham watched the wind sink out of Harding's sails. "No, of course not."

"Nothing further."

Audra sat down and shot Graham a smug glance. He stood up wearily, his hand on Jamie's shoulder, unsure if he was giving or asking for support. "The defense rests," he said.

Cam brought Allie a cup of coffee. She was speaking to his mother with her back to him, so there was no possible way she could see that he was coming, but when he placed his hand on her arm, she stiffened.

Ellen glanced up at her son, finished her sentence, and said she was going to the ladies' room.

"I missed you this morning," Cam said. He felt ridiculous, nervous. His hands were shaking.

Allie nodded. She took a sip of the coffee, mentally noting that Cam had added sugar, and she *never* took sugar.

"So," he said, cutting with his eyes to the door of the courtroom. "Almost over."

"It may be some time. Graham says the State will put up a rebuttal witness. Their own psychologist."

Cam nodded. He felt bad for Jamie, but he didn't want to talk about him right now. He lowered his voice. "Any regrets?" he asked.

Allie looked up at him. Her eyes were wide and clear, the color of oak. "I love you, Cam," she said frankly. "But I still don't like you very much."

The State called Roanoke Martin to the stand

Graham watched him mount the stairs and place his palm over the Bible. It was clear from the set of his head and the slouch in his walk that he wanted to be somewhere else.

Audra walked the psychologist through his credentials. Then, all business, she stood squarely in front of him, blocking him from Graham's view. "When did you meet with the defendant?"

"On December nineteenth, last year."

"And can you give us your evaluation?"

"The defendant clearly understood right from wrong, and suffered no break from reality."

Audra nodded shortly. "Doctor, on the night of the killing, in your expert opinion, did the defendant know that holding a pillow to someone's face would lead to asphyxiation?"

"Yes."

"Did he know that asphyxiation would lead to death?"

"Yes."

Audra glanced at the jury. "Based on your conversation with

the defendant, on the night of the killing, do you feel that he was insane?"

"No," Martin said firmly. "I do not."

"Your witness." Audra marched back to the prosecution table and began to close folders and files as if she had the case all wrapped up.

Graham stood slowly. "Do you recall what time Jamie arrived at your office?"

Martin furrowed his brow, exhibiting enormous concentration. "I'm not sure. I can look it up in my notes."

"Please."

Graham paced while Dr. Martin flipped through a black leatherbound book he had pulled from his breast pocket. "12:05 P.M.," he said.

"Can you tell me without looking at your notes how long the meeting lasted?"

The psychologist blinked owlishly at Graham. "I can't recall," he said.

"Would it help you to check your notes?" Graham said, indulgent.

Martin scanned several pages. "It concluded at 12:23 P.M."

"You had eighteen minutes with Jamie."

"Yes, apparently."

"Did you discuss the night in question?"

"Yes."

"Did you discuss his wife's illness?"

"Briefly."

"Did you cover the prospects for her recovery?"

"I can't recall."

By this point, Graham had advanced on the witness so that he was bent back under the force of the attorney's questions. "Did you explore their relationship?"

"Possibly," the doctor said, somewhat faintly.

Graham let out a long whistle through his front teeth. He stuck his hands deep into his pockets. "You mean to tell me you did all this in eighteen minutes? And based on this no doubt thorough conversation with Jamie, you feel qualified to judge his mental state?"

Roanoke Martin tipped his chin up. "Yes," he said.

"Isn't it true that you listened to Jamie that day, and took into consideration his answers and his affect on that day, and reached a conclusion about his mental state based on what was right before your eyes?"

"Well," Martin said, "of course that entered into it—"

"Nothing further."

Graham went back to his seat.

*I*t was Friday, and everyone in the legal community knew Juno Roarke liked to get out as early as he could Friday and go to the dog track, so it was no surprise when the judge dismissed the jury and announced that summations would begin on Monday morning. No surprise, but simply a disappointment.

Graham loaded his file into his briefcase. Jamie was still sitting beside him. "That's the end of the show?" he asked.

"That's it," Graham said. Summations didn't count. The prosecution had the last word then, anyway. "I just wish he hadn't broken off today. It means another weekend of waiting for you."

Jamie shrugged. He didn't say anything, but Graham knew what he was thinking. *Another weekend you're still free.*

"You've got a ride?" Graham asked.

Jamie nodded. He told Graham to have a nice weekend. Then he turned around. Most of the spectators had filed out the door a few minutes before. Allie and Cam were gone. Ellen was sitting by herself on the bench behind him.

"I didn't know you were still here," he said, smiling at her.

"I'm trying to get a feel for the courtroom without the noise. You know, is it a positive place or a negative one."

Jamie swung one leg over the separating railing. "I guess that depends on if you're the prosecutor or the defendant."

"So," Ellen said, laying a hand on his knee. "What are you going to do when this is all over?"

She looked up at him with such fierce expectation that Jamie almost laughed. "I'm going to Disney World!" he crowed, spinning over the railing to land beside Ellen. Then he sank into the seat next to her and rubbed his eyes. "I don't know," he said. "I really don't know."

"Well, what would you *like* to do?"

He considered this. He didn't want to work; he didn't think he'd be able to program computers very well when he couldn't even master his own mind. He didn't much feel like going back to Cummington either. The point of killing Maggie in Wheelock was so that he wouldn't attach the memories to their hometown; funny how at the time he had actually thought he'd be able to outrun them.

"I'd like to drive through all fifty states," he said, surprising himself. "Or maybe move to the West Coast and get a fresh start." He found himself listing one idea after another, the images tumbling out of him. Ellen put a hand on his shoulder.

Jamie spoke for over an hour, his eyes straight ahead, Ellen beside him. As the pictures developed in his mind, they were more and more real, until he could truly see himself hiking through the Black Hills and taming lions and bowling a perfect 300. He blew his future farther and farther out of proportion. He never considered how much he began to sound like a child, who built foundations on the hopes of being the president, an actor, or a famous quarterback, and who stubbornly refused to believe it wouldn't come true.

On Sunday night Graham called Jamie at Angus's house. Jamie had been reading the paper on the living room floor. "Hello?"

Graham cleared his throat before saying anything. "How are you doing?"

"Good. What's up?" Jamie grinned. "Did they declare a mistrial?"

"In my dreams." Graham hesitated. "Jamie, there's not an easy way to say this, but I don't know if you've thought it out for yourself."

Jamie felt the walls caving in around him. He lay down on his stomach, his chin propped on the floor. "What?"

"Don't bring your car on Monday. I'll give you a ride."

Jamie closed his eyes and hung up the phone.

On Monday, the courtroom was packed. The reporters who had been present for the past two weeks seemed to have spawned another fifty of themselves, so they spilled from the rows into standing-room-only at the back. Some Wheelock residents were there, some Cummington families. There was a space by the door where the armed guards would soon stand.

Graham stood and adjusted his tie. He had dressed in an olive suit today, like Jamie's, a silent show of support. He wondered if any of the jurors would notice. At nine-thirty, he began to speak. "Ladies and gentlemen," he said, "you have been listening to a love story. A star-crossed one at that, but still a love story. This case is about a woman named Maggie, who fell for a man named Jamie, and both were supposed to live happily ever after."

He turned around and stared at Jamie. "But that didn't happen. Unfortunately, this story is about a love that didn't last, because of the physical destruction of Maggie and the psychological destruction of Jamie.

"The law is not only about right and wrong. It also makes a distinction between people who are bad, and people who are sick. That's why you've heard from several psychiatric professionals during this trial. In this case, the State's psychologist offered a judgment on Jamie's mental state based on eighteen minutes. Eighteen minutes. He concluded whether or not a man was capable of taking someone else's life and knowing the consequences in less time than it takes me to shower in the morning."

Juror Number 6 smiled.

"The State's psychologist did not talk at length to Jamie about the person he loved most in this world, more than himself. He did not talk to Jamie about her illness, about her chances for recovery, about the strain that the absence of hope had placed on them. And still he thinks he can offer an expert opinion."

Graham crossed to the jury. "We know that when a bone is placed under too much strain, it will break. So will the mind. You have heard testimony that at the time of his wife's death, Jamie was not able to think clearly, to consider a statement she'd made and to judge it rationally.

"You've heard proof that at his wife's funeral, Jamie was overwhelmed with grief. Is this the way a murderer would act? You've heard how Maggie and Jamie spent their last few days alone. Would a man callous enough to plan a murder take his wife to watch the sunrise in the Berkshires, make love to her repeatedly, take her out to dinner and dancing? You've heard proof from Maggie's best friend that Maggie was going to ask Jamie to kill her, and this woman, Maggie's best friend, does not harbor any grudge against Jamie. Even the police chief who arrested him admitted that Jamie's case could not be considered plainly in black or white."

Graham scanned the faces of the jury. They weren't giving anything away. "You know," he said softly, "I understand what makes you nervous. It's unsettling to hear about a man who loved his wife so much that he'd be capable of doing this. It makes us all feel a little guilty, because we probably wouldn't go to such an extreme. Admitting that Jamie had the courage to do such a thing also forces us to admit that *we* wouldn't. That *we* don't have the same kind of strength, or the same depth of emotion for our husbands and wives and lovers.

"It's very strange to talk about love at a trial like this. More often, you hear about hate. Hate drove him to take out a rifle and gun down all the people on the Long Island Railroad. Hate drove him to set a bomb in a London pub. It's clearly believable to us that hate can spur a person to action. Why not love?

"After all, if hate can steal our sanity, so can love. Love can rob a person of his power of reason. We've heard it all before: *Oh, what can you expect from him, he's in love*. Or, *Love is blind*. Or, *Love conquers all*. Think of the strength we attribute to love in our clichés. Is there any doubt that we're vulnerable to it?"

Graham walked back toward his client, so that when the jury followed him with their eyes they'd see Jamie as well. "If I had a way to enter love into the evidence like the arrest report, I would have. But that isn't an option. What I ask you to keep in mind is this: Jamie is a big man. Six foot four, and in good physical condition. He's strong. But he couldn't defend himself against love. It worked its way past his judgment, past what he'd been brought up to consider right and wrong, through the heavy burden of stress he'd been suffering with for months. If Jamie committed a crime, it was that he loved his wife too much. But is that something for which he should be punished?"

Graham sat down. It was 9:52.

Audra Campbell faced Jamie. "If we could have made Maggie MacDonald hale and healthy again, I'm sure every one of us would have wanted to." She turned to the jury. "There has been so much grief and sympathy in this courtroom over the past two weeks that it's easy to let your heart get carried away in the flow and to forget the real issues. What this case has to be decided on, however, is not emotional but fact. And when you clear away all the pathos, what's left is the evidence."

She began to pace in front of the jury box, making eye contact with one juror or another from time to time. "Mr. MacDonald has no criminal record. He is well-spoken and intelligent and he's been a good American citizen. Mr. MacPhee would have you believe that because of these things, his client shouldn't have to be judged within the framework of the criminal system. However, the law does not say that if you've lived an exemplary life up to that point, you can go over the edge and break the rules just once and get away with it."

She paused with her hand in front of the juror with the red hair. "When you sift through all the extenuating circumstances that Mr. MacPhee has brought into this courtroom, you'll find that the evidence is still there, clear and indisputable. On September 19, 1995, after a period of planning and deliberation, Mr. MacDonald took the law into his own hands and killed his wife."

Audra paused for effect. A juror to her right coughed into his hand. Graham watched the jurors look at Audra, into their laps, at Jamie. He could no longer guess what they thought of Audra or himself. "I'm sure everyone in this courtroom has watched someone close to them suffer. It may have been for a shorter period of time than Maggie MacDonald's illness; it may have been longer. I'm sure you have all experienced some degree of stress in this sort of situation. But none of you broke the law.

"I hope you will remember this when you look at the facts. The *facts,* not the emotions and the grief and the horror. Because although these things have a place, they must be considered separate from the evidence, and the evidence can lead to nothing but a conviction."

She sat down, and beside Graham, Jamie let out the long breath he'd been holding.

Of course, the biggest question I have is: What if, say, we happened to run into each other again, now that you have gone your way and I have gone mine?

I like to think we'd go out to lunch, and even after all this time I could probably still order for you and get it right. But these are not the details I wonder about. Would I show you the pictures of the children in my wallet? Would you twist a wedding band around your finger unconsciously while you were speaking?

Maybe we would talk about it: your leaving. I believe you thought that leaving would set you free; surely you know better now. Even if you take yourself away from the person who holds you fast, if that person still thinks you are his, you always will be.

# TWENTY-THREE

*R*esponsibility makes a man taller. Women too.

Jamie scanned the faces of the jury as they listened to Judge Roarke's final instructions before they disappeared to deliberate the case. Every one of them—even the wizened old guy who looked like a turtle and the round-shouldered woman with the bad dye job—seemed to have grown three inches. Every one of them had his or her attention fixed on the judge's booming voice; and like chrysalises emerging from their spun shells, Jamie realized, the men and women sitting before him were not at all the same men and women he thought he had come to know and understand over the past two weeks.

Not a single juror looked at him. He wondered if this was done out of guilt, or revulsion, or simply because they did not want to give anything away. He wondered how many of the twelve already knew the way they would vote, how many of them felt that retiring for discussion was nothing but a technicality.

Judge Juno Roarke thanked them for their time and patience during the trial. Then he cleared his throat, moving his eyes down the line of men and women as he outlined their duties to the court. "In this state," he said, "the crime of murder in the first degree is defined as murder with malice aforethought." He paused, let it sink in. "In order to reach this verdict, the prosecution must have proved that the defendant's act was premeditated, willful, and deliberate. The prosecution has the legal burden to prove that the defendant exhibited all of these characteristics, beyond a reasonable doubt." The judge explained in detail the meaning of the legal term. "If, after you have heard all of the evidence and applied it to the directions and rules of law on which I've instructed you, you have a reasonable doubt that the defendant is guilty of the offense with which he is charged, then you must acquit him of that charge. If, on the other hand, you are satisfied that guilt has been proved and no such reasonable doubt remains, your verdict must be guilty." He took a deep breath. "Alternately, if that charge doesn't seem to fit, you might find the defendant guilty of the lesser included offense of manslaughter in the first degree, which is defined as intentionally causing the death of a person while acting under extreme emotional disturbance."

Graham turned to Jamie and smiled. It looked forced.

"Now," Judge Roarke explained, "the defense claims that the defendant should be excused from conviction by reason of insanity at the time this act was committed. The legal definition of insanity means that at the time, the defendant did not understand the nature and the quality of his act."

Jamie saw one of the jurors, the artist he had thought to be on his side, nodding in agreement.

"If you find this to be the case," Roarke continued, "you also need to decide if the defendant understands the nature and quality of his acts today." He bobbed his head, as if he was satisfied with himself. "There must be unanimity in your decision. If you have any questions about the law or about your duties, if you need testimony reread or want to see the evidence again, please contact the clerk, and perhaps I'll be able to help you." He picked a piece of paper off the desk before him. "When you come to your decision, this ballot will help clarify your answers." He smiled benevolently at the jurors, as if they had already done something very, very good. "This is the most important part of the trial, ladies and gentlemen. I urge you to remember your sworn duty." He furrowed his brow for a moment. "You can give your lunch orders to the clerk on your way down the hall. Thank you."

Jamie watched the jurors slip through the side door like a string of matched beads. He put his head down on the defense table and closed his eyes. He stayed that way for a long time, until all the buzzing reporters had left the courtroom and Allie had given up trying to get him to answer her and the spectator rows were empty. Then Graham put a hand on his shoulder. "We're going for a walk," he said.

JURY BALLOT

STATE V. James MACDONALD
INDICTMENT NO. 1098-96

( ) 1. We find the defendant GUILTY
      of murder in the first degree.
( ) 2. We find the defendant NOT GUILTY
      of murder in the first degree.
( ) 3. We find the defendant GUILTY of
      manslaughter in the first degree.
( ) 4. We find the defendant NOT GUILTY of
      manslaughter in the first degree.
( ) 5. If you have found the defendant NOT
      GUILTY of murder, did you find him
      NOT GUILTY by reason of insanity
      at the time of the offense?
( ) 6. If you have answered YES to No. 5:
      Does this insanity continue?

Graham had started to walk outside with Jamie, but there were so many reporters smoking and jawing on the front steps that he realized it would be like throwing him into a lion's den. "Let's try up here," he said, dragging Jamie up two flights of stairs to the offices in the Pittsfield Superior Court.

He hated this part of the trial. Now he could do nothing, absolutely nothing, except rerun his witness testimonies and cross-examinations in his mind and find every possibly flaw. In Jamie's case, they had won some battles, and lost others. But the outcome of the war was still in question.

He looked at Jamie, wishing there was something to say, and

knowing that there was nothing right now his client wanted or needed to hear. Jamie was staring out a yellowed window into the parking lot. Graham stepped up behind him and watched the attendant lean into someone's car window and point down the block, offering directions.

"If I forget to tell you, Counselor," Jamie said, still staring outside, "you did good."

Graham shook his head. "I haven't done anything yet."

"Still."

"Can I get you something?" Graham said. "Coffee? Food?"

Jamie turned around and dug his hand into his trouser pockets. "If they take me away, who gets the suit?"

Graham was silent, shocked speechless. "They hold it for you. With your watch and money and things like that."

Jamie glanced out the window again. "I just wondered."

When Graham left him, ostensibly to go to the bathroom although Jamie knew it was because he was lousy company, Jamie wandered off down the hall of the third floor of the superior court. Most of the doors had a smoky glass pane in the center, which made you want to see inside but obscured everything from view. A good number of the rooms were dark, and most were locked tight. It made Jamie smile. At a courthouse, God only knew what kind of criminals prowled the office floors.

He started absently trying the doors. Not because he wanted to get in, but because he could think of nothing else to do, and there was a rhythm to it: two steps, wrist out, twist; two steps, wrist out, twist. When doors opened, he peeked his head in and gave his best good-citizen smile. "Sorry," he'd say to the startled secretaries. "Wrong number."

He wondered if there was a difference between being locked in and being locked out.

The last room on the left-hand side was a copy room. He could see the neon-blue flashes underneath the edge of the door. Someone was in there, Xeroxing something. He thought he might go in, act like a lawyer, wait until they were finished, and then photocopy his hands or his face. He had done that once in graduate school—his cheek and lips pressed against the glass while the flash went off behind his eyes like a rocket. He had done it over and over, trying for the perfect reproduction; but no matter how he shifted position, in black and white he had always looked as if he was in pain.

He opened the door and saw nobody at first, just the copy machine itself, emitting blue rays as if it had gone haywire. He reached over to the green button and shut the machine off, and then he glanced up and saw Maggie.

She was sitting on top of the copier, wearing a sleeveless black turtleneck and jeans, and he did not understand how she wasn't freezing to death like that in January. His fists clenched and unclenched at his sides, and he was vaguely aware of the door to the room closing, sealing him inside. A million questions bubbled up in his throat: *Do you miss me? Did it hurt? Are you healthy now? Do you love me?* But he found himself silent, choked by his own curiosity.

So instead, he watched her smile. He drank in the tilt of her lips and the sorrow in her eyes like a man who has never before known beauty. He thought, *Is she an angel?* And when she nodded slightly, he grinned. Nothing had changed between them. She could still read his mind.

He understood then that heaven was what you made of it, that it differed for everyone, and that you could find it in the most unexpected places. He had been looking so hard for Maggie he had not bothered to notice her when she appeared, thinking that without a requisite halo and a star in the palm of her hand, she was nothing more than a memory. But Maggie, his Maggie, with a rip in her jeans and a smudge of powdered doughnut on her cheek, well, he had been seeing her like this for weeks: in the reflection of a dinner plate at Ellen's house, or staring back from behind the bathroom mirror when he was trying to shave.

"You found me," he whispered, and he slid down the wall to a sitting position.

Allie and Cam were two floors below Jamie, sitting at the end of the hall on a bench and waiting for the jury to return a verdict. Allie was hunched over, her mind running through all the dramatic court scenes she'd seen on TV. The scenario that stuck with her showed a big, burly guard dragging Jamie from the defense bench—

to where, Attica?—with his hands cuffed behind him, while he raised his face to the ceiling and yelled out Maggie's name.

Cam had been rattling away about Angus's estate—as if that was what she wanted to discuss just then—for the better part of three hours. Something about the house, which Cam had rented for Angus when he came from Scotland, and the lease that was coming up. She listened to Cam ask himself questions about security deposits and rental agencies and realtors. "Can I ask you something?" she said finally. "Why are you talking about this *now?*"

Cam didn't skip a beat. "Because it'll keep you from thinking about what the jury's doing. You're wound so tight I'm afraid to sit next to you."

Allie smiled a little. "I don't really care about leases. I just want to brood." She looked up at him. "But it was nice of you to try."

"I learned from a master," Cam said quietly, and Allie thought of all the times he had come home from the station, thinking of the one who got away, or of sexual abuse worming its way into a gold-plated Wheelock family you'd never suspect. She used to sit beside him and chatter like a squirrel, about flower shows or local sales or gossip she'd read on the supermarket checkout line— things Cam didn't give a damn about, but that drew his mind away from the heavier side of his life, if not by interest then by irritation.

"What I was going to run by you about Angus's place," Cam said, "was taking out another lease. Maybe month by month. I thought that when we get out of here today, if Jamie doesn't feel much up to going back home yet, maybe he'd like to stay on in Wheelock. I don't think he knows *we* rented the house for Angus." He turned the brim of his uniform cap in his hands like a wheel. "And he deserves a break for a while."

Allie's jaw dropped. "I think it's a great idea," she said, recovering.

She looked at him, seeing not the handsome features she had always been able to catalog in her sleep, but the more subtle things: the kindness at the corners of his eyes, the way his mouth was bracketed by regret, the hope he held fast with the blunt strength of his hands. Compared to the line of his jaw and the richness of his hair and the other physical qualities she had always admired, these attributes were far more attractive.

She leaned slightly toward him. Cam stared into her eyes, trying to read the signals. *Kiss me,* she thought. *Do this one thing right.*

He leaned forward.

A bailiff walked down the hall, bellowing to the spectators that had spilled from the courtroom hours before. "Five minutes," he yelled, shocking Allie back to the time and the place. "Jury's ready to return a verdict."

When Jamie slipped into his seat beside Graham, he glanced at the prosecutor's table. Audra Campbell was stacking her legal pads and folders.

The courtroom was crowded. The two armed guards, the ones who would take Jamie away, were posted like sentries at the back door. There were even more reporters than during the summations. Jamie did not know most of the people who had come to hear the verdict. He thought briefly of old England, where hanging criminals had been a form of public entertainment.

"All rise." Jamie pushed himself to his feet as the judge lumbered to the bench, but the only way he could keep himself upright was by bracing his palms against the defense table and leaning slightly against Graham's side.

The jury was called in. Three of the people looked at Jamie and then glanced away. Graham told himself this did not mean a thing.

It seemed that Jamie had only just sunk into his chair again when Judge Roarke looked at him. "Will the defendant please rise?"

He felt Graham's hand on his arm, pulling him to a standing position. *Why do they do this? So I'm more of a spectacle? So they can see my knees shake? So they can watch me fall down when I hear the words?*

Judge Roarke turned to the foreman, the retired career army man whom Graham hadn't wanted on the jury in the first place. "Have you reached a verdict?" he asked.

The foreman nodded. He handed the ballot he'd been given earlier to the clerk, who passed it to Judge Roarke. The judge glanced at it, gave it back to the clerk, and nodded. "In the matter of the State versus James MacDonald, on the first count, murder in the first degree, how do you find?"

"Not guilty."

Jamie felt something burst free in his chest, something fuzzy and bubbling that broke through his skin in a sweat.

"On the second count, manslaughter in the first degree, how do you find?"

"Not guilty."

There was a collective murmur behind him, a rush of surprise that sounded like wind through a forest of aspens. The judge continued. "Is your decision based on the defendant's insanity at the time the crime was committed?"

"Yes," the foreman said.

Graham gripped Jamie's arm more tightly.

"Does this insanity still continue?"

"No."

*No.* Jamie turned to Graham, a stupid, silly grin spreading across his face, and he hugged the lawyer so tightly Graham's feet came off the ground. The courtroom erupted into a volley of noise. Jamie could feel Allie's hands, smooth and cool, patting at the back of his jacket.

The judge banged his gavel. "Thank you for your time and effort," he said, speaking to the jury. Then he turned to Jamie. "The defendant is free to go."

A throng of reporters descended on the defense table, held back only by the rail that divided the spectators. They held microphones in front of Jamie's face and blinded him with lights and flashbulbs and tossed questions to him that he fielded with one hand and crumpled in his fist: *How do you feel? Do you think this will affect other euthanasia cases? What are you going to do now?*

Audra pushed through the media to stick a hand out to Graham. "Nice work," she conceded. Her face was pinched tight, her features receding into each other.

Graham shook her hand and watched her get engulfed by the crowd. Then he saw his father. Duncan MacPhee did not come any closer, but he climbed up on one of the wooden spectator benches so that Graham could clearly see him. He stood very tall, his loafers neatly breaking the creases of an Italian suit. He held out his hand, a thumbs-up, and he smiled.

Jamie did not pay attention to most of the questions the reporters asked. He kept thinking of the day he'd been set free on bail, months before, when he'd driven up to Angus's house and had seen the balloons floating in Darby Mac's cornfield. *Congratulations,* one had said, and he'd believed it.

He leaned toward Graham. "I need a ride home," he said, laughing. "I'll pay you extra." He clapped his attorney on the shoulder and told him he'd meet him outside. Then he walked down the aisle of the courtroom and out the door of the superior court, making a beeline to a small, bare fruit tree behind the dumpsters out back where Maggie was already waiting.

$A$llie and Cam had not been able to speak to Jamie alone after the verdict was handed down, but Cam told her that he'd be overwhelmed anyway and she could give him a call or drive over later. He took the car keys out of his pocket—they'd driven over in his beat-up unmarked Ford—but Allie plucked them out of his hand. "I'm too wound up. Let me drive."

So he came to be sitting in the passenger seat of his own car, which he rolled back to a more comfortable position. "I'm just going to close my eyes," he said, but it was less than ten minutes before he had fallen asleep.

He dreamed of Mia. He was standing in the front doorway of his house, and she was on the driveway waving. It was winter and she was wearing a deep purple wool coat that matched the color of her eyes and it was so lovely that Cam could not tear his gaze away. He tightened his hand on the doorknob just to keep from running outside to her.

Then Allie was standing next to him, wearing a sweater he had bought her for her last birthday, her arms folded across her chest. "You're letting out all the heat," she complained, and she went to shut the door.

Cam could feel his heart pounding. She was close enough to see Mia, but she hadn't even thought to look. She kept pushing at the edge of the door. "I'll do it," he said, and with one last glance he shut Mia out of sight.

He realized, when the door was closed, that it was not the heavy oak slab that he himself had picked out for the house. It was new, insulated, with a central grid of nine panes of bull's-eye glass. You could see through the glass, but everything was slightly thick and distorted. Cam stared, making out an edge of what he knew was Mia, and he understood that this was enough.

In his dream, Allie smiled at him. "Are you coming?"

He did not know where, but he nodded. And followed her out of the room.

*T*he adrenaline wore off with every mile she tagged in Cam's car, until by the time Allie pulled into their driveway she did not see how she was going to swing her legs out of the Ford, much less make her way into the house. She was still smiling, but that was for Jamie.

She didn't know what she and Cam were going to do now that the trial was over. It had served as a buffer between them and then as a fragile connection. Now Jamie wasn't an issue. Cam wouldn't be able to win points by sitting beside her in the courtroom, by politely shaking Jamie's hand when he arrived for the day. Now, all Allie and Cam had left were themselves.

She remembered how terrified she had been on their wedding night. It wasn't the sex; they had gotten that out of the way. It was the fact that once they left the reception and got back to the Wheelock Inn, it hit her that she was really going to spend the rest of her life with Cam. Her fingers had been trembling as she unbuckled his kilt and freed the buttons from his crisp white shirt, and Cam had tried to tease her out of it, but her fear was not for that particular evening. She was scared of the next evening and the next and the one after that; of the faith they would have to put in each other, of the overwhelming fact that they were at the bare beginning, and they had so very far to go.

On her wedding night, she'd picked a fight with Cam. He had done something eminently forgivable—he'd torn her stocking while trying to get it down her leg—and she'd started crying. She yelled that he hadn't been thinking, he hadn't been careful, and what kind of omen was *that?* And Cam, always levelheaded, always a hero, had held her until she stopped trying to get free and had kissed her until she believed that if you only concentrated on the here and now, tomorrow didn't so much matter.

Now Allie's hands were shaking again as she turned the key in the side door that led into the kitchen. She fixed her attention on a glass of juice that Cam had left sitting out on the counter. Grape juice. Allie walked into the kitchen with Cam behind her. She picked up the glass. On the white Formica, there was a deep purple stain.

She reached for a sponge and began to scrub the stain. "I can't believe you did this," she said. She could hear Cam unzipping his jacket and hanging it over the back of a chair. She was still wearing her coat, her hat, her scarf.

She lifted the sponge. The ring was a little fainter, but it was still there, clear as day. Everyone knew that grape juice stained. Cam knew. How many times had she told him?

"This is never going to come out," she said, bending to the counter and scrubbing with the scouring side of the sponge. Her hand became raw and her knuckles scraped red.

She was working so hard to remove the evidence that she didn't hear Cam coming up behind her. He covered her hand, flattening the sponge. Soap oozed between their fingers like a fixative. "Allie," he said calmly, "take it easy. Give me your coat."

But she couldn't take it easy. She knew she was acting crazy and felt as if she were watching the whole scene from one of the exposed beams overhead. She knew it was not about a grape juice stain, either. And still, there were a hundred questions running through her mind: What if they wanted to sell the house one day? What if she tried Clorox, straight? Why didn't he see that every time she walked into the kitchen her eyes would be drawn to this mark?

"Allie." Cam pulled her toward him and unzipped her coat and tugged the hat from her hair. He unwound the scarf from her throat. Then he covered her hand with his again. "See?" he said, smiling in a way that reminded her of how, when they were first dating, she had felt a physical loss at not having known him as a child. "There. It's gone."

She looked down. Somewhere, under their spread hands, was a stain. But as things stood, Cam was right. From this angle it could not be seen.

She felt the familiar heat of his skin. Yet now she was also aware of how rough Cam's fingertips were against hers, how mismatched the size of their palms.

Cam turned Allie around to face him. "So," he said, and it was a question.

But to Allie, the word sounded like a beginning. "So," she answered slowly, and she set them free.

# MERCY

Jodi Picoult

# A Readers Club Guide

# About This Guide

The suggested questions are intended to help your reading group find new and interesting angles and topics for discussion for *Mercy* by Jodi Picoult. We hope that these ideas will enrich your conversation and increase your enjoyment of the book.

Many fine books from Washington Square Press feature Readers Club Guides. For a complete listing, or to read the Guides online, visit http://www.BookClubReader.com

# *Questions and Topics for Discussion*

1. To what degree is the title a metaphor for this novel?

2. Are Jamie's actions justified? What about Cam's? Allie's?

3. Who is the author of the "notes" between the chapters? Whom are these snippets addressing? Did you believe this throughout the book?

4. Jamie says, "You know it's never fifty-fifty in a marriage. It's always seventy-thirty, or sixty-forty. Someone falls in love first. Someone puts someone else up on a pedestal. Someone works very hard to keep things rolling smoothly; someone else sails along for the ride." Do you agree?

5. In what ways does Mia's memory of her parents' love influence her relationship with Cam?

6. Who is the most selfish character? The most selfless?

7. In what ways are Cam and Jamie similar?

8.  How is Cameron MacDonald like his namesake ancestor? How is he different? To what extent does the Scottish history of this clan affect his decisions?

9.  What is the significance of the moments in *Mercy* that are magical or somewhat unreal?

10. There is a catch-22 in Mia and Cam's relationship: They have each fallen in love with a person who would no longer exist if they were to run off together. Do you agree or disagree with this statement, and why?

11. Is there a hero in this book?

12. What attracts Allie to Jamie? To Cam? What attracts Mia to Cam, and Cam to Mia? Do you believe that we try to find in the people we love parts of our personalities that are lacking?

13. At the end of chapter 17, Cam "wondered how he had so quickly gone from holding everything he wanted in the palm of his hand to having absolutely nothing at all. He wondered how he could have been so blinded by something shiny and new and elusive that he couldn't at least give equal credit for the strength of something stable, and strong, and his." Do you think his feelings are heartfelt? Do you agree?

14. Why did Picoult choose to make Jamie a pioneer in virtual reality?

15. How has Jamie changed by the end of the book?

16. What will happen to Cam and Allie? To Mia? To Jamie?

17. Is this novel about love, or loyalty? Are they the same thing?